Q-16

and the Fury of
Korangar

A.A. Jankiewicz

To Doris,
Thanks for being on
the journey thus far!

Q-16 and the Fury of Korangar

Copyright © 2019 Agnes Jankiewicz

Flag Photography Copyright © 2019 Agnes Jankiewicz

Cover Art Copyright © 2019 Anthony Letchford

First Edition: 2019

ISBN: 978-0-9959080-6-2

www.aajankiewicz.com

Works by A.A. Jankiewicz

Q-16 Series

Q-16 and the Eye to All Worlds
Q-16 and the Lord of the Unfinished Tower
Q-16 and the Fury of Korangar

Short Stories

The Last Drop' in Water edited by Nina Munteanu
'Skyris' in Brave New Girls Stories of Girls Who Science and Scheme edited by Paige Daniels & Mary Fan
'Impossible Odds' in Brave New Girls Tales of Heroines Who Hack edited by Paige Daniels & Mary Fan
'After the Storm' in Power In the Hands of One, In the Hands of Many edited by Ellen Michelle
'Decoded' in Brave New Girls Adventures of Gals and Gizmos edited by Paige Daniels & Mary Fan

Once more, with gusto, to my family,
For though they do not always understand everything involved with my
creative process, they nonetheless try.

To those who continued to ask for book three,
I thank you for your enthusiasm,
Perhaps this author has done something right.

And to Chris Barfitt,
For his continuous support in all my author adventures,
I tried to keep it spoiler free.
Now here it is.

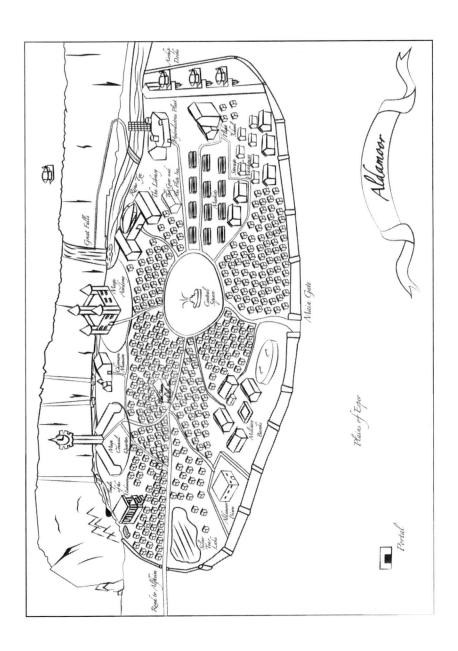

Aldamoor

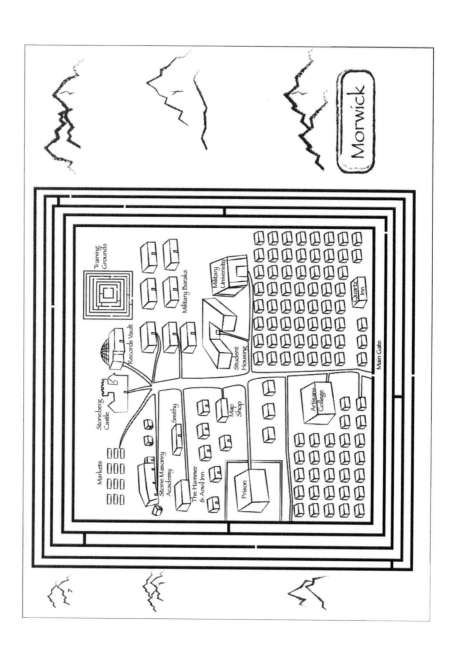

Morwick

Training Grounds
Military Barracks
Records Vault
Stoneberg Castle
Markets
Stone Masonry Academy
Smithy
The Hammer & Anvil Inn
Map Shop
Student Housing
Military University
Quartz Inn
Artisans College
Prison
Main Gate

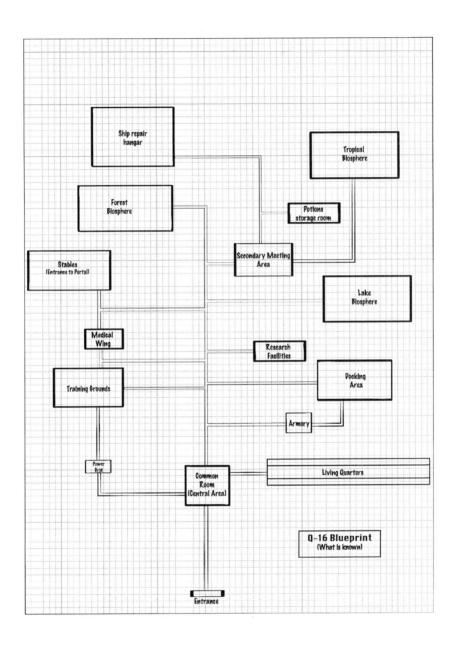

Ship repair hangar

Tropical Biosphere

Forest Biosphere

Potions storage room

Stables
(Entrance to Portal)

Secondary Meeting Area

Lake Biosphere

Medical Wing

Research Facilities

Training Grounds

Docking Area

Armory

Power Grid

Common Room
(Central Area)

Living Quarters

Q-16 Blueprint
(What is known)

Entrance

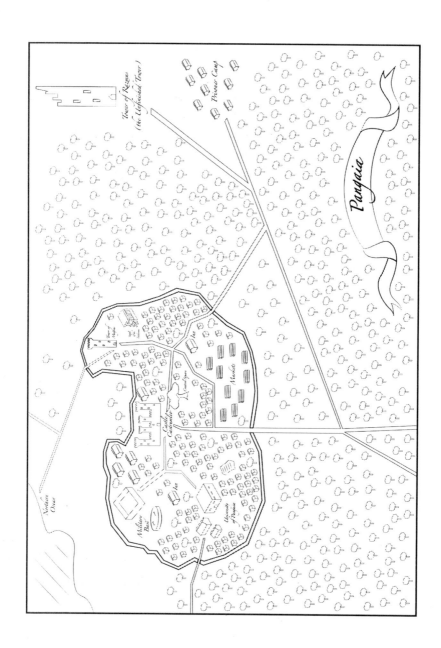

8

The self is a multidimensional creature with many facets. Much like the multiverse it inhabits, the layers work to create a complete and whole being, with some parts more hidden than others. Sometimes, one tries to cast aside fragments of the self, hoping to shape a better version without the flaws in the design. While the removal of these imperfections may be a trial, the more significant task is the acceptance of the whole as it was meant to face the world.

ഇരു

Prologue

A gleaming silver longsword arced through the air, its blade untarnished and reflecting the pristine courtyard of the Citadel of the Unknown in its visage. Its owner, a young man on the verge of exiting adolescence with a head of shaggy tawny hair that fell before his grey eyes, relaxed into a neutral stance. Shocks of a not-fully-developed beard patched his scowl-marked face. Satisfied with the completion of his exercise, Lincerious Heallaws, or the one who had once been referred to as Link, turned on his heel.

He no longer used his nickname when he thought of himself. That part of his life, along with the cursed scar he had once borne, was no more. His life was now in service of his brotherhood, the White Knights. He had struggled to accept when he had first been brought here, torn from his life as he had been. Time, however, had managed to dissipate some of the sting from his removal, and he had managed to do what his superiors had told him he would. He had adapted. This was not to say that the face of a young girl with blue eyes and reddish-brown hair did not appear in his dreams the odd time, as did a kiss he had once rebuked. Annetta had meant something to him once, hadn't she? This, paired along with images of a lake, a base far under the ocean on a world called Earth, a mage of pale blue eyes, a youth wielding a mace, a man with gauntlets hiding claws and another young girl, always with her nose in a book. Sometimes, a creature that he recalled as being called a Hurtz would appear as well. These were all just hazy memories against his continuous training and the monotone routine of Citadel life. He shook his head, removing the thoughts and continuing onward.

He passed by his brothers and sisters at arms, beings of every shape and form from across the multiverse, all dressed just as he was in their pristine white tabards with the tree sigil of the Unknown on them and riveted chain mail underneath. Lincerious paused briefly before leaving to glance at the pale marble of the courtyard and the unyielding high arches which lead to the interior of the building. Above these, visible against the wicked blue and purple swirling clouds, white spires climbed into the sky as if trying to grab hold of it.

Marking the course in his mind, Lincerious continued down to the West Wing of the Citadel, the interior walls just as unmarred in their colouring as the exterior of the structure. His destination having been reached, he stopped before a large arched doorway and, taking in a deep breath, pushed it open. Inside was a levelled auditorium, benches lined in rows which created raised levels that looked down on the main stage. For the most part, the seats were unoccupied, a few other young knights of various species waiting for the lesson to begin. The Unknown, Lincerious had learned, did not discriminate between species or planet, and all were loved and welcomed equally into his service.

The auditorium soon after began to fill, leaving very little room for movement. A hooded figure then appeared below, causing everyone who chatted among themselves to quiet down. No one knew the being's name or face, and he was simply referred to as the Arch Prime. It was common gossip around the barracks that the Arch Prime had once been the One, the right hand of the Unknown in the past, but had retired to found the White Knights. Lincerious, surrounded by his peers, leaned forward on the bench as the Arch Prime raised his arms to speak.

"Brothers and sisters in arms." A voice void of any gender came from under the cowl. "As your journey to graduating your training draws to an end, I come before you today to speak on a matter of grave importance regarding things that have not yet come to pass, and yet, I come to speak to you regarding the purpose we, the White Knights of the Unknown, were founded for as the guardians of the Aternaverse. Before I begin, though, does anyone wish to take a guess as to what that thing might be?"

"We fight for the Unknown, we are his sworn swords, what else but this simple truth could there be?" A creature covered in thick brown fur resembling a great cat with long curved ebony horns stood and boomed.

"You are incorrect, Brother Eddus." The Arch Prime spoke. "While it is true that we do serve the Unknown as his army, that is not the purpose of our existence, for the creator of all could just as easily defend himself against all manner of threats. Does anyone else wish to try and answer?"

A silence fell on the room, as no one else dared to try. Lincerious continued to watch with curiosity to see what the Arch Prime had to say. Part of his mind, however, had begun to drift as he tried to recall his last conversation with Annetta. He then felt the searing heat of invisible eyes fall upon him, causing him to snap to attention.

The Arch Prime then intoned. "Brother Lincerious? You seem deep in thought. Have you any revelations you wish to enlighten your fellow peers with?"

A few snickers from those close by caused Lincerious to grit his teeth as he cursed inwardly, reminded of his days in the Gaian militia where he seemed to more often than not be the butt of many an instructor's taunts, in particular, Layla, who had crowned him with his old nickname.

"Well, if it isn't our weakest, Link," her now-distant voice echoed through his head as he attempted to focus.

He stood, uncaring of what his peers thought and spoke. "To be ready to assist those worlds threatened when the seed of chaos comes."

"In this, you are partially correct." A satisfied tone hid behind the words as the Arch Prime paced the auditorium below. "We must be ready to stand and fight when the seed of chaos comes to threaten the existence of life, for our sacred duty is the preservation of life, life the Unknown has created. Some life is weaker than others, but this does not mean it should be neglected, or thought of as being lesser than others. It is also for this reason that in some universes, there is a sister planet, one race that is bound to another by close genetic makeup and feels a kinship to their brethren. Now, this is not always so, and the White Knights must step in and aid where that aid is needed. We are the last defence in the preservation of life. We must defend when there is no one else left to do so."

Lincerious smiled at that last part as that same image of a young girl with blue eyes and dark-red hair came to mind. She had her back slightly turned to him, and in one hand she gripped a sword, while the other hoisted a rectangular tower shield. This was all contrasted by her wearing an overly large jean jacket with teal sneakers. Though he was separated by universes from her and was not sure now what bound the two of them together, he knew she fought for the same reason.

Chapter 1

Soaring. The dreams always began in the same way for her, with the wind in her face and the mountains capped in snow down below. Trees that were so tiny, they appeared to be only splotches of green dotting the landscape here and there in patterns without end. These and an azure sky before her that stretched into eternity were the only companions in the lone voyage she undertook. To where and why? She didn't know, all she did know was that she had to keep going and there was no time to stop.

A power unknown to her in life surged through her body, and freedom filled her unlike any she knew in life. The sky and mountains were hers as was everything else she could see for miles around in the untouched sanctuary she found herself in. It was hers, so long as the wind beat through her wings...

⁗⁗⁗

Annetta Severio's blue eyes opened in shock, gasping for air. She filled her lungs rapidly with as much of it as she could, and the frigid chill of the mountain peak fully awakened her. She pulled the crimson cloak of her Gaian armour closer around herself as the wind caused her reddish-brown hair to flutter about. It was still dawn, meaning her nighttime excursion had not caused her to sleep through the day, thankfully. This also meant she would not be late for her sparring lessons with Venetor, a long-established morning routine. It was part of the reason she had stayed on Gaia after the battle against Razmus had been won. Her stay was only for the summer, however, and after that, she would need to go back to Earth so she could begin her studies in Police Foundations. She'd found out earlier in the week while conversing with Skyris that she'd been accepted.

"I must have fallen asleep after meditation." She grimaced at herself and noted the time on her C.T.S.. The plan had been to go straight back to Castrumleo upon finishing, so that no one knew she had left the stronghold of Gaian royalty, but it looked like her cover would be blown.

She sighed and got up, stretching her stiff muscles as she did so. She then made sure everything was secure on her person, including her sword, Severbane, which hung at her side in its scabbard, before beginning her walk to the edge of the cliff.

When her great-uncle Venetor had first brought her to the Pendrosian Mountains, and they were to make their descent, Annetta had nearly fainted from fright, fearing her abilities would fail her under so much pressure, but her flight lessons had proven her worries unfounded. Now, at the very edge, Annetta let herself fall with confidence and instinct take over, her telekinetic powers pushing her body against the earth, allowing her to levitate her body and soar. The ability was almost second nature to her by now, and she found it no different than breaking into a run.

A thrill filled her unlike any she had felt on horseback as she flew over the mountain range back towards the city. Stretching out her fingers, she allowed the air current to pass through them, feeling the resistance of the cold wind push against them. As she flew, her mind wandered to the encounter she had just had before falling asleep.

ഇര

Her meditations always began in the same manner, with blinding white light, and moments later, everything else coming into focus around her, along with the sounds of wildlife blaring in her ears. Looking up, Annetta found the branches of trees creating a canopy overhead, blocking out any direct contact with sunlight. She gathered her wits, which generally dissipated after such a journey, and ventured forward to seek out the one person who might have the answers to the question she sought.

Trudging through the forest trail, she soon came upon him in a clearing. He was a mountain of a man with a silver beard, blue eyes and a visage which had been hardened from years of taking command. Dressed in a simple tunic of steel blue with a tattered brown cloak around his shoulders and tan breeches tucked into high black boots, he looked to be a simple woodsman. Intricately embossed brown leather bracers encircled his arms, his hands both clasped under his chin as he listened to someone intently. A large twin-bladed axe rested beside him on the log he sat upon. Beside him was a creature with the face of a badger, long rabbit ears pierced with multiple silver hoop earrings and a thick dark grey lion-like mane that extended onto his muzzle into a beard.

Annetta smiled, seeing the two of them. "Hey, grandpa Orbeyus. Hey, Brakkus."

Both of them turned to her. Orbeyus grinned widely in return. He patted the log he sat upon for her to join him. "Welcome, Annetta. What brings you here today?"

Annetta obliged and sat down beside him. There was an anticipation in her movements that she had trouble masking. "Have you had a chance to go look for him?"

Brakkus, the one who sat to the other side of Orbeyus, flattened his ears against his skull. "Lass, that's just what we were meeting here for."

There was a hopeful glint in Annetta's eyes as she regarded them both. In fact, she half expected Link, the object of her search, to spring out from behind Brakkus at a moment's notice. As the seconds passed, however, it was apparent this was not to be.

"Lass, we honestly tried." Brakkus's great amber eyes were crested with sadness. "We could not find tha lad."

Annetta's eyebrows furrowed. "But that's not possible. You told me so yourselves before that-"

"Annetta, my dear," Orbeyus spoke, his arm outstretched in a hushing manner. "Some things like this are far out of our reach. We just do not have the power to find certain individuals when we are here. Even more so when they do not wish to be found to begin with."

"What do you mean, grandpa?" she asked.

"He means exactly what he says, lass." Brakkus reaffirmed the point.

Confusion flooding her, Annetta turned to Orbeyus yet again, who sat staring out into the distance. She then noticed that etched on his face was a longing she too felt, and then it hit her.

"You never did find grandma in the afterlife, did you?"

More silence passed before Orbeyus spoke. "She always was and has been an adventurous woman. Amelia lived for it, more so than I ever did. I think that was why she followed me to Earth, to begin with, to be honest. Our love for each other did not happen till much later, and even then at times, your grandmother was an elusive and wild creature. The multiverse was as infinite as her thirst for it. It does not surprise me then that she has not appeared to me even once in the afterlife when she could be exploring new worlds."

Annetta nodded. No one had ever spoken much about Amelia to her, save for the story of her heroic death which had been recounted to her by the female Soarin named after her.

A heavy hand landed upon her shoulder, causing Annetta to look over and see Brakkus standing before her.

"Ye may need to let him go, lass. Some souls never want ta be found again."

଼ଉଆ

Annetta then snapped back into the present. The memory still left a fresh sting on her psyche as she tried to come to terms with the possibility of never seeing Link again. Though they had certainly not been more than friends, she still missed him and her having the ability to visit the dead at will had been her coping mechanism for some time now. It had given her a new acceptance over death, one Annetta had not had for many years. Having that taken from her, however, had brought the event into a new and terrifyingly finite light. Despite these feelings welling up inside of her, she did her best to suppress them for a time where they were welcome. Preparing for a lesson with Venetor was not such a time.

Willing herself to go faster, she pushed more to attain a higher velocity and remembering the trick Venetor had shown her, she created an energy shield of psychic fire around her body to go even faster still. She then recognized the spot where she had tied up Firedancer in the glades that surrounded Pangaia, and began to make her descent.

Landing among the foliage, she paused to take it all in. Having grown up in urban Toronto, the scenery always took her aback whenever she ventured outside the walls of Pangaia, the capital city of Gaia and her current residence. The world seemed a different place, with its trees towering overtop like a canopy of well-woven fabric, leaving little chance for the light of day to penetrate through it, save for the flimsy leaves which adorned them. She took a deep breath once she had touched down, and allowed for the scents of rich soil and sap to fill her lungs, a welcome change from the thin mountain air.

Further ahead, she noted the chestnut hide of her steed along with his blond mane. Firedancer, she thought, had been named appropriately for his colouring as she regarded him nibbling on the grass at his hooves. Among the rustling of leaves, Annetta's hearing picked up the sound of movement on the soft forest floor. Her hand went for the hilt of Severbane, though she was fairly sure she knew who it was and turned to where it was coming from.

Appearing from among the leaf filled branches was a creature that resembled a horse-sized black shaggy dog with tan markings around its muzzle, eyebrows and underbelly. Its ears flopped down, and a great big pink tongue lolled out of its open maw, giving it a non-threatening disposition, save for the two elongated sabretooth fangs which protruded from its jaws. Sabertooth dogs, Annetta had learned from Venetor, were once the only mode of transportation in Gaia. Horses had been exclusive to Earth, but were brought over and bred by the aristocracy, in particular, the ladies who apparently had found sabretooth dogs to be too brutish in their disposition if not handled properly. Annetta didn't agree with this.

Dropping her hand to her side, she made her way over to the great beast and wrapped her arms around its neck, her face sinking into its thick fur.

"Hello, Bear. How are you today?" she asked as she pulled away.

The creature, Bear, wagged his short fluffy tail enthusiastically as he nudged her for more attention. Annetta chuckled and scratched him behind the ear, feeling Bear lean into her hand as if attempting to absorb the maximum amount of affection from her touch.

"You should really consider coming back with me to Pangaia," she said. "Then you can get much more pets and ear scratches."

Bear's great amber eyes met that of Annetta's. There was a resolute nature to them that told the girl he could not. Something was preventing him. When Annetta had originally found Bear on her first excursion outside of Pangaia a few weeks back, he had been a complete mess of unkempt fur and wearing a saddle that was torn to shreds which had been fitted onto his back. Since then, she had groomed him as best as she could and removed the saddle. She had even brought him scraps as a way to entice him to follow her back, but the sabretooth dog had shrunk away at every such suggestion. Annetta could only imagine that he was waiting for someone, and perhaps they had been killed during Razmus's reign. She sighed at the thought, feeling if that were so, then there was not much she could do aside from providing some comfort for the large canine.

Withdrawing, Annetta walked over to Firedancer's saddle and pulled out a parcel from her saddlebag which she proceeded to unwrap.

"I hope you like beef," she said to the creature as she lay down a large bone she had rustled up from one of the cooks in the kitchen who knew of her over-the-wall companion.

Bear's eyes widened at the sight of the treat, and he instantly swooped in for it. Laying himself down on the floor of the forest, he began to work away at it, completely forgetting Annetta in the process.

The girl laughed as she swung herself into the horse's saddle.

"There's more where that came from if you change your mind," she told him, and flicking the reins, she was off again.

⬥⬥⬥

Piercing cobalt eyes zeroed in on its prey as fists blocked the incoming jabs and strikes which came at their owner. Countering the latest attack and sure his opponent would not so quickly retaliate, Venetor Severio straightened his posture as a protective barrier of purple and blue psychic fire flared around him. Beads of sweat ran down his temples, their origins visible under the short-cropped black hair that now lay matted against his skull. Trailing down a sharp-featured face, many met their end at the sideburns which curved partially over his cheekbones, emphasizing his naturally grim disposition. He wiped some away with the back of his hand, his fists not uncurling for a single second. His gaze fixated on that of his student, Annetta who was also encased in psychic fire.

"Good, you saw that hook coming this time," he praised her.

Annetta didn't respond to this and instead she teleported from sight. Venetor crossed his arms and sighed, stepping out of the way just as she reappeared aiming her foot at where his head had been seconds prior. His hand then snatched her ankle and flung the girl against the far wall. At the last second, she teleported again.

Venetor closed his eyes as he tapped into his feral form senses and listened for the sound of her breathing. Breath was always the first thing to materialize as a psychic warrior would always take a larger one when they appeared after teleportation.

"And you listened when I said not to wait for permission to attack." He glanced back and saw her standing a few feet away from him.

The two of them now stood in a dim concrete chamber below the main halls of Castrumleo. Faint lights glowed around the room, further accentuating both the light and dark which played on the crisp edges of the walls around them. Both he and Annetta were dressed in just their black beta scale mail armour, the rest of their clothing having been discarded to the side, along with their shoes. Venetor found that it was easier to maintain one's balance on the soles of their own feet. Not to say that he couldn't when fully-equipped. They did train this way from time to time, but today was just a warm up in his mind. They had a long day ahead of them.

Annetta did not reply, her body still tense in a fighter's stance, her arms raised before her. Venetor's lips slightly curled into a smile seeing this, he had told her to never let her guard down, and it seemed that after the few times when he had attacked without warning, the message had gotten through.

"Yield," he said, finally, upon which she relaxed, the word having been chosen to let her know the lesson had come to an end. "You may go and prepare yourself. Our shuttle leaves in two hours. I expect that is sufficient time."

"More than enough for me," the girl replied as the psychic fire around her dissipated and she walked over to the pile of her clothing to begin dressing. She winced from the fresh bruises as she did so but didn't complain, knowing full well she would get no sympathy from him.

Venetor noted the nonchalant tone of the girl and spoke as he pulled on his boots. "We will need to be at our sharpest at this meeting with the Federation, and since it's your first, all eyes in the room will be upon you. Especially with the so-called legends rising up around the White Lioness of Gaia."

Annetta rolled her eyes hearing this. Her little stunt in the fight against Razmus and the choosing of her feral form to be a lion that ironically also turned out to be white fulfilled the lines of a prophecy set out long ago. Since then, Venetor had given her the title White Lioness of Gaia, and all sorts of strange rumours about her person had begun to surface. Some were factual, and many were false, their sources shrouded in mystery. If this was how fast legends were born, she wondered what would be said about her in a hundred years after she was dead and gone.

The King of Gaia noticed her body language and snickered, for he too found the rumours to be absurd. He knew, however, the danger they were both going to be walking into in that meeting, for the Greys still held a grudge against Gaia, even if they did not formally express it.

"I'll have Gladius come for you at the appointed time," was the last thing he said to her as he picked up the remainder of his garb.

Throwing his crimson cloak across his shoulders, he then strode out of the chamber without saying anything else, and Annetta followed not too far behind. Making their way up the stairs into the main hall, they split up in their respective directions.

Castrumleo was by no means as vast as the Eye to All Worlds. It did not need ever-expanding magical properties that continued to generate new doors for portals created due to the wear and tear of the multiverse. It was, however, the oldest and largest of all castles that existed intact on Gaia. Its design was minimalistic and modern in comparison to the grandiose structures Annetta was used to seeing in the media she had consumed on Earth in the past. Half-moon high arched windows dotted the walls of the structure, providing a view of the bustling city of Pangaia below. On the floor, a thick red and gold carpet lay sprawled out, most of it occupied by the feet of those that traversed the main hall, which split off into various other wings of the castle. The walls themselves, the same grey cement-like surface, were adorned with tapestries, paintings and weapons of all kinds, as well as small spherical fixtures which Annetta had learned worked similar to that of light bulbs. They did not, however, run on electricity in the traditional sense as she knew, somehow absorbing the light of the sun and storing it overnight to be used as needed. Venetor had tried to explain it to her when she had asked, but when Annetta equated it to solar panels, he had dismissed that concept as primitive in comparison. She had not asked him to try explaining it further to her.

Thinking no more on this, Annetta turned in the direction of the stairs which led up. As she strode towards them, she caught sight of something from the corner of her eye and paused to get a better look. A young man of light brown hair sat in a chair on a balcony which overlooked the city. He was dressed in a white linen shirt that was tucked into high brown pants and polished leather boots to match, a waistcoat draped over the back of his chair. His angular face was drawn in concentration as he looked out into the horizon before him, a sketchpad laying across his lap with a partially finished sketch in charcoal on it. Black smeared fingers stroked his sideburns as his keen blue eyes tried to gather further meaning from his muse.

"You've got charcoal on your face again, Titus." Annetta announced her presence and leaned against the entrance to the terrace with her arms folded.

Titus, her cousin, snapped out of his daydream and examined his hands. Frowning at the sight of the charcoal on them, he picked up a rag which lay discarded beside the chair, and wiped them down before taking a clean corner of it to his face.

"Better?" he asked as he turned around.

Annetta narrowed her eyes as she took in his features. Were his hair cut shorter and he bulkier, she could have sworn that he was Venetor's blond twin and not his son. Upon completion of her examination, she did find a spot and taking the rag, she did her best to wipe it clean.

Taking a step back, she examined her work. "You'll live, and so might your shirt this time."

Titus grinned sheepishly in return and then sighed. "At least there is that. So, is father having you go to the meeting with the Federation? I've heard a few rumours about shuttle preparation."

"Yeah," Annetta replied and then added, "He keeps going on about how we need to be vigilant and cautious when we are there. Makes it seem like there's going to be assassins at every corner or something."

At this, Titus laughed. "Well, politicians are backstabbers or didn't you know?"

"I thought it was an Earth-exclusive thing, to be honest." Annetta shook her head. "Have you ever gone to one of these things before with him?"

"A lot more than I would have liked to." He adjusted his posture in his seat. "And my father is right, you will both need to be careful when you go. Not in the sense of someone will jump out to attack you, but in what you say. Anything you do say can be potentially used against you in the future or against the throne of Gaia."

Suddenly, Annetta felt more pressure to the whole visit than she liked. It hadn't been an order that she go with Venetor, in fact, he had asked her if she were curious to see how things were in the meetings the Federation took part in. Now, Annetta didn't think it was such a good idea that she had agreed. There was, however, no backing out now for even that, she feared, could bring unwanted attention to herself and Venetor.

Titus seemed to pick up her sudden unease and cleared his throat.

"Believe me when I say this, you'll be fine," he said. "Just smile and nod when cued by other people in the room. My first time in a meeting, I didn't say a single word. Most of them won't even notice you are there."

Hearing the last part, Annetta nodded in response. She got the feeling, however, she would not get away with going unnoticed.

Chapter 2

Puc Thanestorm, known now to the people of Aldamoor as First Mage, sat behind a large desk of dark wood in his quarters in the High Council Tower. Dusk was slowly approaching, lighting the books and scrolls on the various shelves around him in a subtle orange glow, making him reminisce about his quarters within the Lab. He missed them. He still kept his accommodations in Q-16, the underwater fortress on Earth that guarded the Eye to All Worlds which was a castle with portals to other dimensions on the rare occasions that he had time to be there. His time now, however, was needed in the capitol city of the Water Elves to handle affairs of state. Not that he enjoyed it much. Now, sitting over a stack of papers on matters of laws and state, he truly felt the weight of his decision sink in. Honour had driven his choice initially when his friend Iliam Starview had been injured by a Fire Elf infiltrator, but now he was filled with regret. The game of politics was not what Puc had ever wished for. His eyes then wandered to the map of the Eye to All Worlds that was framed on the opposite end of the room. He'd drawn it for Orbeyus many years ago, during days that were far happier than his present.

He stifled a yawn, and he pushed back a handful of shoulder-length black hair, then ran his fingers over the short trimmed goatee. It had been a recent addition of late, partially out of the boredom of routine he experienced. He had grown it out in the same style his father had worn before him, but was unsure if it was a wise decision, and almost every day he had a moment of weakness where he wanted to sheer it off, but he didn't.

Removing the outer layer of his robes, he set them on the back on his chair, hoping the cooling of his body would help jolt him somewhat more awake. There was still so much to do. A knock then, fortunately, came at the door, doing this for him.

"Enter." He turned the page he'd been reading.

The tall wooden door opened and in came a young woman, maybe a little older than Annetta. She was of slight stature with deep brown frizzy hair and dressed in the black robes of the Academy students. Puc recognized her as one of the intern mages that were helping around the Tower while school was dismissed for the holidays.

"A letter came for you, First Mage." She managed to say and quickly handed him an envelope with a red wax seal on it.

Puc frowned. The hour was late for such deliveries, but he rose to accept it nonetheless. He could see the unease in the girl's pale blue Water Elf eyes as she averted his gaze and remembered his own early days of being nervous upon being in the presence of the First Mage.

"I do not bite, young one, if that is what you are worried about." He ran his fingers over the folded parchment she'd handed him. "The wolves at our gates are the ones you should be wary of. My thanks for the letter."

The girl nodded and with a light curtsey, she retreated. Puc paid her no more heed and focused on the insignia that was stamped into the wax of the seal. The sigil was an eye with another eye in its pupil. Puc guessed that if the image were enlarged, the pattern would continue in each eye until it was indiscernible. He knew to whom it belonged. Cracking open the wax, he read the contents within.

To First Mage Puc Thanestorm, he that is of the line of Oberon and Titania,

As these words cannot leave our halls and must be heard by your ears, we summon you to Wyrdland Marsh. Bring only him who you trust most in this world as your companion.

Signed,
The Sisters of Wyrd

Puc lowered himself into his chair, glaring at the cryptic words. He folded the paper and smoothed it out on his desk as he committed the contents to memory. The Sisters of Wyrd had remained secluded from almost all of Aldamoor's dealings throughout the years, and only ever wrote to the First Mage if something beyond the physical realm bade them do so.

He knew there was no point in trying to guess what could be the matter, and for all he knew, they would point out some celestial event on the heavens that would hold no meaning at all to his people. It had happened once or twice before. The part that did stump him was the request at the end.

"Bring only him who I trust most in this world." He let the words reverberate through his throat as he reflected on their meaning.

His most immediate thought was to bring himself, but no, there was something about the wording that indicated there was another that needed to hear what was to be said. They had specifically mentioned a companion in the prose for a reason.

Rolling up the left sleeve of his white shirt, he uncovered a large octagonal watch with a black leather cuff that displayed two different times on it. He flipped open the faceplate to reveal a number pad and typed in a combination.

"117 here." Darius's voice answered him through the speaker on the device.

"05 here," Puc answered. "Have the lads got you busy in the Lab?"

"Nothing out of the ordinary. I mean, aside from the usual teenage fits from Xander and Liam… and, well, Jason has been missing a lot of practice, what with preparing to move into that off-campus residence him and Sarina are renting for school. Why?" he asked.

Puc nodded and stroked his beard as he formulated a plan, then stopped himself.

"Any chance that I might steal you away for a trip to the Wyrdland Marsh?"

⊰⊱

Preparations were set into place early the next day, and Puc awaited the arrival of his old apprentice in the stables below the High Council Tower. He stood a fair distance away from the stalls, with both hands resting on his gnarled wooden staff. His right hand, placed higher than his left, traced the velvety moss which grew in all its green splendour as though the staff had been but a stick in the woods he had picked up on a random walk. His thin jaw twitched as he watched an approaching rider draw closer.

The chestnut gelding came to a stop and the figure riding it, clad in a dark grey cloak, dropped its hood to reveal Darius's face. He seemed older to Puc now as he sat atop his horse. It was not just the short black hair he had taken to wearing or the stubble that was starting to come in on his chin and whiskers. It was the look he carried in his dark brown eyes, the weight of responsibility that Puc was too familiar with in his own face whenever he glanced in the mirror.

"First Mage." Darius inclined his head as he descended from the saddle with a small thud of his boots on cobblestone.

"Just Puc will still do." The older mage gave a slight smile and turned to go into the stables. "I've had a second mount prepared for you. I do not think it wise we waste time if the Sisters of Wyrd have given us a summons."

"Any idea what it could be about?" Darius held the reins of his animal as he led it into the stables.

"I'm afraid not."

Puc led the way inside as stable hands bustled about them, first taking Darius's horse and then leading out another for him. This one was a bay-coloured gypsy vanner. Darius petted the muzzle gently, familiarizing himself with the animal briefly before mounting up again. Puc followed suit on his own horse, another vanner, of solid black.

"I see despite your status that travelling on horseback still plays a role. I was half expecting us to be flown in by airship," Darius teased.

"If I were to allow my fear to rule me, then yes," Puc answered, fastening his staff to his saddle packs before mounting himself. "If, however, I am to show my face as First Mage of this city, then I cannot run from such things. Besides, I would rather this voyage go undetected."

Darius nodded as the two of them raised their hoods. Gentling nudging their horses, took off towards the western gate of the city.

⚜

The journey to the Wyrdland Marsh had taken Darius and Puc off the western road to Alfheim and north, where the waterfalls that created the northern wall of Aldamoor held their point of origin. The trees further north grew thicker and taller, causing their horses to stay on the premade trampled out paths. Not long after, however, the immense sentinels soon gave way to shorter and smaller vegetation that was able to survive the wet environment that composed the marsh.

Scanning the horizon as the afternoon sun beat down on them, Puc soon found what he was looking for and descended from his mount. He led it over to what appeared to be a wooden dock nestled among the reeds. At its edge, a large wooden ferry rested with a few wooden railings built on the sides for support. They secured their horses on the attached beams, and Puc pushed them off the edge with a long pole.

"Have you ever been to see the Sisters of Wyrd before?" Darius asked, trying to break some of the silent tension that was beginning to mount inside of him. "I heard they've existed since the beginning of the world itself."

"Only once, and it was a long time ago," he answered, the same unease present in his voice. "They had summoned young Orbeyus when he had first come to Aldamoor to seek our aid in the fight against Mordred the Conqueror. They wanted to give him their blessing in the task that was to come and to ask me to go with him."

Darius's eyebrows knotted upon hearing this. "I thought you went of your own free will?"

"I did, but the Sisters of Wyrd simply gave me affirmation that the choice I wanted to make was the right one," he replied. "Sometimes, the words of those unknown to us are the trigger we need to start our great adventure."

They soon came upon the shore of the other side of the marsh. Leading their horses across the rickety planks which created a dock, Puc and Darius were quickly greeted by torches guarding the entrance of an immense grotto hewn in dark grey stone.

Puc could sense his old apprentice's unease at the gloomy entrance, for it did not look appealing in the least. He then turned to him and said, "You've nothing to fear in here. As much as I dislike them, the horses would have told us were anything amiss already."

Darius nodded, his shoulders somewhat relaxing as they continued. A grey-cloaked and hooded figure emerged soon after to block their path. Its stature was almost as tall as Puc himself, and it carried a long sword strapped to its back made of gold and silver, its guard resembling a half gear.

"Greetings," Puc addressed it, unfazed. "I am Puc Thanestorm, First Mage of Aldamoor, son of Titania and Oberon. I come in answer to the summons sent to me from the Sisters of Wyrd. I bring, as instructed, one who is closest to me of all, Darius Silver, Mage of Aldamoor."

The guardian examined them from the obscurity of its hood and nodded once satisfied with its assessment. It then turned wordlessly and proceeded to go back into the cave, and the two of them followed along with their horses.

Darius mentally prepared himself to traverse the dark, and was surprised that upon crossing the threshold of the cave to find his senses assaulted by gold-tinted lights from enormous crystal chandeliers which hung from an impossibly high ceiling above. His eyes adjusting, he then noticed that they stood upon an upper terrace, and further below, a sepia marble floor stretched all across, the seal of the Sisters of Wyrd recreated upon its surface in darker coloured stone. The walls of the cave, or room, he then noted, were stacked with shelves of multi-coloured tomes in varying sizes. Scurrying about and oblivious to the new arrivals, female acolytes in grey robes bustled about, moving or replacing volumes of work. Their actions as they worked, seemed mechanical in nature. Two such acolytes climbed up the stairs towards them and only stopped once within speaking range.

"With your permission, we can attend your mounts while you meet with the Elder Sister." The first of the two bowed her head in a humble and respectable tone.

Puc obliged, and removing his staff to take with him, he handed his reins to the second young woman, while Darius did the same. They then continued after the hooded figure, who seemed to glide upon the polished floors. Turning into one of the many side corridors, they soon found themselves in a much narrower part of the cave. Candleholders lined the walls, the candles within half-melted and dripping onto the floors, producing much less light than the chandeliers in the main hall. They came to a stop at a large wooden door which the guardian opened, allowing for them to walk inside. The interior of this room was brightly lit again. More shelves with books and scrolls lined it all around and at its centre was a great stone desk with ornate wooden chairs on either side.

The hooded figure then strode before them, abandoning its watchful post.

"It has been some time now, First Mage Thanestorm, since last our paths crossed," a woman's voice with an old and commanding presence spoke from beneath the cowl.

Dropping her hood, she revealed a long golden braid that was pinned up. Turning around, she faced Puc and Darius. Despite her voice, she seemed only a few years older than Puc himself, with a face of alabaster, sharp features chiselled onto her calm visage. A long, thin scar trailed from one side of her neck all the way across it and ended on the opposite side of her face at her temple.

"Indeed it has, Lysania Chironkin." He inclined his head in mutual greeting.

Darius also bowed his head and felt his jaw go slack upon hearing the name as he tried to form a coherent sentence. He knew it all too well and the history surrounding the one who wore it.

"Lysania Chironkin as in…." he managed to say.

"Sister of Chiron the Creator and founder of the Sisters of Wyrd." She gave a slight smile. "Welcome, Darius Silver, into my halls."

The woman, Lysania, then made her way around the stone desk and in a fluid motion seated herself, then raised her hand to show them both to do the same. Darius and Puc complied.

"I came as soon as I received the letter." Puc broke the silence.

"It is a good thing you did, for the issue at hand is time sensitive," Lysania said. "I summoned you both here today, for I have need of your connections within the realm of humans."

"What is it that you need?" Puc leaned forward in his seat.

"It is not so much a need," she replied, "as it is a request. There is a young human woman I wish for you to locate. She holds sensitive information, and if taken by the wrong people, it can go horribly for all of us. When you find her, I need you to bring her to us for safekeeping."

"That is rather unspecific," Puc stated. "What are we looking for exactly in her?"

"You will know when you meet her, for she will know you without knowing that she does," Lysania told him. "Or rather, I suppose Darius will know, since you no longer traverse their world much."

"Isn't there anything else that you can tell us?" Darius questioned again. "Hair colour, eye colour, a name?"

"These things have been clouded to me from the start. We have only been able to pinpoint that she is in the same city as young Severio and Kinsman," Lysania admitted. "We also know that she will be important in the battle to come, for the seed of chaos has begun to stir, and when it does awake, all worlds shall quake."

Puc's eyes narrowed as he remembered where those words were from, his grip slightly tightening around his staff as he readied himself to leave.

Lysania met his gaze. "These words, Thanestorm, you know to be true. You have known all along."

Puc nodded somberly and rose. "We will do what we can, Elder Sister."

"I should hope so, for our world's sake, and the sake of the Aternaverse."

Chapter 3

Green eyes focused on the screen as his hands pressed various combinations of buttons on the video game controller Jason Kinsman held in his grasp. His training session had been called off for the day, since Darius had received a request from Puc to see him. The summons had been of an urgent nature that could not wait, and so currently, Jason found himself seated cross-legged on the bed in Sarina's quarters within Q-16, engrossed the in the latest turn-based adventure RPG he'd been playing when time allowed. He was dressed in his usual attire of a loose red t-shirt and jeans, his running shoes having been left at the side of the room to prevent him trailing mud, a habit he'd been scolded for more than once. The room itself was relatively spacious, and could have been mistaken for a small apartment, complete with a bathroom and kitchen that were separated by light mocha-coloured walls. Shelves and other furnishings dotted the space in an orderly and homey fashion in complementing colours of green and grey. Jason remembered when Sarina had first come to live in the Lab and how different the space had become since then. It seemed more at case than the utilitarian style the room had taken on over two years ago when she'd first used the hand scanner that customized it to her needs. Jason still couldn't get over the fact that such a thing existed in the Lab.

Beside him, further up on the bed and with her back to the wall was Sarina. Instead of a book in her grasp this time, however, she held a laptop. Her face was obscured for the most part by the large screen as she clicked and typed on the bulky contraption, muttering to herself the odd time. Her auburn hair had grown somewhat longer throughout the summer, and she currently wore it pinned back with a hair clip to prevent it from falling in her eyes.

The clicking stopped, and her head peered over the edge of the screen. "Have you registered for your classes yet?"

"No, I don't get my slot to register for another week. Why?" Jason half turned to face her.

"I was attempting to pick some electives that we could take together," she explained, lowering the screen, her large brown almond-shaped eyes focusing on him intently.

"Oh." Jason paused the game to fully turn his attention to her. "I mean, I don't really care what electives you choose. What did you have in mind?"

"Well…" Sarina pulled something up on her screen and turned it to face him.

Jason squinted as he read what was on the screen. "Biophysics of movement and the senses? A short history of engines? Introduction to herbalism and alternative medicines? You do know an elective is meant to be a class that you can slack off in, right?"

"But don't you want to learn? Isn't that the point of us going to school?" She raised an eyebrow.

"If you haven't noticed yet, not everyone shares your enthusiasm for learning." Jason sighed.

Before Sarina could say anything further, there was a beep from the machine and looking down, she growled. "Unknown's bane, not again!"

Jason glanced down to see a welcome screen with some text on it. "It rebooted again?"

"Yes." She replied in defeat.

The boy scrunched up his nose as he tried to think of their next course of action. When it dawned on him, he said, "Well, no time like the present to go visit the mad scientist in her lair."

₲*⃩

Oblivious to the world around her save for the buzzing of halogen lights far above her head, Skyris Severio found herself completely immersed in her current masterpiece. Keen blue eyes focused on her point of interest as long nimble fingers stained black worked a flathead screwdriver ever so carefully in order to not lose the single screw she had already had to try fitting in twice now, due to the slick surface created by the oil that was present in the joints of her contraption. She stood upon a scissor lift dressed down to only jeans tucked into high black boots and a tattered grey tank top. Suspended in the air, her point of interest was what could only be described as a large mechanical suit. An angry dark silver in colour with currently inactive red eyes, it stood at over thirty feet tall, a variety of multi-coloured cables visible in spots where no armour now covered it. Tubes seemed to protrude from its back and were attached to various other machines and containers sprawled out all over her work area. Her task completed, she took a step back on the platform, retying her loose ponytail to prevent it from slipping more.

Cocking her head to the side, she took the thing in as a whole and grabbing an orange juice jug that lay beside her, she took a swig of it.

As she recovered from the bitter aftertaste, she heard a distinct hovering noise coming from behind her.

Without flinching, she spoke, "How do you like it, Dex?"

The object of her addressing, a large floating oval with a single red eye, hovered closer until it was almost beside her.

"I do not understand the need behind this mechanical suit. It goes beyond any biological need you might have as a Gaian woman in perfect health," it replied.

Skyris, unamused with the answer, simply rolled her eyes. "AI's."

She then removed a flask from the brown leather bomber jacket lined with fluffy sheepskin, which was flung haphazardly over the railing of the scissor lift platform and drank from it. Just as she replaced the cap, her attention was turned to the sound of feet moving along the metal floors of the base. Soon after, Sarina and Jason appeared at the threshold of the room and stopped upon seeing her project.

"What on Earth is that?" Jason pointed, his eyes wide open.

Nonchalantly, Skyris pushed the lever on the scissor lift and allowed for it to bring her down to their level. She then exited the platform and walked over to them, Dexter trailing the entire way.

"I believe in Japanese cartoons they are sometimes called mechs or mobile suits," she explained, finding a rug on one of the nearby workstation tables and proceeding to clean off her fingers. "I can't remember which one I happened across and watched, but it looked cool, and I couldn't stop thinking about how something like it would run, so I decided to make one."

"Wait, you built that thing because you thought it was cool?" Jason recapped, still in shock.

Skyris shrugged. "Why does every invention need a reason behind it? Yes, I thought they looked cool, so I wanted to see what it would take to build one in real life. Turns out the building isn't the hard part, it's the software and coding afterwards which may be a headache."

"It certainly is impressive," Sarina chimed in. "My father would have probably killed for such a weapon."

"Yes, and it's a good thing he isn't around anymore." Skyris winked and took a drink from her orange juice. "So, what brings you both here?"

Wordlessly, Sarina held out the enormous brick of a contraption, to which Skyris raised an eyebrow and lowered the scissor lift. She stepped off the platform and accepted the brick reluctantly. Her hands dropped slightly, not anticipating the weight of the thing and giving it a slight shake, she inspected it from all angles before opening the screen.

"Unknown's bane, you use that to connect to the web? Was it invented by Neanderthals?" The woman gaped at it.

"It's the best on the market," Jason protested.

Ignoring the comment, Skyris walked further into the depths of the workshop, leaving the laptop on a table along the way. She then called once she was out of sight among the many contraptions, "Do you ever bring it out of the Lab?"

"No." Sarina shook her head. "Though, I will have to for note taking once I start university."

There was no reply, but soon after Skyris re-emerged. She carried with her a flat rectangular object, twice as sleek as the machine Jason and Sarina had just brought over. She then handed it to the girl.

"At least ten years if not more on your current model in terms of speed and connection, but still easy enough for you to operate. I'm sure, however, the technology on Valdhar was far beyond this, but I feel its best you get used to Earth technology if you wish to blend in above." She wiped her hands on her pants.

"It's so light." Sarina examined it.

"I'll have to check what's going to be coming out soon to match you up with something decent before the start of school." Skyris grabbed the jacket from the railing and threw it on. "Both of you, that is, and Annetta as well I would assume, once she gets back. Thankfully, humans seem to be in a technological boom, and all of these things change every few months or so."

"Do we know when Annetta will be coming back?" Sarina asked. "I mean, did she even get her acceptance letter to school? Does she have any orientations she needs to go to or supplies she needs to get?"

Jason stifled a laugh. "All this time and you still don't know Anne. She'll come back three days before, guns blazing and stress fueling her very existence to rush everything last minute. That's how every year has gone before."

"As for school, she did get accepted," Skyris replied. "Police Foundations, and I've made sure that my dear brother sends her back early enough so that she can get everything in order."

Their eyes then all met in silence as the same thought flashed across their eyes, the real reason they felt Annetta had stayed behind on

Gaia. Link's death. No matter how much she had tried to mask it when they asked, the truth had become apparent when they found her at his tomb the day after Venetor's coronation.

"Do you think she will be over him?" Sarina inquired.

"Over? No. Not fully, that is." Skyris shook her head. "We don't get over these sort of things. Death has a way of taking a small fraction of our soul with it, and the only thing we can do is to keep going despite the missing pieces."

Jason nodded at hearing this. He couldn't really comprehend what Annetta was feeling, nor did she share any of it with him before he left Gaia. She had remained a rock the entire time, taking on her mantle as the White Lioness of Gaia and playing it without breaking character while in public. He could only speculate and if it was anything like what the potential of losing Sarina felt then he didn't wish it upon anyone else.

⊰⊱

The sound of great bat wings flapping reverberated through Annetta's mind as she closed her eyes and dunked her head into the sink, hoping the sound of rushing water would drown it out. She stayed under only a few seconds, and unable to hold her breath any longer, whipped her head out, shaking it from side to side. She then glared into the mirror in her bathroom, her visage barely visible beyond the veil of the fog that had gathered on its surface. She didn't understand what all these dreams she kept having meant, but the fact that they kept reoccurring bothered her. She'd had multiple instances of similar dreams before, but this was happening every night.

"Why?" she said in a barely audible tone.

Mechanically, she then went about getting ready. She put on her Gaian armour which consisted of a single piece suit of beta scale mail which clung to her body like a second skin and loose woolen dark brown pants that were tucked into polished leather boots. She then donned her red cape with a white lioness stitched into it and fastened it with a silver lion brooch. Deeming her outfit presentable, she then brushed out the tangles from her hair and went to go put on the slightest bit of makeup.

Before Skyris had left to go back to Earth, she had suggested Annetta try using eyeliner to bring out her eyes more. Despite Annetta's apprehension, she allowed Skyris to apply it once and saw that indeed it made a difference. She looked somehow older, fiercer. It made her feel good to have it on, as though a missing piece of her had been found. She had been using it ever since, and had even thanked Skyris on one of their video chats from Earth, something she regularly did with her aunt of late. Thinking on it made her want to call her now, to hear some words of advice on the meeting she was to attend, but she knew there was no time.

Annetta then headed back to her room and grabbed her sword belt, Severbane swaying oddly by her leg as she put it on. She was used to a more modern style of belt, but Venetor had insisted she begin using a ring belt instead, a task which was proving more daunting than she wanted to admit. There then came a knock at the door, causing her to stop.

"Lass, it's time, the gruff, accented voice spoke from beyond.

"Almost ready, Gladius," she replied, fumbling with the belt as she tried to remember how she was to loop it through so it didn't look so clumsy. "I'm having some technical difficulties with my sword belt."

"I can assist ya if that be the case. Ya know how Venetor likes to be on time to these things."

Annetta fought with the belt a few moments longer as she considered the offer, and then caved. "Okay, you can come in."

The door opened, and in strode Gladius. He was nearly seven feet tall, and had the face of a badger with a thick, bushy mane and distinctly-trimmed mutton chops. A brown leather eyepatch with silver filigree covered one eye, across which an enormous scar that had also removed part of his long rabbit-like ear marred his face. His good ear was pierced with multiple silver hoop earrings, which jingled as it twitched back and forth. A leather cuirass adorned his chest, with a green cape that draped from one side, beefy arms covered in short grey fur and scars visible from beneath it, and a pair of matching bracers on each forearm. A large sword was strapped to his back which resembled a massive slab of iron more than a sword, and could only be wielded by one as large as he. Black pants that were tucked into high black boots completed the ensemble.

Annetta gave a nod in greeting and gave him the belt.

Gladius accepted it, and coming closer, he looped the strap of the belt around her. "Now, what seems to be tha problem?"

"Venetor wanted me to start using that military style for tying the sword belt up," she explained. "Except I can't remember for the life of me the steps to do it."

"Well, that can cause some complications, now can't it?" Gladius snickered as he proceeded. "Ya go through the ring, then up from below and down through the loop."

The whole process seemed so effortless on the part of the Hurtz that Annetta felt her ears turn red from shame at not having remembered.

His task completed, Gladius then took a step back to examine his handy work. "Aye, it'll hold. Are ye ready otherwise, lass?"

"Yeah, I don't think there was anything else I needed to take with me," she said.

The two of them then set off, Gladius leading the way through the halls of Castrumleo, as it was customary for the Hurtz lord to lead his charge, the young woman who was the White Lioness of Gaia. Outwardly, Annetta did her best to smile and wave when expected as she passed by the various occupants of the castle, but on the inside, she was not too fond of the attention. When Annetta had been on the battlefield fighting against Razmus and his army just a few months prior, there had been little time to consider the long-term consequences of her actions. She only knew how superstitious the Gaians were about their prophecies, and that she had to try to do something to turn the tide in their favour. They had needed a symbol to boost morale, and she had provided one.

Coming to the front entrance, the two were greeted by the sight of Venetor speaking to some nobles. In addition to his armour, similar to the one Annetta was wearing, he now wore the Gaian crown on his brow. It was a heavy-looking thing, more war helm than a symbol of office, its silver surface inlaid with intricate patterns. At its centre, a fiery crimson gem glinted in the light as Venetor's head moved while he spoke.

The Gaian king then noticed them and excused himself from the conversation.

"Ready?" he asked.

"Now or never." Annetta hooked her thumbs through her sword belt, pleased to find it had not moved since having been put on.

Venetor nodded and then turned to Gladius, who wore a neutral expression on his face.

"Need ye really ask m'lord?" The Hurtz raised his good eyebrow.

Without anything else to say, the trio then left the castle. Walking some distance from the grounds, they then came upon a vehicle which

Annetta could only describe as a small space shuttle. She considered it small, due to being no larger than a minivan from Earth, and from what she recalled, Earth shuttles were much larger in comparison. It also appeared to be solid, with no visible panels along its hunter-green body. Some symbols in red were painted on it, but she couldn't discern what these were and only assumed that they were alien in origin.

"Was there anything else available?" Venetor inspected it.

Annetta tore her gaze away from the craft. "What's wrong with this one?"

"A civilian vessel. A very low-class citizen vessel, and one some among the Federation will point out as a sign of weakness" He turned to face her.

"We're in the process of rebuilding all that was lost, m'lord," Gladius explained. "This was one of tha few vessels left intact after tha purge Razmus performed."

Annetta watched as Venetor sighed in frustration, doing his best to push his churning rage inside away from the surface. The reconstruction of the Gaian space fleet was a daunting task, and one that caused him to have little sleep. There was much rebuilding to do, not only the ships but of Hurtz and Gaian relations after the bloody battle under the gates of Pangaia. It seemed that wherever she went, she heard talks of it, and she could only sympathize from a distance about her uncle's plight. In this, they were both symbols for a nation trying to rise out from the ashes.

"It will have to do, then." The Gaian king frowned as he patted the side of the ship.

&)(&

Not long after she'd boarded, Annetta found herself stepping on a platform that had been connected to the ship to allow entrance into the Una Space Station where the Federation meetings occurred.

"Meetings are not held on any one world to prevent any sort of favouritism among races," Venetor explained as they walked the corridor and exited into a slightly larger room with smooth, dark-grey walls.

In the middle was a small booth with what looked to be glass windows, like a customs officer would sit at in an airport. Annetta noted, however, that the creature sitting inside was far from human-looking. It had a humanoid shape to it, however, its cranium was slightly elongated, and its skin was a jade green with black and red markings all on its face. A set of obsidian eyes looked on at the trio with an apathetic expression to match.

"Elodian," Gladius whispered into her ear as they approached. "It is said that they can pick up any language upon hearing just a few words. Comes as natural to them as breathing does to us apparently, and not ta worry lass, they are not so fearsome as their appearance makes em to be."

Gladius's words rang true, for as soon as the Elodian saw they were within speaking distance, it smiled the strangest of smiles, with its serrated, shark-like teeth. It then addressed them in a language Annetta could pick nothing out from aside from it having a bunch of odd clicking sounds in it.

Venetor responded as if completely clear on what was being said. "Greetings, and just Northern Gaian, please."

"Ah, my apologies," the creature spoke in a clear male voice. "It is required I address everyone in the language of the current Federation head. Will you require T.A.A.'s for today's meeting?"

"T.A.A.'s?" Annetta asked Gladius off to the side.

"Translation and Atmosphere Adjusters," he answered stiffly. "Because there be so many different species which are used to different conditions, tha device was created to allow for us all to be able to communicate with one another and survive in a single room."

The girl nodded, while Venetor continued to speak with the Elodian behind the glass. She then saw the being produce something from under the counter, and upon closer inspection, Annetta saw that it was three large pills. A pouch of clear liquid in what she could only discern to look like a blood bag accompanied each. Venetor took a pair and handed it to Annetta.

"You will need to swallow this." He indicated to the pill. "It contains the necessary nanobots to rewire your brain so that you can understand all speech. It works similarly to how when you cross through a portal, you are able to understand the language of the natives, but on a much larger scale. Its effects wear off in forty-eight hours. The bag is just water, easier to transport this way."

Annetta nodded somewhat sceptically, and watched as both Venetor and Gladius took the pills first, then washed them down with the contents of the bag. She sighed, glancing down at the oblong white pill in her hand. Annetta had never been a fan of taking pills and avoided them whenever possible when sick. Accepting that there was no way out for her this time, she popped it into her mouth and taking a swig from the bag, swallowed. She then waited, but felt no different.

"There won't be any fireworks like after one of Puc's potions, if that is what you are expecting," Venetor spoke as if he had read her mind. "I can tell by the tension in your neck you're waiting for something to happen. Well, it isn't."

The girl sighed, feeling somewhat embarrassed but did not voice her opinion, and instead followed the Gaian king's lead down another narrow hallway that led out of their current whereabouts. The hall was so tight, in fact, they had to walk in single file, Gladius at the head of the group with Venetor behind him and Annetta in the back. A sense of dread came over the girl, her mind analyzing what would happen if they were attacked in such close quarters. Her hand then reached for the hilt of Severbane, and she realized it was still there.

"Won't they disarm us before we go in?" she asked.

"They already did," Venetor replied. "An entire scan was done of the ship and its occupants when we came into the base's reach. Weapons that are in plain view and cannot be concealed are not seen as a threat. Those entering with them acknowledge that they are conscious of bringing something that can be used as a weapon and only do so for self-defence purposes and to show the status of their office. Had the Federation any doubt about what we bring onboard, there would have been a team to examine us in the room we just left."

Annetta found the notion backwards but nodded nonetheless. Who was she to question alien practices?

They continued to trudge down the never-ending hallway until they finally reached an exit which led out onto a balcony that had a control panel at the front of it with a screen. A lavish red velvet sofa made up the edges of the platform, and three matching seats were set in the middle.

Making herself aware of her surroundings, Annetta then focused her gaze further and noticed that they were in an enormous spherical room which contained thousands of other such platforms. Above, a transparent dome that showed the dark of space with a million stars glinted like a haunting chandelier. Trying to make out the various forms aboard the other balconies, Annetta's eyes were then drawn to a platform on the far side of them. This one seemed larger, and a banner hung behind it, bearing a crest with a blazing star inside of a circle on a field of light blue. The girl searched her memory and identified it as the crest of the Federation. Straining her sight further, she could make out little figures, ones she was sure were none other than the Greys. It still baffled her that the creatures were real.

What struck her as odder, however, was the fact that they seemed to be fumbling about in preparation for the meeting. Three of them were huddled in a group on one end, examining a small projection in a heated discussion, while another two made sure everything was set in an orderly fashion on the platform. The movements seemed so uncanny to the girl that she felt squeamish and looked away.

She then felt as though someone was watching her and turned sideways to see the occupants of the balcony beside theirs staring at her in a predatory manner. As soon as she locked eyes with them, they turned away and resumed talking amongst themselves. The creatures in question were small, reptilian in nature with leathery purple skin of various tones, parrot-like beaks and large yellow eyes.

"I see ya recognize the Imap." Gladius whispered into her ear, causing her to turn and face him. "Most likely they know you as well, if their stares are any indication. They've just recently been let back into being part of the Federation after being on trial for their part in Mislantus's plans to take the Eye to All Worlds. Pleaded insane on their fanatic belief in his words. Bunch of sabertooth dog faeces if you ask me."

"Gladius," Venetor hissed. "They have pretty good hearing."

"Aye, and it doesn't stop them from talking about yer niece." Gladius's good ear flattened back, his good eye landing on the creatures in a testing manner."

"Yes, and you know we need to be politically correct here," The Gaian king reminded him.

Before Annetta could chip in her two cents, there came a deafening screech like a microphone being adjusted with the sound on, but much higher pitched. She searched for where the sound had come from, and her attention then turned to the central platform where a Grey was standing at the podium.

"Fellow members of the Federation." It addressed those gathered and continued on in such a manner, relaying fineries and then diving into the minutes from the previous meeting.

Taking her respective seat beside Venetor on the right as he had instructed her in the shuttle, Annetta did her best to stay awake and alert. Her focus, however, was not only swayed by the monotone droning of the Grey about taxation laws, regulations on flight zones, border disputes and the like, but also by the various looks which seemed to gravitate towards their balcony. Even though she could not physically see the pairs of eyes looking her way, Annetta could feel their heat press in on her. She could only hope that these gazes were of a curious nature and that was the extent of their intent.

Chapter 4

Elsewhere, in another corner of space, a star-shaped mask that had been broken on one side glinted in the dark, firelight tinting its surface red. It was not the light of an actual fire, but that of a furious gas giant that lay some distance away from the glass which separated Amarok Mezorian from its blaze. In his time on Gaia, spent aiding Razmus building his tower, Amarok had been secretly reconstructing Valdhar to its previous glory after the floating castle had sustained significant damage in the battle to take control of the Eye to All Worlds two years prior. The fruits of his labour had paid off and the castle was now once again fully operational.

Standing in the now-abandoned audience chamber that had once belonged to Mislantus the Threat, son of Mordred the Conqueror, Amarok found it ironic that he was about to begin the task of undoing the Freiuson family legacy from the throne room of those who had upheld it so dearly. The room was massive, even for the size of an audience chamber. Cold dark walls adorned one end and the walls looking out were made of a transparent material capable of withstanding the harsh nature of space. The vacant throne, a commanding presence of sharply-angled features built of the same materials as the walls, seemed to blend into the floor. The only thing which gave any vibrancy to the hall was the large banner which hung behind the throne, the Freiuson coat of arms, which featured a seven-headed black dragon with ten stars encircling its head on a field of grey. After a more extended stare, it too seemed to be part of the walls, unnoticeable, yet present all the same.

A scraggly-looking figure in a tattered, soiled lab coat then appeared in the doorway holding a tablet in its hand. Underneath the mess of white hair and beard, a pair of intelligent eyes darted back and forth, as if expecting a ghost to manifest in the chamber.

"Enter, mister Abner." Amarok's long white hair glided over his shoulders as he turned to him. "You've no need to fear these walls. I can assure you that the most deadly thing present is speaking to you now."

Lloyd Abner, the man who had once been responsible for creating the Pessumire, the veil-piercing cannon that allowed Valdhar to create portals, took a tentative step forward.

"The coordinates have been set as you requested," he said, jovially. "A sample is required, however, to calibrate it."

Amarok glanced down for a moment before he noted an overturned pewter goblet on the floor. Picking it up, he used his psychic abilities to extend one of the serpentine-like blades on his forearm armour and slashed his palm open. Crimson liquid dripped into the cup and once the bottom layer of the cup was covered in blood, he extended it towards him.

"Will this do?" He pressed the goblet forward.

Squeamishly, Lloyd accepted the chalice. "I believe it will be sufficient for the Pessumire to calibrate a destination. Am I to suspect we are then going to your home dimension?"

A small smile formed on the scarred features of Amarok's lips beneath his mask. "Point of origin, yes, but no, not my home."

⁊ɔɕ

Once all was said and done, Annetta found herself exhausted mentally from having been slumped in her chair for hours. She tried to retain any information she could from the meeting, but most of it was about issues on planets that she'd never heard of. The only points of interest that had managed to catch her attention were the state of the Gaian space vehicle crisis and how Gaia was fairing after their ordeal with Razmus.

When Venetor had stood to speak regarding these issues, he looked as though a cloak of lead had been draped across his back. It was then that she saw firsthand the extent of the burden of what it meant to be a leader of a nation. It was not to say that he didn't do so gracefully, despite the quarrel he supposedly had with the Greys. Whatever his feelings were regarding that issue, they had been shelved. She also noted that Venetor had chosen to omit the detail of Valdhar being spotted in the sky leaving Gaia's atmosphere just as the battle was being won by their side, and wondered why.

Her will finally faltering, Annetta pressed a hand over her mouth, allowing a yawn to escape as they got up to leave their balcony.

"You did a good job of keeping that back," Venetor said, noticing her gesture.

Annetta felt her ears go red from having been caught. "I couldn't help myself."

"I don't think many can, if I be bold enough to say so, lass," Gladius replied as they trio began to make their way back to the ship.

"I remember being present at Venetor's first meeting. He yawned in the first five minutes."

"And father never let me live it down." Venetor rolled his eyes. "I was perhaps twelve at the time. Much younger than you. Orbeyus had just left to go find the Eye to All Worlds, and our father had just disowned him, giving me the title of Crown Prince of Gaia."

"Did my great grandfather ever forgive my grandpa?" Annetta asked. "For leaving Gaia?"

Venetor looked down, the heavy silver Gaian crown resting solidly on his brow. He seemed to swim in his thoughts and then looked forward. "It wasn't until I went to Earth with Skyris to aid him, not until the Federation in all its vanity had finally acknowledged that perhaps they had been wrong and that Mordred was indeed a threat, a conqueror on the scale of which they had not seen before. By then it was too late and the war lasted a decade. It could have easily been stopped in its tracks before then."

Annetta nodded at hearing this.

"Your great-grandfather did forgive Orbeyus for what he did." Venetor continued. "He was even offered back his place as Crown Prince should he have chosen to return, but he had fallen in love with Earth, calling it his home along with his son. He, above all others, understood the value of protecting our sister planet and that never again would it be without a Severio to watch over it. That is why he was so keen for you and your brother to see the same in it."

Annetta's attention was then taken elsewhere as she caught blurred figures standing in the distance by where their shuttle was docked. The elongated grey heads and large black almond-shaped eyes instantly made them recognizable. The Greys.

Approaching their visitors, Annetta noted that all three of those gathered seemed to be wearing orange and grey space suits. Each had the emblem of the Federation on their right side. The closer they got, the more detail Annetta could see in the aliens, features she had not noticed during their previous visit to Gaia. Thin slits were barely visible where their noses were meant to be, and the taut skin which was wrapped around their enormous craniums was not a flawless grey, but one that was mottled with veins visible through it here and there. Their obsidian eyes held a varied texture in them, like a human iris, and at their centres were cat-slit pupils which regarded her and her companions with an indifferent gaze.

"Greetings, King Venetor." The closest of the three inclined their head, a slight smile forming on its almost-invisible lips as it addressed them telepathically.

"My greetings to you as well." Venetor gave a stiff bow and allowed a false smile to lace his face. "To what do I owe the pleasure of your visit?"

The second of the three, unidentifiable to Annetta from the other two, then took a step forward. "We came to ask how the repairs on your ships are going, as well as the quelling of any rebellions which may have arisen since the dethroning of your ancestor, Razmus."

Venetor gave a small chuckle and threw his hands up in their air as if to indicate the ship they had taken to get there. "They go as well as they can. No brigade was ever built in a day, and we lost almost every functioning space vehicle when Razmus took over the planet. He did not believe Gaians should have the power to explore the stars."

"Curious, for yet your ancestor Adeamus travelled all the way to Earth to found the Eye to All Worlds, did he not?" The third turned his attention away from the ship to gaze at them.

"As with any nation, there will always be extremists," Venetor replied. "Razmus was an extremist."

A silence occurred that proved somewhat uncomfortable. Annetta shifted on the balls of her heels, ready to take off at a moment's notice. A heavy hand then landed on her shoulder, causing her to look up and see Gladius hovering over her.

"Aye, but he has been dealt with now," the Hurtz said. "And if I may be so bold as to add, I don't think after the show of power that Gaia managed to demonstrate in its most dire moment will we ever see his like again."

"A very bold statement," the first of the three concluded. "Of course, it was also very fortunate that you had the White Lioness of Gaia appear to save the day. The Unknown, it seems, has greater things in store for your species."

Annetta felt her discomfort grow twofold as the dark saucer eyes of all three Greys landed upon her. It bothered her that she could not just simply come out and say that her transformation had been a fluke, that it was just a coincidence her feral form was that of a white lioness. She had been told, however, to say no such thing to anyone, for it would weaken her position in the eyes of others. Not that this false heroism made her feel any better about herself. In fact, she felt ridiculous to be lying about such a thing.

"It would have been most unfortunate if she hadn't been there," the same Grey said after a moment.

"We were lucky." Venetor's voice removed their gazes from Annetta. "And as you mentioned, the Unknown does have greater things in store for us yet."

There was no challenge in Venetor's, words Annetta noted. The Gaian king's face was neutral as he confronted the Greys in all the pleasant capacity of a monarch that he could radiate. This seemed to placate them, and what tension where was in the air dissipated.

"The unfolding of time will tell," the third of the Greys chimed in, and the group then began to walk away. "Until we meet again, your majesty."

As soon as they left, Venetor heaved a sigh that deflated his presence in the room by half. In place of the superior ruler of Gaia was a tired man, who could barely keep his head level from the weight of the crown resting on his brow.

"I think they're enjoying their elevation a bit much if ye ask me," Gladius grunted.

"It's not long until the election." Venetor removed the crown from his head and strode towards the ship. "Then they won't be singing that tune."

Annetta watched the passenger doors of the craft open. The three of them then climbed in, and Venetor with Gladius went about the task of preparing the ship to leave, while the girl observed curiously.

The question that had been gathering in her mind then formulated without hesitation. "What election?"

"Every ten rotations of the station around the star it orbits, about ten human years, a new planet is elected leader for the Federation. Planets can run multiple times and win up to five consecutive times. The Greys have won four times," Venetor explained, his eyes not leaving what he was doing on the touchscreens where the ship's controls were located.

"I see." Annetta found herself nodding. "Why didn't you mention Valdhar having been on Gaia and having been sighted by multiple people taking off into space?"

Venetor paused and turned his attention entirely to her. "I would think that to be obvious. There just isn't enough proof."

Annetta frowned. It was not the answer she had wished for, and she could only hope that Venetor had some ulterior motive in withholding the information from the Federation.

⁜

Elsewhere, Amarok stood still, transfixed by the star beyond the glass observation deck of the throne room. He observed in silence as the bright purple beam of the Pessumire collided with the blazing orange giant, the light of the cannon slowly taking over and swallowing the star. His good eye took in the sight of the star as it contorted like a rodent trying to escape a serpents grasp and then lay still. The area the star had occupied shrunk, and in its place, something else became visible. A portal.

"One." He smiled.

⁜

"One." A young woman sat hunched over her laptop in a bustling café, her bright green eyes beyond her rectangular glasses fixed on the screen as her fingers flew across the keyboard, messy black hair tied up in a bun. Dressed in worn denim pants and a black and red plaid shirt, Jansen Morrison was far from one who would stand out in a crowd, but blended in perfectly with her surroundings. Taking another sip from the coffee that sat beside her open laptop, she noted that it was empty. Jansen had gotten very good at keeping an even pace in drinking it, and so instead of continually bothering to check the time, her gauging how full her coffee cup was had become her watch. She sighed, unhappy at having to leave already, and proceeded to pack up her things. She had been on a roll the last few weeks, and the once-long hours seemed to zip by in minutes, the words virtually tumbling out of her brain.

"Finish that chapter yet?" A young man with scruffy blond hair from behind the counter, dressed in his franchise-mandatory uniform called to her as he rang another customer through.

Jansen screwed up her face as she tried to think of an honest answer. "I think so. Then again, this is just the first draft."

"Well, when it's published I want the first copy, okay?" He smiled.

She chuckled and blushed a bit. "I'll see what I can do. Take it easy, Travis, and don't work too hard."

"You know me, minimum wage, minimum effort." He grinned and went back to what he was doing.

Jansen nodded a final goodbye and pushed the door of the café open. As soon as she did, she was flooded with the sounds and scents of the bustling city life going on around her. Downtown Toronto was far from idle, especially in the summer months. Cars and cyclists darted back and forth along the roads beside the sidewalks, and multitudes of individuals walked them. Finding an opening much in the same way a salmon would try to snake their way upstream, Jansen joined the conveyor belt of bodies. Confident that her pacing matched those around her, she allowed her brain to fog over and bring herself back into the moment of what she was writing. She was not sure how to describe her process to others, but it was as natural to her as breathing.

What she was sure of was that the process seemed to place her into a sort of trance where the words being formed on the page took over, and everything else around her became hazy. She compared it to the memory of when she had gotten drunk at her best friend Jenny's birthday party in the tenth grade. Jenny's father had provided them with a six-pack of beer, because where he had come from, sixteen had been old enough to drink. The experience of writing, of course, did not have any of the adverse effects that the alcohol had, such as the dry mouth or a headache. All writing seemed to inflict on her was a need to write more, a fair trade-off, she felt. It made her feel accomplished.

Snapping out of her thoughts, Jansen nearly bumped into a discarded pylon beside a chunk of sidewalk that was being excavated.

"Sorry," she said to no one in particular and kept going, checking her shoulder bag every few minutes to make sure no one had swiped her computer. Her mother had always warned her about pickpockets in urban cities, even though she was in Canada, though a deeper part of her admitted the woman was overly paranoid. She was just an average girl amongst average people, trying to do something that perhaps wasn't seen as ordinary, but in a sea of many local artists of the urban strip, she was just a face in the crowd. Still, despite this grounded thinking, she tried to believe there was some meaning behind it all.

Jansen stopped before an intersection and waited in the gathered crowd with her hands pressed firmly to the strap of her bag. She counted down silently for the red halting hand to change to the walking man of pale yellow on the crossing lights. Half oblivious to her surroundings, Jansen felt the gaze of another on her. She focused in on the source of the stare and felt herself lock eyes with a young man across the street. He had short black hair, a sharp-featured face, pallid skin and eyes so dark, they seemed to match the black of his leather jacket. He looked familiar to her, but she couldn't pinpoint from where, nor did she have time to think about it. The lights changed over, and the crowd gathered at the intersection on either side marched forward.

℘℘

A holographic projection of a robotic arm floated before Skyris by her workstation. The Gaian woman was fixed on it intensely, one arm cradling the other, which was raised over her mouth as she tried to solve the latest in a slew of mental problems when it came to her mechanical project. She was once again dressed in her usual attire of a tank top and dark green pants tucked into high boots as well as welding goggles pressed up against her forehead.

The mobile suit, as she learned it was called, had been a spur of the moment idea that she had, without thinking, began simply because she wanted to know if it was possible to create it. She understood the majority of the science behind, it and being a woman with a scientific drive, her thirst for knowledge had pushed her to create. In her mind, it was all a coding algorithm, in the end, a bunch of numbers strung together with either a pure yes or no answer. If the fibre optic cables she had to work with did not seize up when the robot moved its elbow, then the wires in the hands would still carry over the information to have closed fists. If the cables did fail, then it meant the protective tubing around them was not doing its job, and she had to start over again.

"I suppose there really is no sure fire way to find out," Skyris muttered to herself absentmindedly.

Skyris pivoted on her heel and swivelled until she faced another workstation, beyond which, the arm she'd been looking at in the projection was attached to a menagerie of cables that hung around it. It wasn't connected to the body just yet. Skyris felt this was a safer bet when testing. Who knew what sort of chaos would ensue if it were attached?

Fingers flexing, Skyris took a deep breath and closing her eyes, began to initiate the sequence she wanted, typing rapidly on the keyboard before her. Soon, a low creaking sound reverberated throughout the room as the digits on the robotic hand stretched and then contracted into a fist. Satisfied with this first test, Skyris moved onto the next one, punching in commands just as quickly as she had before. So focused was she on her task, that she didn't see the spherical form of Dexter come into the room. The A.I. hovered beside her for some time before making its presence known.

"Miss Skyris, you have a visitor waiting for you," Dexter's pleasant mechanical voice chimed.

Skyris halted mid-command, the arm before her going limp as she stopped. Her loose ponytail glided over her shoulders as she regarded the large red gleaming eye watching her.

"I am very seriously debating removing that stealth function of yours," she muttered.

"I cannot let you do that, Skyris." Dexter's eye moved, following her movements.

"Please," she snorted. "I created you."

Dexter, not swayed by what she said, continued. "I cannot let you do that, because you specifically coded me in this manner to be able to detect hostile lifeforms within Q-16."

Skyris shook her head. "Always the smart one. Well, come along then. Lead me to this visitor of mine."

Dexter bobbed where he floated and then propelled himself out of the room with a light humming sound.

An exasperated sigh escaping Skyris's lips, the woman removed the goggles from her forehead and clasping her bare forearms behind her back, hastily marching after the A.I.. She was led, in turn, to where the living quarters were situated. Frowning at the prospect of someone waiting in her chambers, her private sanctuary, she was relieved to find that Dexter was leading her to another set of rooms. Not that Skyris was anymore thrilled about finding herself in these ones or in the presence of who they belonged to.

The door to the room was wide open as always. Huge shelves with books and scrolls decorated almost every corner, save for a lone grandfather clock as well as some cabinets with jars and other oddities piled into it on the far side of the room. The golden-orange glow of candles filled the space, giving it a far warmer tint than the rest of the cold base. At its centre stood a large dark wooden desk, and beyond it with its back turned, was a tall, thin figure with shoulder-length black hair in navy blue robes looking through some books. A gnarled wooden staff with moss growing from its top lay against the shelf closest to the being.

It took Skyris all of her composure to keep a straight face upon seeing the mage. There had not been many instances since their night in the cave that they had been alone, and the experience had not left her feeling as though there had been much closure. Not the closure she had wanted anyway.

"Thanestorm." She said the name somewhat quietly, still startling the engrossed mage in the process.

Puc turned and placed the book on the shelf it had come from. The growth of facial hair that now covered his jaw caused her to jump just as much as he had from hearing her voice.

"Your face…" she trailed off.

A realization crossed his pale blue eyes as he ran a hand across his beard. "Oh, this? Do you not like it?"

Undecided on the issue, Skyris crossed her arms. "I mean… it looks different."

"With your permission," Dexter interjected. "I should like to go scan the perimeter."

"Go ahead." Skyris waved him off.

There was a hesitance to the A.I. as it continued to float on the same spot for a minute longer. It then hovered closer to Skyris.

"I have read your past history files with the one named Puc Thanestorm," he informed her. "And I am detecting an increased heart rate from you. This may be of use."

A small compartment opened at the bottom of the robot. Skyris held out her hand as a hipflask fell onto her palm. The compartment closed and the A.I. then floated off. "You are welcome."

Puc watched the exchange with a perplexed look. Skyris glanced down at the flask, feeling her face flush as she pocketed it.

"I may have erred in giving him a sense of humour while programming." She cleared her throat.

"Or perhaps it was purposeful in order to diffuse unwanted tension." The mage curled his lips up slightly into something resembling a smile.

"Maybe." Skyris crossed her arms across her chest again. "So, you wanted to see me?"

The First Mage of Aldamoor reached into his robes and produced a letter that he placed on the table before her. Skyris furrowed her brows and picking it up, scanned the contents.

"I was summoned with Darius by the Sisters of Wyrd," he began to explain. "They wish for us to locate a young woman for them. They gave little detail, except that we would know what we were looking for when we would come across it, Darius more so than I. I thought that perhaps you may have some way of tracking odd happenings on Earth."

Skyris ran a hand through her loose ponytail and deeming it insufficient, she pulled the hair tie from it and retied it. "They gave you no information whatsoever? That's like looking for a needle in a haystack, there are over seven billion human beings on Earth. They do know that, right?"

"I believe they are aware of this." He pulled the letter back slightly towards him.

Skyris frowned and reached out a hand. "Well, the odds certainly aren't in our favour, then."

She examined the letter and then glancing up, took note of the helpless look in Puc's eyes. They were eyes she would have once given up her title for and everything she owned. She had waited years to get back to him, even suffered the loss of their child alone and when she had finally made it again, he had rejected her. There was a brief moment where she wanted to turn away, just as he had, but she couldn't. Deep down beat a Gaian's natural instinct to help those in need, to fight when no one else did.

"I will see what I can do." The words felt hollow in her throat as they left it and she handed the letter back to him.

Puc bowed his head slightly, accepting it. "That is all I can ask."

Without saying anything else, he then turned to grab his staff, his body language indicating he was to leave. The lack of resolution surged within Skyris again and stepped in. "Was that all?"

The mage glanced in her direction. "I am not certain what you mean?"

Skyris waved a hand dismissively as she felt a wave of anger pass through her. "Never mind, just go."

A flash of confusion crossing his face, Puc said nothing back and left the way he had come from the stables. Arms still crossed across her chest, Skyris continued to watch after him until he faded into the depths of the lab. She then remembered the flask Dexter had dispensed and withdrew it from her back pocket, examining its cold surface on her palm.

"I guess I won't be dismantling you today, my friend." She smirked and unscrewing the cork, she tipped it back to taste the bitter whiskey within.

52

Chapter 5

A few days after the meeting with the Galactic Federation, Annetta found herself once more sparring in the rink with Venetor. Attacks in the form of jabs and punches flew at her from all directions, and if she didn't pay attention, she was sure to be hit. Blue and purple psychic fire flames engulfed both of their bodies, helping to shield them from each other's attacks.

Annetta staggered back after blocking the most recent attack. Her heart pounded in her ribcage from the exertion.

"Finished already?" Venetor flew at her with his right hand. "Whatever happened to wanting to know all you could about the art of psychic hand-to-hand combat?"

She dodged the attack, her breath ragged and heavy. "I didn't mean all in one go."

"How else are you going to learn?" He flashed her a wicked grin and teleported from sight.

Curling her fists, Annetta closed her eyes and tapped into her feral form abilities, particularly her hearing. Venetor's body reappearing felt like a rippling soundwave as he moved towards her. Annetta's forearm shot up and pushed his fist away from the intended target of her face. Her other fist slammed into his chest, pushing him back.

Venetor fell back but saved himself from landing face first and pushing off with his arm, he cartwheeled into a standing position.

"Not bad at all." He crossed his arms. "I see you've been learning to combine psychic warrior abilities with those of your feral form. This is good."

Annetta's legs begin to turn to jelly, a sure sign her abilities were beginning to drain. The psychic fire shield was taxing on the body, and Annetta had found she could not maintain it for more than an hour straight at a time without feeling it slow her. She had progressed from initially only being able to muster the shield up for ten minutes, but nonetheless, she still had a long way to go with it.

Venetor noted her laboured breathing as the girl went back into a defensive stance and raised his hand up to signal their training session had come to an end.

"I think we can call it a day," he said.

Annetta released the shield, swaying on her feet. She felt a sensation like taking a deep breath after a long dive, and gasped for air as though her lungs were never quite full.

"You need to let me know when you begin to tire from the use of the shield when we practice it," Venetor instructed her. "It is one of the more difficult techniques to learn, and it can kill you if you overuse it without being used to it. Do you understand?"

"How do I know if I've used it too much and it's not just me getting tired?" she asked.

"It is clear you are in better shape and can last far longer without the shield when we spar normally," Venetor continued as he summoned his clothing from the side of the arena to him and began putting on his boots. "The first signs will be muscle fatigue. If you feel weak or like your legs will buckle beneath you, then say you yield. I won't always be of conscious of the signs myself."

Venetor took another look up and down at the girl after he finished with his boots and cloak. "Take a break now, go and rest. You will have a lesson with Atala this afternoon to go over some weapons fighting. I have a meeting I must attend."

"A meeting?" Annetta raised an eyebrow. "Shouldn't I go with you?"

"I don't think there will be a need," the Gaian king assured her. "In all likelihood, it will be a bunch of nobles questioning me as to why I have not remarried yet."

Annetta went over to the wall once she was able to keep her feet steady and began putting on her own shoes. "You've never spoken of my great aunt before. Is there a reason? I mean, I know what happened to my grandmother and why no one speaks of her."

The king smiled faintly as his mind travelled into a memory. "Davena, my wife… she was a beautiful woman, a fierce warrior and a princess who loved her people very much. And stubborn… Unknown's bane, was she ever stubborn to the very end."

He shook his head with his eyes closed, recounting the very last part, a weak smile having formed on his lips. The lids of his eyes then fluttered, and just before the blue irises, Annetta could swear she saw the beginnings of tears. If they were ever there, they quickly faded.

"She died shortly before Razmus and the Hurtz took over the planet, probably around the same time Mislantus was preparing to invade Severio Castle," he said. "Davena had insisted that despite the orders of the Federation, we needed to keep track of Valdhar's movements. She had lost her brother to Mordred's troops when we fought him, and she never got over it. One day, she decided to try and infiltrate Valdhar with one of our cloaked ships that Skyris had been developing. Skyris had told her it was still in its testing phases, but Davena wouldn't listen. The device failed, and the ship was shot down. Because I am now king, I have been under even more pressure to remarry."

Annetta's heart sank when she heard this. He had needed to shelve his grief in order to play the part of being a prince to his people, and now there was no room for it when he was king.

"They don't have a right to ask anything like that of you," she replied.

A small smile then formed on his lips again as he adjusted his cloak pin. "Sometimes I like to think that she was selected to be one of the White Knights of the Unknown, that before her death, the angels came and gave her a choice."

"Who are the White Knights of the Unknown?"

Venetor motioned for Annetta go first and then fell in step beside her as they exited the rink. "A legion of warriors sworn in service to the Unknown. They forsake all their claims, titles and allegiances in their former lives to serve him. In exchange, they are given a second chance at life and training in the Citadel of the Unknown to become the most elite fighting force in the multiverse."

"Do they ever come back to visit those who they were tied to before?" Annetta asked.

What little of a smile there had been on Venetor's face then faded. "No, it is said that because the training process is so long, they assimilate into their units, their past lives having very little meaning to them as they fade from memory. If Davena and I crossed paths again, there is a good chance she would barely remember who I was or what our life together meant to her."

Venetor sighed as he clasped his hands behind his back and continued to walk towards the staircase which led upstairs. He stopped in the doorway, silhouetted by the dim orange light of the arena. "Despite this, knowing she is alive would be enough."

৪১৫৪

Once she had parted ways with Venetor, Annetta found herself back in her rooms. She showered and changed into looser clothing, which consisted of a Gaian-fashioned short-sleeved black shirt with a v-neck opening made of a cloth similar to cotton, and a pair of jeans she had brought with her from Earth. Despite all the luxuries on Gaia, she still found them the most comfortable, even if some of the people of the court frowned when they saw her wearing them. It was not that they found them un-ladylike, since Gaian women often wore pants, but that the material was found to be primitive and uncomfortable.

She lay on her overly-large bed for some time after, her thoughts floating randomly from one subject to the next, her arms crossed behind her neck. Boredom, however, soon had its way with the girl, and she found herself sitting up, wondering what to do next. Her brain naturally defaulted to the activity on Gaia she liked best, and hopping off her bed, she put on her high boots before making her way to the kitchen for scraps to give to Bear.

Not long after, Annetta found herself atop Firedancer, manoeuvring through the streets of Pangaia to reach the gates which led out of the city. Without her crimson cape decorated with a rampant white lioness or her Gaian armour, most people still did not recognize her, and she was thankful for that. It gave her a level of privacy whenever Annetta wanted to leave. She would otherwise need to resort to teleporting out of the city, and there wasn't much fun in that. She enjoyed being able to blend in, even if she got a few awkward stares for her jeans.

Once at the gates, she urged Firedancer past them and out of the watchful eyes of those who stood guard. Annetta then let out a sigh, knowing she was finally free. Scanning the horizon before her, shrouded in forest foliage, she quickly picked out her trail and set off on it. Annetta then rode for some time at a steady pace before she was sure that all traces of the Gaian capital were left behind. The gentle swaying in the saddle added to the experience, further relaxing her along with the afternoon summer heat as she went. Annetta then came upon a somewhat familiar patch of slightly less dense forestry, brought her horse to a stop and dismounted.

Annetta tied Firedancer to one of the trees and removed the bundle from her saddlebags that she had acquired in the kitchens. She began to unwrap it slightly so that the smell of roasted meat could waft through the air and let their rightful owner know that they awaited him.

"Bear! I have something for you!" Annetta called out.

She then strained to hear if she could make anything out among the sound of rustling leaves and birds. She even allowed herself to slightly tap into her dormant feral form abilities, and still there was nothing.

While her mind had been drawn to this issue, Annetta has missed the very subtle cracking of a stick in the distance. It was not until she heard the low muffled voices in the distance from the other side of the forest that she dropped what she was holding and rushed over to Firedancer's side.

Then she saw forms emerging from the woods, her own slightly hidden behind the horse. There were three of them, a Hurtz, a female Gaian and a male Gaian, all dressed in patchwork armour that had been replaced far too many times with parts of animal hide or other armour for it to be distinguishable as having belonged to any single unit. The Hurtz, Annetta noted, was one of the biggest she had ever seen, perhaps close to eight feet tall. Its face was canine in nature, with a thick bushy red mane that was braided with bits of bone and feathers in it, and large triangular ears that were pierced with a variety of metal studs and hoops. A cuirass of black studded leather framed its massive upper body, and strapped to its back were two thick slab-like blades. His companions were a male Gaian with blond hair, blue eyes and a rugged, unkempt beard, as well as a female Gaian with dark eyes and short brown hair that looked to have been hacked off with a sword at the first best opportunity. They were no less impressive with their ragtag assortment of weapons that had apparently been picked up at random. Each of them, she then noted, had Razmus's white lion sewn into the stitched-together patchwork armour.

Coming entirely into the clearing, the trio froze upon seeing Firedancer out in the open. Their hands went to the hilts of their weapons as they scanned the area with alert eyes.

"And what have we here?" the Hurtz spoke in a deep baritone as he stepped towards Firedancer.

Before he got too close, Annetta's hand went to the simple leather cord around her neck, grasping at the wooden replica of Severbane, allowing it to materialize in her hand wordlessly. She sprung out from behind the horse into a defensive stance, causing the Hurtz to stop in his tracks.

"And who might you be?" the female companion demanded as she walked over to join him.

"Just a girl," Annetta stated. "And I would appreciate it if you backed away from my horse."

"You own this fine beast?" the male Gaian stroked Firedancer's neck. "Or did you steal it from some noblewoman along with that sword you're holding?"

Annetta's grip on Severbane tightened. "Who's to say I'm not a noblewoman in disguise?"

"I've known noblewomen in my time," the Hurtz said, "and none of 'em would be caught dead wearing those kinds of pants, disguise or not." The Hurtz reached back and drew the twin blades from their scabbards. "Now, why don't ye step aside and we'll take charge of this beast as was our right under Lord Razmus."

Annetta winced at the comment about her pants, but upon hearing the second part, her suspicions had been confirmed. She was standing face to face with Razmus's supporters. Both hands coiled around her sword and she wished that she'd had her shield with her as her eyes took in the twin blades of the Hurtz.

Despite her discovery, the girl stayed in her fighter stance with Severbane before her. "There is only one king on Gaia, and his name is Venetor Severio the Ironfisted."

Her fate sealed with the words having been said, Annetta watched in a half blur as the trio launched themselves at her. The scene almost seemed surreal, as though she had just woken from a long night's rest and had not been given time to orient herself. This was not, however, wholly true, and Annetta found herself dodging in just the manner she had been taught to do so. They seemed slow, and Annetta wondered if this was due to how intense her training with Venetor had been throughout the past month and a bit. Whatever it was, it was giving her an edge.

Annetta sidestepped as the axe of the male Gaian thrust forward, and tripped him with an outstretched leg. Not missing a beat, she then raised Severbane overhead to stop the two blades of the Hurtz. Infusing the sword with her psychic abilities, she pushed and sent the giant flying back some distance into a thicket of trees, along with his weapons. They crunched from the impact, but Annetta remained conscious of her other foes, Severbane gripped tightly in both hands.

The grunt of the female fighter as she tried to drive her spear into Annetta gave away her location, and the girl sidestepped, grabbing hold of the spear. She tore it from the woman's hand with her psychically enhanced strength, and taking the butt of it, slammed it back into her opponent's gut, knocking her unconscious.

The male Gaian then came at her again, his axe aimed straight for her face. Bringing Severbane before her, she countered the attack, only to be faced with a short sword he had held in his other hand. Annetta then ducked and rolled sideways, returning into a defensive stance.

"You don't fight like a commoner, I'll give you that," he spat. "Who taught you?"

Annetta's brows furrowed. He was clearly trying to give some time for the Hurtz to recover and join him in the fray. Nonetheless, she obliged. "The same one who you refuse to call king."

She then picked up the crashing of branches from off to the side as the Hurtz emerged with a thunderous roar, his snout matted with blood from a gash on his forehead, both massive blades raised like butcher's cleavers. It was an intimidating sight, Annetta had to admit, but she stood her ground. Without so much as flinching, she sent the Gaian flying against a tree to fully focus on the charging enemy.

Before he could reach her and their clash begin, the sound of a horn pierced the forest. Following it not long after was the sound of paws on soil-covered ground as a squadron of guards in black armour with crimson capes, each of them mounted on sabertooth dogs emerged, followed by Gladius on a horse. Gladius rode before them and past Annetta, straight for the enemy Hurtz, and disarmed him in a matter of seconds. Three of the guards closed in around him, while the fourth went to investigate the unconscious female.

"Are there more of ye?" Gladius questioned, his sword pressed against the tip of the other Hurtz's throat.

"That is something ye'd like to know, wouldn't you?" he spat. "Well, ya ain't getting it out of me."

A twig snapped, causing everyone to turn and see the male that had been fighting earlier begin to run. The distraction was enough for the Hurtz prisoner to start breaking free, disregarding the clawing of the sabretooth dogs as he did so and the nicks from the guards spears. A flash of metal then cut through the air, and the Hurtz slumped where he stood with Gladius towering over him on horseback.

"After that one!" he called at one of the startled guards, who quickly obeyed and then turned to the other two. "Secure the woman to bring for questioning, and bury the body."

The steely gaze of the Hurtz's single eye then landed finally upon Annetta. "And you, lassie, mount up. There's trouble at the castle, and all are requested to return back to city walls."

"What's wrong?" she untied and mounted up on Firedancer.

"The prince has fallen ill."

ഇരുന

"Do I really have to do this again?" Liam groaned after having completed his task of teleporting across the training arena in Q-16 to where Darius stood.

Darius, dressed in a black long-sleeved shirt and jeans, did not show a hint of compassion towards the whining of the smaller boy with spiky brown hair. Instead, he regarded Liam's green eyes in a cold, unmoving manner.

"You know, the more you complain, the more times I'm going to make you do it, right?" Darius crossed his arms.

The boy grumbled something incoherent and gathering his thoughts, continued to teleport to where giant X's were marked on the floor in a random pattern with white chalk.

Darius nodded in approval and then turned his gaze to the other side of the arena, where Xander, Annetta's brother, sat on the floor, his face full of concentration. He sat cross-legged with a small tea light candle balanced on his shins, and his hands stretched over it. He was dressed in a dark green shirt, jeans and red sneakers.

"How are we doing?" Darius asked.

Xander's hand dropped in exasperation. "It hasn't done anything. Maybe fire just isn't something I can manipulate?"

"You said the same thing about the cup of water, yet after about a week you were able to move it with no problem," Darius reminded him. "I'll admit that I'm not the best one to be teaching this, and all I have to go on are Puc's notes and books, but I think we are on the right track, don't you?"

Forlorn, Xander looked down at the light again and sighed. "I guess so. Still doesn't mean I don't find it boring."

"I think you and your sister have that in common." He smiled lightly.

"Just where is she, anyway?" Xander asked.

Before Darius could answer, the sound of feet could be heard coming down the hall. Soon after, Jason and Sarina came in through the door.

"How's babysitting going?" Jason greeted Darius with a grin.

"Oh, it's going." Darius indicated to Liam, who was completely oblivious to the new arrivals as he continued to teleport. Darius then turned back to face them. "How's postsecondary prep going?"

"I think we're pretty much done to be honest." Jason shoved his hands into the pockets of his blue and black plaid hoodie. "It's basically just counting down until September now."

Darius nodded and with a hand gesture, indicated for Xander to keep practicing what he was doing. Sure that his pupil was back at his lesson, he then fully turned his attention to Jason and Sarina. "Have either of you heard from Anne?"

The couple turned to one another to confirm that which they already knew and shook their heads.

"No, I haven't heard anything from her in over a month," Jason replied.

"I see." Darius searched his thoughts and then added. "Puc warned me something like this could happen. He said Anne could try to run away from her present in order to not feel the pain of losing Link."

"I don't see why it would bother her so much." Jason furrowed his brows. "I mean, she never acted like this when Brakkus died, and she saw it happen."

Sarina groaned and shook her head. "J.K. isn't it obvious to you by now?"

"Is what obvious?"

"She had some pretty deep feelings for him," Darius concluded. "You could even say she might have loved him."

Darius watched as the recognition of what he had just heard hit Jason, causing his eyes to widen into huge saucers.

The shocked expression then changed on Jason's face to sadness. "I thought you guys were kidding when you said she had a thing for him. You think she's grieving, then?"

"The reason Annetta enjoyed fantasy so much was because it provided an escape from her everyday problems, until the fantasy crept into her life," Darius told them. "Can't escaping to another planet, another way of life be seen as the same thing?"

"I never thought of it that way," Jason mused. "I mean, I started enjoying it because Anne always liked it, I never read much into it. Now when you put it that way though, it kinda all makes sense. I mean, we weren't the most liked kids in school, and Anne would ignore it all by having her head in the clouds."

"Link was also a Gaian," Sarina interjected. "Tied very closely to Gaia with his knowledge of their history, traditions and way of life."

"You sure you wanna do this history major and not psychology?" Jason queried.

"We need to get in touch with her somehow," Darius interjected. "I might not know much about this sort of thing, but isolation doesn't seem healthy."

Jason nodded and rubbed his chin with his thumb. "Might need a techie for the job, and I think I know just where to get a hold of one."

ഇൻൽ

Back at her workstation in Q-16, Skyris typed away furiously as she scrolled through a screen of code on the two glass walls before her. Bits and pieces needed to be updated, and the more she seemed to upgrade, the more parts needed to be replaced, because either variables had changed or chunks of code that served multiple purposes needed to be rewritten to serve only singular purposes. Tedious as it was, Skyris enjoyed the challenge, since it gave her a level of immersion that working with a machine never would. Machines in her mind, though complex to those untrained, were simple to her. A gear could only go forwards or back, and a spring could only compress and uncoil so far. Coding languages were a much different beast, an untamed and wild terrain that was fluid and ever-evolving.

As usual, she was so absorbed in her work that she did not hear the sound of shoes walking across the steel floors until their occupants were already in the room. Only then did she swivel around on her chair to regard them.

"How's the computer working out for you?" She smiled, seeing Sarina, Jason and Darius all standing by the door.

"Very fast and much lighter to transport, thank you." Sarina inclined her head.

"Good." Skyris then noticed Xander and Liam standing behind them. "Uhm… is this some kind of intervention?"

Confused, the original trio glanced back and made room for the two younger boys to join them at the forefront.

"No, we're here because we were wondering if…" Jason paused, trying to find the words to ask the question.

"We were wondering if it would be possible to contact Annetta somehow on Gaia." Darius finished the sentence.

Befuddled, Skyris raised an eyebrow. "Yeah and vice versa. As a matter of fact, I've been talking to her at least once a week."

"What?" all those gathered asked at once in raised voices, causing Skyris to skid back a few steps in the chair.

"Hey now, don't shoot the messenger." Skyris waved a hand before them. "You mean to tell me that she hasn't contacted you guys at all? Aren't you guys like her best friends?"

"We are, which is why we are concerned," Jason stated. "Anne hasn't spoken to any of us in weeks."

Skyris furrowed a brow as she thought long and hard. The others were not exaggerating their claims that Annetta was not contacting them, this was clear to see from the concerns on their faces.

"We think it may be her trying to deal with the loss of Link," Sarina said. "Darius has a theory that's what's happening."

"I see." The woman pursed her lips and rose from her seat. "Follow me."

Chapter 6

Annetta rode alongside Gladius as they returned back through the fortified front gates of Pangaia. The citizens paid them no mind, and it was clear that word had not gotten out yet about Titus's condition. She really wanted to ask Gladius what had caused her cousin to fall ill, but from his pace, as he headed towards Castrumleo, it was clear that it was not the right place to do so.

They handed the reins of their mounts to attendants once they reached the courtyard, and continued on foot, Gladius now following Annetta. Once inside the main building, it was clear that here too, not everyone was aware of any mishaps. It made her wonder just how serious this illness was, or if perhaps Gladius was exaggerating it into something it wasn't. A serious expression crept onto her face, which bordered on anger as she lost herself in these thoughts. This caused more than one noble and servant to scurry out of the way, thinking she had urgent business with the king. She also allowed Gladius to pass her, not sure where it was he wanted them to go

When they reached a door at the far end of the east wing, she glanced up at the Hurtz. "So are you going to tell me what's up with Titus, or do I have to just keep guessing?"

Gladius didn't reply, and pushed open the door with one of his large hands. Inside, Titus lay on a bed with a small breathing apparatus attached to his face. Scans were being performed on his body, x-ray-like holograms of data hovering over top of him. Beside the bed, a dark-skinned man stood by, observing more data on a set of touch screens, moving things around occasionally.

"I can't tell ya, because we don't know," Gladius finally said.

"What happened?" she prodded further.

"Apparently he was drawing on the balcony as he always does in his spare time, and all of a sudden, he went rigid and began to have a seizure. They managed to stabilize him, but he's been asleep ever since." The Hurtz folded his arms and allowed Annetta to come further into the room.

Once she was inside, he closed the door behind them and added, "And this needs to stay secret. No one can know that the prince is in this condition. We already have skirmishes with those still loyal to Razmus, like what you saw. Imagine how bold they would be if they knew this?"

64

"Of which they will not know." Venetor's voice came from behind them, causing the duo to turn around.

He leaned against the far wall, with one foot up against it as though he would launch himself off of it at a moment's notice. His arms were folded across his chest and his shadowed face looked extremely gaunt and worn.

"Has there been any change, m'lord?" Gladius inquired.

"None, but he is stable for the time being." Venetor removed himself from his place against the wall and walked over to join them.

"So he just had a seizure and no one knows why?" Annetta summarized.

"There is no history of such a thing in our bloodline. The only thing I can think of is poison." Venetor stated.

The man who had been looking at the touchscreens then turned to face them, his bright keen green eyes directed at his sovereign. "There are no traces of anything inside of him that would cause such a reaction, my lord. It was the first thing I ruled out."

Venetor turned to the girl. "Annetta, meet Doctor Cassius Sano. I don't think you were ever formally introduced, since you were unconscious the last time both of you were in the same room. He is the court doctor."

"Seems to be a trend with my patients not having their wits about them." Cassius inclined his head towards Annetta with a small smile. "Anyways, I did run tests, and there are no traces of any poison we know. Did his mother's side have a history? It could just be a very late manifestation."

"I will look into it, but I don't believe she did." Venetor's crossed arms dropped to his side. "Should anything change, notify me immediately, and under no circumstances is anyone outside of this circle to know."

Venetor then turned to leave and Annetta followed him, her mind teeming with a thousand questions. "Do you think this is all of this because of the rebels?"

Venetor stopped and pivoted on his heel to face her. He then leaned in close so that no one around could potentially hear. "If it is the rebels, then it's poor timing, else it be someone who already knows what my goal is. I plan to have Gaia run for the upcoming Federation election. Titus's condition could be used against me, as a sign of weakness. The Greys will use any advantage they can get their hands on in order to

65

make the other candidates look unfit to govern, and quite frankly, I'm getting a little tired of them being at the top."

Annetta nodded. She now understood what Venetor was doing by hiding this, but at the same time, she did not like it. There was something in Venetor's eyes that threw her off when he spoke of the election, and she guessed that it had something to do with his need for more power. She'd heard subtle warnings about this in the past from Puc. Perhaps she was interpreting wrong, though, and he was genuinely interested in the betterment of the system. A firm hand then landed on her shoulder, breaking her away from all meditations

"Tell no one of this or of what you saw." Venetor gave her shoulder a good squeeze and then withdrew.

The Gaian king then turned and began to walk away, a heavy aura hanging over his visage. Annetta watched him go, and in a quiet voice, she answered. "I won't, I promise."

ഇരഌ

Holed up in the First Mage's chambers, Puc read over his latest set of notes. The hour was late, and the candles dotting the room glowed in a lazy orange light, not dissimilar to how the mage's eyes seemed to droop. Since his visit to see the Sisters of Wyrd with Darius, Puc had been consumed with the task of trying to identify who it was they were supposed to find. Though his other duties as First Mage took up much of his day, the rest of his time was dedicated to this one single objective.

"You will know when you meet her, for she will know you without knowing that she does." He repeated Lysania's words absentmindedly and closing his eyes, he leaned back in his seat. What did it all mean? He could only guess that Lysania's words meant that they were looking for someone who had tapped into their psychic abilities without having realized it and could read minds. Generally, individuals who were able to do so and were unfamiliar with the laws about such abilities were found by angels, taken aside and educated, but there were also some cases where these people were never found if their abilities were minor enough. The gift was not strong in all, and if untrained, it was passable as someone knowing a few parlour tricks. If this was the case, however, what made this individual different?

He had, as a result of this conclusion, began looking through his old notes on scrying. If perhaps he could modify an existing spell to look only for those with psychic abilities who were female, then perhaps he could make their search easier. It also ran the risk of being more difficult if the spell chose to locate every female being with the potential to carry those abilities. He needed to be more specific with who he was searching for, and yet he couldn't be. It was a closed circle.

His train of thought was interrupted when someone knocked on the great wooden door of the room.

"Enter," he said dispassionately.

A moment of silence followed, but then the entry crept open, and in came a familiar figure with a neatly-trimmed brown beard and hair to match. Dressed in his military uniform consisting of a long blue coat with large brass buttons that were shined to a point as well as his high black boots, Iliam Starview cut an impressive figure of authority. The now general of the Aldamoor forces made it his priority to do so no matter the hour when he was on official business.

"So," he mused as he looked around at the various open books and scattered papers. "This is where the First Mage of Aldamoor hides during the hours of the night?"

"I believe the more accurate word is research," Puc replied, only half paying attention.

Iliam rolled his eyes and slumped in the chair before him, stretching out his legs so that they rested on the very edge of the table, but didn't disturb the books. "This is exactly why I dropped out to become a soldier."

Puc ignored the boots, knowing Iliam was trying to bate him, and continued to read. "I always thought it was because you were a good shot. That, and, as you stated yourself, because it would help you get women."

Iliam let out a throaty laugh as he sat up straight, which in turn caused Puc's lips to curl upwards slightly.

"Well, I did get the woman," he chuckled. "We're to be married in the fall. Did you get my invitation, or is it buried in this artistic mess of yours somewhere?"

"I did. Worry yourself not. I will be there."

"Well, that's promising to hear." Iliam smiled. "So, what about you and Miss Skyris?"

"What about her?" Puc lowered the parchment he'd been studying.

"Well, she's back on Earth. I just figured you two would have picked up where you left off is all," Iliam stated.

Puc rose from his seat to stretch and strode over to the window with his back turned to the Aldamoor general. "There has been nothing between us since her return to Earth, nor will there be."

"I don't believe that for one second." Iliam scoffed. "I saw the way you looked at each other; that's not something you give up so easily, and I know you, Thanestorm. If she'd told you to, you would have burned Gaia to the ground in her name."

Puc mulled the words over as painful memories surfaced to the forefront of his mind once more and ended upon his reunion with Skyris in the cave just a few months ago. He felt himself suffocating in these recollections, and was overcome with the overwhelming need to push them down.

"Did you know that we had a son?" he asked finally.

"You guys have a kid? That's great! When do I get to-"

"He died at childbirth." Puc shut him down from further commentary.

Iliam sat with his mouth hanging open for a little while before he recomposed himself. "I'm sorry."

Puc then turned back around to face him. "It is the greatest of ironies in my life that despite being one of the most skilled mages in existence, I cannot save those who matter to me most when they are in need."

Iliam nodded upon hearing this. "Well, for what it's worth, you did save thousands against the Fire Elves. Not bad for a kid who started off from the streets, I would say."

"No, I suppose not," Puc acknowledged, with a bitter note to his tone.

Unable to comfort his friend, Iliam rose to leave. "My original reason for coming here at such a late hour has not been addressed. It's about Tamora."

The name of the captive Fire Elf leader that had attempted to attack Aldamoor brought a scowl to Puc's face. "What is it?"

Iliam sighed as he glanced down at his boots and then back up at Puc. "She's has been acting rather odd in her cell. I am told from reports by the soldiers posted there she's gone mad. She keeps ranting nonsense, and they found her yesterday scrawling things on the wall with her food."

Puc narrowed his eyes at hearing the last bit. "I will see about it first thing tomorrow morning. Does anyone else but these soldiers know?"

"No one."

"Then keep it so, and make sure they speak to no one until we know how dire the situation is."

𝔰𝔬𝔠𝔯

Somewhere in a deeper and less-travelled part of space, far from any major ports or planets, a lone cargo ship hovered lazily, its dark brown metallic exterior blending in with its surroundings as though it were nothing more than an asteroid. The only thing which gave it away was the orange glow of the main engines on its far side.

Inside, Matthias Teron sat stretched out lazily in the pilot's seat, his black boots resting on the control dashboard, his old assassin's cloak thrown haphazardly onto the back of his seat. A look of boredom could be seen on his angular and mostly clean-shaven face, save for the patch of hair under his lower lip. His hands, clad in his signature metal-plated gauntlets with hidden extending claws, held a thin, transparent tablet that was littered with information. Azure eyes scanning the contents, he would from time to time swipe his index finger up or down, or tap on an article.

When he had announced his plans after the liberation of Gaia to continue his pursuit of Amarok, now presumably on Valdhar, there had been no objection. Those he had grown closest to while he dwelt in Q-16 had understood his vendetta against Amarok Mezorian, the one who had once been his teacher and his greatest adversary. They knew better than to stand in his way. There had also been little need of convincing those gathered how important it was to track down Valdhar, since he had not been the only one to see it.

Valdhar, also dubbed the castle in the sky by those who saw it, had once been a fortress belonging to Mordred Freiuson, also known as the Conqueror, and had after his defeat by Orbeyus Severio in the Great War, passed to his son Mislantus, who had then, in the throes of vengeance, gone after Orbeyus's heir. Though he had been defeated, Valdhar had survived and this was a problem. This was due to Valdhar possessing the Pessumire on board, a cannon capable of firing a beam which was able to create portals to other universes. Such a weapon could not go unchecked.

Matthias had followed Amarok's trail based on any scrap of information he could find, but now that trail had run dry, and he found himself with no options but to try searching the old fashioned way on the D.U.N.E. or the Distributed Universal Network Exchange. The concept behind it was quite similar to that of the Internet found on Earth, except the D.U.N.E. connected to different planets using strong satellite signals. It also, unfortunately, shared its Earthly cousin's problem of signal strength when roaming through space, and so the spot Matthias currently occupied was positioned close to an orbiting satellite around a small moon.

Not finding anything of use, Matthias sighed and exited the window he had currently been browsing, laying the rectangular slab across his legs, he stretched, running his hands through his wild shaggy brown hair. He was all out of ideas, and the burnout of searching the D.U.N.E. was beginning to cause a slight throbbing behind his temples. He then gazed through the tinted windows of the cockpit into the vastness of space, the twinkling light of stars dotting it without end. It was funny to think that by the time their rays reached him, many would be gone, snuffed out by time. Nothing was eternal, that was the law of the multiverse, unless you believed in the Unknown. Who knew, though, perhaps there was a universe that went on and on with no end. In any case, Matthias knew he would never see it, for no one knew what each universe was like. He had been lucky enough to see the other four he had visited with Annetta, Jason and their companions.

As his mind then wandered back to the Lab and all those he had left behind, he remembered a certain conversation that he'd had with Venetor. It was not really of significance, except for a burning question it had branded into his mind. Where was he from? He had never cared before, not while he had served Mislantus and when his family had been murdered by the tyrant and Amarok, he had been too young to remember what planet he had grown up on, or even in what galaxy. Valdhar had become his home, and that was all that had mattered. When he was older, he had asked about his origin, even requested a test be done to confirm what species he had been.

"We are all one unit aboard this ship," the scientist he had been speaking with told him. "One under the banner of the seven-headed dragon of Lord Mistlantus Freiuson, known to his enemies as the Threat."

That was the only answer he had ever gotten, and he had never bothered to ask again, burying it in the back of his mind. It was not until Venetor Severio had brought it up that the desire had awakened in him to know. Now, like the creeping tendrils of a vine, it continued to grow and ensnare his brain in his spare hours, when he was too exhausted from his pursuit. Looking down once more at the board on his lap, he picked it up and entered a new search for his last name, Teron. Pages of various tidbits of information showed up, and he began to scour them for any trace of information about a couple with a young girl and boy. He didn't have much else to go by, not even his parents first names, was his last name even Teron, or something he had been given aboard Valdhar?

As he scrolled, his eyes paused on an image, a family of four. He wasn't certain for sure, being unable to remember their faces, but they fit the numbers he was searching for. He glanced at the caption under the photo.

"Teron family, killed in a deadly forest fire," he read out loud. Scoffing, turned the search off again. "Just what exactly am I hoping to find anyways?"

Then it came, a notification at the top of the screen, blinking incessantly with the phrase "new message" written in a sans serif typeface. Lazily, he tapped it to reveal its contents on the screen. Reading through the short passage, he quickly straightened and slid the screen into a compartment in the dashboard, causing everything to light up in a brilliant display of various bits of information on the various screens. His fingers typed rapidly across a keyboard on the glasslike surface of the control panel as he set his course.

"Game on, Amarok." He smirked and shifted the gears into go.

ଔଓଔ

Night had fallen on Gaia, and Annetta found herself alone again in her chambers, changed into a clean set of blue cotton pyjamas. After the incident with Titus, she had been forced to stay on castle grounds in case the thing which had afflicted the prince was contagious in nature. She had no idea how such things worked, but in Annetta's mind, if it were indeed contagious, then it would have already started affecting people, wouldn't it? She remembered when Xander had come down with strep throat and for about a day, her mother told her that they couldn't play video games together because she needed to keep her distance from him in order to not get sick. Due to being young, she had, of course, disobeyed and ended up staying home a week as a result.

Unable to sleep, Annetta found herself wide awake, staring at the stark white ceiling that was tinted blue in the dark. Her mind floated from subject to subject with no particular aim aside from biding the time until she was able to close her eyes and drift off. She thought of the start of college and what it would be like, having heard all the horror stories of how difficult it was compared to high school. She also thought of her friends back on Earth and what they could possibly be doing, as well as her family. Her mind also drifted to Link and their final conversation over the C.T.S. that they had had. This brought a bitterness to her that she couldn't get over and she turned onto her side, hoping to dispel them.

She was forced out of her thoughts seconds after, when she heard a cry of terror echo down the corridors and bolted up. Moving off the bed, Annetta felt her bare feet touch the cold marble floor of the room as she looked around for her shoes and put them on. She then grabbed Severbane in its scabbard from the chair it rested against and tying the belt on, made her way out of the room towards the sound. It was not difficult to find the room where the cry had originated from, due to the small crowd of people which had gathered outside, consisting of Gladius in his usual gear, a very sleepy looking Atala and a few of the castle militia with their weapons drawn.

The girl paused a few feet away, not sure how to react to the sight, and it was not until Atala turned her golden eyes in her direction to beckon her forward that she moved.

"What's going on?" she asked in a whisper.

"Would that we could tell you, lass," Gladius replied, also in a hushed tone.

"It's complicated," Atala interjected harshly before being blocked out yet again by the commotion from inside.

Being closer to the room now, Annetta could hear exactly who was the one uttering the sounds. It appeared that Titus had awakened from his sleep.

"The end times awake, and make all worlds quake," he spoke in a raspy and feverish voice in between howls of pain. "Abandon hope and end lives, in this the seed of chaos thrives."

Annetta shifted back a pace uneasily, her hand wandering to the leather-wrapped hilt of Severbane, tracing it for reassurance.

72

"He's been on and off like that," Atala explained. "Started about half an hour ago, with him just screaming bloody murder. The king rose first, followed by the guards posted at his doors, and then we were alerted of the happenings."

Annetta furrowed her brows as she tried to make sense of it all. "Is it a fever?"

"Aye, it's what the physicians think." Gladius nodded. "Though them lines he keeps repeating. I've heard em before and I don't like-"

"They mean nothing," Atala snapped.

Gladius flattened his good ear along with the stub, and wrinkled his snout. "Aye, but I still don't have to like it."

Before anyone else could speak, a very weary-looking Venetor emerged from the room dressed in his beta scale armour and cloak. His face was covered in thick stubble and dark rings encircled his tired eyes. It was the look of a defeated man, and Annetta barely recognized him because of it.

"How is he?" Atala asked.

The king turned to regard her. "He is stabilizing. They gave him some sedatives to calm him, and he seems to be coming around."

"Do they know what caused it?" Gladius probed further.

"We do not as of yet." Doctor Sano came out of the room with a transparent tablet clutched in one hand. "Heat stroke is a strong suspect. The prince had spent all day outdoors, and this sort of side effect is not uncommon."

"What can be done in the meantime?" Venetor queried, running a tired hand along his forehead and through his short hair.

"Rest, and as I mentioned, no word to others of his affliction," the doctor stated, and then added, "If I may have your leave, my lord, I must go run some further tests on this latest blood sample taken from the prince to rule out any infection. The other acolytes will keep watch over him in my stead."

Venetor gave a gruff nod in return. "Do as you must."

The doctor then left without another word, his white overcoat billowing behind him. Soon after, Venetor left as well, followed by Gladius in tow, who did his best attempt to engage the sleepy king in conversations of a positive manner. This left only Atala and Annetta before the doors, along with a few more of the guards.

The general of the Gaian forces let out an exhale of exasperation. "I fear there is nothing more that we can do for young lord Titus in his present state, most of all you, White Lioness of Gaia. You'd best go and get some sleep. Tomorrow will be another day."

Annetta bobbed her head in reply and sleepily began to make her way back to her chambers. She then paused and looked back at Atala. "What about you?"

"I am a soldier first before I am a commander, and there will be a change of the guard to relieve me in due time. Worry not." Atala crossed her powerfully muscled arms before her as if to prove a point.

"Okay," Annetta said in a small voice and left for her chambers.

As she walked, however, she could not shake the feeling that there was something larger at play. Something weighed on her as she mulled over the seconds leading up to her departure and the longer she did so, the heavier it all became. Above all the images and words exchanged, a set that had been uttered by Titus in his fit seemed to burn most in her mind.

"The end times awake, and make all worlds quake. Abandon hope and end lives, in this the seed of chaos thrives." She muttered them to herself, trying to gauge meaning from them.

Hearing them said through her own lips, she knew there was only one person who could provide an answer to them, and she hurried to her room to await dawn.

Chapter 7

As promised, Puc made his way to the prison the very next day. Accompanying him were Iliam and two other guards, both wielding traditional Aldamoor military staves with bayonet knives on their tips. They were dressed in crisp dark blue uniforms, decorated in silver trimmings and buttons. The First Mage wore in his usual navy blue robes, not having bothered to change his attire since ascending to his new station. As far as he was concerned, he was still the same individual he was before the official swearing in, and he refused to wear robes that would suggest otherwise.

The locals moved aside as the party strode down the cobblestone streets of Aldamoor, earning a glance every so often in wonder of where they might be heading. Though the majority loved the First Mage and respected their newly-appointed leader, there was always cause for some wariness when he was seen traversing the streets with an armed escort. For all they knew, he was going to arrest someone or conscript a child to the Academy if they had been found using magic. Puc reflected on the latter. He had been a street urchin when he had found himself before Kaian's father with Iliam after the two of them had been caught using magic to steal food. He felt a certain sense of irony thinking about this now that the two of them practically ran the city because of that chance meeting. It was because of this meeting that he had become Orbeyus's advisor and helped to found the Four Forces. Looking up, he noticed the slowly-nearing sight of the squat grey building that was the prison and hurried his pace, causing the others to follow suit.

Once inside, they were greeted by the prison warden, a gruff-looking elf with short brown hair in a green sleeveless tunic with gear designs tattooed all along his exposed muscular arms. He wore large leather bracers that covered his forearms and each held several small knives.

"First Mage." He inclined his head in a bow. "How can I be of assistance?"

"Good day, Warden Wallhammer. I have heard from General Starview that there has been trouble with Tamora," Puc stated.

As hardened as Warden Wallhammer looked, his disposition instantly shifted upon hearing the name, and his face paled a little.

"She has been causing a disturbance these past few weeks," he began. "At first the guards paid it no mind. They thought she was attempting a new tactic to unnerve them, but when her behaviour began to escalate, they grew suspicious that there was an illness of the mind at work."

"I should like to see this for myself," Puc said. "Everyone I ask is vague about the details of what she is saying."

"Nonsense, I assure you First Mage," Wallhammer insisted.

"Sometimes in nonsense, there is a hidden truth we do not always see at first glance." Puc shifted his grip on his staff. "Now, I would like to see her if possible."

Though it was clear Wallhammer was unnerved by the prospect of going to see her, he nodded obediently and led the way down the corridor to Tamora's cell.

Her cell was located in the permanent residency wing of the prison and was much larger in comparison to the smaller ones that were closer to the front of the prison. Puc had always guessed it was to prevent interaction with prisoners who had a longer duration or permanent stay in the facilities. Less chance to plot an escape with those who would be returning to the outside world.

Coming to her cell, Puc had expected a great many things, but was still taken aback to see her in the state she was. She sat barefoot sprawled out on the floor, her prison uniform tarnished and stained. Her long flowing dreadlocks had been shorn off to prevent the smuggling in of any weapons, and her short platinum-blonde hair was tussled atop her head which lolled from side to side, swaying to the beat of some unheard tune. An upturned bowl where her rations had been served in lay some distance from her, and her hands appeared to be stained.

What disturbed Puc more than this image of the fallen Fire Elf leader was what he saw drawn behind her. There, painted upon the wall in the very food Tamora had been given to eat, was an enormous emblem of a seven-headed dragon.

"What is it?" Iliam inched closer to the bars of the cell. "And why does it look familiar?"

A low rumbling laughter came from Tamora and continued to grow until it reached its crescendo in a shrill and mad cackle. Her ruby red eyes glistened as she faced them and leapt to her feet in a speed neither Puc nor Iliam thought she would possess in her current state.

"Why, it is the mark of the one I am to marry, don't you see?" She grinned as she spun around and pressing a hand against the wall, her fingers raked across the sign in a loving fashion. "The dragon, him that is the end. The Unknown's true bane and striker down of stars. Bringer about of darkness eternal, flame to destroy all other flames, the beast, and I am to be his bride."

Puc looked over at Wallhammer and Iliam, whom both glanced back at him in confusion and bewilderment. Keeping a cool head about him, he spoke. "And when is this event to take place?"

Tamora paused what she was doing and bound towards the bars of the prison to grab hold of it with sinewy fingers, causing all those gathered except Puc to take a step back and place their hands on their weapons. A devilish grin spread across the Fire Elf's face in victory upon seeing the reactions, and she placed her face in between the bars, as if to squeeze it through to get closer to Puc.

"When the stars will fall and the keeper awakes, then freed my lord shall be," she whispered and lapsed back into laughter, throwing her head back. "When the winds will howl, the stone shall split, the tides will lower and flames extinguish!"

Puc turned to those that had come with him. "I think I have seen all that I need to this day. Keep this as quiet as possible. I must go and seek answers."

Saying nothing else, the First Mage of Aldamoor left.

಄಄಄

Their attempts to reach Annetta on Gaia having proven fruitless the day before, Jason, Sarina and Skyris crowded around the screen to try again. When Skyris had told them how she had been communicating with the girl, they had insisted she connect them, which had led them to the control room filled with its many glass screens and monitors.

The group felt somewhat out of place with Skyris seated on the large rotating chair and typing away on a glass table. She was dressed in her combination of a brown fur-lined bomber jacket, black tank top and military green pants that were tucked into high black boots with a pair of goggles propped up on her forehead, which reminded Jason of something a character in an 80s action film would wear.

"It is first and foremost a military base," Skyris reminded them as she typed in the sequence needed to reach Gaia. "A communication device with video capabilities is a mandatory piece of equipment."

"Not on Earth it ain't." Jason scrunched up his nose.

Skyris turned to regard him. "I highly doubt that your military would disclose such technology to the public. Chances are they're already using it."

She then returned to her typing along the glass keyboard and finished inputting the remaining numbers.

"While we're on the subject, what does Q-16 stand for anyway?" Jason continued to prod.

"If you're looking for meaning, it has none," Skyris stated. "It was a random selection of a letter and number to hide its location from the enemy on the grid."

"Like latitude and longitude?" Sarina asked.

"Simply put yes, but it was more complicated than that," the woman said. "Orbeyus had his whole own system for it. He would have been better at explaining it if he were here."

"Man, Anne is gonna be so jealous when she finds out we know." Jason beamed. "We tried for so long to figure it out, and Puc would never tell us."

"Or we could just tell her when we talk to her now," Sarina added.

"Yeah, maybe." He grinned.

The trio watched as the screen before them went black, a small version of the camera they were on becoming visible in the right-hand corner of the screen showing their live feed. This was as far as they had gotten last night, and when Annetta had not picked up after fifteen minutes, they had called it a night. If she did not today, then they would have to try again until they got a hold of her.

"She could be training with Venetor." Skyris leaned back in the chair, stretching out. "He may have taken her to the Pendrosian Mountains, and if they went there it was probably a trip of a few days."

"She's been training with Venetor?" Jason's eyes widened. "Now I really have no hope of beating her in single combat."

"Here's a thought, train harder, and if you're that worried, pray you never cross swords with her," Skyris mused.

"Yeah, right," Jason muttered under his breath.

Before anything further could be exchanged between the trio, the screen lit up. A figure with long reddish-brown hair appeared on the screen. It took Jason a good moment before he realized that he was looking at Annetta. She wore traditional Gaian armour, consisting of beta dragon scale mail and a crimson cloak clasped to her right shoulder with a silver rampant lion brooch. It was not just the armour that threw him off. There was something about her face that made her look harder than she had just months before, as if the last semblance of her childhood had been cast off from her. He had a good idea why that could be, as he reflected on the conversation that he'd had with Darius and Sarina.

"Hey, Anne." Skyris greeted her. "Some of your friends missed you and wanted to say hi."

The confusion that had been present in her blue eyes left Annetta as she recomposed herself and moved a few strands of her bangs out of her eyes that were becoming too long.

"Uh… hey guys." Her voice came crisply through the speakers. "What's up?"

"What's up?" Jason raised an eyebrow in a light-hearted manner. "More like what's up with you? No postcards, no phone calls. Come on, Anne, you're killing us here with the silence."

Annetta cringed a bit hearing this. "Sorry, I guess I lost track of time."

"Well that's a pretty lame excu-" Jason began his sentence, only to be elbowed gently by Sarina to stop.

"What Jason meant to say was that we were worried if the rebels had perhaps taken control of Pangaia again." Sarina leaned in closer to where Skyris had indicated the microphone was.

"Oh, that." Annetta shook her head. "No, things have been pretty stable on that front, and I've been keeping in close contact with Aunt Skyris for that reason."

"Right, just not us." Jason sulked.

An awkward silence fell after this comment and Annetta shifted uncomfortably on the screen.

Despite his usual lack of perception, Jason took note of this and without waiting further, he dove right back in. "Look, I'm sorry about Link and everything that happened. I didn't realize how close you two were until Darius laid it out for me. I should have been a better friend when you needed one."

The hardness at the corner of Annetta's eyes softened hearing this, and it seemed to de-age her by a decade.

"I'd be lying if I didn't admit to hoping each day that I'm here on Gaia to hear the horns sounding the arrival of a stranger come to the castle and it turns out to be him." She heaved a sigh. "The logic part of my brain knows better, but part of me doesn't want to let go. I'm sorry

I didn't keep in touch with you guys, I guess so I was so busy trying to keep myself occupied that I didn't realize half the summer was gone already."

"Forgive and move on, it's what we always do." Jason shrugged.

Annetta nodded with a small smile and then muffled a yawn with her hand.

"Is Venetor letting you sleep? You look as if you've been up all night," Skyris commented.

"I was, but with good reason," she replied. "Titus has... well, he's gotten sick, but it's not a normal kind of sickness. I was actually hoping that Puc would be around so I could ask him about it."

Sarina's interest then piqued, hoping to put her knowledge she'd gathered from the mage to good use. "What kind of symptoms?"

"It's difficult to explain," Annetta began. "I wasn't there when it happened, but apparently, Titus was outside sketching on the balcony and he just started having a seizure, and he's never had them before. He was asleep for a while, but then he woke up in the middle of the night, saying all sort of nonsense. There was one line that everyone heard and I wanted to pass it on the Puc, see if he knew anything about it."

"What was it he said?" Skyris pulled out a notepad from her coat pocket along with a pen.

"The end times awake, and make all worlds quake. Abandon hope and end lives, in this the seed of chaos thrives," Annetta repeated the phrase. "Does it mean anything to any of you?"

Skyris jotted down the words and read them over several times before flipping the notebook closed and putting it back. Jason and Sarina both stayed silent.

"Well, I got nothing." Jason threw his hands up and let them slap his sides as they fell to emphasize his point.

"I'm afraid I don't have anything either." Sarina shook her head.

"Neither do I," Skyris responded as well. "But you're right, Anne. If anyone knows, it's probably Thanestorm. I'll make sure he gets them. Keep us in the loop if anything else happens, and more importantly, don't forget your friends."

"I will, and why do I get the feeling this is something I'm not going to be able to live down for a while?" Annetta groaned.

"Brought it upon yourself." Jason winked.

"I'll try to remember that." She chuckled. "Okay guys, I need to get going. There's another meeting Venetor wants me to attend in his stead. He's been spending most of the day with Titus."

"Okay, see you Anne." Skyris waved as did the others.

The connection ceased and the screen went blank.

"I think I'm going to pay a visit to Aldamoor in person." Skyris got up from her chair and turned to leave.

Jason and Sarina glanced at each other to confirm their thoughts, before turning back to face her.

"You sure that's a good idea?" Jason asked. "Wouldn't it be easier to just call him on a C.T.S.?"

"It would, but I've been down here for months now, and I think it's a good idea if I get a change of scenery."

There was another awkward stare between the two youth before they glanced at Skyris once more.

"Are you and Puc…" Jason fumbled with his hands as he tried to think of a way to finish of the sentence without being too forward. He had sadly not realized in time that even the beginning of that sentence had already implied something.

Skyris did not miss a beat, only slightly raising her eyebrow before turning to face them fully and replying. "Oh, Unknown's bane, no. We're two very different people now, and whatever joined us before, well… it's just not there anymore."

"Wait… so when Matt and he fabricated that story so they could get the Aldamoor troops to Gaia on time…" Sarina tried to piece the information together as she recalled the accusation Matthias had made when storming into the Mage Council chamber during Tamora's lengthy trial.

A slight smile formed on the woman's lips. "My brother Orbeyus once said that the only true form of anarchy in this world is love. He was right."

She said no more to them and left without another word.

෨ඏ

The perspiration off of Darius's iced coffee dripped onto the table he occupied in the coffee shop. He had been to over a dozen like this over the past week or so since he went to go see the Sisters of Wyrd with Puc. He had been charged with the finding of a young woman whom he was told he would be able to identify when the time came. His current locale was of average size, painted in the earthy tones most chain coffee shops chose in the area, complete with a sitting area by a fake fireplace surrounded by couches. A few occupants were present, mostly post-secondary students on laptops who were cramming for summer school finals.

Lysania had not given them much to go on, and so Darius had been left mostly to his own devices to improvise. For some reason, he had decided that visiting coffee shops would be a good way to possibly bump into someone he had never met. Perhaps it also had something to do with his need of late to be in the outside world to just observe life.

Since having become Puc's apprentice, Darius had spent most of his life in the company of Annetta and Jason to keep an eye on them for his master. In that time, Earth had become a second home to him and the people that inhabited it fascinated him. They were just like the people of Aldamoor but different, sped up. Everything on Earth was faster than in Aldamoor, and sometimes it moved so fast that it had a tendency to get ahead of itself and forget the meaning behind why it was going so fast to begin with. This was especially true in downtown Toronto, where he currently found himself. Everything here was always on a pulse down to the last second. Through the windows outside, cars, public transit and bicycles stood congested on the streets. On the sidewalks people mostly in business attire walked towards their destinations with hurried paces, stopping only long enough for the streetlight signals to tell them to go yet again.

After a while, it drove one mad to keep looking at it, and Darius turned his attention back to the black moleskin notebook he carried with a map tucked into an inside flap on the cover, and began copying out spells in order not to forget them. Mages stored spells in their memory, and while they were skilled at remembering many of them, the mind could only store so much information at a given time. Purging of spells that were not needed for certain situations was therefore mandatory in order to keep only the most relevant things stored.

Scribbling down another sentence into the notebook, he took a sip of the iced coffee, its taste overtaken by the amount of sugar put into it. It was revolting.

"Unknown's bane, how can people drink this?" he grumbled.

He then looked over at his watch and noted that it was well past when everyone would be gathering in the Lab, and he still had to commute to get back to Annetta's house and the teleportation device. Shutting the notebook and tucking it under his arm, he got up, taking the cup with the over sweetened ice coffee or, more aptly, liquid sugar and threw it into the garbage by the exit.

Before he could notice, he nearly walked into a young woman with an olive-skinned complexion in rectangular glasses. She was dressed in an overly large sweater that seemed unnecessary for the Toronto summer heat and clutched a bulky laptop. A cap hid part of her messy black hair that seemed to tumble out of it in all directions.

"Sorry," She muttered quietly and darted out of the way.

As quickly as she had bumped into him, she was gone behind the walls which obscured the counter from the street view. His thoughts quickly went back to what he had been thinking earlier about city life and shaking his head, he left the shop.

Chapter 8

The spacecraft's rumbling engines slowed as it exited the Speedway, spat out at the exit Matthias had specified. To his immediate disappointment, there was no sign of Valdhar floating through space.

"Would have been too easy." He sighed and got out of his seat.

Checking the coordinates that he'd received, Matthias wondered if there was a point in even going to them, or if he was already too late to catch up to Amarok. He was half-tempted to go find the nearest satellite and plug himself back into the D.U.N.E., but something in the back of his mind prevented him from doing so. It was a need for closure.

Resolute in what he wanted, Matthias maneuvered the craft towards his intended destination. It was a planet that was small in size, perhaps no bigger than Earth's moon, with a surface that was covered in dense red-tinted vegetation, green bodies of water and no signs of a higher civilization on it. This did not mean that there was none present, though. Many of the ascended races, as they called themselves, had reverted back to living closely with nature, spreading themselves out among the stars in order to not overuse the resources on their homeworlds, even if it meant building colonies in space. The latter of these was generally the last resort, mostly due to the funding involved. Space exploration and expansion wasn't cheap.

Pinpointing where the exact signal had been from, he began to make his descent into the atmosphere. Passing through the hazy clouds, he then realized that the vegetation he had seen from space was no vegetation at all. It was instead the rusted remains of a metropolis. A chill went down Matthias's spine as some faint memory from his childhood tried to poke through the veil of his mind, only to be pushed back down by his present situation.

The ship touched down without so much as a bump, and Matthias checked the readings on his dashboard yet again to verify the atmosphere's composition, radiation as well as temperature of the surrounding area. The last thing he wanted was to spontaneously combust upon exiting his ship without the proper gear. Everything came back as being negative for any anomalies. Matthias still grabbed a breathing apparatus off the wall in the back of the ship and fitted it over his mouth and nose before stepping outside. He wasn't one for taking chances with faulty equipment.

Matthias wrapped himself in his cloak, checked the apparatus once more, and opened the doors. His shoes were immediately caked in the orange flaky substance once he emerged. Upon closer examination, it looked to be ash. The small harmonica-like apparatus attached to his mouth gave him a level of comfort as he breathed in and out harshly through it. He also extended his claws to full length to further strengthen this feeling, and pressed forward.

Once he'd covered some distance, Matthias flipped open the Communication and Time Synchronizer that he had taken with him. He entered the coordinates into the device and watched as a small hologram popped up to show a map projection with his proximity from his target, which flashed as a glowing blue dot. Prior to his leave, Skyris had given him a crash course on the C.T.S. in case he needed to use any of its other features.

"I have to hand it to Skyris, the woman knows her tech," he mused and moved forward.

As he progressed, the dot continued to flash with a greater intensity. A tension laced his muscles as he prepared for a possible confrontation, moving through the charred remains. His surroundings did not surprise nor appall him in the least. The rust-coloured ash was a byproduct of the amount of iron in the atmosphere, not uncommon in cities as large as the one whose grave he currently traversed. He had witnessed the aftermath of such carnage at the hands of Mislantus the Threat. Those planets that had not bent the knee to his will were left in a flaming mass of chaos, a beacon across the galaxy marking his presence as Valdhar sailed away through space to claim its next prize. Where before, Matthias was immune to what such a thing had meant, now he understood just how many lives had been senselessly lost all because one deranged Gaian had wanted to have it all.

His target was now a few paces from him and on the horizon, Matthias could see the remains of a much smaller building, a house perhaps. Miraculously, all four walls still stood mostly intact, but the roof had been burned away. Where once there had been a proud arched doorway, there now remained a charred and slanted remnant that was twisted by time.

The azure orbs that were his eyes glanced down once more at the C.T.S. to confirm his location. Inhaling through the respirator, he ventured into the building. The rusted dust blanketed everything inside the structure, giving it the illusion of having gone to sleep. Matthias knew better. He was disappointed to find also that this was where the trail he had been following ended. What could Amarok have wanted in a house in a desolated city?

Something then crunched underfoot, causing Matthias to stop where he stood. Looking down, he noticed something under the ashes and knelt down to pick it up. It appeared to be a flat glass screen that was chipped and cracked on the one end, where he had stepped on it. An image of a young boy and a girl flickered in and out of the frame as he continued to gaze at it. There was something familiar about them.

"A rather poetic homecoming, wouldn't you agree?" A voice he knew all too well spoke behind him.

Matthias's back tensed as he lowered the frame. "So, you're here after all."

Out of his peripheral vision, Matthias saw the glint of a mask that resembled a star, the two lower points curved downward like fangs forming around the mouth guard. It had been partially burned on one side, scarred flesh exposed underneath, along with a dead eye. Wild long white hair sprouted from behind it and around like a mane. He tilted his head a little further to confirm who it was, and then fully turned around.

"Amarok Mezorian." His fists tightened at his sides.

"In the flesh." He raised his hands, the stud covered armour encasing the entire length of his arms and a grey tabard with the seven-headed dragon of Freiuson upon his chest. "Welcome home, Matthias Teron."

"Home?" The younger assassin shifted his feet as he went into a fighter's stance.

"Oh come now, don't tell me that you don't recognize your own house? The very one you were forced to flee when Mislantus's troops stormed this sorry excuse for a rock."

Matthias wrinkled his brow, causing the exposed part of Amarok's face to grin.

"You don't remember, do you?" he chuckled.

"Should I?" Matthias flexed his hands. "Everyone here is dead. What does it matter?"

"Ah, but here is the fun part, it does. Did you think it was mere coincidence that Mislantus stopped at this backwater planet?"

Matthias was beginning to grow frustrated with the amount of talking going on. "He was collecting psychics for his army. End of story."

"If that is the story you wish to feed yourself." Amarok sighed as he paced around Matthias in a circle. "It's a pity, a real pity that you went down the path you did. I once really thought you would be my protégé. I could have shown you the truth…"

"The only truth I seek is your true death." Matthias lunged at Amarok, clawed gauntlets extended before him.

The elder assassin did not miss a beat and dodged by leaping back. The studs on his arms came to life in a sea of steel tentacles that came at Matthias in a counter.

Letting out a guttural roar, Matthias twisted and turned as he tried to evade them. A few nicked his arms and he could only hope that his opponent had not laced them with any poison, a tactic Amarok was known for employing.

"Enough of this," Matthias muttered. Teleporting, he ended up on the other side of the house. A ball of psychic fire sprung from his hand, and he set it loose.

A swarm of the tentacles moved to block it, forming into a single solid shield before Amarok. The fire blazed on impact, halting on the metallic wall. Matthias teleported back, as to not get caught in the flames, and only had seconds to react at another swarm of steel tentacles as it raced after him with all the ferocity of a horde of bloodthirsty insects.

He teleported again and ended up beyond the structure, but had underestimated his safety when another set of tentacles wrapped around his legs and arms. He was about to teleport once more when another of the spikes found its way to the small of his back.

"I wouldn't do that if I were you." The elder assassin clicked his tongue. "Unless you wish to see which of us is the faster, and I have to say, I think babysitting those brats has slowed you, or is it age, perhaps?"

"If killing me is your plan, then get on with it. I'd rather not have to keep listening to the sound of your prattling voice."

"Oh, I'm not going to kill you." Amarok snickered. "No, I'm going to give you a front seat to events that are to come. It's going to be quite the show, I hear."

He felt the spike from his back move away, but as it did, he sensed Amarok move closer until he was beside him. He could feel his ragged breath blowing into his ear. "But before I let you go, there's something I need."

Matthias half anticipated a killing blow, despite Amarok's words, and so when it did not come, his muscles relaxed in confusion, only to seize up again when a sharp pain seared through his left arm. Looking down, he saw a gash and a stream of blood leaking from it into a vial held by one of Amarok's tentacles.

"Only a Teron's blood will hold the coordinates," Amarok explained cryptically. "That's a part no one but those present there when the prison was laid down knew. Mislantus just thought he was attacking another Gaian outpost and capturing psychics, but there was so much more to it than that."

Matthias's eyes widened. Amarok laughed. "Enjoy the show."

Before he could say or do anything else, Matthias felt the restraints on his limbs drop, and whirling around, saw no trace of Amarok. He grabbed at his blood-stained arm, teared at his shirt and made a makeshift bandage. His eyes shifted from side to side to be certain that he had not missed any trace of his former master. Amarok, it seemed, was gone, and in his place, a well of questions had risen.

හ○ශ

The clattering of horse hooves on cobblestone streets overpowered all other sounds on the main street of Aldamoor as Skyris entered the city. Without the urgency of a Fire Elf attack, the capital of the Water Elves looked much like it had in her youth when she would come to visit with her brothers. Narrow, tall and mismatched buildings lined the horizon, framed by the great waterfalls on the far side, along with the high stone walls that encapsulated them. The Council Tower, now restored, loomed over top of these, its great clock face beaming down at all the residence with its gleaming white faceplate.

Skyris smiled at the familiarity of it all and looking up from under the hooded cloak she wore, she turned her gaze westward. There, she could see the airship harbour and the multitude of vessels that were in various stages of departures, arrivals and docking. She remembered how much she had loved them in her youth, enough that she had once snuck out of her rooms just to be able to visit the harbor. The excursion had resulted in some mischief involving a trip on one of the vessels, the Tessa, without a proper crew and then the crashing of said vessel into the harbour because neither her nor the young elf that had commandeered her father's ship had known how to stop it. The woman chuckled to herself as she recalled the mortified looks on Puc and Venetor's faces when she had emerged. Only Orbeyus had kept his cool demeanour about it.

"Those were the days." She sighed under her breath.

Her gaze then turned back to the tower, and she remembered what she was actually here for. She cursed herself inwardly for a moment as she came to realize that having volunteered herself for the mission perhaps hadn't been the best idea. Ever since she had come back, her encounters with Puc had been awkward. She knew what she still felt for him, yet he no longer reciprocated. That flame had been further snuffed out when she had told him on their initial reunion of the son they had lost. She had mostly offered to go speak with him due to how panicked Jason and Sarina had been about getting prepared for their first year of university. It was a stress she remembered herself. Having a compassionate heart, or so she told herself, she had proposed to go in their stead.

"Unknown's bane." She grumbled and nudged her mount, a mare of pure black with a long wavy mane and tail, forward.

The remainder of the trip took an eternity, and when she finally dismounted at the base of the tower, her legs felt like lead hitting the stone. Once she located a post used for temporarily tying up horses, she secured the reins of her steed, stroked its neck reassuringly and sauntered up the stairs to the door. She was then met by two guards at the entrance, their navy blue long coats neatly ironed and their silver buttons shining pristinely. Each also carried one of the bayonet-like war staves, which with the soldiers' current stances, made them look like spears.

"State your business with the Council," the one on the left, a woman with short cropped black hair and a thin angular jaw demanded.

Skyris removed the cowl of her hood. "I am Lady Skyris Severio, sister to King Venetor Severio of Gaia. I am here to speak with First Mage Thanestorm."

The guard who had spoken looked over at the other, a male in his late thirties with a medium length salt and pepper beard, who nodded in approval to her. Skyris then understood that the woman was not a full-fledged soldier, but a trainee having a field lesson.

"You may enter." The woman bobbed her head and paid Skyris no more attention.

Relieved at not having been turned away, Skyris continued inside and began to make her way towards the office of the First Mage up the stairs. She received a few curious glances in the halls from those who passed her by when they recognized her eyes were not the typical feral blue of Water Elves, but nothing more. They were growing used to visitors from other worlds again, it seemed.

Skyris reached the door and paused with her hand held up to knock. She then lowered it to smooth out the creases in her cloak she had worn not to stand out too much, and ran a hand through her loose black hair which fell well past her shoulders. She then finally knocked on the door.

"Enter." Puc's commanding voice came from the other side.

The hinges of the door creaked open and Skyris peered inside. The entire study seemed to be a flurry of books, scrolls and parchment. Many would call it a disaster area, but Skyris knew the look of an artistic mess when she saw one. She was prone to them herself when engrossed in a projcct. Puc stood over his desk reading a scroll. He had shed his heavy dark blue robes due to the summer heat and wore only a loose white linen shirt with leather bracers over the cuffs. Time had not ravaged him, she thought, as she gazed at his lean physique before stopping herself when his eyes moved to look at hers.

"Skyris." Her name escaped his lips. "What are you doing here?"

Clearing her throat, she stepped forward. "I… I need to speak to you. It's about Titus. He's ill, or at least that's what Annetta said when I spoke with her."

"Ill? Does Gaia lack physicians now?" he mused.

"It's not like anything they've ever seen." Skyris took another few steps into the room, closing the door behind her.

Puc's brow furrowed as he rolled his scroll back up and walked around his desk to clear a space on one of the chairs for Skyris. He then motioned for her to sit down and waited for her to continue.

Skyris inhaled deeply as she took a seat. "Apparently, he had a seizure of some kind and was out cold. The next thing the doctors knew he was thrashing madly and talking gibberish. They couldn't diagnose him, and there's no history of anything like that in either the bloodlines."

The First Mage of Aldamoor gazed down at his desk reflectively as he thought on what to say. Skyris could tell he was taking the matter seriously from the way his brow creased. It was a quirk she had picked up on in their long conversations over the years, though perhaps this had changed with age, too.

"I will consult other mages on the issue," he replied, finally. "Perhaps there is something which can be done for Titus. I make, however, no promises on the matter."

Skyris then reached into her pocket and produced her notebook which she held out to him. "There was one thing he did say that was more coherent than all the rest, or so Annetta said."

This piqued the mage's interest as he took the notebook from her and then looked back up. "You spoke with Annetta? How is she? I have heard nothing from her since her decision to stay on Gaia for the duration of the summer."

She bit back the twinge of guilt as best as she could before plunging back into the conversation. Skyris had had no idea that Annetta would isolate herself that much from everyone else.

"She's doing well," Skyris continued. "She's been training with Venetor most of the summer, and I suspect from the general lack of communication, healing from her wounds inflicted on her through the loss of Lincerious."

Puc's lips tightened on hearing the last part of the conversation, and Skyris felt a slight wave of déjà vu pass over her saw this reaction. Another bout of silence followed this as the two of them seemed to not wish to look one another in the eye, like magnets that repelled rather than attracted.

"Time heals all wounds," Puc said finally as he flipped open the notebook. "Was there anything else?"

Skyris looked down in hesitation at her feet before she faced him anew. She got up from her chair and loomed over the desk. "No, it's just as I wrote in the notebook. He said the following words in his delirium: The end times awake, and make all worlds quake. Abandon hope and end lives, in this the seed of chaos thrives. Does this mean anything to you?"

Puc's grip tightened slightly around the notebook, he flipped it open to the indicated page and skimmed over it before looking back up. "Is this exactly what he said? Word for word?"

"Word for word." Skyris nodded.

"Understood." Puc closed the notebook and handed it back to her. "It is good that you came to me with this, I do know these words... however, it will take time before I can give a concrete answer upon their meaning. As to what part they play in Titus's affliction, I do not know, but I can speculate. A heavy illness may at times bring out the fanatic in us."

"Right." Skyris sighed, her eyes catching the grandfather clock in the room. "I should get going, even if just to message Annetta and let her know that everything will be all right."

"Yes, that would be best." Puc came around the desk. "You know, you could have just sent me a message through the C.T.S. about this, no meeting was required."

Skyris felt a twinge of patronization in his voice and glanced at him with a coldness of her own. "Who said this was the only reason I came to Aldamoor?"

Saying nothing else, she then left the room.

ಬಂಜಾ

The tavern doors swung behind her as Skyris entered the inn known as the Gear and Flute. She smiled as a wave of nostalgic images wafted past her, along with the smells of various pipe weeds being smoked and the daily pub fare being ordered by patrons. Wooden cabin walls greeted her on all sides adorned with paintings or parts of old airships that were hung on display. Tables and chairs were filled with male and female elves as they chattered away, engaged in their own conversations and paying no mind to the newcomer.

Skyris's gaze caught and hung on a painting of an airship going over the falls when she heard a distinct voice speak to her from behind.

"I take it you've never seen an airship before."

The words ringing in familiarity to her, Skyris turned to see a woman around her mid-thirties with long chestnut-coloured hair flowing past her shoulders, dressed in an Aldamoor officer's navy long coat that hung open to reveal a white blouse beneath with dark brown pants tucked into high polished black boots. A mischievous smiled formed on the woman's lips as she eyed Skyris.

Realizing who it was, Skyris cracked a grin and not giving it a second thought, she walked over to embrace her.

"Seen plenty enough in my day now, I think." She chuckled as she pulled back from the hug. "How are you, Maria?"

"I've been doing well. What brought you to Aldamoor? Do you have time to stay?"

"Well, I'd lie if I said I wasn't hoping to run into you," Skyris replied. "I've been getting a bit stir crazy in the Lab."

The two of them made their way over to the far corner of the establishment where an empty table stood, and slid into seats on opposite sides of one another.

Maria was then quick to flag down one of the servers, who made their way over. "Two pints of the dark stuff and make sure there is little foam."

The server, a female Water Elf with short dark hair, gave a quick bob of the head before disappearing to the bar. The two women smiled at one another once she had gone, in the contentment of one another's company.

Skyris was the first to speak. "I'm sorry I didn't seek you out sooner when I first got here. It's just that there was a lot going on."

"Things were rough here as well with everything that happened with the Fire Elves." Maria waved her off as the server returned with two pewter steins that held a frothing liquid in each. "Action was needed, and not talking. Now, there's plenty of time for talking."

"To talking then." Skyris raised her stein.

"To talking." Maria grinned and clinked the metal cup against hers before taking a drink from it.

Skyris did the same and then noticed a silver cuff around Maria's wrist. "Is that what I think it is?"

Maria looked down and rolling up the sleeve, she unveiled the two-inch silver cuff on which was engraved a design meant to look like gears clicking into place with one another, with roses entwined among them.

"I'm engaged." She beamed.

Skyris smiled broadly upon hearing the revelation. "Congratulations! When, and more importantly, to whom?"

"Iliam Starview." Maria grinned. "We're thinking sometime in the fall maybe, so things will have had time to settle back fully to their old routines."

"Starview? You mean Thanestorm's childhood friend? The one with the terrible jokes once you get a couple of pints in him?"

Caught mid-way through taking a sip of her drink, Maria stifled another laugh before turning her attention fully to Skyris. "The one and the same, though I've tried to curb the jokes as best as I could. Some habits, however, die hard."

"Could be worse, I suppose," Skyris mused in a joking manner as she tipped the stein back, tasting the bitter liquid go down her throat.

The Water Folk woman smiled again as she looked down at the table and noticing a ring of liquid from the condensation, she began to run her finger through it, playing with the patterns it produced. "What about you and Thanestorm?"

Skyris nearly felt her drink go up her nose at hearing this, and it took all of her resolve for it to complete its journey. Swallowing, she then turned to regard her. "What about it?"

"Don't act like I've forgotten about you two." Maria looked up at her. "I mean, you both introduced Iliam and I to one another all those years ago. I remember how you both looked at one another."

Skyris took another long swig from the tankard before placing it on the table again, albeit somewhat louder than she had wanted to, resulting in a hollow slamming sound on the well-worn wood. She then ran a hand through her black hair before gazing back up at her companion.

"I'm not sure where this sudden interest in Thanestorm and I is coming from with everyone I seem to encounter lately but, whatever bound us all those years ago is no longer there," she said. "Those days of childish gallivanting around the caves of Aldamoor behind my brother's back, the long nights under the stars in the war camps of old and the times shared beside campfires in the company of our other friends… it's all gone now. We've both changed, him and I, and there's no going back to the way things were before. It means nothing."

"But it meant something before." Maria took a sip of her drink.

"Past tense," Skyris muttered. "I'm afraid now there's a void between us that won't be so easily fixed. The heart isn't a machine, no matter how many people try to compare it as being such. You can't just swap out the damaged parts and keep going. I know, I've tried."

Maria nodded as her gaze turned back to the condensation on the table. She then glanced back up again. "So… you'll still come to the wedding though right?"

"Have you ever known me to pass up a chance on free beer?" Skyris cracked a grin and took another deep drink for emphasis. "Of course I'll be there, and this time I promise to not crash any airships."

"Oh don't you worry about crashing airships, we'll be doing that at the bachelorette, if you make it, that is."

The two women both chuckled and clinked their steins in the promise of the aforementioned.

Chapter 9

The days blended together at Castrumleo. Annetta had no recollection of the last time her uncle had held court himself or trained with her. The stagnation of it all had begun to weigh on her so much that she had taken to going and practicing alone in the arena just to give her something to do. It wasn't the same without another person there, though. She'd tried interacting with Gladius, Atala and the other castle occupants, but everyone seemed to be so caught up with their tasks that every conversation Annetta struck up with them seemed forced.

Annetta walked out of the castle, having completed her latest bout of training, and wandered out onto the stone steps in front for a change of scenery. She picked an area off to the side of the entrance and sat down with a huff, feeling all her tense muscles sag into relaxation. Her gaze then shifted from her boots to the bustling streets below the stairway that led to it. Grey cobblestone glistened silver in the sunlight as busy city dwellers went about their daily tasks, oblivious to the fact that the proclaimed White Lioness of Gaia was watching them.

A female voice then interrupted the silence in her mind. "It's almost hard to imagine that just months ago almost everyone here was enslaved by Razmus and made to work on his tower."

Annetta turned her head and found Atala half-hidden in the shadows of the building, leaning against a stone pillar which held up an overhanging roof closer to the doors. She didn't dislike the Gaian general, but she found the woman to be all business all the time.

She shifted somewhat uncomfortably on the stone. "How would you have them reacting?"

"More afraid." Atala walked closer to Annetta, "Tenser. Suspicious of every corner and everything, but I suppose this is just not our way. We are, after all, Gaians."

Annetta wrinkled her nose at this and turned back to watching the streets. She sensed the comment had been meant to compare her reaction to a human one. She almost leapt up to retort, saying she was human, but then she remembered she was also Gaian. It still felt odd to know that at times. Earth had been her home all her life.

Despite having turned her attention away, Annetta could still feel Atala's molten gold eyes on her, and unable to bear the heat, she turned back around to face her. "Is something wrong? I mean… worse than it was before?"

"I could lie and say that Prince Titus is getting better." Atala crossed her powerful arms across her chest. "But that would be just that. A lie. No, I'm afraid his condition is deteriorating and the doctors cannot figure out why. They found him last night scrawling on the walls. It was meaningless mostly, except for the references to the seed of chaos and some drawings of constellations. The latter has been taken to astronomers for verification to see if they hold any significance."

The girl frowned, taking in the information. There was something more behind the defensive manner in which Atala stood, this much Annetta could see, and she too got up. "Look, you don't have to sugar coat it to me. If it's bad, I get it, and I can tell you're not here just to chit-chat. What do you need me to do?"

"I feel that the only ones who may be able to help him are the Water Elves of Aldamoor, even if Lord Venetor wishes to keep this under wraps," Atala concluded.

Annetta licked her lips anxiously. "I spoke with Aunt Skyris just a few days ago. She's already taken the information to Puc."

"And you haven't heard anything back?"

Annetta frowned further, the sensation of her ears flattening against her skull becoming prominent. "No."

The older Gaian woman closed her eyes pensively and nodded. "I fear we may not have time to wait much longer. The Crown Prince's life is in danger, as is the security of the Gaian throne should Venetor continue to neglect his duties. Not to mention sending multiple transmissions could catch the eye of some unwanted listeners, if you get my meaning."

The girl nodded, remembering what Venetor has said about the Greys and the Federation. She then felt what was coming next. "So you want me to cut my vacation short and go back to Earth, is that it?"

Atala shifted on the balls of her feet and looked out into the crowd below, as if hesitant to meet Annetta's gaze. "That is what I am asking, yes. I don't do so with ease. I know how eager you were to spend your summer on Gaia and to learn more about the people you are descended from, but if you are as your title suggests, then you will understand why I'm asking this. Your family needs you to fight when they cannot."

Annetta bobbed her head. It was the reason she had bothered to fight at all.

"I'll go." She said. "But I'll need to get to Earth somehow, the portal Aunt Skyris created from Severio Castle is closed up now, I think."

"A ship will be prepared for you to leave within the next few days with a pilot to drop you off via space pod. I suggest trying to get a good night's sleep, not everyone has the stomach to sleep onboard."

Annetta then watched as the general turned to leave, but she stopped just as she reached the doors. "I think it would also be wisest if you tell Venetor it's your own idea to leave. In the state he's in, he may see it as you being forced to do so, and he may be reluctant to let you go. Though he may not show it outwardly, he has grown fond of you, like a daughter."

Before Annetta could say anything further, Atala was already off, the castle doors closing behind her. Left alone again, she gazed out into the streets, contemplating her latest predicament.

ഇൻരൈ

Lush trees billowed in the breeze just paces from where the wide river poured into a larger body of water. The Lake biosphere within Q-16 had of late become a favourite for Liam and Xander, who, after having been shown it by Jason and Sarina, had taken to going there whenever they had completed their lessons. With no school, they had a lot of free time, and they also had no curfews they needed to worry about.

Liam picked up a smooth, flattened stone that was roughly the size of his palm. Satisfied upon his examination of it, he turned sideways with an outstretched hand and flicked it out onto the lake. He watched as the stone skipped five times before it sunk.

"Damn," he muttered.

Xander, who sat stretched out on a boulder, watched as his friend attempted again and again to skip stones.

"What exactly are you trying to do?" he asked.

"I want to see if I skip them far enough if they'll hit like some invisible force field or something," Liam said. "There's gotta be an ending to this biosphere somewhere."

"Honestly, I don't think there is." Xander sat up properly and stretched. "I think it might be like a portal or something."

"Inside of the Lab?" Liam raised an eyebrow. "No way, how? That would be kind of stupid and besides, how would they get it here?"

Xander thought on that for a moment and shrugged. "Well, I mean, the portal to Severio Castle is technically in the Lab as well."

"Oh yeah, I guess it is." Liam pursed his lips. "But I mean, this place has an actual door, not a portal, so I mean it can't be... can it?"

"Man, I don't know. I'm not some portal expert or something. Maybe Darius knows, or Aunt Skyris."

Before Liam could say anything else, the sound of snapping twigs could be heard coming their way. The duo turned and stood frozen, even though their intuition told them both to run. After all, they had been warned not only by Darius but by Jason, Sarina and Skyris to not wander off too far in the biospheres, or biodomes as they were sometimes called, in case there were still creatures around from when the blackout had happened. It had been a time when the shields in Q-16 had weakened to such a point that creatures from some of the unchecked portals had made it into the Lab, and it was believed that some were still around.

The boys tensed further when over the hill came a creature not of their world. It stood upright like a human, but had the facial features of a bull, and was covered in coarse fur. Its densely muscled frame was dressed in heavy plate and chain mail armour. It was a Minotaur.

"Are you the defenders of Earth?" it spoke in a clear dialect, its great nostrils flaring as it gazed down at them.

Slack-jawed, Liam and Xander looked back up at the creature. Their time off had suddenly become that much more interesting than skipping rocks.

༄༅

It did not take long for Jason and Sarina to assemble Skyris and Darius in the common room area after Liam and Xander showed up at the foot of Sarina's door with a Minotaur in tow. A large wooden table had been scrounged up from the discarded furnishings, the majority of which were mismatched couches. In the middle of the table lay Jason's C.T.S., the leather band of the watch neatly folder under the faceplate as though it were a display piece in a store. He had decided that having Puc there, at least through the communication device would be a good idea. Despite Darius having stepped in on a majority of issues and despite Jason not wanting to admit it at times, the older mage's wisdom was irreplaceable.

The seven of them stood around the table as the Minotaur, who had introduced himself as Stonefist, explained the reason for his visit.

"There have been rumours of activities west beyond the city from wide expedition hunters that packs of Fenrikin have been spotted accumulating together, the largest packs ever recorded, and what's more, of no blood relation to one another."

"Why's that unusual?" Jason asked.

"Fenrikin won't travel if they aren't from the same pack," Sarina interjected. "They'll get territorial if they spot one that isn't part of their family."

"Yes, unless they are held in thrall by another, then they will obey their master." Stonefist nodded. "Which is why Lord Snapneck believes that something is amiss in the west. Some even speculate that the giants could be returning."

Jason wrinkled his nose. "That's not possible, Anne and I brought down that mountain where Yarmir's lair was and all those creepy statues that he'd gathered. That was supposed to be all of them, wasn't it?"

"It is possible that Yarmir had a second lair should his first one be discovered." Puc's voice came through the C.T.S. **"It is not unheard of in the records I have read on giants."**

"That still doesn't explain why there would be no activity for so long. Why now?" Darius frowned.

"Uh, yeah, Anne dropped a mountain on him," Jason reminded those gathered.

"My sister did what?" Xander's eyes went wide, having never heard the story.

"Yes, this is true." Puc's usually neutral tone came through with subtle concern. **"If, however, we speculate the worst, then it is also possible that perhaps Yarmir had already used the hydra spell on himself prior to leaving that cave, in the event that he could meet his demise. Doing so would ensure that he would survive no matter which of his lairs was attacked."**

"Lord Snapneck has requested that a portion of the Four Forces military be sent to aid in the defences of Morwick in the event of a siege." Stonefist reached into a pouch on his belt and produced a small black tablet of stone with marks carved into it that had been inlaid with silver ink, and placed it gently on the table before them.

Skyris moved closer to the table and looked over the contents. "So let me get this straight, some of your hunters saw large packs of Fenrikin, and you just want everyone to drop what they are doing to go send parts of their army to you? Now, I'm no expert in military matters but, if I can chime in, then that just sounds paranoid from where I'm sitting."

The youth gathered in the room went silent upon hearing this. The air instantly became colder, as though the temperature had dropped several degrees to match the blueish tint of the Lab itself.

Stonefist's nostrils flared at hearing the declaration. The uncannily human eyes on the bull head narrowed.

"Last I checked, it was Jason Kinsman and Annetta Severio who led the Four Forces and not... Skyris... sister of King Venetor the Ironfisted." Stonefist intoned in his baritone voice. "And when Gaia was in need of aid we did drop everything to come to its aid."

"Stonefist is correct." Puc's came through the C.T.S. once more. **"Both Jason Kinsman and Annetta Severio lead the Four Forces. Annetta, however, is not present at the current time and so we cannot grant anything without her being present. As a favour, I can lend five hundred troops to help in fortifying Morwick until we are able to contact Annetta in regards to her decision on the issue. Will this suffice?"**

Another bout of silence followed. Jason, Sarina, Darius, Liam and Xander all looked over in the direction of the Minotaur, while Skyris stood stone-faced with her arms crossed and looking down at the floor.

"I thank you, First Mage Thanestorm, for your support." Stonefist inclined his head to the C.T.S.. "When can Lord Snapneck expect an answer from the rest of the Four Forces?"

"I will try to contact Annetta," Skyris offered reluctantly. "She's not on Earth currently, she chose to remain on Gaia after the battle against Razmus."

Stonefist nodded. "I shall let him know, and I will depart at once."

The great creature then began to turn to move, the hooves thudding heavily against the metal floor. When those gathered around the table were certain that he was out of hearing range, they all exhaled as the tension in the air dissipated.

"Just what were you thinking saying that to him, Skyris?" Puc's rang from the C.T.S.

"The same thing everyone else here was thinking?" she crossed her arms. "He didn't exactly give us any proof that they are actually in danger of an attack and last I checked, the resources of the Four Forces haven't had time to recover from the battle against Razmus. It's called conservation of force, or did battle tactics change in the last two decades since I was last involved in a war?"

"It was still brash and arrogant to say in front of an envoy," Puc stated, **"Have you forgotten how short-tempered Minotaur can be? You could have invited open rebellion then and there over something as small as sending a few troops to help qualm any possible unrest their monarch is feeling. Orbeyus spent years cultivating a friendship with them, and I will not see it dismantled before my eyes by his sister, of all people."**

"I like to think I have more than a base intelligence in such matters," Skyris spat. "And I also like to think I can smell paranoia where it's present."

"Unknown's bane, you Severios are all alike," Puc groaned. **"Brilliant warriors but bloody recalcitrant in demeanour, and prone to creating mutiny."**

Jason and the others watched the exchange between the two with wide eyes, and were glad that the entire thing was taking place over a C.T.S. instead of in person.

Skyris gritted her teeth at the last comment as she bit her tongue from saying anything further, or tried to at least. "Yeah, well, you seem to attract us Severios like mayflies into your life, so I suppose you are part of the problem. Now, if you'll excuse me. I'm going to go and attempt to contact Annetta."

The Gaian woman then pivoted on her heel and left the room without another word.

Regaining some of his composure, Puc spoke once more. **"I will go about organizing those troops. 05 out."**

A third wave of silence proceeded to radiate through the room as the gathered youth stood dumbfounded around the table.

Xander was the first one to speak. "What... What just happened there?"

"Well, that encounter just had enough unresolved tension to put Puc's chemistry set to shame." Jason cringed and sucking in some air clasped his hands together. "Right then! Who's up for a movie to forget what just happened?"

⬥⬥⬥

As dawn crept over the land on the day following her talk with Atala, Annetta, shrouded in a dark green hooded cloak, found herself riding atop Firedancer outside the walls of Pangaia in the forest. The feathering on the gypsy vanner's legs seemed to blend in with the wild grass as though he were treading water, while Annetta manoeuvred him steadily along in order to avoid any potential potholes. Sunlight peered through the leaves above, heralded the start of another day, causing the girl to subliminally acknowledge how fleeting her time was on Gaia. It was for that reason exactly that she had risked sneaking out and ventured on her current course, past the dense foliage.

Her destination didn't take long for her to get to, and the trail leading up to it was still fresh enough that she was able to find it with little difficulty. The decaying structure of a house beckoned her in welcome as she dismounted and walked the rest of the way. She lowered the cowl of her hood carefully as her eyes found the site.

There, before her, nestled among the tall grass was a white marble slab on which was carved a visage of Lincerious Heallaws, or as she had known him by in life, Link. The sarcophagus had been created by Puc through magic to look this way, but no body lay inside it. It was only Link's sword, which had been found at the site of the explosion that had destroyed Magnus's Tower. His body was never recovered, and this lack of closure had been a pain Annetta had carried with her for almost two months now. Her hand reaching out, she touched the cold stone and slid down, crumpling up beside it.

Though she had shed no tears in all the time that had passed, now, a sob erupted from her lungs rawer than anything she had ever felt. It was even sharper than what she had felt with the loss of Brakkus, whom she was able to still visit from time to time through meditation. With Link, there would be no such encounters.

"You know, I half hoped that you'd been fooling us this whole time," she managed to get out of herself, a tear-streaked face glancing up at the marble. "I stayed here thinking maybe, just maybe, you'd show up one of these days at the castle, but you never did, and now it's finally hit me that you're never coming back."

The tears continued to flow, violently and uncontrollably as Annetta shook from being in sorrow's thralls. She was so lost in it that she didn't hear the soft padding of paws approaching her until something warm and wet pressed up against her back. Startled, Annetta pulled away to see Bear standing behind her, his great amber eyes watching her thoughtfully. At least they appeared to be, until a great pink tongue cascaded out of his mouth and the giant creature started panting again with a jovial, but vacant expression. Despite the pain,

Annetta managed a small smile and getting up, she hugged the creature, burying her face in its fur.

She then withdrew and looked up at him, wiping the remainder of the tears from her face. "I'm going to have to leave soon, and I'm not sure when I'll be able to come back to see you. Do you understand what that means?"

The creature continued to survey her, its maw hanging open as it watched her without any sentient indication. Annetta sighed, having confirmed what she had already thought, and turning back to the tomb, she patted the corner of it.

"Watch over him for me when I'm gone," she said to Bear, and mounting up on Firedancer, she was off again.

೩೦೧೩

Leaving Firedancer in the care of the stable hands, Annetta made her way back towards Castrumleo. Once in her rooms, she quickly changed into the traditional scale mail armour she had grown used to wearing around the premises, and throwing on her crimson cape, she made her way out while fastening Severbane to her hip.

Zigzagging through the slew of castle staff, soldiers, nobles and officials, the girl strode towards the chambers Titus had last been kept at. Turning the final corner to them, she noted both Atala and Gladius standing guard at the door. The Gaian general nodded and let her pass.

Once inside, Annetta saw that the scenery had not changed much. Titus still lay on the bed, his eyes closed, light breathing being the only sign that he was still alive. Beside him, seated on a stool and unmoving, was Venetor. The King of Gaia's eyes were glassy, as though he lacked sleep, and a fortnight of facial hair clouded his face, his mighty hands clasped together supporting his chin.

Not sure how to proceed, Annetta wrapped her hands behind the small of her back and cleared her throat.

Venetor awoke from his trance and turned to face her. "Annetta, I didn't hear you come in."

"I didn't think you would," she commented as she came closer and crouched beside the bed. "How's he doing?"

Venetor frowned as his eyes went back to Titus. "He sleeps. There hasn't been much change, but his breathing is lighter, which the doctors assure me is a good sign. He will wake soon, a warrior's blood flows through his veins."

Annetta nodded as she gathered her thoughts and got back up to stand straight. "Uncle Venetor, I think it may be time for me to return to Earth."

"Is your summer over already?" He raised an eyebrow. "It can't be."

"It's not," she confessed. "But I think I can be of more use on Earth, maybe get some answers about what's happened to Titus. The Water Elves may know something that could help him get better quicker."

Venetor turned away from her and Annetta could sense a tension brewing within the monarch at having been confronted with such a piece of information. His eyes settled back on Titus as he processed it.

"Since when have the Water Elves been friends of the Gaians?" he spoke after some thought.

"Since they swore an allegiance to the Lord of the Axe, your brother and my grandfather," she stated. "I already spoke with Aunt Skyris about what was going on, maybe if I go back, I can speed things up and get some answers."

Silence followed and Annetta almost turned away to leave when Venetor turned back to face her yet again. "You would do this?"

Annetta stiffened, not expecting him to take the news so well and without a fight. "Whatever it takes. I'm the White Lioness of Gaia after all, right?"

Chapter 10

The next few days flew by for Annetta as preparations were made for her departure. With Titus remaining in stable condition, things had returned to normal, with Venetor attending meetings and solving disputes. He'd gotten so far behind, however, that this didn't mean Annetta saw him any more than she had during the time he'd sat vigilant by her cousin's side. She'd expected this would be the case, though, and didn't force any interaction between them. The few times she had seen him were when she stood beside his throne, dressed in the Gaian armour she had been given, while Venetor held audience with whoever was scheduled.

"The presence of the White Lioness of Gaia will be a reassurance to those we speak with," Venetor had told her on the first day he'd asked her to stand with him. "You are also the heir of Orbeyus, and should things have gone differently, it would have been you here as queen."

The words echoed in her mind as Annetta was forced to come back into the present, after the king's resolution of the latest issue resulted in an elderly Gaian woman kneeling before Annetta and kissing the hem of her cloak reverently. Uncomfortable as the gesture made her, Annetta remained still and did her best not to betray her feelings. It hadn't been the first time something like this had happened, but it didn't make her cringe any less.

The room itself was of a moderate size, with two twin doors on the far end. The throne itself, a seat carved of what Annetta thought to be white marble, stood on a raised platform on the opposite end of the room against the wall. Banners and pennants adorned the walls, a white rampant lion present on a red and white field on every inch of wall where it could be placed.

His tasks for the day having concluded, Venetor rose from his seat and reached for the heavy warrior-like crown on his head. Removing it, he inspected the master craftsmanship and the way the sun captured the crimson gems, causing them to come alive with flame. Placing it on the cushioning of the seat, he exhaled and faced Annetta.

"I suppose you're rejoicing in not having to do that anymore." A slight smile formed on the corner of Venetor's lips.

"Would it be terrible if I said yes?" she asked.

Venetor chuckled. "No, I suppose not."

His face then lost its grin as he turned his attention to the door on the far side of the room. "Come with me."

Annetta scrunched up her face, but obeyed and trailed after Venetor. They crossed the halls into a part of the castle that seemed older than others. Here, the doors hadn't yet been replaced with their more modern sliding counterpart like the room Annetta occupied, and the large rock slabs on the walls were smoothed out with age. There was a coldness to the hall as well, not uncomfortable, but the kind that occurred from stone not having been exposed to any sunlight for a long period of time. The journey ended with both of them before an enormous ornate wooden door on which the likeness of a rampant lion had been carved into. The girl frowned, still unsure of his purpose for bringing her there.

"As King of Gaia, I occupy the older part of the castle," he explained, pushing the door open.

Annetta had expected, despite the old door, that everything on the inside would be high-tech and full of gadgets. Instead, she was confronted by walls on either side filled with shelves that climbed to the ceiling stacked with books. The ceiling itself was a map of the galaxy Gaia found itself in, from what Annetta could discern, painted in navy blues with golden writing to show planets, stars, moons and so forth. The floor was painted with a map of Gaia's five continents in an array of tans, greens and blues. Annetta felt guilty about stepping on it as she made her way inside. A large mahogany-coloured four-post bed stood on the far side of the room with a matching dresser, and before them was an enormous wooden desk that would have put Puc's to shame. In fact, the more Annetta looked around, the more she realized how similar the room was to Puc's study, minus the artistic mess of books and parchment.

"The history of over ten generations lies in those shelves." Venetor placed a hand on one of the closest shelves, running a hand down the wood. "Not all Severio, of course. There were kings and queens that were not of our bloodline that were elected to power."

"Did you have to read all of these?" Annetta asked.

"Do I look like Thanestorm to you?" The King of Gaia laughed. "No, but I have read many."

Annetta felt silly for asking, but it seemed the natural thing to do, and fell silent. She watched as Venetor advanced further inside and pulled out a chest from under his bed.

"I had been saving this to give to you at the end of the summer before your return to Earth," he said as he began to open it. "I seem to recall you had a jacket that you would wear everywhere that I've not seen since the battle against Razmus."

The girl's brows furrowed and then softened when she realized what it was Venetor had pulled out of the chest. In his hands, he held a jacket made of what looked to be red leather. On the left side of her chest, a white rampant lioness was embroidered.

"It's made of beta dragon hide, but fashioned to look like the style of jackets worn on Earth." He handed it to her. "It's flame resistant, and will not disappear when you change into your feral form, much like the scale mail armour."

Annetta accepted it, the texture a soft velvet in her hands. Eager to try it on, she removed the cape from her shoulders and put it on. It fit like a glove.

"Thank you," she said, admiring the intricate stitching.

Venetor nodded. "Never forget where you're from, young Severio, and remember when you wear it."

೫೦೦೩

Elsewhere, in the darkness of space, a singular light flashed brightly as a beam shot forward. Without the slightest hint of encountering anything, it plunged into an invisible wall, like a spear having hit its mark. The wound of its intended target then grew and festered, until a hole surfaced in its wake. From within the floating fortress and beyond the translucent walls, Amarok watched with an insatiable hunger as the Pessumire hit another of its intended targets. He didn't move from his spot until the veil-piercing cannon's afterglow faded from the skyline.

"A miss." Lloyd Abner's voice came from behind, and the ruffled-looking scientist joined him.

Amarok glanced sideways slightly, his good eye focusing on the new arrival. He then turned his gaze back to straight ahead.

"From our side, it would appear so," he said after a moment. "But what if I told you that, in actuality, we had just hit a star in another universe on the other side of the portal we just made?"

Lloyd stroked at the scruff on his chin absentmindedly. His eyes peered with a greater intensity into the hole that had just been made.

Without betraying his intent, Amarok's good eye continued to follow the scientist. Then he saw it, the glimmer of recognition. In the reflection of Llyod's pupils, he saw the contents of the now-obliterated star begin to spill out of the portal and float carelessly on the sea of space before them.

৪০৫৪

After a spaceship bearing the White Lioness of Gaia left for her home, Venetor found himself walking towards Titus's room. When he'd made sure Annetta was safely on the ship, he'd turned his attention to matters of state that he had been ignoring and could do so no longer. He was not particularly proud of that, since negligence was part of the contract each Gaian monarch swore to not allow to happen. There had been a few instances in history where it had led to riots and uprisings, but he hoped that a few days of his absence would not be enough to bring that about.

Reaching the final stretch of corridors, the king soon found himself standing before the door and watched it glide open. On the other side, he was greeted by the sight of Titus laying peacefully asleep on the bed. No traces of the fitful states he'd been in before could be seen creasing his brows. His face that had over the last few days been contorted and twisted in cries of a chaotic nature was now veiled in a mask of peace.

Venetor grabbed a stool some distance away from the prince's bed and sat down, content to watch his son sleep without pain. The feeling brought a sense of déjà vu to him as he remembered when Titus had been just an infant.

Shortly after his birth, he had contracted Ghost Shock Fever, an illness that was said by the more superstitious of the locals to be caused by the shock a spirit received after having entered its new body and the craving it had to leave it once again. Despite Gaia's many medical advances, Ghost Shock was not something they had been able to cure. There were higher rates of survival in the present, but to those unable to afford the treatment, it generally meant certain death to their child. Titus had thankfully been born into one of the wealthiest families on the planet, and such care had been within his reach, something Venetor, having experienced it firsthand, hoped to rectify for future generations of families. No one deserved to lose a child, no matter the circumstance.

His thoughts were interrupted when he heard the thudding of heavy boots and jingling of metal approach the room. Gladius then popped his head inside.

"How fares the lad?" he asked in a whisper as he stepped over the threshold of the room to stand beside Venetor.

"He seems at peace, but I missed the physician, so I've no update on his actual status," Venetor whispered back.

Gladius's good ear flicked back and forth, his good eye assessing the sleeping youth. "Do ye think it means he's getting better?"

"It's hard to say. I don't think we'll know until he does wake up. If he does."

"He'll wake, m'lord." Gladius's ears went flat against his skull for emphasis. "He did when the Ghost Shock took him, for all we know this could be some adulthood lapse. It's not unheard of. Once ye carry the predisposition, it's in ye for life."

The King of Gaia continued to sit beside the bedside without saying anything. What he hated most was how powerless he felt in the face of it all. He was Venetor Severio, named the Ironfisted. He had singlehandedly killed Razmus, fought countless wars prior, and yet he could do nothing to aid his son but watch and wait. His jaw muscles twitched in the effort to hold down the enraged scream that threatened to escape him.

"No parent should ever have to bury their offspring," he said, finally.

"And ye won't, m'lord," Gladius assured him. "But he may wake to find he needs to bury you instead, if I can be so bold as to say. Ye haven't been getting much sleep."

"I've been getting enough," Venetor retorted.

Gladius let out a throaty sigh. "Ye can't lie to me, Venetor. I am sworn to ye, or do ye not remember that? I can feel everything yer feeling, and I know that ye are tired."

Venetor cursed himself internally as he remembered the bond between him and the Hurtz warrior. The bond obviously had its uses, some more beneficial than others. This was one of the less beneficial ones. He opened his mouth to protest, only to be shut down by the singular piercing glare of Gladius's good eye.

"Ye have a kingdom to rule that is still recovering from the wounds of the blows dealt to it when Razmus took over, and ye claim to be vying for a chance to lead the Federation to boot. I think ye need that rest more than ya realize. Now, I know ye are my liege lord, but I'm ordering ye to take it."

Venetor couldn't argue with what was being said by the Hurtz. Despite this, however, his mind in its sleep-deprived state still tried to come up with some valid arguments.

"On yer feet, soldier," Gladius barked, causing Venetor to respond to the drill sergeant's tone. "I want ye in yer chambers and asleep within the next hour. Is that clear?"

At first, Venetor thought the Hurtz was joking around, but when the steely gaze did not yield, he stood at attention. "Sir, yes sir."

"Good, I want ye in fighting shape tomorrow. This country needs ye to shape it with both hands and live up to yer namesake, Ironfisted. Now, at ease soldier, and do as ye were told."

The tactic, though strange to Venetor at first, had put the fight back in him in just seconds. He was after all, first and foremost a warrior, even if he wore a crown.

"My thanks, old friend." Venetor gave a curt nod.

"I wouldn't thank me just yet, soldier," Gladius replied with that same glint in his eye. "There's still a war to fight, even if ye don't see it."

Venetor, though exhausted, still managed one of his signature smirks, and pivoting on his heel, left the room.

Gladius watched him go, unconvinced that the king would do as he asked. He began to move after him, but not before he caught one last glance of Titus.

"Don't ye ruddy think about dying, lad, or I'll box yer ears out in the afterlife once I get there," he threatened and then hurried after Venetor.

ଔଔ

The hour was not certain, but what was were the events which took place around that given time. It was dark, save for the stars twinkling on the sky through the open window. Somewhere in the distance, the sound of grass blowing on the wind and being caressed by its might could be made out, along with the occasional wildlife making itself known to the sleeping world. The streets of the great city of Pangaia were mostly asleep, aside from the guards which patrolled them and the occasional citizen which found themselves to be up and about.

Silence stretched all the way to the great fortress of Castrumleo, the castle of the presiding monarch of Gaia. While inside, minimal staff could be seen at work in these late hours, and there was an overall stillness to the usually bustling nature of the stronghold. Even the lights in the halls had been dimmed to further give the illusion of nighttime.

One room, however, strayed from these conformities, unyielding to what was expected in that given hour. Despite the dark, despite the silence and despite all that told it to lay still in that given moment, the one named Titus stirred and the eyes of the Gaian prince opened.

Chapter 11

Wires hissed as they were melted together by the flame coming from small blowtorch Skyris held over them. A blast shield obscured her face, and her arms were clad in heat-resistant gloves up to her elbows to protect her from any potential drip off coming from the wires.

The focus she so vigorously poured into her task was broken when she heard the sound of feet coming her way. She shut off the torch and removed the blast shield, picking off loose strands of hair that had stuck to her face. She then turned to find Jason, Liam, Sarina and Xander all standing some distance from her, with Dexter hovering closely behind.

"Hey guys," she said. "Uhm... this some sort of intervention or something?"

"Huh? Oh, no." Jason shook his head. "Dexter said he found a spaceship that isn't registered or something, so he needed to tell all of us."

"An unrecorded extraterrestrial vessel," Dexter corrected. "I have the coordinates for you in order to obtain a visual."

Skyris stretched her arms as she stood up. "Right then, okay, let's go have a look."

She then led the group down the corridor towards the control room of the base. The room was one Skyris took particular pride in, having designed much of it herself, along with most of the programming in Q-16s security system. It had been a labour of love which had spanned the better part of her life, and as far as she was concerned, would be part of her legacy long after she was gone, if not her only legacy. The metal-paneled room with its glass walls that acted as monitors took up much of the space. Inactive, it looked rather plain, but when the glass walls were filled with the various diagrams and images, it was something else. Ironically, the technology was out of date according to present day Gaian standards, but there was something homey about it to her.

"Coordinates, please." Skyris pressed her hand on the central panel and made the screens spring to life.

Dexter froze where he hovered, and his normally red eye changed to blue. The screens around Skyris and the youth populated first with a variety of numeric sequences, which then translated into a world map that zoomed in on the specified coordinates. A live feed followed soon after, showing a crater. Thankfully, there looked to be no human civilization in sight, and the only witnesses were the now torn-up coniferous trees in the surrounding area, and a curious black squirrel that now poked its head over its edge of the torn-up land.

Jason whistled at seeing this. "Someone likes to make an entrance."

"That looks like the crater Venetor's pod made when it landed," Sarina said. "It's about the same size as well."

Skyris studied the scene keenly, pinching the screen closest to her to zoom into the image on it. "The blast radius is consistent with that of a Gaian space pod, so I do agree with Sarina, but neither Annetta or Venetor said anything about someone coming to Earth."

"I don't put it past Annetta to have forgotten," Jason scoffed.

Both Sarina and Xander shot him a glare at the comment, while Liam remained neutral.

"What? Her track record hasn't exactly been the best this past summer. I'm just stating a fact."

"Unless they were worried someone might be listening it to the communications." Skyris frowned.

"Couldn't they have used a C.T.S. to let us know, though?" Jason leaned over and squinted at the screen. "I mean isn't that sort of the point of having them?"

"Technically speaking, yes and no," Skyris answered. "But that's a topic for another conversation. Whatever the reason, this individual didn't send anything, so there's a chance that they are not friendly."

The room went silent after Skyris said this, and worry lined the faces of those present. It was then also that she saw those gathered for what they truly still were, children.

"That's worst-case scenario." She crossed her arms and the looks dissipated temporarily. "In either case, someone needs to go there and investigate."

"You mean teleport there and see?" Jason pointed to the camera feed.

Skyris nodded. "Exactly."

Jason bobbed his head in acknowledgement and turned to Sarina. "Guess there's only one logical choice for who should go."

"Hey, what's that supposed to mean?" Liam puffed out his chest defensively.

"It means exactly what I just said." Jason narrowed his eyes at his younger brother. "No way you and Xander are coming with. You're way too young for this."

Skyris watched the exchange between siblings. She remembered how she was always at the receiving end of those types of comments from her own older brothers, but said nothing initially. Her resolve only broke when she saw the look of belittlement crawl over Liam's eyes as he got ready to step down from the fight.

"And how old were you and Annetta when you stood against Mislantus?" Skyris questioned Jason.

The youth glanced at her half in anger and half in confusion. "Older than they are."

"But no less experienced?" she prodded further and seeing Jason's resolve falter, she continued. "A thing to keep in mind when you forbid those younger than you to do things. Try to remember how you felt in their shoes and thoroughly assess the situation before passing judgement. You may find you are overestimating the risks and removing a valuable learning experience for them that may one day save their lives."

"But you just said that whoever landed, there's a chance they are hostile," Sarina interjected.

"As there is also a chance that they are not," Skyris reminded them. "Besides, you're just teleporting in and out, it's not like they can follow you here if they are psychic, because they don't know the location of the Lab."

Jason wasn't convinced by this. "What if they've previously been in the Lab? Amarok came down here just fine the last time, and who's to say it's not him?"

"That would have been one of those security updates I told you about I was doing," Skyris replied. "When the blackout happened, the DNA database of who could and couldn't teleport in got erased, standard procedure for rebooting the system. I had to manually plug everyone in. Only matching signatures can pass in and out now."

Hearing this argument, Skyris saw Jason's posture relax a bit, even though he crossed his arms. "Okay fine, they can come with us."

The two younger boys instantly grinned ear to ear at hearing this, only to be shot another look by Jason. "But if I say you need to teleport out, you do so, got it?"

"Yeah." Both Liam and Xander nodded.

Jason closed his eyes, sighed and turned to Sarina, grabbing hold of her hand. "Right. Let's do this then."

"I'll be monitoring the situation from here. Get out if you sense any danger at all," Skyris told him and watched as the youth that had been standing before her vanished from sight.

೮⊃⊂೮

Jason felt his feet impact the earthy ground, causing some dust to rise around him. Sarina, who had held onto his arm, let go and looked around.

"Where are we?" she whispered.

Before Jason could provide an answer, Liam and Xander also appeared a few paces away. The latter boy, from what Jason could tell, looked as though he would throw up at a moment's notice.

"Do we... really have to do that again?" Xander squirmed, clutching his stomach.

"Only way back, we don't have a teleporter," Jason said, and then turned his attention towards where the crater was.

Sarina took a few paces towards it, while remaining at a cautious distance. "Do you think they're even still in there?"

Jason strode over to be closer to her. "As much as I don't like or trust him, I feel like Dexter would have said something if a lifeform had exited the pod."

A wave of uncertainty passed along those present, as their eyes darted from one another. Sarina was finally the one to break the cycle and rolling her eyes, she began walking towards the crater's edge.

"Sarina, what are you doing?" Jason pivoted after her.

"What apparently the rest of you aren't capable of," she replied, and kept going.

Jason watched with frayed nerves for only a split second before jogging over to join her, followed by Xander and Liam. The closer the edge crept upon them as they walked, the higher the tension they felt, until the centre of the crater unveiled itself before them.

"It's another meteorite," Xander concluded, squatting and leaning over to get a better look.

He was sent back seconds later, landing on his rear when he was spooked by the side of the thing melting away.

"What the?" he managed to say as he scrambled to his feet and moved back a few paces.

"Get down." Sarina warned everyone, causing those present to drop to the ground on their stomachs.

116

The sound of feet on a metallic surface followed, and upon coming into contact with the ground, Jason heard them pause. Then nothing. The muscles in his back tensed as he waited for some form of possible attack he would have to flee, or the sound of some horrible beast charging their way, but nothing came.

"Uh… guys? Was that you up there?" a familiar voice called from down below.

Jason, while still remaining cautious, crawled to the edge of the crater, and as soon as he set eyes upon who it was down below, he cracked a wide grin.

"Anne!" he shouted as he got up and scrambled down towards his best friend.

Below in the crater, Annetta stood wearing her Gaian armour with a large tan canvas duffle bag at her feet. Jason swore she looked tougher than he remembered, and it had nothing to do with her physique, but rather her face, and more specifically, her eyes. There was a sharpness to them that he didn't remember before. Or had it always been there and he had never noticed it before? Whatever it was, it dissipated when the serious expression on her face melted into a smile.

"I thought I heard you guys up there. Took you long enough." She smiled and gave Jason a one-armed hug when he came closer.

"Well, you kind of gave everyone a scare at the Lab, if I can be honest." He reciprocated and took a step back.

Xander looked as though he would jump for joy when he saw who it was and ran down to meet her. "Sis!"

Annetta grinned back at him and gave him an embrace as well. "Hey, Xander! Did you get a head taller when I wasn't around, or did I get a head shorter from all the poundings I got during training with Uncle Venetor?"

The younger boy beamed back upon hearing the comment, and then looked at her thoughtfully. "I think you might just be getting short."

"We thought you'd be staying on Gaia the whole summer. What changed?" Sarina asked.

Annetta's jovial face darkened. It seemed to make the girl age a decade. "It's Titus… things have gotten really bad."

"Don't they have doctors or something on Gaia that can help him?" Jason tilted his head slightly to the side in disbelief. "I mean, Venetor kept rubbing in how much more advance Gaians were to humans and all."

The girl in armour nodded in agreement. "That's the whole thing, they can't figure it out."

Her ears then seemed to perk up in an animalistic style as she looked around and then turned to those gathered. "We should get going. I can hear a car engine closing in on us, and we don't want to be found when they get here."

"How can you hear anyone coming here?" Liam, who'd remained silent until now, asked.

"Feral form abilities," Annetta replied, and then turned to Jason. "To the Lab?"

Jason looked at those gathered briefly before focusing back on Annetta. "To the Lab."

Grabbing hold of the duffle bag at her feet, Annetta then vanished, followed by the others. The only indication of them having been there to begin with was a light wafting of dust that followed, and not long after, settled anew.

Chapter 12

The red Gaian sun beat down fiercely on Titus's black cotton shirt and pants as he sat in a reclining chair on one of the many balconies located in the upper levels of Castrumleo. His sketching supplies lay scattered on a table beside him, pencils and charcoals of various thickness and sharpness. A large sketchpad sat in his lap as he worked away furiously on his latest muse, the charcoal seeming to be one with his fingers. It was the ruins of Magnus's Tower, which still hadn't been completely removed from their resting place. It wasn't that there was a lack of workers, but rather that the site itself had come to stand for something to the Gaian people in the last few months. Titus often watched as pilgrims from far and wide came to lay tokens of their gratitude on the ruined stones in honour of the two that had sacrificed their lives trying to stop Razmus, even if their efforts had been in vain. Because of this, now, the once dead stones were transformed into a meadow of freshly lain flowers, candles and trinkets. Some of these had been placed as far up as the jagged intact columns that crested the horizon.

"The people are trying to petition to have a monument erected to commemorate both Layla and Lincerious," Atala's voice said from the entrance.

Titus paused from his scribbling and glanced sideways to see the woman walking towards his side. "It would be a nice tribute if they do. Has father heard of this yet to approve it?"

Atala shook her head. "I'm afraid your father wasn't thinking of much else except you these last few days. Annetta and I were the ones attempting to fill in for his absence."

"Right, I haven't seen her around. Where is she?" he asked.

"I'm afraid her absence is partially my doing, my prince." Atala folded her arms as she came to the edge of the balcony to look down. "When you weren't waking, we feared the worst, and I asked Annetta to travel back to Earth so that she could relay to Puc and Skyris your condition. I feared if she continued to communicate in an electronic manner, then someone could potentially hack the signal."

"And end father's plan to vie for the position of being head of the Federation," Titus concluded as he put down the charcoal. Rubbing his blackened thumb against his pointer finger, he watched as the concentrated smudged spread up and down the length of it, creating an ashen shade to his skin.

The golden-eyed woman nodded. "That is correct."

The Crown Prince of Gaia frowned at the confirmation. "Well, I hope that since I am better we are able to call her back for the next few weeks before her school starts."

"I'm sure she would like that, my prince."

Titus bobbed his head thoughtfully. "It was different with her here, you know? I didn't feel as alone as I once did."

His mind wandered to his days as an only child in the castle. He'd had tutors aplenty, but he had never had many friends, not people he could truly consider friends because he was, after all, the future king of Gaia. The children of other nobles were expected to accept him, and he knew from a very young age he would never get an honest answer out of them. Annetta had been different. She didn't see a prince, but a person, her cousin that she had just learned about.

Shaking off the thought, his gaze then turned down as he set aside the piece of paper he had been working on and flipped through some of the other works in the leather portfolio. These had already been sprayed to prevent smudging. When he found what he was looking for, he pulled out the paper. Unlike most of the rough sketches he worked on when he was trying to relax, this one was fully detailed. It depicted Annetta dressed in her Gaian armour, Severbane drawn as she looked out into the distance, with Severio Castle in the background on one side of her and Castrumleo on the other, her cloak fluttering behind her and dividing them.

"I was working on this to paint and then give to Annetta to take home," he explained. "Like when Mother painted Severio Castle for Arieus and Aurora."

Atala walked over from her spot at the balcony and peered over the prince's shoulder at the drawing. "One of your finest works, if I may say so. Davena would be proud of how much you've improved."

Titus returned a weak smile and sighed at hearing his mother's name. "Sometimes I feel when I'm drawing that she's here with me, still instructing me on what I was doing wrong. Even after all the lessons, she would always find something that could be done better."

"She was a perfectionist, my prince," Atala replied.

He gave another nod, turned his attention back to the drawing he was holding and placed it back into the portfolio. He then resumed his work on the sketch he'd been working on when she'd come in.

The Gaian general watched him for a little longer before she decided to speak again. "My prince, I must ask you... do you recall anything from when you were ill?"

The charcoal in Titus's grip snapped just as she asked this, but the youth's expression remained unfazed. Concentration took over his features.

"I'm sorry, but I don't," he replied and blew the pieces of broken charcoal off the page, then grabbed a fresh piece to continue drawing with from the case on the table beside him. "Everything from when I slept is hazy in my mind."

"I see." Atala frowned slightly but said nothing else and shortly after she began to turn to leave the balcony.

Titus looked away from his work just as she was about to get out of hearing range. "There was one thing I do remember."

The woman stopped and craned her head around slightly. "Oh?"

"I remember something about the seed of chaos." Titus's brows knotted. "I think I dreamed also about a city being destroyed and a great tower falling, but I think that was just me recalling the battle against Razmus."

"It's not uncommon," Atala agreed.

They didn't speak anymore, and Atala resumed her walking away, leaving Titus to his sketching. Free from the mental burden of conversation, he allowed his mind once more to wander, his eyes focused on the page and the dark strokes of the charcoal. As he did this, he did not realize that the thing he was drawing on the page was no longer the stone of a tower, but dark wings.

₧₧₧

Annetta felt her feet touch down on the steel flooring of the Lab. Bathed in the blue-tinted halogen lights, she smiled at the familiarity. Despite having been away, nothing had changed. It had also incidentally been the first time she had attempted to teleport directly into the Lab and, all limbs accounted for, it looked like she had been successful. She hadn't been sure, however, where Jason, Sarina, Xander and Liam had wanted her to go, and so she had chosen the common room meeting area for her destination. The couches and chairs had thankfully not been moved, and so she hadn't ended up teleporting inside one of them or tripping onto one in the process of her entry.

'I'm in the common room, by the way.' She sent the message out telepathically to Jason.

Not hearing a reply back, she put down her bag. Found the closest armchair, slid into it and waited. Not long after, she heard the shuffling of feet on steel. The forms of her friends and brother, along with Skyris and Dexter hovering in tow behind them soon emerged from the corridor farthest to her.

Her smile widened upon seeing them and she stood up. "Hey, guys! What's up?"

"You not telling us that you were coming mainly," Skyris stated as they closed in. "You could have given us some warning."

"I'm sorry." Annetta's smile faded. "Atala was worried if I sent out too many communications, the Greys would catch on that something was up, and well..."

Skyris's concerned and flustered look faded at hearing this. "You don't need to say any more than that. If there's one thing I'm familiar with, it's the Greys."

A silent acknowledgement passed between the two of them and Annetta made a mental note to speak with Skyris in private about the whole thing. She then turned back to everyone else. "Where's Darius?"

"He's off doing some stuff for Puc, I think," Jason replied. "He's been in and out a lot with that kind of thing. Not to mention the Minotaur thing that happened a few days ago."

"Minotaur thing?" Annetta wrinkled her nose.

Jason crossed his arms and nodded. "Yeah, Snapneck sent an emissary requesting the aid of the Four Forces because they saw Fenrikin packs banding together, and he thinks Yarmir isn't dead or something like that. If you ask me, it seems kinda paranoid."

"It is paranoid," Skyris confirmed.

"I'm not sure if I can fully agree with that," Sarina added. "I agree with what Puc said, and I think him sending some of the Water Elves was a good call."

"Better safe than sorry. Puc did the right thing." Annetta adjusted the pin of her cloak that had shifted out of place slightly. "If it's okay with you guys, I kind of want to change out of this Gaian armour. I didn't realize how grimy-feeling you get while travelling through space."

"Not much different than your airplanes." Skyris chuckled. "Same concept, just more sky."

A small smile formed at the corners of her lips, and grabbing the bag on the floor Annetta then left in the direction of the living quarters in Q-16.

෫෬

Jason, Sarina, Skyris, Xander and Liam watched as Annetta left. As soon as her form vanished, the tension in the room dissipated as those gathered exhaled in unison.

"Okay, can we talk about the whole Gaian armour thing now?" Jason motioned rigidly with his hands in the air.

Skyris glanced over at him. "What about it?"

Jason found himself at a loss for words as he attempted to think of how to explain what he wanted to get across. "Well, I mean, it's Anne and she was in Gaian armour. Don't you think that's a bit odd? I mean, she knew she was gonna be landing on Earth right?"

Sarina mulled over the words he said. "You're right. It's odd that she didn't change into something resembling human attire, but I don't think that's cause for alarm J.K."

"Yeah, I mean you have to admit, that cape is pretty sweet," Liam added, to which Xander also nodded.

Jason growled in frustration, raking a hand through his hair. "I don't know... I just... I feel like something is off."

"J.K., do you remember the conversation we had about Annetta trying to escape reality?" Skyris crossed her arms as she leaned against the closest sofa. "The armour? The something off that you are feeling could just be that."

"You could also just be thinking something is off, but it isn't," Sarina offered. "You haven't seen her in over a month, after all."

Jason frowned at hearing this. "I don't know if that's it. Even the whole not announcing she was coming... I don't buy it. She could have let me know through our abilities. Last I checked, the Greys couldn't read minds, same as any other psychics. It's forbidden."

Skyris switched the dominance of her feet underneath her before turning her attention back to the conversation. "While this is true, there are some in their ranks, just like the First Mage of Aldamoor, who have the privilege of being able to do so, and not all of them have honourable intents sadly."

Jason's gaze turned back to the hallway Annetta had gone down. He didn't like being kept in the dark, and he knew Annetta was definitely hiding something. It was the speed in which she had tried to leave the room in order to be alone. He shoved both hands into his pockets in defeat.

Xander glanced down at the C.T.S. on his wrist. "Jeez, I should get back. I can let mom and dad know that Anne is home."

"I'll go with you," Liam added and took off after his best friend.

"I should also be getting back to what I was working on," Skyris admitted, having looked down at her own C.T.S. Pivoting on her heel, she began to walk away with Dexter floating lazily behind her.

Jason and Sarina watched as the trio departed to their various destinations. Once alone, Sarina huddled closer to Jason, slipping an arm under his. Despite this, the frown on his face persisted.

"Something's wrong with Anne," he repeated once more, mostly to himself out loud. "I can feel it."

"She's still probably grieving over Link. I mean, it has only been a month."

His shoulders sagged at hearing this. "Right. I wish I could help her somehow."

"It looks like with Anne you just need to give her space." Sarina withdrew from him and began walking towards where her room was. "She'll come around when she's ready, I think."

"Or she'll grind her teeth into dust from the effort of not saying anything." Jason rolled his eyes and followed Sarina without another word.

⊱⊰

Corina Benedicta, now head of the kitchen staff upon the retirement of the previous one, was one of the thousands of servants who dwelled within Castrumleo, and had been overjoyed with the rest of the staff with the reinstatement of Lord Venetor the Ironfisted in his rightful place as the king of Gaia. Like the others, she'd felt the wrath of Razmus Severio when he had taken power, in the form of the Hurtz he had taken control of. It had been a frightening time to be anywhere near the capital, but this fear was thankfully short-lived due to the battle against the Four Forces and the White Lioness of Gaia that had come to the aid of the Gaians when they needed her most.

Though the mental wounds many carried because of it were still fresh, most Gaians had tried to move on with their lives as though it were a bad memory. There was no place for weakness in their society. Everyone, no matter their rank or status in life, had precious warrior's blood flowing through their veins, and in the eyes of the Unknown all were worthy of such a calling, should they choose it. Corina was not one such Gaian, and she felt no shame in it. After all, someone had to make sure the great lords and ladies of Pangaia were well-fed, had their clothing cleaned and their desks dusted, so why not her? As far as she was concerned, this was her battlefield, and she would do everything in her power to make sure that she was victorious.

Her current mission carried her towards Prince Titus's chambers. A silver tray which contained a variety of smoked meats, preserved vegetables and aged cheeses cut into small pieces were stacked onto their respective plates with toothpicks in each. A steaming pot of tea stood beside these, along with a cup that was turned upside down, white porcelain decorated with gold filigree. She had handpicked each one to ensure it was the best quality when she had been asked by Lord Gladius to bring up some refreshments to the prince who had spent most of his day in the confines of his room working on one of his art projects. She'd also made sure to wear her finest crisp black uniform over her slightly plump frame for the occasion, as well as pin up her long salt and pepper hair into a tight bun. She had even insisted to the lesser staff that she should be the one to carry up the tray, an honour if ever there was one.

Once she reached the final set of steps that led to the prince's rooms, Corina paused and inhaled the cool air sharply to calm her nerves. Her entrance and exit needed to be fluid and smooth. She wouldn't engage in conversation with the prince unless he asked first, and needed to act as though she were invisible in the process of her task. Saying a silent prayer to the Unknown, Corina pushed open the door lightly.

Whatever grace she'd just asked for hadn't come, and upon seeing the happenings of the room, the entire tray dropped from her outstretched hands, spilling onto the floor. Before her, the wall that had once been a pristine cream held the immense drawing of a dragon with seven heads surrounded by ten stars. The rest of the area that had been blank was now filled with scribbled writing. The content of it made little sense to her as she tried to follow it, and reaching the end, she saw who it was that had been responsible for its inscription. On his hands and knees in the far right corner, covered in charcoal was Titus.

"The end times awake, and make all worlds quake. Abandon hope and end lives, in this the seed of chaos thrives," he repeated again and again as though the words held no meaning while scribbling away.

At a loss for what she was witnessing, Corina backed out of the room without even bothering to pick up the discarded tray and ran to notify Lord Gladius.

⁫ ⁪

Atala clicked her tongue as she walked up and down the length of the wall in Titus's room, inspecting what was written on it. Her golden eyes committing every inch to memory. "It's as we feared, whatever fit he was having, he has relapsed."

Venetor stood some distance behind, examining the wall as well with his arms crossed. "He was fine this morning, I don't understand."

"I don't think we fully can understand it." Atala turned to face him. "Whatever this affliction Titus has, I don't think it's of natural causes, and these repeated phrases prove it."

"Then what does it mean?" he unfolded his arms and strode towards her.

"What it means, my king, is that I think there is something greater at work here, and I say this as not a very religious Gaian." Atala pointed to the writing on the wall. "This sentence: The end times awake, and make all worlds quake. Abandon hope and end lives, in this the seed of chaos thrives. It's repeated again and again all over the wall, along with other lines. The way in which they are composed…. I think it may be part of some prophecy."

Venetor moved closer to the wall and inspected the charcoal scribbles that were written all around the great black dragon on the wall. He wrinkled his nose in distaste. "This is some hoax. It has to be."

Another set of feet could be heard walking along the stone floors from the opposite end of the room. Venetor turned around to see it was Doctor Sano. The physician stopped upon making eye contact with him, and straightened before speaking. "I'm afraid it's no hoax, my king. I examined your son again, and there is nothing wrong with him physically. Whatever this is, it's something in his mind."

"Send for a psychoanalyst then," Venetor commanded.

"As you will have it, my king." Doctor Sano nodded and left the room just as quickly as he'd arrived.

Atala watched the doctor leave, then turned to Venetor. "We can't let anyone know of this. We'll need to do something about that kitchen staff that found him."

Venetor sighed wearily and began to leave the room. "Speak to her, but nothing more. The last thing I need right now is to have more rumours spread."

"I will see it done."

The Gaian king bobbed his head before looking back at the wall. "I want someone with Titus at all times from now on. He is not to be left unsupervised, and before this is taken down, I want copies sent to Skyris with an encryption on them."

Venetor then left the room, leaving Atala to contemplate the wall on her own. She narrowed her eyes and focused in on one particular area. The longer she glared at the writing, the clearer it became, until she was able to read it without any trouble. Her eyes widened when she realized what it said, and just to be certain she was not seeing things, she recited the words out loud.

> *"While peace restored and violence quell,*
> *Darkness breaks a forgotten spell.*
>
> *The end times awake,*
> *And make all worlds quake.*
> *Abandon hope and end lives,*
> *In this the seed of chaos thrives.*
> *Black beast of seven minds and crowned in ten,*
> *The catalyst of its end living in man's kinsmen.*
> *In the prison among the stars it waits,*
> *Raging to govern all fates."*

Atala felt a chill go down her spine and looking around, she found a discarded piece of paper. Grabbing a piece of charcoal from Titus's pencil case, she quickly jotted down the contents of what she'd just read. She then ran out of the room in pursuit of her king.

Chapter 13

As soon as Annetta had managed to change out of her armour and into jeans, a black t-shirt, her beloved teal sneakers and the red leather jacket she'd received from Venetor, she decided that it was time to go see her parents. It wasn't until she'd seen Xander at the crash site that she realized how much she had missed them. She had been so caught up in being on Gaia and experiencing it that she had lost track of time. Like Jason, she had not even called them and now this bothered her. She made a mental promise to herself to do better in the future.

Materializing in her room, Annetta found that it had remained virtually unchanged. The posters of fantasy films she liked occupied much of the space on her walls, as well as a few of the drawings she'd done in the past. Her desk on the far side of the room had its shelves filled with books and a few trinkets she had left from her childhood, such as the dragon and knights she and her brother had played with when they were younger. There were also some photos of her, Jason, Sarina and the others that she had placed in frames. On a corkscrew board to the left, she also had drawings of maps that she had made for the various places she'd visited. She was not sure how accurate they were, but she liked to think they at least gave one somewhat of an idea of what they looked like.

She left the room soon after and closing the door, took a good look at the poster on it that showed a red and a white dragon ready to do battle with one another, then made her way downstairs.

Annetta descended the stairs and found her mother seated on the couch with a book in hand. Though it had only been a few weeks since Annetta had seen her, it felt a lot longer, and she was glad that her mother hadn't changed. Her chestnut hair was cut slightly shorter, just above the shoulder, a style she had adopted over the last year, and she had one of her around-the-house t-shirts on, which was an indication that she was not going to be running any errands. Her eyes wandered from the page and looking up, she stuffed a bookmark between the pages before jumping to her feet. "Annetta? You're home."

Annetta smiled gingerly, and seconds later, found herself being embraced by her mother. Instantly, despite everything she had been through, she felt like she was a child again, and every problem that she'd ever had disappeared. She withdrew just a little, her smile widening. "Yeah, I came back."

Just then, Arieus popped out from around the corner carrying two mugs with coffee that he nearly dropped. "Annetta?"

Areius put down the mugs on the coffee table as quickly as he could, and reached out his arms, embracing both Annetta and Aurora tightly at the same time, causing them to laugh. Annetta sighed contently. No matter how far and wide she travelled, home was where her family was.

"So how was it?" Arieus let them go. "And I thought you weren't coming back until the end of summer."

Annetta took a step back and followed Arieus as he made his way into the living room. "It was great. I was going to stay longer, but there were some things happening with Titus that … it's a long story, and I'm not sure where to begin actually."

Aurora sat down again on the couch, leaving a space between her and Arieus. "We have time if you want to talk."

Annetta was about to say something about how it was all too complicated. She didn't want to worry her parents and yet at the same time, she didn't want to dismiss their interest. Her mind made up, Annetta settled in and began to weave the tale that had been her last few weeks on Gaia.

☙❧

Fingertips clicking away on her keyboard, Jansen finished the passage she'd been working on and leaning back in her worn leather office chair at her desk, she sighed. She had opted to stay in her room and work today instead of going out to the coffee house before work. Her supervisor at her part-time job at the grocery store had called her in for extra hours. Lord knew she needed the money before another semester of school started. College wasn't cheap. A feeling of warmth spread through her as she read over the scene she'd just written. It was as though she had been in the room with Annetta upon her reunion with her parents. She still couldn't fathom where the inspiration was coming from, but whatever it was, she would not argue with it.

Seeing what time it was, Jansen got up, stretched, then saved the file a consecutive time before turning off the word program and powering down the laptop. She checked if she'd packed her lunch and the latest book in the series she'd been binge-reading before she slid her knapsack on. Jansen grabbed her keys and then went to put on her sneakers before going to close the door. The routine had almost become a dance to her at this point, and she barely noticed half the steps, resulting in her sometimes needing to backtrack to make sure she had actually locked the door. Today, thankfully, was not one of those days, since she was running five minutes behind schedule, and every second counted.

With a quick flick of her wrist, the apartment she occupied was locked, and she was off, making her way down the hallway towards the elevator. Growing impatient with how long it was taking, she decided to use the stairs, and again thanked herself internally for only being on the second floor.

Jansen left the building and once again found herself walking towards the main street where her bus was scheduled to come in. She noticed her one strap was tighter than the other, and pulled off the bag to adjust it, while still making a steady pace towards the stop. The buses were known for sometimes coming earlier, though not often, thankfully. Not wanting to be late, however, meant she was unable to look straight ahead and shortly after, found herself colliding with another person.

"Sorry!" Jansen panicked as she snatched her backpack from the floor, scrambling to her feet as quickly as she could to remove herself from the embarrassing situation.

The person she had crashed into looked somehow familiar to Jansen as he picked himself up off the floor. It was a young man, about her age, tall, with short black hair and dark eyes that contrasted his light complexion. He was dressed mostly in dark clothing, the only thing varying in shade was his grey t-shirt that was mostly hidden by the black zip-up hoodie he wore.

"No worries." He brushed off some of the dirt from his jeans as he got up. "You okay?"

Jansen couldn't help but also noticed that the individual she had bumped into was also quite handsome, and found herself struggling not to blush or say anything she deemed stupid. "Uh... yeah, I don't think any brain damage happened."

So much for the latter part, she cursed herself, until she saw the young man's face light up into a genuine smile.

"Well, that's good to know. I don't think I'm insured for that."

Jansen felt herself relax a little upon hearing that he shared a similar sense of humour to her, and smiled back. Instinctively, she then reached out her hand. "I'm Jansen Morrison."

The young man shook it, his grip firm and warm. "Darius Silver."

Jansen's brows furrowed slightly at hearing the name. She then, however, noticed the bus coming to her stop from her peripheral and withdrew her hand. "Nice to meet you. Sorry, but I've gotta run, that's my bus I need to catch for work."

The one named Darius nodded. "I'm sure we'll bump into each other again."

Jansen bobbed her head and jogged towards the bus, pulling out her monthly pass to flash for the driver. Once on board, she seated herself by the window. She took another glance at the young man she had just met as the bus began to speed away and then shook off her current train of thought. What were the odds she would meet someone with the same name as one of her characters?

೫೦೧೪

The squealing of the drill overpowered all other sounds as Skyris removed one of the screws she'd deemed unnecessary in the left shoulder socket of the mobile suit. She examined the part and then pocketed it for reuse in a future project. She hooked the tool back to her belt and exchanged it for a pair of needle nose pliers, which she then tapped against her lower lip, analyzing her latest work on the project. Deeming the pliers insufficient, she put them back in her belt, and reached in with her hand into the joint, locating the various coloured wires and beginning to untangle them for easy access.

Her work was interrupted by the sound of movement on the floor some distance away. Not wanting to get too engrossed in her project, she withdrew her hand from inside. She grabbed a rag to wipe down her grime-covered fingers. When she deemed them clean enough according to mechanic standards, she reached over for the jug of orange juice on her desk, popped it open and took a swig. She swallowed and was greeted by a familiar acidic taste, followed by a burning sensation as the liquid travelled down inside of her.

Skyris's eyes then went to the door just in time to see Annetta appear in their frame. The older Gaian smiled, seeing the jacket the girl wore. "Looks like you got a wardrobe upgrade."

Confused, Annetta glanced down at herself before realizing what Skyris had meant and smiled back. "Oh, yeah… uncle Venetor gave it to me before I left to come back to Earth."

"Oh I know, I helped him design it. My brother is far from style-oriented. He's more concerned with the utilitarian uses of clothing."

Annetta chuckled and walked further into the room. Her eyes then went to the giant mechanical being in the room. "Uhm…so… what is this?"

Skyris pivoted around to her creation. "Oh, this? A challenge. I got really bored one night and found myself surfing the internet, and I came upon this cartoon which had giant robots piloted by people, so I decided to see if I could make one. It helps me unwind when I'm not working on coding upgrades or any of the other work that needs doing around the Lab."

"So you're just building it for fun?" Annetta pointed at the thing.

"As an exercise to stretch the limits of my potential." Skyris corrected as she opened the bottle and took another drink from it.

The girl nodded, even though Skyris could tell she didn't fully understand what she meant. Not that Skyris expected her to.

"So, how was Gaia?" she put down the jug and leaned against the table cluttered in a variety of wires and metal parts.

"It was…different."

"Different?" Skyris pursed her lips. "I guess that's as apt a description as any considering you were raised on Earth."

"That's not what I mean." Annetta bit her lip as she tried to rephrase it.

Seeing the girl's anxious body language upon thinking she gave the wrong answer, Skyris waved a hand dismissively. "No, trust me, I get it. Believe me, I've travelled to enough worlds to know what it's like to find yourself in a place that you think is the same as where you come from because the people look similar, only to be thrust into a totally different culture than anything you've ever experienced. I only have to look as far as the Water Elves for examples."

Skyris then looked off to the side as she remembered some of her time in Aldamoor and smiled slightly at the waves of memories in her mind.

"Is it true what they say about you and Puc?" The younger girl broke the silence.

Skyris felt the weight of the words plunge into her as though she had been forced into an ice bath. "Where did you hear that?"

"Jason may have mentioned it at the feast after Venetor's coronation." Annetta shifted her weight from one foot to the other. "Though he didn't seem convinced it was true."

132

Skyris straightened her posture as she looked over at her. "It's true."

There was another pause, this one more so due to Annetta looking away and clearly feeling silly for asking, from what Skyris could observe.

Skyris sighed and cleared her throat. "It's hard to imagine, I guess, at least with how he is now, I suppose, though he wasn't always that way, and neither was I the way I am. We were younger, without the scars that now decorate us."

Annetta's brow furrowed at hearing the last part. Skyris took a deeper breath than normal as she prepared to continue. "Our union was never approved by my father, nor Venetor. When they found out, they were furious, and I was made to return to Gaia, though not without…"

The words stopped in Skyris's throat, her hands curling at her sides into fists. "Puc and I had a son."

"You mean I have another cousin on Gaia?" Annetta's eyes widened. "Or is he in Aldamoor?"

Skyris shook her head. "No… he died shortly after."

"Aunt Sky, I'm sorry, I had no idea…" The words tumbled out of the girl's mouth clumsily.

Skyris had heard it all before. She then drew upon the inner shield she had created over the years to quell the emotions that tried to rise each time she spoke of the event. It was a block she had been taught to bring up whenever the darkness of recounting it tried to take her. "He's in a better place. It was just not meant to be in this life, but it's also why some scars are too deep to heal."

Annetta gave a brief nod. "I understand."

A third pause began, but this time it was Annetta who stopped it from progressing. "There's another reason I needed to talk to you, Aunt Sky. It's about what Uncle Venetor is planning."

"It better not involve trying to marry me off." Skyris fumed and took another drink from the jug.

A chuckle escaped Annetta. "No, no, nothing like that. It's about the Federation. He wants to run to be the head of it. I just thought you should know."

Skyris gave a curt nod. "It has been his ambition since the start. To put Gaia back in power."

"I don't see how that's a bad thing, though." Annetta's brows furrowed.

The woman smiled lightly, amused by Annetta's innocence on the whole subject. It was times like this that she remembered just how young the girl was and how new she was in the game of politics. "Make no mistake, Venetor does have the good of Gaia at heart, but further beneath this there is a far simpler motive, much darker and far more primitive in nature."

Annetta leaned in to hear more, and Skyris leaned in to meet her. "He wants to be in control."

೮ාೲ

Matthias had felt compelled to stay on the planet after his encounter with Amarok. At first, he could draw no connection to the abandoned and savaged remnants of a living space, but the longer he stayed, the more it seemed to come back to him. It was as though someone had covered his vision in a veil, and only by remaining in the place it had meant to cloud in his mind, did his memory return. The table he sat at now held more meaning than when he had first arrived. He could recall his father speaking with him and his sister, telling them stories of long before they were born, while their mother sat in the overstuffed armchair in the corner, reading her book and occasionally shaking her head when her husband's tales got too tall. The armchair, along with much of the other furniture, had now perished, but the table had remained mostly intact.

In his search through the partially-demolished house, he had come across a small trapped door just beside the foot of where the entrance had once been. Once he'd opened it, he found a small chest inside, and in that, an assortment of scrolls and books. Now the contents of that chest lay sprawled out on the table before him while he poured through them, trying to make sense of what he had found. There were some maps of star systems, faded from age but still legible from the dark blue papyrus-like material they had been drawn on. There were also a few old notebooks, which made Matthias question why his family had used such primitive technology to record vital information if it was so important. Perhaps longevity hadn't been something they had been concerned with?

He closed his eyes as he struggled to grasp some meaning about them, and the only memory he could recall was both of his parents hunched over the pile he had sprawled out on the table at his father's work desk. There was a paranoid concentration visible on their faces as they discussed what it was they were looking at, but Matthias couldn't make out any actual words.

He ran a hand through his tousled shaggy brown hair, blinked and refocused on the mass of assorted works before him. His brows knitted together as he struggled to find a pattern of some kind, anything at all that could help him gain some understanding of what he was looking at.

"There must be some relevance to all of this," he muttered, slamming his hand on the table in frustration.

The impact of the blow, he then noted, had reopened his wound that Amarok had inflicted on him, causing fresh blood to begin to travel down his forearm and make its way onto the page. Noticing the mess, he withdrew his hand from the table and began to wipe his gauntlet-clad hand on the bottom of his cape. Doing his best to wipe the blood from under his nails, yet still leaving them stained a dark pink, he huffed and got ready to abandon his quest. That was, until his eyes ventured back to the papers one last time.

Gently lifting the pages one after another, Matthias was greeted by a curious site on one of the larger maps. Where the blood had fallen onto the page, he saw now that it had congealed like mercury under the influence of a magnet and was being drawn to ten points around the outer edges, all with lines linking to the middle. Lifting it carefully, he watched as the blood began to resume its regular consistency and began to drip down the edge of the page onto the floor without damaging the paper it had just been on. Perhaps there was more to these ancient scrolls than Matthias gave them credit for, even if they seemed primitive to him.

A smaller scrap of paper that had been stuck to the back of the map then fell away and floated down onto the floor. Matthias bent down to pick it up.

"I cannot for the life of me be the one to end his life." He read the words out loud. "Though he is not of this world and perhaps, even as the Apostles of the Unknown claim, soulless, he is still my son. A parent should never have to bury their child. No, his course shall be decided hundreds or perhaps thousands of years later, when I am long gone. Let it be known that I, Freius, spared my beloved son by imprisoning him between the point of ten stars, for fate has named him the seed of chaos."

Matthias then noticed in an open book the sigil of Mordred and Mislantus, a black dragon of seven heads with ten stars circling over it. A chill went down his spine, and though he had never been the superstitious sort, tales from his youth about the being who would end the world spilt to the forefront of his mind. Amidst these thoughts, one memory became most prominent...

⁊⁓

Matthias watched as the man with dark brown hair and a short cropped beard wearing plain woollen clothing tucked him into bed. Azure eyes focused on their task. The young boy always felt safer when he was around, as though nothing could ever touch him.

"There, all set." The man smiled and got ready to rise.

"But Da, I'm scared." Matthias pulled the covers up further over his face.

The man, Matthais's father, sat back down at the bedside looking at his son. "Is it because of that story old man Thaddeus told by the fire? The one about The End?"

Matthias looked down at the fabric of the covers before deciding to admit to his shame, and nodded.

Matthias's father cracked a wide grin as he chuckled. "You've nothing to fear. Go to sleep, Matty."

"Oh yeah, well, how do you know?" he frowned.

The man shook his head and reaching out, he stroked Matthias's head. "Because, Matty, our family are the keepers, and the secret to where the seed of chaos lies is in us. So as long as we are around, then The End cannot come."

Matthias still looked unconvinced at hearing this. "What happens when you die?"

"When I and your mother pass on, then the secret will remain with you, just as it has with every Teron for hundreds of years."

"What if I forget?"

Another faint smile appeared on the man's face, his hand going from Matthias's forehead to his chest. "That which writes itself on the hearts of those who once witnessed will remain forever."

⁊⁓

His jaws hanging slightly parted, Matthias felt himself being pulled back into the present. His body tingled numbly, as though he were freezing. He knew what he needed to do and where he needed to be. Scooping up the remaining papers, he turned in the direction of his ship.

Chapter 14

The morning after her return, Annetta found herself at her desk with her computer booted up. She felt thrown off from her schedule of the last few weeks, and needed something to take her mind off it. She scrolled to see what her required course materials were for college. Just before having left for Gaia, she had heard back from two local colleges that had accepted her into their Police Foundations programs. It had then been a matter of her and her parents sitting down and figuring out which one was closest, had the highest post-graduate employment ratio, and so on. The entire time, her parents had also droned on about if she was sure this was what she wanted to do, to which, Annetta had responded with, how much more different would it be than some of the things she already did while in the Lab?

Opening her online mailbox, the girl cringed to see that in the six-week absence, she had amassed over two hundred emails. Perhaps signing up for all those promotions back in the day had not been such a good idea.

"They really should make junk mail illegal," she grumbled and began to mass delete those that she deemed to be spam, leaving only the relevant ones to read.

Once she had finished sorting, she saw the first one had to do with school, clicked on it and began to read its contents. When she finished, she moved on to the next one, repeating the pattern. Most of it was generic congratulatory literature that she glanced at for about thirty seconds before moving it into designated folder she had made, and then proceeded to move onto the next one. It wasn't until she got to the email that listed what her school uniform, shoes and books were that she read through it thoroughly.

After a few frustrating attempts, she was able to set up her school ID online and began the process of registering for her courses. Unlike high school, she had designated blocks to pick from which consisted of four main classes and one elective, a course that she got to pick from a list which was not related to her course. There were some Annetta thought that could be useful to her, like Introduction to Psychology, but the part of her that still enjoyed Science Fiction and Fantasy gravitated towards something completely unrelated.

"Apocalypse Now: The Study of Prophecies and World Religions." Annetta read the course name out loud and felt a chill go down her spine. "Course material will explore the ways in which prophecies from around the world herald the end."

The girl bit her lip as she thought about it for a moment, then hit the select button to complete her block registration. It would be fun to sit in a class and talk about would be predictions, she thought, instead of having to live and interpret ones that had been laid out in real life. She wanted that escape into something fabricated again, she longed for it. Ever since she had found out about the Lab and the much larger world she inhabited, she had craved to have a little piece of the world that was still make-believe. There was something liberating about having a place where one could be safe and not have to worry about the troubles in their everyday life. The only other thing, or rather person, that had made Annetta feel this way had been Link, and she had not realized it until he was gone. A tightness formed in her gut as she dwelled on it for a second, but then a picture formed in her mind. Everything was the same as it had been moments before but with the addition of Link lying on the couch and flipping through one of her old fantasy graphic novels. She smiled. Perhaps there was still some form of fantasy she could indulge in that would not make her think of her own life. Sighing, she closed the browser on her computer and proceeded to shut it off and go about starting a new day.

∞⌘

Word had reached Puc of Annetta's return, and the First Mage of Aldamoor made swift arrangements to visit Q-16. Like the others, he hadn't heard from the girl in over six weeks, and the silence was deafening. He remembered the state she had been in during their last encounter, and he wondered if the retreat on Gaia had done her any good.

Once back to Q-16, he descended from his mount in the stable. After having made sure his horse was adequately settled in, he strode inside. As he walked, he did his best to avoid the work area Skyris generally inhabited. Their last encounter, though over C.T.S., had not gone well, and he thought it best to allow some time to pass before they encountered one another alone and face to face.

His journey concluded at the end of one of the steel corridors. Puc stood before the entrance to the training arena behind the Calanite Diamond wall that acted as a safeguard and separated it. Inside, he could see the shapes of Sarina, Xander and Liam on the benches, while

Annetta and Jason sparred in the arena with dull-edged weapons. They seemed to be equally matched.

Both combatants were dressed more for the gym in their sweats and t-shirts than fighting in a war, and the mage could only speculate that the following bout was meant more to test technique than the prepare them for training in their full gear. Perhaps Annetta had wanted to make sure she'd not forgotten what she'd learned. The Unknown only knew she did everything possible to get out of training when she could. Left unsupervised on Gaia for six weeks meant she more than likely had avoided training. Puc's suspicions were then confirmed when the sword Annetta had been wielding flew out of her hand and clattered on the floor some distance away.

Then a peculiar thing happened, and Puc noticed that the girl, unlike Jason, had not been wearing any shoes. Her knee drove upwards, slamming into Jason's elbows and caused him to lose his grip on the mace. He staggered back a pace, a flustered look spreading across his face as well as one of pain. The girl, on the other hand, resumed back into her weaponless battle stance with her feet shoulder length apart, profile sideways and both hands before her with fists curled. A small smile spread across the mage's thin lips. Perhaps she had been practicing after all.

A roar then erupted from Annetta as she charged for Jason at full speed. The youth did the best he could to brace himself against her attack, but it was clear he was not prepared to deal with the situation at present. Annetta's fist then sailed through the air, hitting a wall created by Jason's forearms. She then threw another punch and then another and another, all the while causing Jason to have to move back. When he felt he was being pressed into a wall, he finally teleported to the other side of the arena to catch his breath.

Puc took this as his cue to enter. "I do hope that display I just saw was a genuine one of confusion due to a friend having picked up a few tricks while away, and not an accurate portrayal of how you would react to a fighting style you had never encountered on a battlefield before. The Unknown help you if it is."

Both the boy and girl stopped, turning around to face him. Where once there would have been scowls to greet him due to such a comment, now, there were warm smiles in their places.

"Am I allowed to say something in between?" Jason placed his hands on his hips, then looked over at Annetta. "Jeez, Anne, next time you decide to pull a hitman, give me some warning, okay?"

Annetta chuckled, rubbing her knuckles. "I'll try to remember that, but Puc is right. What if I'd been the enemy?"

"Well I... you're not." Jason crossed his arms.

"It is the same mistake you were making a few months ago while engaged in a fight with Sarina," Puc reminded him. "You cannot seem to separate your friendships from sparring, and it is costing you dearly."

Where before, Jason would have retorted with everything he had, he now only sighed and dropped his arms to his sides. "I know, but it's just so hard."

"Focus on the weapon being used to attack you." Puc moved closer towards them. "And remove the image of the one you call a friend from your mind."

Jason nodded and went over to pick up the practice mace that had been knocked out of his hand. Puc's gaze then turned to Annetta. There seemed to be a hardness to her that he'd not seen before, or perhaps he was imagining things due to lack of sleep finally.

"Anything I need to brush up on?" she asked.

Puc shook his head. "No, it is clear that you have been practicing. Though if I can make a suggestion, I would say do not plant yourself so firmly on the ground. You will not have the same flexibility of foot in a pair of sturdy boots."

"Thanks, I'll keep that in mind, and can I ask just one more thing?"

"Yes."

Annetta's face then screwed up. "What's up with the beard?"

Puc's eyes nearly widened, but he did his best to show that he was not fazed by what Annetta had just asked. "I thought it was time for a change."

"Well it's tripping me out, I'll say that." She put her hands on her hips. "Did I ever tell you about the one time my dad shaved his moustache off when I was little and I didn't recognize him when I came home from school?"

"No, I do not believe you ever did." Puc noted from the corner of his eye that Jason had gone over to speak with Sarina, Xander and Liam. He then glanced back at Annetta standing before him. Despite everything his mind told him, the girl seemed perfectly normal on the exterior, in fact, she seemed to be thriving. Nonetheless, the words came out of him. "How are you feeling?"

The mage then watched as the armour in Annetta's eyes came loose, she looked over to see her brother and her friends engaged in deep conversation before looking back at Puc. "Honestly, I feel like... like I've aged a hundred years on the inside while the rest of the world stayed young."

Puc could only nod upon hearing this, having travelled down the road of grief all too many times. It was a feeling that despite all the curses and spells he knew, he still deemed the worst. He'd been victim to its dark quicksand-like embrace and the damage it could do.

"I am sorry I cannot be of better counsel to you in these matters," he managed to say after a few moments. "Though I have had to witness the deaths of those I cared for, it never gets any easier, but it is true what people say. Time does heal wounds, or at least it manages to patch up the holes left by those gone enough for us to be able to carry forward."

Something resembling a tear formed in the girl's eye, but when she blinked it was gone. In its place was the armour once more. "Thanks. I'll try to remember that."

A short silence then passed between them before Annetta spoke again. "I should probably tell you the real reason why I'm back, because it's got nothing to do with homesickness. I came back because Titus's condition isn't getting any better, and everyone on Gaia is at their wit's end as to what's going on with him."

"And Venetor is too proud to ask for my aid himself?" Puc concluded.

"What? No, he's just not exactly himself with how it happened," Annetta retorted. "What do you have against Venetor anyways? Does it have something to do with you having been with Aunt Sky?"

Puc's jaw twitched. "Unknown's bane why is everyone bringing Skyris and I up of late, it's like a plague. Who told you that?"

"Well aside from your beard doing a poor job of hiding it all over your face, Aunt Skyris did. I asked because of what Jason had mentioned at the coronation feast. Ever since, I can't help but feel that your tension with Uncle Venetor has something to do with that."

Puc tried flexing the muscle in his jaw to prevent it from twitching anymore as he glared at the girl. Another bout of silence passed between them as he reviewed the information in his head, trying to think of what to say back. The more he thought on it, however, the more it seemed like he was trying to make excuses for the truth that so painfully lay before him and the truth of it all was that lying never did anyone any good.

"There is merit in what you say," Puc finally spoke. "Though the full story is far more complicated."

He had expected a stream of questions to follow, as was typical of Annetta in most such situations when he was vague, but instead, all that he got was a nod from her.

"You don't have to go into detail if you don't want to," was all Annetta said, and then walked across the arena to pick up the practice sword she'd dropped and put it away on the training rack.

The mage watched the young woman as she moved around the arena. There was something about the way she had acted and said those last words to him. It almost made him forget he was speaking to Orbeyus's heir and instead was conversing with Orbeyus himself. They made him want to tell her, and for the first time, he realized, that perhaps he finally saw his past charge as more than just that.

He exhaled roughly, adjusting the grip on his staff. "It is a tale I am willing to share, should you be willing to listen."

Sliding the sword into its place, Annetta turned around with a look of surprise. She had not expected him to touch on the subject further and as he prepared to speak yet again, the sound of feet coming in their direction overpowered what he might have potentially said. In came a Minotaur and two Water Elf soldiers, all three covered in the grit and grime that came with battle.

"We must speak with Lady Annetta Severio and Lord Jason Kinsman," the Minotaur spoke in a low baritone voice. "The matter is of great importance."

⁖⁗

What occurred after the Minotaur emissary and the two Water Elves showed up seemed like a blur to Annetta. She recalled they had walked to the common room area where a large table was placed, and that all the remaining members of Q-16 had gathered, minus Xander and Liam, who'd had to go home since it was past their agreed upon curfew. It was not until the Minotaur began to speak that Annetta felt herself snapped into the present moment.

"It is as Lord Snapneck feared," the great beast spoke. "Yarmir has somehow survived the battle fought against him and is now amassing another army. This time, we fear, he means to eradicate Morwick once and for all. His scouts have already been spotted raiding outposts. It is at such an outpost that I, Spearstone and these Elves here were stationed."

Arms crossed, Annetta listened patiently without interruption. A neutral expression had placed itself on her face. It wasn't that she didn't care for the plight of these soldiers. Venetor had often stressed when she'd attended audiences with him in the throne room always to appear distant when speaking with those below her in the chain of command. A leader couldn't show being swayed one way or another until he or she had had time to think about the consequences.

Beside her, Jason and Sarina too observed without speaking, though Jason's face said what he didn't verbalize. At least not until Spearstone finished speaking.

"This is awful." The corners of Jason's eyes crinkled as he gazed down at the table. "We have to go to their aid."

To the other side of Annetta, Puc and Darius also stood with impartial looks, though it was clear there was much more going on in the eyes of both mages.

"Is there an estimated number for troops?" Darius pressed his hands on the table and leaned forward.

"We've no clear count yet," Spearstone confirmed. "The full extent of Yarmir's forces dwell within the caves he is using to hide, and he is making sure we don't get an accurate count."

"Either that or he is already throwing everything at you that he has," Sarina added as an afterthought.

"It would not be unlikely, all things considered," Puc stated. "We doubted he would attack, and yet here we are. He could have been informed of the additional troops pouring into Morwick and decided to try a desperate last stand, or he does indeed have a vast army that he does not mind utilizing as cannon fodder due to his ranks being so populated. There is no certainty in either assumption."

Skyris's voice then came from further behind those gathered around the table. "I think everyone in this room has forgotten to ask one fundamental question, and that is, why?"

Jason turned to regard the woman, who was leaning against one of the small sofas with her arms crossed as though the brown Sherpa-lined bomber jacket was doing nothing to stave off the cool of the Lab.

"Why what?" He frowned.

"Why did they bother to start trying to attack now," she clarified as she dropped her arms and walked over to the table. "Was there any incident that may have prompted them to try attacking Morwick? Was there a piece of information they might have gotten wind of that made Yarmir think that this would be the perfect moment for him to unleash his supposedly pent-up fury?"

"Lord Ironhorn's death." Annetta narrowed her eyes.

Skyris snapped her fingers and pointed at the girl. "The death of a king."

"There is more to it than that, I'm afraid," Spearstone stated and motioned for the first of the two elves who had accompanied him to step forward.

The soldier reached into the satchel that he'd been carrying and produced the charred remains of what those present could discern as possibly once having been a war staff like the soldiers of Aldamoor carried.

"These are no ordinary giants," the elf holding out the remains spoke. "They come wielding fire and brimstone."

Puc's analytic gaze went directly to him. "What exactly do you mean by that?"

"Exactly what we are showing you, First Mage," the second elven soldier replied. "These Giants weren't like the ones we faced long ago with Lord Orbeyus. They're changed somehow, and can wield fire magic as though it were their own."

"The priests have ancient carvings which speak of this on Aerim," Spearstone intoned. "It is foretold that upon the arrival of the Final Cataclysm, that giants shall wield flame as though it had always been their birthright. Or so one of the signs claim to be."

A bout of silence followed this. It was clear to Annetta from Puc's constant expression that he placed little merit in what was said, and so she didn't tense up. Jason and Sarina she observed, however, did.

Jason cleared his throat as he attempted to regain composure. "Final Cataclysm as in the end of the world?"

"It is what the ancient carvings call it, yes," Spearstone confirmed. "It is also said in these scriptures that an army unlike the world had ever seen could save it from occurring."

Skyris, who had been silent until now, crossed her arms again with a huff. "I don't buy it still."

"Don't buy it? What's there not to buy?" Jason shot her a questioning look.

The woman shook her head. "It's a little convenient that suddenly these giants that were supposedly defeated before by Annetta and yourself now show up being able to throw fireballs or whatever it is that they do when it says it in scriptures. If you ask me, I smell manipulation and trickery."

"So you don't believe the end is coming?" Spearstone glared at the woman.

Skyris shot him a stern look back. "Only the Unknown himself knows the day and hour of a world's end. Even then, it is only one world out of thousands."

Puc was quick to interject right after. "What I believe Skyris means to say is that there may be missing facts that are not being picked up on. The giants could be using illusion to give the appearance of such to create confusion and fear among ranks. It was not unheard of before from them."

This comment seemed to calm Spearstone, and the bunched-up muscles in his neck relaxed. "Guerilla warfare tactics you think, then?"

"It's not out of the question." Annetta jumped in. "If it is Yarmir, then I could see him doing something like this. Our fight against him with Jason proved that. He didn't reveal the Hydra spell on him until Jason left to gain the upper hand against me. This wouldn't be that much different."

She then looked over to Jason and tapped into her telepathic abilities. *'What do you think J.K.? Should we investigate?'*

Jason's eyes moved to her, but he didn't turn his head. *'I think we should, Anne. He seems worried, but I agree with you and Skyris. Yarmir may be playing us or trying to divert attention from something else that could be way worse.'*

Annetta gave the slightest nod before turning back to Spearstone. "We will gather the rest of the Four Forces and come to Lord Snapneck's aid. We won't abandon our own, but we will do so with caution. I agree with my Aunt Skyris and with Puc that something doesn't add up here. It could all be a trap to throw us off. We need to be careful, now more than ever."

Spearstone bobbed his head. "Yes, of course, Lady Annetta. When can we expect you?"

"A fortnight, I think." Annetta turned to Puc who nodded in agreement and then locked eyes with Spearstone. "You'll have to forgive me, but I'm not the best with estimating, so I still turn to others for help in that."

"Understandable. I shall go and relay this information to Lord Snapneck with your permission." Spearstone stated and looked over at the two elves that had accompanied him. "They will need us back in Morwick."

"As you will, soldier," Annetta inclined her head slightly.

She then watched as the trio left. It wasn't until they were well out of sight that some of the tension the meeting had brought in with it vanished.

"That was well done, Annetta," Puc commented. "Perhaps your summer on Gaia had some merit to it."

Annetta turned to face the mage fully. "Uncle Venetor had me sitting in with him on a lot of meetings dealing with raids from people who were still loyal to Razmus, or other small disputes. Sometimes just listening and trying to offer some aid was the best outcome, even if, at times, it was clear the people were trying to take advantage of the system. The key is to know when you could be potentially set up. A psychic warrior needs to always be fifty steps ahead."

A small smile crept into the corner of Puc's eyes and mouth. "A wise observation."

"I have those sometimes." The girl cracked a grin.

"I'll begin contacting the other leaders with your permission," Darius announced and after a nonverbal approval from Puc, left the room.

Jason sucked in some air and clasped his hands before him. "Guess I should let my mom know I'm going to be gone for a few days. If she lets me in the house after this. Some days I'm really starting to doubt it."

"You'll be fine, J.K. She is your mom, after all," Annetta said.

"Yeah, but you don't know her like I do." The boy rolled his eyes and left the room with Sarina.

Annetta chuckled, running a hand through her hair. Her eyes then landed on both Puc and Skyris standing at opposite ends of the room. Her aunt cleared her throat, shoved her hands into the pockets of her coat and began to make her way out as well, leaving Annetta entirely alone with the mage.

It was then that Annetta finally noticed the dark circles under Puc's eyes. "Are you feeling okay?"

The neutral expression didn't leave Puc's visage. "The virtues of being First Mage. Sleep is generally optional in the profession."

Annetta cringed at the thought of no sleep. Her own had also been fragmented of late due to her dreams. Her mind then went back to Titus and the fits he'd been having on Gaia before she left. He was also victim of insomnia.

She then internally built up her courage and spoke. "Puc, can I ask one more thing before I go?"

"Go on," he intoned.

"What is the seed of chaos? When Titus fell sick on Gaia, he would repeat something about it over and over again."

A moment of silence followed, during which Puc's gaze went across the slew of maps spread out on the table. "How much do you know about the religion known as Unaverisim?"

"Does it have to do something with the Unknown?" the girl questioned.

"Yes, it is the religious system that worships the Unknown in his purest form," Puc stated. "In addition to the Unknown himself, there is another, and that is Khaos. Where the Unknown is the embodiment of all good, Khaos is the embodiment of destruction and, as its name suggests, chaos. Some go as far as to interpret this as evil, while others take the words at face value only. The seed of chaos is a reference from a prophecy to a being called Korangar."

Annetta nodded, hearing this. "I think I remember that name from somewhere before... Mislantus said something about it just before I killed him. Something about Korangar's shadow overtaking all."

"It would not surprise me in the least that Mislantus would reference Korangar," Puc said. "Mislantus's father, Mordred, boasted that he was the descendant of Freius, the Gaian said to have enslaved Korangar in the first place, and thus saved the multiverse from ending. It was for this reason that he believed his bloodline was destined to rule all worlds, upon discovering his origin."

Annetta looked down at her feet as it all finally clicked into place. "That's what started the Great War, wasn't it? Mordred went to my great-grandfather with his findings, and I'm guessing he didn't approve."

Puc shook his head, reaffirming her thought. "No, he did not. In fact, Mordred threatened to raze all worlds to the ground that opposed him."

Another pause then occurred, and Puc spoke again. "To go back to your original question, Korangar was said to be the embodiment of Khaos, a manifestation of his seven forces, or aspects as they are sometimes called. It is also said that when Korangar is freed again, he will destroy all worlds."

The girl gave a shallow nod and watched as the mage took his leave to catch some of the much-needed rest he required. One other question, however, had welled up inside the girl and she gave voice to it. "Do you think what's happening with Titus has some connection to the Minotaur and the giants new abilities?"

Puc turned one final time as he picked up his staff from where it rested against the table. "If it is the end of the world that you fear young Annetta, note that the world is always ending for someone, somewhere."

Annetta then said no more, and the two of them parted ways for the night.

Chapter 15

The darkness permeating Valdhar exploded into an array of colour as the beam of light coming from it collided with the blazing form of a star. No sound came from beyond the large windows of the throne room's observation deck, but Amarok could hear the thunderous collision filling him despite this. It was a beautiful sound, the symphony of an ending life, the crushing of a cycle. Pessumire could not and would not be stopped as it tore through the remaining chunks of molten rock.

"Ten," he murmured to himself, his good eye squinting against the intense illumination.

As the light faded, he then saw it. A gem trapped and floating in space. A smile formed on the elder assassin's lips as he beheld before him the object of his search. To many, if unexamined by the naked eye, they would simply pass it by thinking it nothing more than some distant nebula of yellows, blues and greens. Amarok, however, knew the truth of it.

He moved away from where he had stood towards the communication hologram panel by the throne and activated it. Seconds later, a blueish-tinted small form of Lloyd Abner showed up. The scientist looked to be even less himself than before. His white hair was a disheveled mess, a growth of beard covered his face and his clothing was in a total state of disarray.

"Yes, Lord Amarok?" The hologram wrung its hands as if attempting to make them clean of something.

Amarok's mask glinted as he gazed down to where he knew the camera sensor's to be. "Do you see it?"

The hologram image looked sideways in response. "Oh my, does this mean we've completed the final set of coordinates on this puzzle?"

"The portal to the Temple of Creation nebula," Amarok replied.

"Fascinating, a portal to the prison among the stars. I bet we're the first ones to see it since it was sealed all those years ago. It's quite the honour, I would think. Well then, what is the next course of action, Lord Amarok?"

The assassin looked away, his good eye drawn back to the portal as he formulated his plan. Caution was needed to pull off the feat he planned, and there would be no second chances. His mind clear and ready, he uttered only one word. "Forward."

The next day found Annetta, Jason, Sarina and Puc on route to the Eye to All Worlds. Puc had called for a meeting of the other leaders to discuss their plan of dealing with the giants. It would be, he decided, the easiest place to amass troops, and with the help of Skyris's miniature Pessumire cannon, they could create a large enough portal to get everyone through at once. Already, colourful tents were being hoisted up around the castle, and troops populated the grounds. The mage noted that this time around, there was less of them than in previous battles. The fight against Razmus had taken its toll on their resources, and some of those soldiers were still recovering. Even with all of the medical innovations of the Water Elves, sometimes there was no substitute for rest.

The First Mage looked over at his young companions, who rode silently beside him. Grim expressions lined their faces. This was not a meeting they were looking forward to, and unlike previous times, they understood its magnitude.

Annetta, dressed in her traditional Gaian armour with the crimson cape displaying a white lioness on it, attempted to stifle a yawn by drawing the back of her forearm to cover her mouth. The gesture caused Puc to look over, and he then saw the bags under the girl's eyes. A pallid tint had also crept over her features, as though she were coming down with a cold.

He would need to think of mixing something together to help her get a good night's rest. "Are you well, Annetta?"

Startled from her stream of thought, she raised an eyebrow. "Yeah, I'm fine. Just didn't sleep too great, is all. You know how it is. Pre-battle anxiety."

The mage gave a short nod and continued onward. Among the chaos of the war camp, he could see the top of the larger tent used for meetings by the leaders of the Four Forces, and angled his horse in that direction. Coming within sight of the tent, the group descended from their mounts and upon giving them to a few elven squires to take care of, entered inside.

The interior of the tent was plain and minimalistic. A large wooden table stood in the middle, littered with a series of maps. Large candle holders were placed around the room, as well as a selection of smaller ones on the table, out of range to be knocked over by potential hands pointing anything out. Behind it stood the remaining leaders of the Four

Forces. There was Mother Natane, the Ogaien matriarch whose race bared draconic features. Doriden Windheart, the recently appointed Alpha of the Soarin stood beside her, his feathered wings tucked in behind his back and his teal mane braided neatly to reflect his station. To the furthest right of these stood a Minotaur clad in gold Gyldrig chainmail and a blue tabard placed over top, with gold trim that seemed to be stretched to its limits. A pair of axes sat in his thick brown leather belt that was also pleated with gold and silver accents. On his head rested a war helm with a crown fashioned into it.

"Lord Snapneck?" Annetta asked as she fully entered the tent.

The Minotaur turned to face the newcomers. Aside from the hyper-intelligent blue eyes, Snapneck was virtually unrecognizable from a few weeks ago. He had grown at least a foot in height if not more, and his muscle mass had tripled since their last encounter against Razmus and the Fire Elves. He was now perhaps the biggest Minotaur the youth had ever seen.

"Talk about a growth spurt," Jason whispered to Sarina, who only shook her head in response.

"Lady Annetta." The Minotaur bowed his head. "Or should I now be saying White Lioness of Gaia?"

"Annetta still suits me well enough without the lady part added to it," she replied with an air of confidence.

Snapneck inclined his head further at this. "As you command it, so it shall be said."

"All formalities aside dude, I think we have some battle plans to go over." Doriden crossed his arms as he hovered over the table.

This cue brought the others closer into the room to huddle around the table. While the elder leaders spoke, Annetta, Jason and Sarina did their best to remain silent and absorb what was being said. If the last few years had taught them anything, it was that they still had a lot to learn when it came to leading armies, especially after some of the blunders made during their battle against Razmus.

"Has there been a count of any kind for us to know the numbers we are dealing with?" Puc inquired amid the conversation.

"Yarmir has hidden his forces," Snapneck stated. "Aside from the masses of Fenrikin packs, we have no idea of the magnitude of what we would be up against."

The mage frowned at this. Neither Annetta nor Jason liked the sounds of it either. For all they knew, they would be severely outnumbered, in which case a different plan of attack would be needed.

'Is it just me or is this starting to sound more and more like a suicide mission?' Jason spoke telepathically to Annetta, doing his best to keep eye contact on what was going on in front of them.

'I can't say, it could go either way,' she replied.

Jason furrowed his brow and blinked a few times as he tried to remain slightly focused on what was going on before him. *'You can't be serious, Anne. Snapneck has no numbers counted, and I'm hearing these guys picked up some new tricks since we last saw them.'*

'And so have we,' Annetta reminded him.

Doriden's voice overpowered their thoughts then. "No matter what we think we are dealing with, at the end of the day we need some numbers, so if Minotaur scouts haven't brought us anything concrete, I offer to send out some Soarin and see if we can detect anything from the skies. The giants won't suspect us, and we can hide easily enough in the taller peaks."

"I will send an airship with some mages on board to provide your scouts with additional cloud cover," Puc added. "Until we have at least a rough estimate, I would advise against a full frontal attack of any kind."

"By waiting we give Yarmir a chance to grow stronger." Snapneck protested. "A series of guerrilla attacks would keep them on their toes."

Natane then stepped in. "It would be a waste of resources. Our armies have not yet recovered from our efforts against the Fire Elves and Razmus. We should preserve and use wisely."

"I agree with Natane in this." Puc leaned over the table examining the map of Morwick. "We should not be hasty in our efforts to spill blood. There will be more than enough opportunities for this in the coming fight."

"Well, we've not heard from our leaders as of yet." Snapneck tucked his thumbs into his belt and looked at Annetta, Jason and Sarina. "What say you?"

'One of these days...' Annetta heard Jason's voice echo in her mind with frustration. The girl, however, didn't show any signs of discontent in her bearing, despite feeling the same as her friend. Her time on Gaia, as well as the events leading up to her changing into her feral form for the first time, had made her realize just how much power

a symbol like a leader carried within them, even if they themselves didn't always feel as powerful as others thought them to be. With this, there also came the responsibility of not showing weakness, at least not in public.

"I will have to agree with Puc and Natane on this," she said. "We need to send out scouts first and not be hasty with our resources. Once the party is sent out and we get more information, though, I do think small teams of guerrilla fighters should be sent out. We don't want Yarmir getting too comfortable."

Annetta then looked over at Jason to see what he had to input.

Jason's response came not long after all eyes fell on him. "I'll second that. Walking into unknown territory blind when information could be gathered beforehand seems a bit rushed. Same time, though, we don't want them to get comfortable."

"Then it is settled, I would think." Puc moved away from the table. "I will go forward with preparations for the scouting ship."

The young Soarin leader flexed his feathered wings in anticipation. "Guess we'll need those scouts, then."

"I should return to my troops then if everything is sorted here," Snapneck said, then glanced over at Annetta and Jason. "With your permission, of course."

Annetta gave a firm nod and watched as the Minotaur King made his way out. The others followed soon after, until only Annetta, Jason and Sarina remained. The three of them stood around the table, their silhouettes elongated by candlelight and made to move by the swaying of the flames.

"Here we go again, I guess." Jason sighed. "You'd think by now I'd be used to this."

"I don't think anyone ever gets used to it," Sarina stated. "At least from my understanding, humans never do, and you were primarily raised as one."

"Gaians don't exactly seek out war, either," Annetta interjected. "Sure, they call themselves a warrior race, but they don't provoke war. That's not what the Unknown intended them to do, they're meant to be peacekeepers."

"Never got that impression with Venetor." Jason shoved his hands in his pockets. "Guy seemed to revel in training and fighting when he was here."

A small smile formed on Annetta's lips. "Oh, he does, but never once did I see him plan a campaign to take over another planet or anything like that if that's what you're thinking. Heck, we had our hands full with Gaians who still supported Razmus and were hiding out in the wilds."

"Is that what he had you doing, then?" Jason mused. "Cleaning up after the show?"

Annetta rolled her eyes at this. "You think Venetor had me there to go around killing Razmus supporters?"

"Well, I mean, you never did tell us what exactly you were doing there." Jason reminded her. "You've been pretty secretive."

"We're worried," Sarina added right after. "You haven't been the same since you got back."

At this, Annetta's defences dropped a little and for a split second, the commanding aura of the Four Forces leader, the White Lioness of Gaia vanished. "Oh, I mean I guess a lot happened, but I didn't think…"

"Didn't think it was noticeable?" Jason raised an eyebrow. "You really are gullible sometimes, Anne, but I guess it's good to still have you underneath there."

Annetta chuckled at the assessment. "Sorry, I guess having been on Gaia and around nobles kind of rubbed off on me."

Her face then went serious as she looked away from them and at the pile of maps on the table. "And I guess with what happened to Link."

The three of them nodded consecutively and silence occurred right after. It was an event that none of the youth present really wanted to go back to, but there it was, the elephant in the room.

Doing his best to change the subject, Jason cleared his throat. "So when do we all have to start calling you Lady Annetta like Snapneck? Also, should I begin to practice my curtsy?"

Annetta's eyes widened as she looked up from the table, a perplexed look as though she were a deer caught in headlights. The effect on her previously-drawn face caused both Jason and Sarina to start grinning. For added effect, Jason pinched the sides of his tabard and put one leg in front of the other, clumsily lowering himself slightly before going back up. Seconds later, the infection of joy spread and Annetta too found herself giggling, causing the other two to join in.

"Never. Now can it," the girl deadpanned and left the tent with the echo of her friend's hoots.

A night sky glowing in blues, golds and purples loomed over a landscape of craggy lifeless brown hills with sparse vegetation. A light breeze blew through the blades of dried-up blue grass, which swayed lazily in its thrall. It had been so for ages, untouched and unclaimed by any, and was meant to be for all of eternity.

Fate, however, had different plans for the world, and the signaling of this cosmic change in its destiny was heralded when the light of ten distant stars began to glow in the eccentrically-coloured sky. Not long after this, another object appeared that was brighter than the others. This last light in the sky didn't intend to stay still. It was like an angered sibling hurling towards the world with a single blazing fist. It entered the atmosphere and collided with land, shaking its foundation to the core.

Some distance away, a figure with a broken star-shaped mask appeared and watched dispassionately as the blazing carnage unfolded. His single good eye took in the roaring fire and smouldering remains that had once been the Freiuson stronghold. On a bent, armoured arm, a black cloak snapped back and forth as if trying to escape his grasp, silently screaming for help, but there was none to come. Amarok Mezorian would not move from his vigil.

His steadfast determination was rewarded some time later when among the flames he spotted something moving, gasping for air as it stumbled among the debris. Orienting itself, the shape then noticed the assassin and straightened its posture. It then strode towards Amarok at a steady pace.

As the shape neared Amarok, it became clearer and more defined. It was a man in his mid-thirties, dressed in nothing more than a torn pair of pants, and this fact didn't seem to shame him in the least. He carried his well-muscled, powerful frame as though he were wearing one of the finest suits of armour. Square-jawed, with a growth of facial hair and short blond hair to match, he seemed ordinary enough, someone Amarok would never have looked at twice. It was the man's eyes, however, that gave him away for who he was. Despite their rich blue hue, they were void of anything that was of the life-giving force of the Unknown.

Amarok stretched out his arm with the cloak, which the man snatched without so much as a nod of appreciation. The assassin turned his head ever slightly, long white hair gliding across his shoulders, and caught the faintest glimpse of an enormous tattoo across the man's back as he threw on the cloak.

The man stood with his back still to Amarok, unmoving, and after a while, a voice emanated from him. "To whom do I owe my thanks?"

Amarok then knelt and lowered his head. "No one of importance but a humble servant."

The man turned his head slightly as he regarded him. "Then you know who I am?"

"I know what you are," Amarok replied.

The dead eyes regarded Amarok, analyzing his being with something resembling interest, but this too died. Looking forward again, the man reached out with his hand. At first, it seemed as though he would come into contact with nothing at all, but just as his fingers extended their full length, it was as though they scraped at an invisible layer of something. Light flooded from the crack, and soon after, on the other side of the peeled-away existence before them, lay an opening into another world. Unlike the world they were in, it was alive and vibrant, deer-like creatures with red hides and velvety green antlers looked at the newcomers with vacant expressions bordering on curiosity.

The man then turned back fully to Amarok. "Let's begin then, shall we?"

∞∞

On Gaia, in the dead of night, Titus opened his eyes, tears having been falling from them in his restless slumber.

"The end times awake," the Crown Prince of Gaia whispered in fear.

Chapter 16

The sound of anvils and blades being sharpened filled the air, along with the scents of oil and leather as Puc trudged through the camp, making sure everything was prepared for the upcoming possibility of a siege. The mage's dark blue robes billowed around him like a trail of smoke in the afternoon winds that surrounded Severio Castle. Had those present not known any better, they would have thought it the illusion of some spell. Much like the robes themselves, Puc's mind was being blown this way and that as he tried to focus not only on his troops, but also on the Four Forces as a single entity. He cursed himself silently for having told Darius to focus on the other mission of finding the woman the Sisters of Wyrd had told them of. He would have much rather had him by his side now.

"Thanestorm." Natane's voice pierced the camp noise.

Puc stopped in his tracks and pivoted right to see the Ogaien leader beside a large black horse whose mane and tail was pure fire, an Aiethon. He had never been comfortable around the beasts, his unfortunate history with regular horses further propelling such discomfort. As always, however, he did his best to mask it, as he'd learned to mask many other feelings. Hiding things beneath the surface was sometimes the only way to move forward.

Natane stood dressed in her simple Ogaien garb, which consisted of pale brown hide pants and a tunic which contrasted the red and orange of her skin. Overtop of this was draped a cloak made of heavier furs for the Aerim winter in the Minotaur world. Her oval, draconic-featured face held little resembling human and elven emotions. It was only in the large green cat-slit saucer eyes that the flame of intelligence burned, along with the knowledge of a life long lived.

"Great Mother." Puc inclined his head in respect.

"I would have words if you would hear them." The Ogaien woman indicated to her tent that stood not far from them, to which the mage nodded and followed her inside. Once there, she began to speak again. "Dark have been my visions of late. I do not like what tales they tell, if they are meant to be glimpses of the future into which we are all headed. I did not speak at the meeting, for I know naught the intent of these dreams. There is no clear indication if Tiamet is their creator for the purpose of warning, or if some other malicious force tries to find ways of undoing us. I have only ever held the greatest of respect for you, Thanestorm, even if you are a male."

Puc gave another shallow bob of the head. "I thank you, Great Mother. What is it that brings you such malcontent?"

Natane turned away from the mage, and with crossed arms, she walked over to the fire pit which had been set up in the middle, white and red coals glowing in its centre. She gazed at them, full of remembrance. "My dreams of late have been clouded with unnatural occurrences. Again and again, they repeat in their content, different and yet always the same. Worlds shattered, lives destroyed. I have had nightmares involving the end of the world, but never on a scale like this, and never so frequent. Each night in my dreams I am forced to watch as a beast of seven heads, black as night, devours not only the Yasur Plains but also that of the Eye to All Worlds, Aldamoor, Morwick, the Trafjan Cliffs and countless others I know naught of."

Puc listened without interruption to what the Ogaien leader was saying. A chill went down his spine as he recounted in his head his last meeting with Tamora in person. She too had drawn on her cell the symbol of a seven-headed beast, a dragon to be exact.

"This beast, was it draconic in nature?" he asked.

Natane looked up at the mage, and he detected a hint of shame in them, as though she had been hiding something from him that she had just been caught on.

"It was." She turned away and folded her arms. "But this thing… with its gaping maw of cinders and ash was not of Tiamet. It was of the underworld."

He furrowed his brow. "You think these visions may be connected in some way to the giants choosing to attack?"

"Perhaps not directly, but I feel something greater is beginning to stir, Thanestorm, something we are not equipped to deal with, even with the son of Arcanthur and the heir of Orbeyus to lead us. I may be misinterpreting these dreams as more than they are meant to be, but I do feel that they are meant to be a warning against something to come."

The First Mage shifted the grip on his staff as he took this all in. "It is no secret that with each battle our ranks have been weakened, and skirmishes such as these do not help us recover, though if I may offer some of my insight into this, how is this any different than the Great War when we all served?"

"You know well how it was different. Our Gaian allies have long since abandoned our conflict. We have only ourselves to depend on in these times."

Puc couldn't argue with her there, nor was he inclined too because it was true. Though never an official force in the Four Forces, Gaia had made up a significant portion of it with its warriors, a great many of them having been psychics, skilled pilots and the like. Orbeyus had brought many assets to their cause as the son of a king who had given up his title in the pursuit of a higher goal. Now, Gaia was nowhere to be seen, and it was beginning to show.

"We are winning battles, but we are losing the war," Natane finally chimed in again.

"Not yet," the mage spoke. "Not so long as we have the White Lioness of Gaia."

"A symbolic title." Natane huffed. "Nothing more."

"As Orbeyus's black lion was also a symbol," Puc reminded her. "Though she may not have known it at the time, I believe Annetta did the right thing to remain behind on Gaia for a few weeks, to show a connection between Earth and Gaia once more. She may be the one to re-forge that which was broken."

A smile began to form on the serpentine-featured face of the woman at hearing the last part. "Perhaps Orbeyus was right to choose you as his advisor after all."

Before Puc could say anything further, he was cut off as the sound of a deep horn filled the tent.

৪৩৫৩

Annetta rose from the cot she was lying on as she heard the baritone horn blasting. She could feel the vibrations from the instrument all throughout her body, rattling her bones as though they weren't even attached to her muscles. It was disorienting, and it could only mean one thing.

Jason and Sarina, who were sitting on another cot close by, perked up at hearing the deafening sound. A look of worry etching their faces. They were no strangers to the sound, either.

Still dressed in her scale mail, Annetta walked over to the large rugged-looking wooden table in the centre of the room and withdrew her red cloak that had been thrown over the back of one of the four chairs that encircled it. She threw it over her shoulders and fastened the pin to one side as she had been taught. She then moved her attention to her sword belt and the straps on her tower shield. It looked smaller somehow, as though it had shrunk over the past few years. She was now able to hoist it up in one arm now with ease.

"Starting to look like those drawings of yours, Anne," Jason teased her.

Annetta glanced over at her friend while using her psychic abilities to tie her hair into a braid. "Huh? What do you mean?"

"Oh, nothing." Jason shook his head. "It was just funny how you got up at hearing the bell and started getting ready. Seemed like something out of one of those movies we used to watch."

The corner of her mouth bent in a half smile, but before Annetta could say anything, the blaring sound of the horn returned, blotting out all potential conversation. She frowned.

"What do you think it means?" Sarina asked as she put on the belt holding her sabre.

The muscles in Annetta's back tensed as a third blast came right after. "Whatever it is, it's not good."

The flap of the tent then opened and in came a flabbergasted-looking Skyris. There was a wild look in her blue eyes, and it was hard to tell if she had been sleeping and the horn had blasted her awake, or if she had just arrived at the camp. Knowing the Gaian princess, it was most likely the latter, since she had last been seen working on one of her projects in the Lab.

"An army approaches Morwick," she informed them through strained breaths. "We have to get moving."

"The spies came back already?" Jason questioned.

Skyris shook her head, her loose black braid coming partially undone as she did so. "They didn't even have time to send anyone out. Ran into the messenger from Morwick just now as I came into camp, he was on route to notify Lord Snapneck."

"Is the cannon ready?" Annetta asked. "We won't be able to get everyone through on time otherwise, and if there's an attack-"

Skyris raised a finger in the girl's direction. "You get ready to lead the charge. I'll take care of the cannon."

With that she disappeared again, blending into the chaos that was already beginning to brew outside from the rushed preparations.

"How did that saying go again? Out of the frying pan and into the fire?" Jason ran a hand through his hair and scratched at the base of his skull.

"Sounds about right." Sarina nodded.

Annetta didn't reply to what was said. She looked towards the tent opening and watched as the flap swayed back and forth in the wind from the movement on the other side. Though she did her best to control how she felt, deep down inside, she was beginning to feel the tendrils of that same wind rise.

Matthias pulled into the dock at the Casvenian Space Station, locked the ship into place and parked the craft at the assigned port. He'd already paid the docking fees upon approaching and was thankful for the fact that, despite Amarok having taken control of Valdhar after Mislantus's demise, he'd not bothered to close any of his accounts. This had made his travels that much easier through space for supplies, fuel and the most vital, information.

It was for this last part that Matthias had docked, though it was also for the fact that his engine was in need of refueling. He took care of the latter first, along with arranging for any supplies he was missing. Once everything was secure, Matthias then went to his intended destination. He wove his way through the high-volume traffic of bodies in the station, his shoulders tense and ready to pounce at a moment's notice as rain poured from the artificial atmosphere. One never knew when someone would recognize his face from Mislantus's ranks and rat him out, and Mislantus hadn't been liked. He'd always been aware of the latter fact, but it had been different when he served under the Freiuson banner. The side had been chosen for him since childhood, and there had never been an alternative, not until his journey to Q-16.

He turned the corner and came to a stop at a beaten-down holographic sign that had a picture of a dragon curled up around a tankard. Three-dimensional smoke rose from its nostrils as it slept, and the words 'Dragon's Den' flashed above it. Matthias smiled fondly at the name, remembering another such den on Earth, and proceeded inside.

A few of the patrons at the bar turned to regard him, but past that paid little attention and resumed their own conversations as well as drinks. The establishment reeked of cheap spirits and the bodily odors of a thousand different species. Matthias had to use all of his willpower to avoid pinching his nose, and he was generally very tolerant of such things. It was the reason he'd suggested on the place for meeting. He thought no more on it, then picked his way across the dimly-lit establishment.

A head of bushy and wild grey hair with large traces of black still in it poked out from one of the booths on the far side, and Matthias quickly hastened in its direction. He then slid into the seat on the opposite end of the table, and a wiry smile spread across his face.

"Long time no see." Matthias folded his hands before him.

The man before him was obscured by the gloom of the bar, and a puff of smoke further clouded this. It wasn't until he leaned in under the light of the lamp that Matthias got a good look at him. His face was lean, with deeply-tanned skin from exposure to one too many close encounters with stars. His steel-grey eyes glared at Matthias in a calculating, yet casual manner while he puffed on a thickly-rolled cigar.

"Well, well, it if isn't Teron." The man blew a large circle of smoke at Matthias, stretched out, and put his lanky legs on the table. "I take it you found what you were looking for, then?"

"And then some." Matthias bobbed his head. He then leaned in over the table.

"Come to pay in person then? Bold move, all things considered." Smoke rose from the man's mouth like the open maw of a great fire-breathing beast. "You know there was a group of bounty hunters here, and I'll wager they've got your name in their database."

"Newsflash, Corin, I no longer work for Mislantus. Now, are you willing to part with some more information or not?"

The man, Corin, took his feet off the table upon spotting the sour look shot his way from the bartender, removed the cigar from his mouth and put it out in the ashtray he had on the table. "Look, I'm only telling you what they are as a courtesy. I'm a member of Tetraptor, aren't I? Part of being in the guild is information harvesting, so as I said before, it's gonna cost you. The question isn't if I will part with more information, so much as can you afford it."

Matthias gritted his teeth, tasting the smoke in his mouth now. He wanted to threaten the facts out of Corin, to bend him into submission with the same tactics he'd used while serving Mislantus. He had to strongly remind himself that this wasn't how he did things anymore. Corin had proven to be a valuable ally, having let him live after their initial encounter had created a resource of endless applications. He reached into his pocket and retrieved a clear flat rectangle that he placed on the table and slid it over.

"I believe the contents of that chip will be sufficient." Matthias folded his hands again, and gave a closed-lip smile.

Corin turned the rectangle towards him and watched as numbers formed on the transparent piece. He then looked up at Matthias with a mouth wide open.

"I took the precaution of adding a little extra to my usual fee to make sure I have your undivided attention and loyalty in this manner," Matthias stated.

The man pocketed the card safely in his duster coat. "What do you wanna know?"

"I need to know where Amarok has taken Valdhar."

Corin glanced sideways on the table, where a clear liquid in ice lay perfectly still. He picked it up, ice cubes clinking along its edges, and took a good long drink.

"Tetraptor probes picked up Valdhar disappearing into a portal a few days ago," he said. "If you're of the superstitious lot, then the coordinates he disappeared to were of an apocalyptic nature. They're said to be one of the possible locations for Korangar's prison, and if I gotta be honest, he's not a guy I ever wanna cross paths with. I might be old, but I ain't looking for my world to end, if you get my meaning. Too much else to do, and I would like to finally get that chance to retire from the guild one day."

Matthias rose from his seat at hearing this. While he knew most of what Corin had said, he'd still needed confirmation from another living and breathing being. The horror in his eyes disappeared when he heard a glass break and the sound of raised voices from the bar. A group of creatures stood by the bar and were pointing in their direction. Matthias's arms and neck tightened.

"Looks like your fan club has arrived." Corin smirked.

Matthias cursed under his breath, threw up the cowl of his hood and walked quickly out the door, the claws in his gauntlets extending as he left.

❧☙

The prison cells of Aldamoor were not by any means luxurious. Yellowed plaster walls stained from the condensation of the city marked their every stretch as a reminder of what they were meant to stand for. This was a place where the things that were meant to be forgotten went, the things that were meant to be swept under the rug.

164

Tamora knew she was such a thing, had been such a thing. As a child, she had once found solace in the great city, the capital of the Water Elves, but that had all changed when she had witnessed her first Fire Elf raid on the city. It was then that she had learned exactly what she was, and where it was she came from. It was then that she learned why she had been an outsider all those years, the freak on display at the Academy. She'd learned she was destined to lead her people, and now destiny had another calling for her, greater.

It had all started in whispers at the back of her mind. A tingle at the base of her spine, as though someone had massaged it there, and the feeling lingered long after. She could not comprehend it at first, what it meant, but then the dreams had begun. Mottled and chaotic at first with no purpose, they were like the land itself in the beginning of time. As the whispers continued and the dreams reoccurred, however, Tamora began to realize that what she was being drawn into, being made part of, was far greater than she could have imagined. In these whispers, she heard the promises of a new life and of the great love the one who named himself as the beast had for her. In her dreams, she bore witness to the cities he laid waste to for her as a testament of that love, and the thousands he burned. The utopia he created for her, a world on fire.

Tamora sat on the floor, smiling as she looked up at the wall where she had repeatedly painted the dragon with the meal she had been given to eat. The guards always came to remove it, but she would then paint another and another, but always making sure to never do so with the same meal to throw them off. Her stomach presently felt like an empty pit of acid as it recalled subconsciously not having been fed due to her act. The meal remnants on the wall had spoiled. They were dry now, crusting, but it didn't matter. He would come for her soon, she knew, and then they would be together. All she had to do was keep waiting.

"Soon, my love, soon." The words echoed in her mind, stronger and more frequent than before as imitating the rhythm of a beating heart.

She closed her eyes, and did the best she could to centre herself as she focused on the words. Tamora then felt it, like the peeling away of layer upon layer of her existence, the lifting of all burdens past. Her eyes opened, unable to stay in the state of euphoria the feeling gave.

The wall before her, the one where she had painted the emblem of the dragon, now stood with a gaping hole in its middle. Chunks had been torn away, as though someone had taken a pickaxe to it, and was only beginning to break through. Where there should have been a tunnel going through various rooms on the other side, however, there lay something Tamora had not expected.

Staring at her through the portal was a man, a Gaian perhaps. He was tall, broad of shoulder, with short-cropped blond hair and a growth of facial hair on his square jaw, as though he had not shaved in several days. He wore nothing, save for a pair of torn trousers and a black cape which snapped on the wind behind him. His hands were bandaged up to his elbows, and so were his feet up to his knees, as though he had been injured, but there were no signs of blood.

"I have travelled many worlds to find you." He said.

Tamora would not have given second thoughts to the man, thinking him irrelevant, but there was one thing that set him apart, his eyes. There was an intensity to them that she had never seen. The more she peered into them, the more she realized that before her was the source of the voice she had been hearing all along. She bowed before him, pressing her face to the cold stone floor.

She then heard feet padding along the ground, and another bout of silence. Something softly touched her shoulder. Tamora looked up to see the man kneeling beside her, his bandaged hand caressing her arm.

When he saw that he had her attention, he took hold of her hand and pulled her up to stand. "Rise. You do not need to bow before me. I am no god."

Tamora found herself struggling for words, her mouth dry. She tried swallowing to clear her throat, but was left with a harsh and sticky residue which made it difficult to speak. "I have been waiting for what seems like my entire life here."

A grin stretched across the man's lips when she said this. It was genuine, she knew, but his eyes remained the same despite this. The combination of the two made it seem forced, unnatural. It then faded into a small smile that seemed much more in place on his face.

He then took Tamora's hand and pressed the back of it to his lips and withdrawing, he looked deep into her eyes. "Worry not. The wait is over."

In a single fluid motion, Tamora then found herself scooped up into the stranger's arms, still looking directly at him. He then began to walk towards where he had come from. That was when Tamora saw it, the world beyond that she had not seen at first. A landscape of green

166

skies, set ablaze. It was beautiful and as she gazed at it longer, she realized it was the one thing she had always wanted.

Chapter 17

There was no time to organize a charge. Instead, Annetta and her companions did the best they could to steer themselves to where Skyris was creating the portal that would lead them to Morwick. Already the twelve foot miniature replica of the Pessumire, the original being over thirty feet, stood poised and ready to fire. Its large circular arc creating a halo around the cylindrical cannon as the midday sun beat down on it.

In all of the chaos, Annetta hadn't even bothered to look into getting her horse re-saddled with Jason or Sarina. Firefoot was still on Gaia, and she had no idea when she would see him again, so she'd been granted a temporary mount in replacement. The trio jogged past tents, doing their best to evade those that were still straggling to organize. Upon reaching the outskirts, they found themselves entrenched in a sea of soldiers, with no way to get to the front.

Annetta, frowned and seconds later found herself shooting up into the air. She picked a spot she saw as empty near the front and landed. Jason followed her lead, holding Sarina as he did so.

"Picked up some Superman moves while on Gaia too," Jason mused.

The girl turned to him, a weak smile forming on her face. "Just a different way of thinking about our powers."

Her attention then waned from him and she looked to the cannon where Skyris, dressed in chain mail and a red tabard overtop with a black lion on her chest, tinkered with it. Strapped to the woman's back were the two short swords she'd carried with her into battle on Gaia, and her raven black hair was tied into a neat braid, a stark contrast to its typical dishevelled state. Concentration lined her usually good-natured face, making her appear enraged from the effort of calibrating. The youth all knew better than to approach when that look occupied her.

"You'd all best take a step back," she informed them and punching in the last few keys on the touchscreen keyboard, did the same as the machine hummed to life.

Annetta turned to look back at the crowd of anxious soldiers who did their best to hold the lines. In the past, she'd addressed them from atop whatever horse she rode, the colours of the Four Forces snapping on the wind in her hand, Severbane raised high. It seemed almost a lifetime ago, all of it, and yet had it not been mere weeks since their battle against Razmus and his supporters on Gaia? Now, the thought of doing so made her weary, for what could she offer those before her that they already didn't know except for a temporary mask of relief, the one that said battle was a glorious thing. Annetta was learning that it was anything but that. She chose to say nothing, and turning around, gazed at where the cannon tore through the fabric of their world.

The silence continued. Sarina leaned over to her and whispered. "Aren't you going to say anything to them, Annetta?"

The weight of the words crushed down on her and despite her skepticism at the moment, Annetta then withdrew Severbane from its scabbard in an exaggerated motion and raised it skyward so that the engraved lettering on one of the sides was visible to those behind.

"Severed be he who forgets," she spoke loudly as she read the words on it, and turned to face the crowd. "These were the words etched into this sword by my ancestor, and all these years later, their meaning is just as important now. They remind us to not forget what binds us not only to our lands, but to those we hold oaths of kinship to. If we forget that, then we are indeed severed from who we are. Though my surname is Severio, I will not forget. Who here is willing to do the same with me?"

Saying the last part, she pointed her sword at them, a singular roar of 'I will' coming from the thousands before her. Her words having made their mark, she withdrew the sword. "Let's show these giants what Water, Wind, Fire and Stone combined can do!"

Removing the shield from her back, Annetta used psychic energy to strap it onto her wrist firmly as the soldiers continued to cheer, building themselves into a frenzy over the fight to come.

"You're getting pretty good at that, Anne," a voice came from beside her.

Annetta turned to see Darius in his dark blue mage robes not far from where she, Jason and Sarina stood. When he had made it there, she had no clue, but she was glad that he was there nonetheless.

"Took you long enough. I didn't think you were gonna show." A faint smile appeared on her lips.

Darius shrugged in response. "Blame the First Mage of Aldamoor. He's the one sending me on errands."

Before any of them could say anything more, the portal completed opening. A blast of strong icy wind blew through it, sending a chill down Annetta's spine. Her armour didn't accommodate for the cold, and she guessed neither did anyone else's. It would have to be a luxury they'd do without. The heat of battle would warm them this day.

Annetta took one brief glance at those around her, in particular, her three companions, Jason, Sarina and Darius. Though all of them held the same apprehension in their gazes, beneath the surface of it was another emotion. It was the one the girl used as fuel to fire her will. Trust. It was trust in one another that had gotten them this far, and hopefully would prevail again today.

Annetta's grip on Severbane tightened as she looked yet again at the portal forming before them. Sparks of energy crawled along the edges of it as it widened across the horizon, swallowing trees and sky. Inhaling the crisp air that was now coming through, she removed all doubt from her mind and focused on the fight that was to come.

೮೦೧೪

Before Annetta or her companions could orient themselves with the frigid land surrounding Morwick, they were thrown into the midst of a battlefield. Dark skies above with light snowfall didn't help to improve the state of combat, along with the high winds blasting through the landscape. The rocky ground around them already lay littered with the bodies of Minotaur soldiers, Fenrikin and giants.

Huddled close together with Jason, Sarina and Darius, Annetta did her best to hold ranks as the first of the enemies came upon them. Weapons clashed as soon as they were in range. Annetta threw the full weight of her shield at the closest giant, knocking him off balance from his attack, and countered with her own set of sword strikes. Finishing him, she watched as the giant fell to the ground before moving on to the next target, and the next and the next.

The further the girl continued, however, the more she began to feel something was not right in her gut. It was not to say that it was something wrong with her surroundings, but more so that it was something wrong with her. Her stomach churned ever so slightly, as though she were having a case of stage fright. Her sense of smell, too, seemed to be heightened, and so she assumed it could also be hunger. Regardless of what it was, from where the feeling could originate, Annetta had not a clue, and pushing down the questions about it to the back of her head, she continued on her path. A single misstep now could mean her demise.

170

"Damn, maybe I shouldn't have skipped lunch," she muttered to herself as she swung to block an enemy sword and parry it away.

Her distracted thoughts caused the girl to not see a large club from the side as it swung towards her. A direct hit in her midsection caused Annetta to sail through the air, clutching at her now bruised and most likely broken ribs. She landed with a thud, her fall cushioned by the body of a Minotaur warrior. Knees buckling slightly, she struggled to rise, propping herself up with Severbane. Before her was the giant. Over eight feet tall, with light blue tinted skin, white unkempt hair swirling in all directions and fangs on its lower jaw almost as yellow as its beady eyes, the creature stalked towards her with an ugly grin of victory on its mug.

Among the haze of her pain, Annetta also noticed that he had sawed-off horns on his forehead like Yarmir had when they had fought him. She didn't dwell long on this, and quickly brought Severbane back to eye level, her father's shield raised in her other hand as she did her best to ignore the pain in her side.

"Pain is weakness leaving the body," she breathed out in a raspy voice.

The creature was now within hearing distance, the foul grin stretched to the limits of its monstrous face as it raised its club yet again and slammed down. Annetta braced herself for impact as she raised her shield to block. Splinters from the wood danced around the girl's face as they fell and she braced her arm, throwing psychic strength into it to prevent it from breaking. Grunting, she pushed the giant back, enough to allow his stagger to give her sufficient time to reorient herself into her fighter stance.

As hard as she tried to focus, however, Annetta still found that her senses were somehow dulled, unable to work to their full potential. It was as though someone had thrown flour in front of her eyes, covering everything in a white tinted haze. Sleep deprivation was the only other thing the girl could compare it to. While she had been missing sleep, it was not enough to warrant such a reaction, or so she thought. There was also the question of the feeling in her gut.

The giant roared and charged at her anew, swinging its club in makeshift arcs. Annetta parried the weapon blow for blow, and eventually gaining the upper hand, she flung it from the giant's grip. The creature growled as it gaped at its open hands, then back up at

Annetta, a snarl forming on its face. Her eyes lit up in horror when she noticed what it was that seemed to be forming in the creature's hands.

She would not have believed it had she not witnessed it herself. What started off as orange and red sparks on the giant's palms soon after turned into crimson flames. The creature hurled the fire at the girl, who blocked it with her shield. The impact of the ball made her fall back, stumbling yet again, but not forgetting to keep the shield up. The Calanite diamond interior of the shield rippled through the enchanted wooden exterior as it absorbed the blast. Somewhere in the distance, she thought she heard the sound of her name as it echoed through the wind, but she paid little attention to it. Her quarrel was with her current nemesis. Annetta rose quickly, with her shield before her.

A vicious grin continued to line the face of the giant as he created yet another ball and hurled it again with all his might. Annetta did her best to duck out of the way for the second attack. The flames singed the end of her cape, which she quickly put out with her foot. The distraction was enough to give the giant the opening he needed and seconds later, Annetta found herself being hoisted up into the air by him.

While he was quick, Annetta was quicker. Teleporting from his grasp, she reappeared some feet in the air and slid her blade between his shoulder blades. The creature toppled and the girl yanked the sword free.

Staggering back a few paces, Annetta felt another wave of nausea pass through her and shook her head. The sound around her also seemed to amplify as this happened, making even the slightest ringing of steel sound like cannon fire.

"I must be losing my mind." She gritted her teeth. "Either that or I've got one killer migraine coming on."

The shapes of Jason, Sarina and Darius soon emerged on the horizon, causing her to relax ever so slightly. Jason raced at the head of the group, dressed in his chain mail and black tabard with a red lion on it, a bloodied Helbringer in his hands.

His face looked worried. "Anne, we tried calling you, but you didn't answer. All I saw was you fighting that giant, and then you were gone."

"It's complicated," she replied.

"Like fire-wielding giants complicated?" Darius asked, to which the girl shook her head. "Yeah, we already know that."

Before further banter could be exchanged, four Fenrikin charged towards them, their enormous maws with enlarged canines snapping to pierce both armour and flesh.

The group moved back in a synchronous fashion, only to have Darius get the edge of his sleeve hacked into by the closest beast. The creature tore into the fabric, causing the entire sleeve to rip off. Darius gave a feral growl in response and leaping at his opponents, his body melted and shifted into what looked like a large man with the head of a panther, covered fully in black fur. Dagger-like claws worked away at his opponents, sending those he was not busy with scurrying. The frenzy of the fight having taken him, he chased after the deserters.

"I guess that solves that," Sarina managed to say.

"Yeah, but not the immediate problem." Annetta pursed her lips as she looked around, struggling to focus. "There has to be a central point to all of this, something that can be attacked to end the fighting."

"Like what? A king in chess?" Jason asked.

Annetta turned to her friend. "Something like that, yeah. I mean, every army has its leaders. Take out the head and the rest generally surrender."

"You mean Yarmir or this clone of his," the boy replied.

Annetta nodded and glancing back, she saw the mountain in the distance that had been pointed out to them on the map as being the base of operations for the giants. If something was truly there, then that would be where she could get some answers, or at least destroy whatever was giving the giants their newfound powers.

Feeling her psychic abilities flow through her, Annetta used the surge to begin to levitate off of the ground ever so slightly. She slid Severbane into its scabbard, then slung the shield across her back, the leather belts springing to life with her psychic abilities as they tied it to her.

"Cover me," she commanded those below, and shot up into the air.

It was still hard for Annetta to comprehend that she could actually fly, even if the physics behind it were pure logic based on her own psychic abilities. Flight was a fancy of children, of who she used to be. The ground below her shrunk and soldiers turned into tiny dark moving dots over the horizon of the frozen land. The sight below made Annetta somewhat dizzy, but she shook it off as previous nausea returned. Feeling energy flow through her hands freely, she focused her sights on the task at hand as her gaze turned towards the mountain. She flew towards it, her crimson cape snapping this way and that on the intense wind as it billowed behind her. She could see why her friend had made the comic book hero comparison, and smiled lightly at the thought as she pushed forward, her arms at her sides the entire way.

Once within range, Annetta stopped, still in midair. She was feeling, of all things, out of breath. The trip couldn't have drained that much of her power, could it? She had done far more strenuous things under Venetor's guidance and in past battles. Perhaps it was the lack of sleep.

She inhaled a breath of the cold air so deep, Annetta thought her lungs would turn to ice and burst. She focused her energy into her hands and blue sparks encircled them. She placed one hand so it hovered over the other, and then watched as a ball of blue and purple flame formed in its centre and grew. It had been some time since she had used psychic fire, in fact after her battle against Mislantus, Annetta had avoided it as much as possible until Venetor had convinced her otherwise.

"It is a part of you as much as everything else." She remembered his words vividly. "Your rage, the thing that drives you, is just as important as feelings of love. They balance each other out. Embrace it, and let it be part of all of who you are."

Annetta drew herself back into the present and felt the blazing heat of the ball she held in her hands. It was now the size of a basketball and still growing. Her anger, she had realized years before, stemmed from bullies, and this made it that much easier to channel on a battlefield. With a heave, the girl threw the blazing ball and watched as it crashed into the mountainside, blasting a hole in it.

She was thrown off balance not long after, as another ball of flame shot up and grazed her arm. Annetta hissed as she clutched at the wound. While her armour was untarnished, there would be a red welt underneath it to greet her in the aftermath. Picking out the one responsible from below, she created another ball of flame and hurled it back in retaliation. The giant screamed below as it caught fire, blue and purple engulfing his body.

Another wave of nausea followed, and the girl felt something warm trickle down her upper lip. Bringing a hand up, she wiped to see blood smeared on her fingers.

"The hell?" A thousand questions surged through her mind as she tried to make sense of it.

She was not to get an answer, however, when not one but another two blasts of fire came hurling towards her. Annetta teleported to the side, missing the blasts and watched as they collided with one another and exploded into a frenzy of flames.

Gritting her teeth, she glared down below and shot a ball of psychic fire in the direction of both offenders. A precautionary thought then crept into the back of her mind. If all giants now had this ability to throw flames, then why should she wait to retaliate? Her right hand went down to the pouch at her belt, which contained energy potions. She had only three, but she could make them count. She had to. She wanted to. She had never needed more than one potion on a battlefield before, what harm could it do?

Her mind made up, she began targeting the giants one after another, while occasionally dodging the odd attack. She could feel her energy draining her with each blast she expelled, doing the best she could to push back the part of her that was still a teenage girl and squirmed at the thought of harming anyone to the point of death. These were monsters, she told herself, and pounded the notion into the forefront of her mind with a zealot's fervour. It was the only thing she found that worked in times like these, a mental shield against the acts she was committing.

She reached into the pouch and grabbed one of the vials. Annetta then clenched the cork between her teeth as she ripped it out and poured the liquid into her mouth as quickly as she could. The action had almost cost her a blow to the head from another blast, which she managed to teleport from in the nick of time. With her strength renewed, she continued her rain of fire, executing each blast with the proficiency of a machine gun. Time seemed to lose meaning as she continued, her hands beginning to throb from the heat of the flames she expelled again and again. The meaning behind the assault, too, began to slightly lose meaning. All she knew was that she had to push on. Her friends needed her, and she remembered the words she had said only a few years ago. That she would fight because nobody else would.

What happened next, she did not remember exactly, except that everything blurred into a darkened haze of battle and crimson.

Chapter 18

Annetta awoke and found herself staring up into halogen lights, which greeted her with their signature buzzing sound. The scene was disorienting, and she immediately wanted to jolt up, except that she found she couldn't. Looking down, Annetta saw that she had been stripped out of her armour into a white nightgown, and was strapped to a medical bed with thick brown leather belts. The thought that followed right after was not a happy one, and she began to move around with more force. Had it all been a dream?

To Annetta's relief, Puc appeared around the corner of the room seconds later and rushed towards her, navy blue robed billowing and all. The First Mage of Aldamoor, unfortunately, looked worse for wear and it was clear that unlike her, he'd not had a decent sleep in quite some time. He had, however, in all of the chaos, managed to shave off his beard, which she found odd. Skyris was the next one to hurry in, dressed in her usual tank top and leather bomber combination, nearly knocking him over in the process.

"How is she?" The older Gaian woman hovered beside the mage as he strode across the room.

"Conscious, though I do not know if she is coherent." Puc stopped at the foot of Annetta's bed.

Tension brewed as the two of them watched Annetta, not saying anything else. If she hadn't known any better, Annetta could have sworn that they looked scared of her. She wriggled around a bit more under the heavy belts, which caused Puc to tighten the grip on his staff and Skyris to take a step back.

Confused, Annetta did her best to hold her head up. "Uhm... hey... did I... did we win?"

A sigh of relief came from both, and relaxing, they walked closer to the side of the bed. There was still something off about the way they regarded her, and Annetta couldn't understand what was causing such a reaction. Had someone died? Panic rose inside of her as she replayed how she had found out about Link's passing in her head. She was not ready to relive something like that, not now, not yet, and if she could help it somehow, not ever.

"The giants were defeated, though the cost was great." Puc's neutral reserve didn't shift despite his obvious underlying apprehension.

Annetta's chest tightened as she asked the next most important question on her mind. "Where are Jason, Sarina and Darius?"

"They're at their university orientations," Skyris said. "Jason and Sarina, that is. We made Darius all of the necessary paperwork, and he's now at your orientation. You'll both be attending the same program."

"Orientation?" Annetta questions. "But that's not for another week."

Skyris glanced down at her feet before looking over at Puc, and then back at the girl. "You've been mostly unconscious for that long."

"Unconscious?" Her eyes widened. "Just… what exactly happened to me and why am I tied up like this? The last thing I remember was being up in the air and trying to level the mountain with psychic fire."

"A reckless move." Puc's gaze fixed on her. "Which left you open to attack. Unknown's bane, Annetta, did Venetor cause you to forget reason in the span of six weeks? Since when has making yourself an open target like that been a good idea?"

Annetta felt the familiar sensation of ears flattening against her skull. Puc was right, what she'd done was extremely reckless, but it had been a sacrifice she'd been willing to make to win the battle.

She felt her courage return, and her gaze met his. "Yeah, it was, and I'll admit it, but you didn't answer my question. Why am I in here?"

The girl then looked to Skyris for clarification, but her aunt's eyes deflected her gaze and went to the mage.

Puc adjusted the grip on his staff and looked down at Annetta. "You were injured quite severely. The straps were put in place so you would not move around while the healing took place. One of the injuries you sustained was a blow to the head, which is why you may have difficulty remembering anything. You were conscious when you were brought to the medical tent, however, I had to resort to using magic to stabilize you before you were brought to Q-16 for a full examination. The magic may have erased some of the memories from that time. It is an unfortunate, but sometimes necessary side effect."

The answer didn't satisfy Annetta. There was something about the way Puc had delivered the answer to her that made her suspect he was hiding something. "What else? Look, I need to know what happened out there. How did we win? Did my efforts with the psychic fire work?"

"I think it is best you rest, Annetta," Puc stated. "While you may be awake, you are still very weak from the ordeal. I will be more than happy to tell you everything in detail when I deem you can fully function again. Your body does not need any more stress at the given time."

"Well, if I'm stuck in here and you won't tell me more, can you at least let me out of these straps?"

Puc opened his mouth as if to speak again, and then shut it. Beside him, Skyris folded her arms across her chest with a concerned look. From what Annetta gathered, something terrible must have happened for them to be this troubled and for them not to want to worry her with the details after she'd just woken up.

After a long minute, Puc finally took a step forward, and with a simple wave, the belts fell away to either side. Annetta sighed with the burden being lifted from her, feeling lighter.

"I do this under one condition: That you will stay in that bed. Understood?"

"Won't move, I promise." The girl raised her hand.

Puc nodded, turning on his heel and began to leave the room. He was at the entrance when he spoke once more. "I will be back shortly with some potions to check in on you."

Skyris lingered for a little while longer after. Her usually jovial face was lined with worry, and it seemed to add ten years to her ageless features. She was the last person Annetta wanted to see upset about anything, and it made her insides twist at the scene.

"So, what made Puc shave it off?" she asked, trying to change the subject.

It took Skyris a moment before she caught on to what she was getting at. "Hm? Oh, the beard. I think he realized facial hair and fire don't mix well together."

Annetta cringed at the thought, then laughed as she pictured a panicked Puc trying to put out a beard that was much longer than the one he'd had in real life. She then saw Skyris too had a smile on her face, but it faded all too quickly once she noticed that Annetta was watching her.

Skyris dropped her arms to the side. "I'm going to go and contact Gaia, see how Titus is doing. I'll come back as soon as I can."

A short bob of the head being all that Annetta had time to show, she watched Skyris leave. Loneliness and isolation crept in once she was gone. She did her best to push them aside and settled herself into the bed more comfortably. As she gazed up at the ceiling, she wished that they would have at least left her with a book to pass the time.

Skyris trailed behind Puc after having left the room, an air of determination enveloping her as she pressed forward. Being shorter than the mage, it took significantly more effort to catch up to his long strides, not that this deterred her in the least.

Confident that they were both far away from the room, she spoke. "Just how long do you plan to keep her in the dark like this?"

Puc stopped with his back still turned to her, his staff coming down onto the steel floor in one final thud that seemed to echo around them. "You saw as well as I what transpired on that battlefield."

Skyris folded her arms across her chest. "I did, and I also feel like she has a right to know what exactly happened."

"In due time." The mage turned to face her. "She has just become conscious. I did not think it beneficial to bring to light the situation at hand. How exactly would you react to hearing that the alliance your grandfather built might well be in shambles?"

"It's more than that, and you know it." Skyris pointed back in the direction of the room. "What was that thing?"

"I cannot be certain," Puc replied. "Though, if my hunch is correct, then I daresay I wish I did not know the answer, for then we are all in grave danger."

The hardened edges of Skyris's face softened, her arms going down to her sides as she looked into Puc's pale blue eyes. He was no older-looking than she was, but there was an agelessness to his eyes that made them look much more wearied than his visage. The spell had drained him, and though it had been a week since he'd performed it, it remained behind in the form of the dark circles under his eyes. Worst yet, Skyris knew that he wouldn't stop to rest. It was a trait she had admired in him once, but had made her worry that the mage would drop dead in his study one day.

"What will you do now?" she asked.

"I think its best now to get her parents here and let them know she is doing well," he said. "After that I must return to Aldamoor for a time to do research, it would be also beneficial I think for me to take a blood sample from her to study further. While away, Tamora also managed to escape, though how, I am not sure. When last I saw her, it appeared that she had gone mad."

"Mad?" Skyris frowned. "Wasn't she already?"

"Not like this." He shook his head. "Just promise me that while I am away, you will try not to cause her undue stress? If you find you must tell her, so be it, but do not throw everything at her at once. The spell I placed should hold as a seal. I am, however, uncertain how long it will hold in place and stress seemed to be the trigger for it. You should warn the others as well."

Satisfied with the answer, Skyris nodded. Puc then turned away from her and began to make his way towards the stables to arrange his return to Aldamoor and the responsibilities of First Mage. She continued to stand, watching as his silhouette minimize and vanish. She had not wanted him to leave just then. Though Skyris had never considered herself a weak woman, being a Gaian, she was not without fear, and fear was what she felt in that moment.

೫෧

Jason picked absentmindedly at the nicks and scratches on his C.T.S.'s faceplate as he waited for Sarina after his orientation. The hall of the university he found himself in looked much like a high school, but as though someone had given it one of the mushrooms from Alice in Wonderland that caused everything to grow larger. In this case, large enough to fit adults in the seats instead of just teenagers. It wasn't just the desks and chairs, though, even the halls and rooms themselves, in general, seemed larger, so large that Jason felt invisible. The lecture hall he had just been in could have fit at least five hundred students with ease and still had room for a few stragglers to stand at the back and listen to what was being said. Despite telling himself over and over again in his head that he shouldn't like it, he kind of did. With all the responsibilities of the Four Forces that had rested on his shoulders, he liked for once to be nothing more than just another face in the crowd.

The polished silver knob on the brown wooden door beside him twisted and from the glass panels on either side, he could already see the mass of students that was pressed in close to leave the room. Knowing the chaos that would ensue, Jason stepped aside just as the sea of bodies geysered out of the room and spilt out into the hallway. His attention was fixated on the exit as he waited to see a head of auburn hair appear amid the students.

"Ready to go?" a voice asked from beside him.

Startled, Jason pivoted to see Sarina already standing beside him. She wore a dark green blouse with a black leather jacket and washed out jeans that covered a good part of her green and black matching sneakers. Her hair was half pinned up, parts of it falling out around her neck and shoulders in a messy fashion. Had he known any better, Jason would have guessed that she was human.

"Uh… yeah." He nodded and adjusting his backpack, he extended his hand, which she reached out and took. The two of them then began to make their way towards the exit of the building while trying to remember the layout of it and not get lost in the maze of lecture halls and tutorial classrooms.

"I don't think I'll ever get used to this." Jason sighed. "Everything looks the same and it's so… big."

A small smile formed on Sarina's face. "I can recall you saying that about a certain other place, and you seem quite at home there now."

Jason connected the dots to what she was saying and couldn't help but crack a grin. "Yeah, but that's just the Lab, this is different. No destiny, no…"

He paused, which also forced their hands to come apart. His mind flashed back to the most recent battle in Morwick and the things he'd seen there. A small shudder crept through him, but he did his best to mask it. Exhaling, he looked down at his shoes and then back up at Sarina.

Sarina took a step towards him and entwined her hand in his once more. "J.K., she's going to be okay. Look, I don't know what happened out there exactly, but whatever caused it, we'll find the source of it. I don't think that was just some trick Annetta picked up on Gaia."

"What if it was, though?" Jason asked. "She's been acting differently since she came back to Earth."

Sarina shook her head. "In any book I've read about Gaians, I never came across it. Besides, if it were a common occurrence, then my father would have weaponized it somehow, and I never heard him or his scientists talk of anything like it. Unless it's some Severio secret passed down through generations, which I don't think it is. You saw how she was when Puc finally brought her down."

Jason closed his eyes and pushed the image back. "I try not to remember."

The two of them began walking again. If Jason had not been blessed with any sense of direction, he was sure they would have both been lost at the first turn.

"We should go see her today," Sarina said as they neared the doors to the exit.

Jason turned to regard her with a raised eyebrow. "Oh I... yeah, I guess we should, though she's still probably out cold."

"We won't know until we get there," she reminded him. "We made it clear to Puc that unless it's an emergency, neither he nor Skyris was supposed to contact us in case we were in class."

Jason gave a silent bob of the head in reply. Their next course of action set, they headed back to the apartment.

„›‹›

The scene having been written, Jansen exhaled as she leaned back in her chair. Such a rush. She loved when the words she typed flowed out of her fingertips. There was nothing more satisfying than it in the world. She knew then and there that if the book ever got published, this would be one of the signature scenes in it as long as her editor wouldn't axe it. She was so enthralled by her achievement, however, that Jansen didn't notice the time, and glancing down at her computer screen, she was forced to scramble in order to make it to the bus she needed to get to work.

She grabbed all of her essentials and stuffed them into her backpack, taking a quick glance in the mirror to see if she had anything on her face. She then slipped on her black runners and not bothering to wait for an elevator, dashed down the stairs and out of the building.

As smooth as her escape out of the confines of her apartment seemed to be going, it was not meant to last and soon, Jansen found herself running into a stranger. Tripping over the dangling shoulder strap of her messenger bag that she clutched in her hands as she ran, she fell face first onto it. Looking up from amidst strands of loose blonde hair from her ponytail, Jansen groaned as she was forced to watch the bus speed away from the stop.

"Just my luck," she grumbled as she scanned the ground to make sure nothing had fallen out of her bag.

A hand then found her upper arm and began to pull her up. "You okay?"

Jansen looked over to see that the person she had run into, and her face flushed red at seeing it was none other than the youth that had introduced himself to her as Darius Silver.

"Uhm… yeah, I guess," she answered, pulling away and dusting off her pants while taking one last look around to make sure she didn't lose anything.

Her eyes then turned to the bus stop in longing, as a million excuses for as to why she would be late for her shift began to formulate in her head. She couldn't exactly tell her supervisor that she got carried away while writing a scene in her book. Perhaps her bus had gotten a flat tire, and everyone had been forced to take a detour bus would work this time around? She cross-checked her mental notes to see if she had used it before.

"That was your bus, wasn't it?" Darius's voice cut through her train of thought.

Jansen turned to him. How could someone have brown eyes that were so dark? She found herself hypnotized by them for a split second. Hearing the question, she snapped out of it. "Yeah, it was the one I take to work."

"Anywhere I could drop you off to make it up to you?" The young man indicated back to the parking lot behind them. "I feel kind of responsible, having been in your way."

Jansen looked past his hand to see he was pointing at an old-looking black Mustang, the year of which she would never have been able to guess, except that it was vintage. Usually, she would have thought twice about getting into a car with a total stranger, but weighing her options as she glanced back at the now-empty bus stop, she was wondering if now was a good time as any to break the rules her mother had beat into her head as a child.

"Sure, if you don't mind." She nodded. "I work at the mall right off Ellesmere Road."

Darius pursed his lips as he fished around for his keys in the pocket of his black jeans. "Yeah, I think I know the one. I have to go by there anyway. I'm picking up a pair of steel toes for school."

Jansen relaxed a little on hearing that she wasn't a total burden and followed him. "What are you taking?"

"Police Foundations," he replied as he unlocked the doors. "Though to be honest, it wasn't my idea completely. I have a very persuasive friend with a fiery personality."

Jansen pulled the handle and found herself assaulted by the smell of a leather interior. She hadn't taken Darius for a car guy, but then again, she'd only just bumped into him the second time. She slid in as she listened to what he was saying. "Oh really? I have a character who's thinking of taking the same thing in a book I'm writing. Think I could bug you for some notes?"

Darius pulled on his seatbelt and started the car engine. "A writer? That's pretty cool. What kind of stuff do you write?"

"Fantasy, I guess." She shrugged. "Though there's some science fiction mixed into it."

"Oh really? That same friend I mentioned loves reading that stuff, or at least she used to." He continued talking as he sped off onto the main road, merging with the midday traffic. "She hasn't had much time lately with all the family stuff, and the part-time job she's working."

"Sounds like you guys are pretty close," Jansen said, taking the opportunity to check her makeup in the mirror and adjust the eyeliner.

Darius kept his eyes on the road. "We're like family. I've known her since we were kids."

Jansen made an 'o' shape with her mouth and nodded before staring out the window. Her mind still swam in the aftermath of the last scene she'd written. Had she not been in a car with a total stranger that she felt compelled to make conversation with, Jansen would have put in her headphones and zoned out to the latest round of music she had acquired to fuel the next thing she planned to write.

"My friend Anne used to do that whenever we were driving." Darius's voice cut through her thoughts again. "Any time her dad would take us anywhere, she'd just stare out the window. Still does it on occasion."

"Your friend?" Jansen looked over at him.

"Yeah, Annetta, but everyone calls her Anne for short."

Jansen felt a chill go down her spine at hearing the name. It had to be a coincidence though. "Oh, that's actually the name of my main character, Annetta Severio."

"Oh really? Cool. It's not a very common name." He flicked on his turn signal. "She'd probably be interested in reading it if you ever get it published."

"That's the plan." Jansen smiled and saw the sign for the mall come into view. "Anywhere here is fine."

Darius nodded and pulling into the mall's parking lot he stopped at the curb beside the closest entrance. Jansen removed her seatbelt, collected her things and opened the door.

"Thanks for the lift," she said.

184

"Any time, I'm sure we'll run into each other again," he replied. "Though not literally, I hope."

Jansen cracked a wide grin. "For sure."

She closed the door behind her and then ventured inside.

෨০෬

Darius pulled into an empty spot in the parking lot and turned off the ignition. Quickly checking to see that no one was in sight, he flipped open his C.T.S. and dialed the number he wanted.

"05 here." Puc's voice came through moments later.

Darius inhaled, composed himself and said the only words he knew that his former master needed to hear. "I found her."

Chapter 19

Annetta sighed after having completed counting the tiles on the ceiling for the tenth time in the last few hours, and turned over onto her side on the cot. The mattress coils squeaked, further reaffirming just how uncomfortable the bed was. If only she could get up to move around just a little bit... but she couldn't. She'd promised Puc that she wouldn't leave the bed. Being out for a week cold, she could understand just why the mage had been so adamant about her staying in one place. There had been a lot of hushed talk among him and Skyris, which could only mean, she concluded, that her injuries had been incredibly severe.

Despite all of this rationalization, however, she was getting bored. The room didn't have a television she could watch, she hadn't a book or a magazine to flip through, and the only music she had was the constant buzz of halogen lights overhead, which was beginning to drive her slightly mad. She was about to get up despite the promises just to walk around the room at least, when she heard the sound of voices coming in her direction. When she realized who they belonged to, a smile lit up on her face.

Soon after, Jason and Sarina came in. As soon as they saw that she was awake, they froze in the doorway.

Annetta propped herself up on her elbow and resting her forearms on the bed. "Hey guys, you okay? You look like you've seen a ghost."

Jason was the first to cave out of the duo as he ran to her bedside. "Anne! Is it really you? Are you awake?"

"Uhm... last I checked." She furrowed her brows. "Why?"

Sarina took a few steps closer until she was just feet behind where Jason stood. "You mean, you don't remember anything?"

"Well, not everything." Annetta sat up as best as she could. "I remember us crossing into the portal to Aerim and fighting the giants and the Fenrikin. I flew up to destroy the mountain with psychic fire, and, well..."

Annetta felt the pressure built in her forehead as she struggled to remember anything at all that could indicate just what had caused her to go unconscious. The problem was, there was nothing solid for her to grab onto as evidence of just when the triggering event had occurred. She massaged her temples with her thumb and forefinger in an effort to disperse the tension.

"I can't remember anything past that." Her hands dropped to her sides. "Everything is just a haze."

"Nothing?" Jason confirmed.

"Is it so hard to believe?" she asked.

Jason swallowed hard and looked over at Sarina as if seeking her insight on how much he could say. Annetta was tempted to throw in a comment on the fact, but decided it was best to keep silent. Jason squatted beside her at the foot of her bed. He lowered his head, gazing at his hands that rested over his knees. "I don't know where to begin, Anne, if you can't remember."

"Just tell it like it is, J.K., you know I wouldn't want it any other way," she stated, now growing concerned herself.

Jason stood wordlessly and looked down, studying her with his green eyes. He then raised his hands. "It might be best that I just show you what happened, otherwise I don't think you'd believe me if I just told you."

A tight feeling of suspense entered Annetta's gut, twisting as Jason's hands came towards her. Though they had both been taught to not use their hands in any manner that could betray their actions as a psychic warrior, projection, or the ability to project memories into another person's mind, was not commonly used enough. Physical contact would make the process easier.

As soon as Jason's hands touched her forehead, Annetta felt herself drawn back to the battlefield around Morwick. She found herself standing right beside Jason, who was fending off a giant with the help of Sarina. Seconds later, a ball of fire struck their opponent and sent him to the ground. Jason looked up, first in relief and then in horror. Where just moments before, he'd seen Annetta floating above them and dispelling a blazing display of psychic fire, there now was a being he had, even with all of the things he had been exposed to over the last few years, thought he would never see. Enormous bat-like wings beat through the air, its body covered in crimson scales. A serpentine tail swished back and forth, and from the tip of a graceful long neck, a head with horns jutted out, topped with eyes as green as the most vile of poisons, with teeth the lengths of swords protruding from an elongated great maw. Annetta felt the hairs all over her body stand on end as she was made to confront the one thing from all the books she had read that up until this moment had still been fiction: A dragon.

Frantically, she searched for where she could have fallen, where her own body was, but she could only go as far as Jason would, since it was from his point of view. The creature soared overhead and without recognition of friend or foe, it lashed out with great column of flame that spilled forth from it. A chill ran down the girl's spine. The creature was one thing to see it in a movie and another to be standing mere feet away from. The projection then sped up in time, and Annetta was bombarded with images at an incredible fast pace. The journey of whirling faces and images took her all the way to her current accommodations in the Lab where she had lain unconscious.

"You foolish boy!" A voice she recognized cut past the projection with a boom.

Annetta looked up to see Puc grabbing Jason's wrists as he pulled them apart. There was an urgent violence to the mage's body language that she was not used to seeing, which soon after transformed into concern as he knelt beside her in his place.

"Unknown's bane, I thought I had more time before she awoke to warn you not to use Projection for this. The shock for her system could be too great. Annetta, can you hear me?" he asked, his pale blue eyes darting from each of her eyes to check on them.

"I…I think so," she managed to say. "But I… I need answers. What the hell happened to me?"

Relief showed on Puc's face when she spoke, but was quickly replaced by sadness. "I am sorry, Annetta. I wanted to have more time to research this…"

Anger surged through her. "So when exactly were you going to tell me that I turned into a monster on the battlefield that couldn't tell friend from foe? Did it even occur to you that I had a right to know?"

"Anne, you need to calm down." Jason stretched his hands towards her. "Puc placed a seal on it using a spell, but we don't know how well it will hold. It happened when you were using psychic fire, and there's a good chance that anger is what triggered the change."

Annetta stopped and looked down at her hand, which was already in the process of curling up into a fist. Exhaling, she made it go limp before glancing back at those that had gathered in the room. In addition to Sarina, Jason and Puc, Skyris stood at the very back, with a hand resting on the doorframe. Further still behind them, Annetta could see two other figures she had not expected.

"Mom? Dad?" Her eyes widened as Arieus and Aurora passed by Skyris and into the room.

Puc stood and took a few paces back to allow her parents through. They then knelt in his place beside the bed. Though both Arieus and Aurora had begun coming down to Q-16 after the initial battle with Mislantus, they didn't do so often, and not without purpose.

"How are you feeling, dear?" Aurora asked.

"To be honest, after what I just saw from Jason I'm not sure," Annetta admitted.

Another thought then ran across Annetta's mind. "The Four Forces... the Minotaur, the Ogaien, the elves and the Soarin-"

"They can wait, Anne." Arieus placed his large hand over her smaller one. "Right now, you should focus on rest."

"I've rested enough, Dad," she pointed out. "A whole week, apparently, and I'm missing my orientation."

"Darius will get you the material you need," Skyris chimed in. "I made sure you were both in the same block. You don't have to worry about it."

"Then what am I supposed to worry about, because apparently turning into a dragon or my grandfather's alliances aren't on the list." Annetta frowned.

"We just need time to know what you can and cannot do without possibly disrupting the seal until I am able to place a more secure one," Puc said to her. "And even then I am not certain how long it will hold. You need to think of it as a band aid. Should you strain yourself without proper stitching, the wound can begin to bleed again."

"How long till you can put on this new seal?" she asked.

"I do not know, and even then, I do not know how well it will hold. I have never seen anything like this. This magic, it surpasses even the time of Chiron."

"Magic? So this is a spell?" she inquired.

"I cannot say, Annetta," Puc answered her. "It is my only explanation for it at this time."

Annetta sank back into her pillow. A wave of exhaustion fell over her from the information. Her mind swam as she did her best to piece everything together, and the images of the projection Jason had shown her continued to assault her.

There was one memory that stood out above the rest as she closed her eyes for a split second. In it, she saw herself in the room she was in now. Puc, Jason, Sarina, Darius and Skyris were among those gathered, trying to hold her down. Mixed in were also Soarin, Ogaien and other elves, maybe even Minotaur, she could not discern. There was another thing she was focused on more than these. It was the sound of her own screaming as she tossed and tried to rip free of the grips of all those she loved. Her eyes, as Jason saw her, were not her own, but a feral bright green that covered the whole of them. A cat slit pupil with flecks of yellow darted back and forth, while sweat-matted hair plastered against her as she struggled against the combined weight of all those there. She could barely recognize herself, and it disturbed her in a way nothing ever had before. She had been distraught and even sick after battles before. Nothing really ever prepared you for how to react to death, but this was different. She had watched conscious beings die before, but how could you fight the enemy when the enemy lived within yourself?

∞⟨∞⟩∞

A fading sun gave the last of its light to the ruins that were once the ancient city Edran. Decaying stonework made of various shades of brown poked through here and there from the tall grasses which surrounded much of it. It was hard to tell that a mere six weeks ago, this ancient site had been witness to a battle where the forces of Aldamoor had clashed with those of the Fire Elves. It was hard to tell that the area had been occupied at all in any recent years until tonight.

The one who prophecy named as the seed of chaos watched as the orange sun faded to red on the horizon and fell behind him as its light was then compensated with hundreds of torches igniting. He turned around, the edges of his sleeveless long vest made of patchwork leather whirling around him like smoke. It had been given to him by his bride to be, the one he had chosen, Tamora. He was not certain just how he had stumbled across her in his mental searches of the multiverse while hidden away in his prison for what seemed like eternity. One minute, she hadn't been there in his mind, and the next, she had. It was simply fate, or as some called it, the will of the Unknown, though the Seed very much doubted that ignorant fool had anything to do with it. No, it was he himself who was responsible, his will alone. It was their passion for a shared singular thing that had brought them together, he knew, their desire to watch everything burn. Their love of a world on fire.

He watched as the flames of those gathered parted in the middle into two columns, lighting the way for a shadowy figure. As it came closer, the shape grew smaller, more defined. He gave the slightest twitch of his lips upon seeing Tamora materialize fully. The one he would call his queen had stripped off the tarnished rags he had found her in and was now dressed in the hide armour of her people. Her fierce and untamed platinum hair flowed down past her shoulders in thick dreadlocks, contrasting the crimson of her eyes.

He stretched out his hand towards her, and when she accepted it, he gently pulled her closer to him until they stood side by side. The one known as the seed of chaos then turned his attention to the gathered masses and raised his free hand.

"My brothers and sisters, if I may call you that," he addressed them. "I come before you this night in this sacred place to wed one of your own, so that we may be one. I come not only because of this, however. I have heard of your plight and of the hardships you have all faced at the hands of these Four Forces. I come to let you know that the time of your suffering will end."

Cheering could be heard as some of the torches flickered from being raised higher in praise. He smiled lightly at this recognition, then turned his attention fully back to Tamora. The leader of the Fire Elves looked back at him with a hazed longing in her red eyes. Taking a step back and letting go of her hand, he walked over to where a barren bush grew, its dead thorn-covered branches shooting up in various angles as if trying to reach out to him. He bent down, grabbed a handful of the branches and weaved them together into a circlet. The headpiece then seemed to come alive as leaves sprouted from it. Small orange flowers flecked with red resembling roses bloomed as he carried the crown over and placed it gently onto Tamora's head.

"With this crown, I give you dominion over my heart," he proclaimed. "Now, I ask… what does my bride bring for me in dowry?"

Tamora looked out into the crowds and outstretched her hand. "I give you the armies of the Fire Elves. Let those who served me now also serve you."

Satisfied with the words, the one known as the seed of chaos nodded, then he looked to the other side, away from the torches and into the dark. "What say you, acolyte of shadow?"

"I think." Amarok emerged from the dark. "That this dowry is worthy in the eyes of Khaos. May it serve you well."

He then locked his gaze with Tamora. "Then let it be known then that I, the seed of chaos, take Tamora of the elves who worship flame to become one with in this lifetime."

There was another swell of cheering, louder than the others. The flames seemed to dance in Tamora's eyes as he that was the seed of chaos gazed down at her. Leaning in, he cupped her face in a single hand and kissed her, making it known that the dragon had wed his bride.

Chapter 20

The tide crept in on the brown sandy shore of the beach's edge, washing away any remnants of footprints. Not far from it, a pair of worn teal sneakers with white socks stuffed into them rested beside a fallen log, a light breeze fluttering through the tall grass that shaded it from the afternoon sun.

Annetta stood in the lake with her jeans rolled up past her knees, the water midway up her calves. It was warm enough within the Lake Biosphere that the normally frigid water was tolerable for once and, there was something peaceful about watching the waves come in and then roll out. Peaceful was good for her condition, or so Puc claimed.

Ever since the incident, Annetta had been put on a stress-free schedule, void of anything which would bring her anxiety or strain, things which could trigger another potential episode. She hated it. What if the incident had nothing to do with her condition, as he called it? Puc, of course, would not hear of it. His mind was made up on the subject, and until he was able to learn more about her condition, then she was to steer clear of anything which could act as a potential trigger. This included training. Despite all the whining in the past about it, Annetta had never felt more miserable in her life.

Thinking about it, she reached down her shirt and pulled out the thin leather cord which held Severbane in its shrunken form. She marvelled at the intricate wood carving, studying every detail of its making. When she had finished, she summoned her sword, the miniature being replaced in her hand by it. The weight of the blade felt good in her hands, it felt right to hold it again. Her fingers pressed with more force into the soft leather of the hilt as she adjusted them into a proper hand-and-a-half position. Her feet automatically moved into a widened defensive stance and before she knew it, Annetta found herself being swept up in images of imaginary fighters with no defined features. Severbane thrust forward as she cut the closest one down to size and then another and another.

"Uhm… didn't Puc say you weren't supposed to do any sort of training?" Jason's voice pierced the illusion she'd created.

Annetta stopped herself, nearly dropping Severbane as she did so. She turned around slowly to see both Jason and Sarina. She cursed herself inwardly for being caught.

"What he doesn't know won't kill him," she replied. "I mean, unless that's what you're here for now, to babysit me."

Jason snorted and shook his head. "Right, like that would end well."

Satisfied with his answer, Annetta began to wade ashore, dismissing Severbane back into its pendant form and slipping it over her head. "So, what are you here for then? What's up?"

"We wanted to come see how you were doing before we head back up." Sarina stated. "We both have our first classes tomorrow."

"Right, that thing." Annetta nodded.

A pause followed. Annetta looked over at Jason and Sarina standing ashore side by side. Despite it only having been two years, the two of them looked older, wiser and far more capable than the two youth that had come to know of Q-16 at the start of their journey. A pang of grief filled Annetta for a second as she wondered if her and Link might have looked like that together were he alive. She suppressed it, however, as fast as it came. She then looked down at the water once more, focusing on the gentle waves as they brushed past her legs and fused with the shore.

"You okay Anne?" Jason asked.

Annetta glanced up at her friend again, her mind fully in the present. "I'm fine. Look, just because I stared off into the distance doesn't mean anything, okay? I've been prone to daydreaming way before this thing."

"Sorry, I was just worried." He frowned.

"Well, don't be. I'm not incapable of taking care of myself," she snapped.

"Anne, we know," Sarina interjected. "But if you saw what Jason and I did then you should understand…"

"What? That I'm some kind of monster?" She scowled, coming fully ashore.

"You're not a monster, where did you get that from?" Jason raised an eyebrow.

Annetta walked up to him and stood but mere paces from his face. Despite her being shorter by about half a head than he was, at that moment she towered over everyone with her presence. "I saw everything you did, J.K., and if you think you can just lie to me about what you thought when you saw me, then you're either really ignorant or really stupid."

Another pause followed as Annetta caught herself breathing heavily before Jason. Never in her life had she felt she was being lied to in such a capacity. It was as if no one was willing to tell her the truth and worse yet, she couldn't help but feel that deep down, that this was just the surface of it all.

"Dragons are not monsters if the legends about Korangar hold any truth to them." Sarina broke their staring contest.

"Korangar? I keep hearing that name." Annetta looked over at her.

"If the legends are to be believed." Sarina began, "Then Korangar was once a simple man of humble origins. He was not a great lord, nor a powerful king, though he was a fighter as fierce as what any title could bring to his name. One day, however, he was punished with a terrible affliction, the likes of which no healer could determine the cause of. It was then assumed that whatever had befallen the man was a curse of Khaos's origin."

"What was this affliction?" Annetta asked.

"It's hard to say because all of the stories conflict, and the ones my father told me as a little girl don't all add up," Sarina confessed. "What they did share in common was that his soul had broken up into multiple aspects of evil. The seven evils, to be exact: Avarice, murder, narcissism, false-speech, overindulgence, vainglory and deification."

Annetta absorbed the information. "And the dragons?"

"It was said that the only way Korangar could be bested was by a dragon. It's suggested that's how my ancestor Freius was able to enslave Korangar for all time. Again, though, there are no facts in any of this." Sarina ended with a shrug.

Annetta frowned a little. While the story was interesting, it did little to lighten her mood.

Jason took a step forward. "Anne, we'll get to the bottom of this. I mean, maybe it's some genetic Gaian adrenaline booster or something. You were shooting psychic fire on that battlefield like crazy."

"We've both used it before, though."

The youth shook his head. "Not like that. You were literally raining fire down on everyone, and seconds later, you changed. It was like… I don't know, the fire made you go out of control or something."

"You're not helping," Annetta growled.

Sarina sighed at the banter. "We know it's not your fault, Anne."

Annetta's shoulders slumped. She walked past the two of them to where her shoes and socks lay. Getting as much of the sand off her feet as she could, she began to put them back on. Her mind swam in guilt as the faded memories of her friend tried to resurface again.

"This isn't like you, Annetta." Jason strode over to her. "The Annetta I grew up with wouldn't skulk about this or-"

"The Annetta you grew up with also didn't turn into a thirty-foot fire breathing dragon and hurt people she cared for," she snapped. "I saw the look on everyone's faces when I came to, and your memories confirmed it, so don't try to sugar coat it. What I did out there, even if I wasn't in control, was against everything I ever stood for, and I don't think I'll ever be able to forgive myself for it."

She could feel the beginnings of burning tears start to form in the corners of her eyes as she said this. It was a harsh truth, but one that she had admitted to herself. Even if this thing had been suppressed, the Annetta Severio everyone knew would never be the same again. Unable to look them in the eyes, her gaze fell downwards as she slumped on the log she was sitting on. A few of the tears she wasn't able to hold back fell onto the sand, creating small circles in it. She then felt a hand on her shoulder.

Jason's voice then filled the silence. "Anne, I know you don't see it in yourself right now, but trust me when I say this. You aren't alone, and we're going to get to the bottom of this."

The sound of feet then followed. Annetta continued to look down at the ground and when she finally did move, found that she was utterly alone by the lake.

⚯

Matthias's escape from the port was not without any complication. After his flight from the bounty hunters, word had spread that the right-hand assassin of Mislantus had been sighted, and like a pack of rabid dogs, more hunters came to try their hand at him.

The ordeal had forced him to take a route back to Earth through outer rim planets, dodging any ports, which would potentially be a hub for hunters on the lookout for him. It had also meant a more extended trip and a larger need for fuel and supplies. His luck had seen him through most of the trip, but his last transaction at a spaceport had cost him, and he found himself hurtling towards Earth with a pack of ships at his heel firing at him.

He still had a fair distance to pass before the ship was within the protected zone of Earth. Once there, no ship could touch him. The Greys didn't take too kindly to anyone without a permit going within satellite detection distance of Earth, knowing full well that the humans were always watching for signs of alien life and were not yet ready to handle the discovery of it. A cloaking device was needed for that, and Matthias was fortunate enough to be in possession of one. Skyris had been thorough in her designs.

"I owe that woman a whole bottle of aged spirits when I get back," Matthias mused to himself from the cabin as warning strobe lights flashed from the damage he'd just taken.

The ship shook around him with the pressure of another hit, Matthias glanced at his radar to see that his left engine was leaking, and it was only a matter of time before it gave out fully. While cloaking worked for Federation standards, bounty hunters had their ways of getting around them and the ones on his tail were no exception to the rule.

Picturing the shape of it, Matthias moved a panel from underneath where the wheels were stored for descent, and plastered it over the hole like a makeshift band-aid with his telekinetic abilities. He wasn't sure how much more abuse the ship could take, made by Skyris or not.

He then saw it, however, a small glint on the horizon that was drawing ever closer. He had been uncertain at first, but upon closer inspection of the massive red eye which was the centre of a storm, he grinned in recognition of the planet the humans called Jupiter. Once he passed it, he would be in the restricted zone.

"Sorry boys, but not today." He grinned, and pushing everything he had into the ship, he sent it into full speed ahead.

Chapter 21

As all things come to an end, so too did Annetta's quarantine by Puc, along with the beginning of college. Her uniform, boots and textbooks had all been picked up by Darius, who'd attended the orientation the previous week, and so when the morning of her first class came, she was ready to dive in head-first, or so she liked to think.

That first morning, she navigated her way through the college halls with Darius in tow. After some consultation with a school map and a few students correcting her course, she managed to locate the class where their Introduction to Health and Wellness course was to take place. It was a plain-looking room painted in a washed-out greenish grey with a whiteboard at the front, a podium and what Annetta could only assume would be the professor's desk. Three rows of tables, each one on a tier making it higher than the previous level, faced the front, and behind each table were neatly pushed-in chairs. The large rectangular windows that were located on the far side all had their blinds pulled down halfway, giving them the illusion of sleepy eyes that looked in at the new arrivals. To their surprise also, there was not a single soul in the room.

Annetta took a second glance at the room number and then back on the sheet, confirming they were in the right place. She shrugged, entered and placed her backpack on the chair beside her before lazily sliding into a seat.

"You think everyone is running late?" she asked.

"It's possible." Darius rolled up his jacket sleeve to check the time on his C.T.S. "Looks like we still have ten minutes before class officially starts. Besides, you saw that coffee shop lineup."

"You're telling me everyone was waiting in that thing?" Annetta recalled the lineup that wound almost all the way down the length of the cafeteria hall.

"Caffeine, every college kid's addiction." He snickered.

Annetta rolled her eyes at the sentiment. "Give me one of those energy-recharging potions any day over enduring that."

"I can arrange that." Darius grinned.

Before either of them could say anything else, the doorknob turned and opened. A young man that was at least six feet in height with short tawny hair dressed in a crisp school uniform peered in.

"Uh, hey," he said. "You guys here for the Introduction to Health and Wellness course for Police Foundations?"

"Yeah." Darius turned around to face him nonchalantly. "You're in the right place."

The man looked at them with a confused look. "Uhm… didn't you guys hear that we were supposed to meet up at the track for initial cardio testing before coming here?"

೫୦୯୫

As quickly as they heard the news, Annetta and Darius found themselves racing towards the track. Despite their best efforts to be on time, the duo made it with only bare minutes to spare.

"Severio and Silver, I presume." An older man with a balding pate and short-cropped blond greying hair stared down the two of them from behind his clipboard. "Nice of you to join us ladies. Did you pick up coffee for the rest of the class?"

Darius stood with his mouth slightly open as if to say something, but it was Annetta who chimed in. "If we'd known yesterday, then it wouldn't have been a problem. Did you see the lineup?"

A few of the students that stood around the instructor snickered, though not loudly. The instructor's mouth did not so much as twitch at the words, and his steel grey eyes seemed to bore holes into them. "Cute, Severio, but in this class I won't tolerate mouthing off. Now get in line with the others. We're going over the obstacle course once everyone changes and you will be timed."

Annetta didn't protest and did as she was told. She watched out of the corner of her eye as Darius followed behind her.

"While most of class will be done in your gym equipment you are expected to come in full uniform to class. You will also be marked on the state of your uniform." The instructor continued as he walked down the line and paused in front of Annetta. "Those shoes better be shined tomorrow Severio or I will take off marks."

While she didn't show it, Annetta groaned internally. Just what had she thought she was getting herself into when she decided to take this course? It had seemed ideal at the time, with what all of her experience fighting on a battlefield. She had forgotten one key fact, however, when she had been filling out her applications, and it was that despite all her prowess, she would be forced to take orders just like any other soldier.

೫୦୯୫

"Why didn't you mention anything about the shoes?" Annetta groaned at Darius at the end of the day after having endured three classes in which she had been forced to do twenty push-ups each when the instructors had seen the state of her boots. Her arms burned in protest as she pushed open the last set of doors to get out of the main campus building.

"Honestly? I thought you had read the orientation material about uniform presentation," he replied, fumbling in his pocket to get his car keys.

"If you don't recall, I was unconscious. A quick-notes version would have been appreciated," she grumbled.

Darius couldn't help but chuckle. "Come on, Anne, you've been fighting intergalactic threats and training with weapons for three years, and you're sore over a few push-ups? The world really is doomed if you're its defender."

"Can it," she fumed. "Next time I'm not saying anything so you can do them with me."

"Aw, was that why you mouthed off? My hero." He gave a mocking smile, then laughed when he saw Annetta's face begin to turn slightly red. He then remembered what Puc had told him about setting Annetta off by accident and stopped immediately. "Sorry, I shouldn't have said anything just now."

Annetta cocked her head to the side in confusion and when she realized what it was that Darius meant, her own face turned sullen. "Right... don't remind me."

They walked in silence until reaching the car. It was the same dastardly-looking black beast that Puc had insisted on driving around while masquerading as Jason's uncle a few years back when they had gone to visit Jason's father in the mental health institution. The rectangular angles of the vehicle aged it greatly in comparison to the other cars in the parking lot, and the roar of the engine whenever Darius turned the key didn't hide it any better. It was all in all, the opposite of subtle.

"I'm sorry I brought it up, Anne," Darius spoke again finally once he had cleared the parking lot and was in the process of turning onto the main road.

"It's fine, and I think I'm starting to get used to people walking around me like they're on eggshells." She gave a half-hearted smile in response. "Even if it's annoying. Sometimes I wish I could just forget."

Darius pondered for a bit before switching lanes. "So let's do that. Why don't we see if J.K. and Sarina wanna go out to see a movie or something? You know, like how we used to."

They drove on in silence for another few minutes, Annetta watching them pass by the suburbs which were close to the college. After some thought on the subject, she shifted in her seat to look at him. "That doesn't sound half bad."

"Great, so you give them a call and organize things, and I'll be back at your place by six-thirty?"

"Where do you have to go now?" She furrowed her brows.

"There's something I promised Puc I would see to," he replied.

She shook her head with a grin at this. "Passed all your exams, made a full mage and yet you're still doing what he tells you to."

Darius glanced over briefly at her. "Hey now, Puc is First Mage of Aldamoor. That's like the Pope and Prime Minister all rolled into one."

"Yeah I get it, but I can still find it funny." She smirked.

Darius then pulled into the driveway of the Severio residence, the small two-story house greeting both of them in the shade of a lush maple tree. Annetta took the reversing of the gears as her cue to leave and opened the door while Darius still had his foot on the brakes.

"See you in a bit, then," she said.

Darius gave her a nod and once she shut the door behind her, he reversed out of the parking lot. Annetta then stood watching as the black car sped away. She sighed and looked down at her boots, knowing what she would be doing until it was time to leave.

ഇരു

By the time Matthias reached Earth's atmosphere, the ship was running completely on fumes. He threw his telekinetic abilities into the very design of the machine, keeping the pieces all running together and hoping he'd be able to make a landing. He was certain if he let go of his concentration for even a second, it could spell the end of the small ship. Going down in flames was not how he wished to die.

Sweat trickled down his brow, matting his hair against his skull as azure eyes strained looking out the windows while clouds parted before him. His gauntlet-clad fingers were pressed into the navigation points on the glass panel surface. Any more pressure, and he was almost certain it would shatter, but the multitasking of keeping the ship together and running versus worrying about the navigation table took priority.

Finally, the last of the clouds vanished and Matthias was presented with a nighttime landscape that was… well, it had been covered with grass a few years ago. His panic increased when Matthias found that he was headed directly for a slumbering construction site.

"Unknown's bane! Like I need this right now." He gritted his teeth.

Matthias searched for options, but found none and decided to take the only logical course. Abandon ship. He grabbed the few books and scrolls that he'd taken with him. He then quickly searched the window for an unoccupied area of land and teleported from the ship.

Mere seconds later, the vessel collided with the machinery and torn the earth. The blazing ship mixed with the fossil fuels from the construction vehicles, and an explosion ruptured forth. Matthias's knees buckled as he was blown back onto a patch of tall grasses that had been untouched. Clutching the scrolls and books to his chest, he watched in horror as the site went up in flames.

He opened up his C.T.S. and promptly dialed the only number that made sense.

"05 here." Puc's voice came through the device.

"09 here…" Matthias breathed heavily. "I'm gonna need a cleanup crew where I'm at, and you might wanna make it fast."

He then punched in another number and fell back into the grass with exhaustion, lifting his wrist up to his face. "I've sent coordinates. 09 out."

He then shut the C.T.S. and letting his arm drop he, allowed the flames burning in the distance illuminate the world around him. He only hoped that there were no authorities in the area before help arrived.

഼഼

Darius pulled into the parking lot of the apartment building he had been staying at these past few weeks. Sure enough, as he had predicted, Jansen stood at the bus stop waiting patiently for the public transit vehicle that would whisk her off to her next destination. He couldn't exactly pin what it was about her, but there was something that drew him to her. Perhaps this was what Lysania had meant when she had told him and Puc that he would just know when he met the person he was seeking. His suspicions had only been confirmed after her admitting what it was that her book she was writing was about. It couldn't be a coincidence, and he had to know more.

He stepped out of the car and shutting the door behind him, Darius leaned against the trunk, watching as a bus came into view. He then closed his eyes and visualized the words of the incantation he had committed to memory. He muttered the words under his breath and opened his eyes upon hearing an enraged Jansen.

"Aw man! You have got to be kidding me!" she groaned as the bus sped by her, a sign that showed in glowing orange letters 'Out of Service.'

Darius took this as his cue. "Jansen?"

She whirled around at hearing him, her blonde hair spilling out of her crochet hat. Confused, she surveyed the scene until her eyes met his. She hugged the laptop bag that she'd been holding in her hands tighter, but remembering that she was waiting for a bus, she stood still in her spot.

A small smile formed on Darius's lips. "Where you off to?"

"Work," she said without any hesitation. "They asked me to do an evening shift, but when it's dead they let me have my laptop in the back for breaks to write."

"Pretty accommodating of them." He nodded. "You need a lift? I'm guessing that bus that just passed was the one you were waiting for."

"I thought so, too, but I guess not." She frowned. "Are you headed in that direction?"

"I'm meeting with friends for a movie, it's along the way," he replied.

With some reluctance, Jansen began placing one foot in front of the other as she made her way towards him and the car. Darius slid around the side, opened his door and hopped into the driver's seat. The door beside him opened and he was joined by Jansen, who promptly put on her seatbelt.

"I should really start paying you for gas the number of times that you've already rescued me from irregular public transit," she mused.

Darius turned on the ignition and began to reverse out. "Honestly, I wouldn't feel right about it. It's literally right on the way. I'd have to stop at a set of lights sooner or later."

Jansen nodded and the two of them drove in silence for a little while, passing by an urbanized landscape. Telephone poles, buildings and trees blurred by them, only coming into focus whenever they stopped.

"Maybe I could grab you coffee, then, or something. Do you drink coffee?" Jansen's voice rang again out of Darius's periphery.

"I mean, I have an idea, but I don't know if you'd be up to it," he confessed, coming to a stop at a set of red lights.

"Oh, and what's that?"

"How about we go out for a coffee together?" he asked.

The young woman shifted beside him as if a little uncomfortable, and Darius realized seconds later how the question had come out.

"I mean…" He ran a hand through his hair. "I meant as two people just wanting to get to know one another."

"Isn't that technically a first date?" Jansen cocked her head to look at his.

Darius sighed and shook his head. He'd buried himself into a hole. "If looked at from that perspective, but I didn't mean it that way. You seem like an interesting person, and I don't know many people outside my circle of friends. I wouldn't mind just going out to a coffee shop to hang out. You seem really interesting. I've never met a writer before."

Silence prevailed yet again as they drove. Darius cursed himself inwardly for having said anything about meeting up. He could have just as easily asked her to go and hang out with him, Annetta, Jason and Sarina. Right after that thought, it occurred to him, however, that none of them were supposed to know about the nature of his mission.

"When you put it that way, it doesn't sound half bad," Jansen answered as they finally pulled into the parking lot of the mall. "I wouldn't mind getting to know you, too."

Darius glanced over at Jansen as she unbuckled her seatbelt. She looked up to meet his eyes with her own, green orbs dancing in mischief. He gave her a tight-lipped smile, trying to remain looking cool.

"Great, when's your next shift?" he asked.

"Tomorrow, but I don't work the next three days after," she said as she opened the door and as gently as she could, she closed it.

"After tomorrow at six-thirty?" Darius shifted his gears into drive.

"Sounds good to me." She smiled and closing the door behind her, left with a smile.

Darius watched her until she was out of his line of sight. While part of him didn't approve at what he was doing, deeper still, he knew if the Sister of Wyrd had taken an interest in Jansen then he had to obey them. She could be in great danger, the kind that neither he nor his friends could rescue her from. He reaffirmed this point in his mind with a nod to himself and then drove off towards his next destination.

Chapter 22

Frigid winds slammed against the stone walls of Stoneberg castle, the ancient stronghold of Minotaur kings. Despite the chill, fires roared inside, and the light of thousands of candles illuminated through the windows, making it seem as though each room were bursting at the seams with life and a joy that could stave off even the greatest of winter storms.

In reality, however, much of the castle was silent. The giants had been defeated, but at great cost. It was a cost so great that the minds of many wandered from their loyalties to the Four Forces.

Lord Snapneck found himself in the ranks of these who doubted. He sat at the foot of his throne as he once had when he was younger and his father had held court. In his great clawed hands, he examined the crown inlaid with blue gems, the crown he had inherited from his father, Lord Ironhorn, or as he should have been known, King Ironhorn. Why did the kings of Aerim not use their full titles? His father had never explained that to him. He never would now that he was dead. Sure, Snapneck had advisors, other Minotaur elders who could educate him, but it would never be the same, it hadn't been. The part that was his father would forever be missing, and he was beginning to understand why.

Since he had met her, Snapneck had believed that Annetta Severio and Jason Kinsman, along with the Four Forces, were the saviours of all worlds, and that he could depend on them in his time of need. Now he was beginning to see the truth of it, the great lie. Annetta Severio and her companions didn't care for the Four Forces, they just used them, like a hammer which pounded steel. His father would have been alive were it not for Annetta's will to go to planet Gaia, her home planet, to liberate it. It was Annetta also that had changed into the great beast that had obliterated nearly half his army because they had been in the way. The flesh on his mighty hands dug into the metal of the crown as such thoughts continued to seep in. She was no saviour of his or his people as he had thought, she was a fraud.

"My lord." A thin voice came from the doorway.

Snapneck looked up to see a female minotaur servant dressed in the customary blue tunic of his house. "Yes? Speak."

"There is a traveler, a flatfooter male that wishes to see you."

His blue eyes were red-rimmed from lack of sleep, but Snapneck still stood up from where he sat and placed the crown on his brow, then turned to ascend to the throne. "Did he say who sent him? If he's sent by Annetta, then I want him dead."

"I come not of this Annetta you speak of."

Snapneck spun around as he reached the top of the stairs to see a man in a patchwork hide jacket of different shades of tan and brown standing a few feet behind the servant. His square jaw was covered in blond stubble and deep blue eyes glared at Snapneck in defiance of the respect a monarch should have. The king dismissed her with a nod of his head, to which she scurried out, leaving the two of them alone. He seated himself on the throne, looking down at the man. He seemed ordinary, and yet at the same time, not. Snapneck could not remember ever seeing a man enter Aerim and not be bundled up from head to toe due to the cold, yet this man's chest was fully exposed underneath the jacket, and he wore no boots.

"Then where do you come from and for what purpose?" Snapneck's nostrils flared as he observed him.

The man ignored Snapneck as he walked around the room with a sureness that would have unnerved most. He ran his hand down the side of the wall as if he were reverently absorbing the entire history the room had ever seen. Snapneck shifted uncomfortably on his throne.

"Where I come from really has very little relevance," the man admitted. "I was but a simple farmer once, trying to get by. I worked hard and I loved fiercely, but then the Unknown saw it fit to place the weight of the world on my shoulders. Sounds like something this Annetta has done to you."

"My quarrel with the Severio woman is of no concern to you," Snapneck spat.

The man raised his hand into the air, his index finger pointed skyward, but was barely focused on Snapneck. "Ah, but you see, she is a concern of mine. I recently learned that she's responsible for having hurt my wife."

"Wife?" Snapneck tilted his head in curiosity.

"Yes, the Lady Tamora," he stated as he continued to assess of the room. "You may remember her from the battle on Edran."

The battle flashed before Snapneck's eyes as he pictured it all crystal clear in his mind. It was the battle that had kept him from having been at his father's side when he had met his end at the hands of the one they had called Razmus. Despite the rage building in his muscles, he did his best to remain calm.

Snapneck leaned back in the throne, stretching his bulk to its full height. "And what makes you so sure that I would betray Annetta Severio and the Four Forces?"

The man then finally turned his full attention to Snapneck. His blue eyes seemed to be void of something that the Minotaur king could not exactly pinpoint, which made his skin crawl. It was as though they held no soul.

"I can offer you something Annetta Severio never could," he said. "I can offer you peace."

છ૦ભ

Venetor Severio found himself immensely bored as he forced himself to stay awake during the latest Federation meeting. The Greys were particularly lengthy in their droning this day, and it made him remember just why it was that he'd never wanted to be king in the first place. His jaw muscles twitched as he did his best to suppress a yawn without opening his mouth. He was a warrior, not a bureaucrat.

"The next order of business is the disappearance of life on the natural reserve planet Galecto Kelper Twenty-Three…"

At hearing this, Venetor focused back on the conversation, his gaze turned slightly to the right, where Gladius stood unmoving. He raised an eyebrow to the Hurtz, silently asking him if he had not overheard what was being said. Gladius bobbed his head slightly in reply and Venetor turned back his attention fully to the Grey speaking below.

"While at first it was believed to be only a band of poachers having taken interest in the rare horned gazelle which inhabited the planet, reports are coming in that several other planets now too are showing a lack of life forms on them as well, these not being reserves of any kind. As these are planets which held no sentient beings, this item is not being held as a priority on the agenda for this meeting, and will be scheduled for the following general meeting to be held in a week's time."

Venetor couldn't believe his ears at hearing this. He looked around him at the various balconies on which other representatives of species within the Federation sat or stood listening to what was being said. As far as he could tell, many of them were void of any emotion on the subject, their eyes glazed over from the continuous monotone speech, with only the odd balcony-dwellers seeming to register anything dimly resembling worry that the topic was being dropped so lightly.

He took this as his opening to do something, and strode towards the control panel on the far side of the balcony which faced outward towards the masses. Placing a hand on the touchscreen, he activated a holographic live feed of himself, and then spoke. "I would prefer not to leave this unattended for so long. When was it that these reports first started coming in?"

The Grey at the front seemed offended and looked back to the wall where the Federation banner hung to see a hologram of Venetor's projection hover before it. He then turned back to face outwards. "The reports of Galecto Kelper Twenty-Three were received a few days ago, and were followed by five other smaller natural habitat planets. These, of course, have no correlation to the ten destroyed stars that were discovered just weeks before that."

Venetor's eyes widened at hearing this. "Ten destroyed stars, and you didn't think this was significant enough to even mention at a meeting of the Intergalactic Federation? Then what in the Unknown's bane are we here for?"

The eyes of all those present shot in Venetor's direction. The Gaian king felt their tension resonate on him like the heat of a burn on skin. The floor was his, and he knew what he was going to do with it.

Venetor inhaled deeply and felt the tension build in his chest. His blue eyes looked out over the balcony at all who would hear his words. "For too long have I watched as those who need our aid have been neglected. A planet is made void of life and we are told nothing of it? Ten stars have been destroyed and no one failed to mention it? Is this what our system of government has fallen to? Let it be known that I, Venetor Severio, king of Gaia, do submit my planet's name in the forthcoming election. Let it be known that I, as well as the rest of Gaia will not stand for such withholding of information."

He chose the last of his words deliberately and made sure to focus on the Greys when he spoke them. Turning around, he then sat on the plush sofa that rimmed the balcony and watched as the seeds of discontent he had just sown began to grow.

It hadn't taken Puc long to locate Matthias once he had contacted him. The C.T.S. was easily trackable by Dexter, and so it had taken the A.I. mere moments to project a map with coordinates to the mage. The trickier part had been, of course, getting Matthias out and making sure there was no trace of his ship to be found in the wreckage before any of the local authorities came. He'd been lucky that despite the construction, he had landed in the middle of nowhere, and the nearest town with law enforcement was still a good twenty minutes away. By the time they arrived with the fire department, all that was left were some smoldering construction vehicles that had been ignited by some unruly youth with firecrackers. Matthias, on the other hand, was once again thousands of miles away under the Atlantic Ocean within the confines of Q-16, debriefing the First Mage of Aldamoor.

They were in Puc's quarters, which, despite the mage spending most of his time in Aldamoor now, had remained unchanged. Stacks of scrolls and books lined the shelves behind the large wooden desk in the centre. On the desk, a dozen red candles were lit, flickering from the movements on the room's occupants. The slow and steady swing of a pendulum could be heard coming from the grandfather clock. Where candles and wax did not touch it, the desk was littered with various open scrolls and books, on top of these the most prominent being the one Matthias had brought with him of his parents' notes.

"In truth, I would not have believed it had I not seen it myself," Puc concluded as he gazed down at the open tome. "And part of me still resists believing this as true."

"If what's written in here is true and Amarok opened the portal, then we have a serious issue on our hands." Matthias sat hunched over the writing, with his hands folded under his chin. "And if I can be blunt, then it's one I don't think either the Four Forces or the kids are ready to handle."

Puc stood from his seat and strode over to the shelf farthest from his desk. He then removed a particularly tarnished-looking tome, carefully dusted it off and placed in on the desk to reveal its cover to Matthias.

The assassin narrowed his eyes at seeing it. He could recognize that emblem anywhere, having seen it plastered on every tabard, banner and shield since his youth. The seven-headed black beast that had been Mislantus's coat of arms.

"There are only a handful of scholars who know the true origin of Korangar." Puc glanced up at him. "Only those with access to the library of the Sisters of Wyrd have ever lain eyes on this book, or had a copy in their possession. As First Mage, I am privileged to the latter."

He flipped open the text to a random set of pages, one of which was covered with undecipherable script, while the other held the intricate drawing of a man's portrait. There was nothing extraordinary about him. He had short neat hair, was clean shaven, and had light-coloured eyes, if the black and white shading was any indication.

"Korangar was once no different than any living being," Puc began. "He was, in fact, a Gaian farmer with no great ambitions in life other than to marry the woman he loved and start a family of his own. He loved his land, his king and his people."

The mage then turned the page of the tome to reveal more writing and another image beside it. The one depicted the same man kneeling before two beings clad in celestial robes. One had long flowing hair that was highlighted in red pencil, while the other had short hair that was spiked. They seemed to be placing something within the back of the man that looked like a blinding light.

"One day, the angels came proclaiming that they had isolated the root of Khaos, evil as it were within the multiverse, but there was one catch, they needed a host to cage it within," Puc continued. "The only way it could be housed was to have a host that was yet untainted by Khaos's power. It was then that a Gaian named Freius volunteered his son, knowing he did so for the good of the people."

"Wait, I thought Korangar was enslaved by Freius," Matthias interrupted.

"Oh, he was." Puc's pale eyes gazed at the assassin. "But what most texts neglect to say is that he was enslaved by him twice, once to become the vessel of everything that led to the end, and second when his father realized that he had both doomed and saved his people. For while he had found a vessel for evil to be encased, he had also given it a way to walk all worlds and destroy them."

The assassin looked more intently at the mage this time. Though tired and worn by the journey, Matthias pulled all of his focus into absorbing the words Puc said. The mage continued.

"Korangar became so consumed with the aspects of evil within him that he was no longer able to discern right from wrong. It was in this state that Freius made up his mind, to commit Korangar to his prison on a planet far from anyone's reach. He, as any other Gaian, did not have the heart to kill his own son, and was unsure if doing so would just pass on the burden, and decided to imprison him where he would do the least damage."

The page turned yet again to reveal the drawing of a cloudy nebula, the shading on the page so detailed that it looked as though it were a photograph. Matthias reached out to touch it. It was familiar to him.

"I remember seeing this in my father's collection," he confessed after having combed his memory. "My mother and he would study it almost every night, looking for any anomalies or changes that had occurred within it, as though they were terrified of someone breaking it. Before Amarok left after I confronted him on my home planet's surface, he said that only a Teron's blood held the key, or something to that effect."

Puc nodded thoughtfully. He felt the weight of his years settle on his shoulders as he pieced all of the facts together. "Whatever you do, do not relay any of this to Annetta, Jason or Sarina just yet. We have had our own slew of calamities in your absence."

৪৩৪৩

Annetta, Jason and Sarina all waited outside of the theatre as they watched the awkwardly large rectangular car pull over the last of the speed bumps and into the parking lot. All three of them knew it was Darius, and Jason could only stifle a chuckle while Sarina poked him in the ribs as he found a place to park.

They watched as Darius got out of the car, dressed in a black pullover hoodie with dark jeans, and ran a hand through his short hair as though he were checking to make sure it was all in place. He then locked the car and made his way over to them.

"Hey guys, sorry I'm late," he greeted them.

"No worries." Jason shook his head. "Puc give you a lecture about how if you scratched his baby then he'd turn you into something unnatural?"

"Something along those lines." Darius stifled a laugh. "Did you guys manage to pick out a movie yet?"

"We tried but it's been so long since any of us have been in the theatre." Annetta pursed her lips. "We actually didn't know what's what."

Darius formed his face into an 'oh' as he came closer and looked past his friends. Thick plastic walls guarded a variety of posters as he walked by them, inspecting the row thoroughly.

He then finally paused beside a poster of what looked to be the silhouette of a young woman. She carried in her hands a sword as well as a gun. In the background behind her was a desolated landscape.

While it was not their normal flick in terms of theme, Darius found himself spinning on his heel and turning to face them regardless.

"How about this one?" he asked.

The trio frowned, inspecting every aspect of the poster. It was not like a novel where one could read the synopsis to determine what the film was about. Not without access to the internet then and there.

"Could be interesting," Jason finally said. "Why not?"

Sarina and Annetta agreed, exchanging nods with the boys. Standing in front of the movie theatre reminded Annetta of the time they had taken Link to go see a movie with them. She remembered the curse Link had placed on him that gave him the crescent moon scar and also remembered how fiercely Darius had fought to protect her, thinking Link was a threat sent from Mistlantus. She smiled to herself as she spaced out further. Link, or Lincerious as he had been later introduced to her, was one of the most truthful people she had ever met. He would never had gone out of his way to work for the enemy.

"Right, I guess that settles it." Jason's voice cut through her thoughts. "You coming, Anne?"

Annetta's eyes focused on her surroundings again to see Darius holding the door of the theatre open for them, Sarina nowhere in sight and Jason standing close to the door. She felt herself flush red.

"Right, sorry." She muttered and walked in, hands in her leather jacket pockets. It had been the first time in a while that she'd had a chance to wear it without worry of boiling to death in the summer sun.

Purchasing their tickets, the group then made their way to the designated theatre located on the lower floor and settling into the seats they picked, waited for the screen to go dark and hold them in thrall.

ℴ∞ℚ

"Man, was I the only one who had that ending go over their heads?" Jason said as they got onto the escalator leading up while the rest of the people they had been with dispersed after the showing like ants.

"It was a cliff hanger, they're clearly setting it up so that it can be made into a sequel," Darius explained.

While the two boys spoke, Annetta found herself dwelling on the protagonist of the film. She'd been a soldier who had been thrown through a portal that had been discovered in an ancient temple into the past. There, she had not only become involved in a series of battles, but also fell in love with one of the soldiers she fights alongside. At the end of the film, however, he dies saving her. She returned to the future, but the final shot implies that she's pregnant with the man's child. Her brows furrowed as the escalator pulled them up, the scene of the man dying in the woman's arms prominent at the forefront of her mind. What would watching Link die have been like? She envied the woman in some ways for having been able to say goodbye to the man in the film.

"Hey, Annetta." Sarina touched her arm gently.

"Oh, sorry." Annetta blinked a few times. "I was just thinking about the movie and uhm…"

She bit her lip, how exactly did she broach the subject to someone else about what she was going through? It seemed an impossible thought that any of her friends would understand.

"You're thinking about Link, aren't you?" Sarina read her thoughts as though they had been written on her face.

A feeling of being made completely vulnerable filled Annetta. "Yeah… that scene in the movie just made me think what if…"

Before she could continue, they reached the top of the stairs and saw that the doors were being crowded around. People were taking photos with cameras and pointing at the sky. Annetta looked over at her three friends, whose eyes were just as wide as her own and they rushed to the door, half expecting to see a spaceship.

"Snow in September?" Jason blurted out when they got closer.

Sarina turned to glance at him. "It's not unheard of in Ontario, is it?"

Darius raised his head to try and see above the crowd. "No, just not common."

People chatted amongst one another and a few were outdoors trying to catch the tiny flakes that fell from the sky. Annetta couldn't discern what was so strange, why everyone seemed on edge. Not until she looked at the ground and saw the colour it had turned. Not thinking twice or about what her friends would say, she stepped outside and placed her hand, palm up out. She watched as a single flake came to rest in the centre of her palm. Closing her hand, she opened it again to reveal a black smudge where the flake of ash had landed.

Chapter 23

Venetor felt the water trickle down his face as he looked up into the mirror. His breathing was still heavy from his sparring against Atala, who had agreed to a match with him, though he felt she was holding back ever since his coronation. He could always tell it when he faced someone, there was a block in their eyes which prevented the fire from fully coming through. Annetta had not had such a block, the girl had always attacked with everything she had, determined to beat him. He missed it. He missed her too. She had been a breath of fresh air in the palace after the events of the battle against Razmus. Her curiosity about Gaia and its people was comparable to that of a small child asking questions of their parent. It had taken his mind off the other matters at hand, but she was gone now.

Venetor left his washroom and strode over to where a fresh set of Gaian armour had been left out for him. He changed into it quickly, feeling the beta scale mail cling to his body like a second skin, moulding to his shape. He then put on the looser black pants that went overtop the lower section of it, and the high black boots. Finally, he fastened the thick belt and pinned the red cloak to his left shoulder. He was about to stride out to go to his meeting when he realized he was forgetting something.

He turned around and was forced to acknowledge the presence of the crown at the far end of the room. The helm-like headpiece sat on his desk, collecting the rays of the sun through an open window which caused the gems on it to glow as if alive with firelight. He hated the thing, it was so heavy to wear. To him, the crown was a representation of all the things he had never expected to have nor wanted. In truth, Venetor had never forgiven Orbeyus for abandoning him to it.

"It should have been yours, brother, along with all the problems that come with it." He sighed, and using his telekinetic abilities, he watched as it floated over to him and rested on his head.

He was never meant to be king, he had been a second son, and all too many times Venetor had wondered how his life would have turned out if Orbeyus hadn't gone to Earth to find Severio Castle and to found the Four Forces. He often pictured himself as a decorated warrior, standing beside his brother's throne, the general of the Gaian forces, the Ironfisted. For his whole childhood, that had been his dream, until the day at the beach where Orbeyus had taken that dream from him and left him a kingdom instead.

Venetor knew he had no more time to waste, and left the room to be greeted by Gladius outside his door. The one-eyed Hurtz bowed and followed after him once he'd cleared the doorway.

"You don't have to follow me around like this anymore, Gladius," Venetor reminded him. "You're a free Hurtz now, a lord, in fact."

"I might be a lord, yer grace, but I am and will always be your friend first," the Hurtz informed him. "We've been through far too much for it to be any other way."

Venetor didn't turn to say anything, but smiled to himself. He cleared that emotion from his visage before he stepped through the door leading into the throne room where he was to have his audience. The two dark wooden doors had no guards before them, and Venetor parted them with his abilities.

As they opened, he saw that the room was mostly empty save for a few lords dressed in their finery of lavish and colourful suits and gowns. Beside the throne, Atala stood, looking as haughty as ever. She had a way of making people feel inferior in her presence, and Venetor could practically feel that energy vibrating off her now as she looked down at those gathered. Were it not inappropriate, he would have chuckled at the scene. The sight reminded him of a lion terrorizing mice.

Venetor seated himself on the throne and got a good look at those gathered before him. "My lords and ladies, I hear you have want of my attention this morning."

There was unease among those gathered as they looked at one another. Finally, a small older woman who found herself at the front summoned the courage to speak.

"Our meeting here today," she began. "Concerns the line of succession of the Severio bloodline."

Venetor's brown furrowed at hearing this and the Gaian king stood, walking down two steps, closing in on those gathered. "And what exactly is it that you find yourselves so concerned with?"

"Well, my lord, ever since you took power," a young lord this time spoke, "it has always been assumed that should you pass and he prove true to his vows, Prince Titus would ascend to the throne should the people find him worthy of such. If the rumours are to be believed, however, then…"

Though not the tallest of stature, Venetor's presence filled the room as he descended the stairs, crimson cloak trailing behind him. A tension filled his muscles and threatened to burst into fighting, but he did his best to suppress it. His burning blue eyes that bore into each noble there, however, were a different matter entirely.

"And what is it exactly that you feel you need to worry about? I am in perfectly good health, as is my son Titus, as well," he managed to say through gritted teeth.

The same lord who had spoken before and now found himself but mere feet away from Venetor swallowed hard as he did his best to try and loosen the high collar of his suit jacket. "Well, my lord, you see, no one has seen the Crown Prince for some time and... rumours have begun to spread. We need to know what your backup is in the case of an emergency."

"Rumors and nothing more." Venetor glared at those gathered. He then turned back to make his ascent towards the throne. Once at the top, he veered around to regard them once again, his cape swirling around him like fire. "Though if succession for House Severio is what you fear so much, then you should know who the next of line would be and has always been."

"Lady Skyris?" the woman who had spoken first asked.

The Gaian king shook his head and seated himself, looking down at the crowd below. "No, my fellow nobles. The choice in this matter is far more obvious than that. It is the only choice since its revelation that would ever make sense. The White Lioness of Gaia would be your queen."

As soon as the words passed his lips, those below began to mutter among themselves, which soon escalated into angered vocalizations of their own opinions on the matter. Venetor steeled his ears against it and prepared. He also hoped no rumour of the dragon incident had somehow managed to spread.

"A child raised on Earth?" A young nobleman with shaggy blond hair and a hawk-like nose raised an eyebrow.

"The prophesized saviour of Gaia," he reminded them. "There will come a day when a world split in two will cry out for the white lion to rise anew. Those words do not necessarily mean just in that moment of crisis. No, so long as Annetta Severio draws breath, she would risk her life and position for this world. Though young and not raised here, she understands what it means to be a Gaian far better than some who would call themselves natives."

This seemed to quiet those gathered for a short while until the same youth spoke out again. "Is it true then also what they say about you running for Gaia to become Head of the Federation?"

All eyes fell to Venetor. He felt the muscles in his back stiffen as he attempted to sit up straighter on the throne.

"It is true," he confirmed. "I have every intention to run for and have Gaia become Head of the Federation. For too long have we had to take orders from the Greys and be unable to give aid where it is needed. I say it is time we change all of that. Gaians are a warrior race, we are made to fight, and we are also made to protect those who cannot do so for themselves. That sacred right was taken from us when the Greys barred us from going to assist Earth, our sister planet, in their time of need against Mislantus the Threat. I for one never again want to look my niece in the face and tell her that we couldn't help. This is not who we are. It is time we retake our place as the flame of justice against the dark in this universe."

The speech had stirred a sense of patriotism in those gathered as they clapped their hands. Some of those present even had hints of tears glistening in the corners of their eyes. Venetor decided to deliver the killing blow.

"Gaia has not yet fallen. What they have taken from us, we will win back with blades in hand."

೮೦೧೪

The kettle hissed wildly on the mantle as Arieus reached over and turned the dial on the stove off with a defined click. He then poured the water into the set of mugs that he'd put out for the youth which were currently convened at the kitchen table. Annetta, Darius, Jason and Sarina all wore expressions of worry as they sat hunched over without speaking. From the living room beside the kitchen, the television could be heard blaring the news as a reporter gave the latest details on the ash that had been falling from the sky for the past hour and had subsided suddenly.

"They keep saying it's from that explosion at the steel mill downtown, but I don't buy it." Darius wrinkled his nose as he looked over at the TV. "Ash doesn't stay airborne long enough to travel that far, not from something like that."

Aurora, who sat transfixed on the couch in front of the television turned to look at them. "No, you're right, it wouldn't, but the general public won't know that and buy into it. They'll use anything to prevent panic from spreading."

Arieus placed the mugs with steeped tea in front of the teenagers before looking over at the television where footage of the ash was shown as it trickled down from the sky. "The question remains, however, if a steel mill isn't the culprit, then what actually caused the ash and is it something we should be concerned about?"

Another bout of silence followed. The report drew to an end and the scene on the television then cut to a battle that was being fought somewhere else in the world.

"I don't get it." Jason chimed in. "How can they just keep fighting like that among one another?"

"Simple, actually," Sarina interjected, lowering the cup from her lips. "They've never been confronted by a force that was beyond their fellow man."

"What's that supposed to mean?" Annetta raised an eyebrow.

"Aliens, duh." Jason blew on his tea and took a sip. "Though if I gotta be honest, I'm pretty sure people meeting them in the here and now would probably flip, and not in a good way."

"Why? I mean, if they aren't trying to invade you, that is." Sarina looked over at him.

"Humans have a tendency to shoot first and ask questions later." Darius stated. "Not everyone, but all it really takes is one idiot with a gun."

Arieus turned his attention from the television. "Darius is right. There are a lot of people who have aggressive reactions to the unexpected, and all it takes is one person to create a lot of miscommunication, panic and fear. That's why the angels are so strict with which planets know about the existence of magic and alien worlds. Until a world is ready for such a revelation, it's generally best to keep it in the dark, so to speak."

"I don't think Earth is ever gonna be ready, to be honest ." Jason rolled his eyes, looking at the screen, and then turned back to his mug.

The television turned back to the footage of the ash falling from the sky and the fire at the steel mill where firefighters frantically worked to keep it under control. The more Annetta looked at the screen, the more difficult she found it to believe. Her gut told her there had to be more to it. She gripped the sides of the mug she held tighter, feeling the heat seep into her fingertips.

"Dad." She looked over at her father. "When J.K. and I first went down to the Lab, you said something about external forces that didn't want to make their presence known to humans. Could this be one of those? Like the unicorns who have learned to hide their horns?"

Arieus pondered the words. "Honestly, I don't know Anne, I can't recall a creature who could create ash like this. It's beyond me."

"There is mention of ash falling from the sky heralding the arrival of the end in ancient human texts," Sarina thought out loud.

A shiver passed through Annetta's back. "You mean the end of the world?"

"Human texts." Aurora rose from her seat and walked over to the table. "But if you read the texts pertaining to the teachings of the Unknown, then you'd also know that only the Unknown itself knows when a planet's time has come, and not all planets are meant to end at once."

Arieus nodded. "It's true, and some scholars have even argued that's why sister planets exist, so that one can come to the aid of the other in their time of need."

Jason finished the contents of his mug and then placed it down gingerly. "Somehow I get the feeling Gaia won't be making any rescue efforts if Earth needed them. The Greys didn't let them come to help against Mislantus, and I'm pretty sure they wouldn't now."

Annetta decided it best not to mention anything about Venetor's plans with the Federation. She also thought it best not to defend her uncle as to why he hadn't showed up at the time, even if it wasn't Gaia's fault. The Greys had been petty, expecting help when others needed them more and held a grudge against Gaia because of it. Instead, her eyes focused on both of her parents. They seemed older somehow, almost as old as Venetor himself, if not slightly more, while Skyris, on the other hand, seemed much younger than him. A strange thought then occurred to her. "Hey... this is going to sound awkward but... mom, dad, how old are you, really?"

Arieus looked over at Aurora and the two of them seemed to beam a strange sort of smile as though they were about to laugh at some inside joke. They then turned back to face the youth. "You mean because of the way Gaians age? Well, we're much younger than we appear... in fact..."

He lifted his hand where his wedding band was, a smooth silver piece with no etchings or markings on it and removed it.

Her eyes widened from shock as Annetta watched her father transform before her eyes, the grey completely fading from his hair and his laugh lines smoothing out. Her mother too seemed to de-age when she removed her ring. When the process was finished, they both looked no older than Skyris, perhaps even a little younger than her. Annetta had never been good with knowing how old people were.

"Whoa! What?" Jason's eyes widened.

Arieus looked at the ring as he raised it before the youth. "Puc had these made for any Gaians who chose to stay on Earth, such as myself, Aurora, Talia and Arcanthur. They make us appear to age at the same pace as normal humans. We have to be careful, though, and remember to keep them on at all times, and if not, then there's a potion we take before removing them that will keep the illusion going."

"What happens when you'd both get really old? Gaians can live up to three hundred years." Annetta furrowed her brows.

"We would need to move and get new identities, but that won't need to happen for a very long time," Aurora stated.

Annetta nodded, her eyes still wide from the revelation. Her parents slipped the rings back on, becoming their "old" selves as she had known them. Since meeting Venetor and learning about Gaians, she'd half suspected such a truth, but hadn't dared to ask. She hadn't been ready then for another change in her life, another false truth about her existence shattered. Her time on Gaia, though short, had changed that about her. Annetta then looked back to the screen where the news continued to loop through the same footage of war, the falling ash and weather reports in the area. She then recalled the words Puc had said to her not long ago. The world was always ending for someone, somewhere. She knew looking around the room, however, it would not end for anyone here today.

୨୦୧

Another day of political meetings having ended, Venetor found himself yet again in his chambers. He would have preferred another battle at the front gates with Ramzus over what he had to put up with some days.

He removed the crown from his head and made it float over to its place on the far table from him. It settled with a light metallic thud on the wood. He decided to keep the rest of his armour on and then left the chamber. He had one more stop that night.

The few guards that were on duty saluted as he passed, which he dismissed as quickly as they did so. He appreciated the gesture, but he was in a hurry.

Venetor then made his way down the stairs into the lower level of the castle. He could practically feel the air become chillier as he descended the stone steps, a sure sign that he was now underground. Here, there were no large windows to bring in the moonlight, only the lights that were installed.

When he reached his destination, Venetor paused before the pair of Hurtz guards who stood at least two heads higher than him and were at least double his size across the shoulders. Both had canine features, long, braided manes and were armed with halberds, in addition to the swords they carried at their belts. Their postured straightened when they saw Venetor approach.

"Krexus, Haroldus." He nodded to them. "At ease, soldiers."

The one on the left with large cat-like ears, Krexus, inclined his head. "Had we known ye were coming, my lord, we would have made sure to have more lights on down here, especially the stairs."

"There's no need for such trouble." Venetor shook his head.

Haroldus, the second Hurtz with twitching hare ears, flattened them against his skull. "Trouble? My lord, we'd have more trouble if ye'd trip, fall and break a bone or two."

A wiry smile lined Venetor's face, showing he was sincere in what he had said to the two guards. That smile then faded. "How has he been today?"

"Quieter than most days," Krexus stated. "Would you like to see him, my lord?"

He nodded and took a step back, watching as the two guards leaned their spears against the wall to begin the process of opening the double-doored room. Though it pained Venetor to do this, he knew at present there simply was no other way. Once opened, the Gaian king took a deep breath and entered.

The interior, to Venetor's surprise, was quite neat and organized. The large bed at the side was made, and there was no indication of anything having been upturned or destroyed. He then looked over to the other side. There, sitting at a desk with a lamp illuminating his face, was Titus.

In the time he had spent down in the room, Titus had completely foregone shaving, and his once neatly-trimmed sideburns were now blended with a scraggly beard that covered his face. Though he was not permitted any sharp objects in the room, he had been allowed to have a barber come in to attend him, and so the choice had been his own. His red-rimmed eyes were fixated on the papers he had, scrawling out something on them. His hands were a blur on the pages and Venetor wondered if he'd even be able to read what he was writing. More importantly, he wondered if his son would respond.

"Titus?" he asked in a quiet voice.

The scratching of the charcoal on paper stopped. Titus looked over at his father, studying him with those sleepless eyes of his, and Venetor gazed back, searching in them for his son.

The pause was long, drawn out and soon, Venetor found himself getting ready to turn and leave, the muscles beginning to coil in his legs to the physical response of the action he wanted them to perform.

His mind made up, he turned, only to hear a response. "It's good to see you too, father."

Venetor peered over his shoulder to see Titus fully focused on him. Relaxing a bit, he turned back.

"How are you feeling today?" he asked somewhat stiffly.

"Coherent." Titus swung his legs around on the chair and stood to face him.

Venetor noted the considerable amount of weight his son had lost as well. He had not been robust to begin with, but the looseness of his clothing was beginning to show it. Had he not been eating the food sent to him?

"Coherent is good." Venetor nodded. "Do you... do you remember anything from the days before?"

It was the same question Venetor always opened with when his son was feeling better. He felt like a broken record, but how else could it be possible to hope to gain some insight as to what was going through his head? He'd had doctors brought down in the past, both physical and psychological, but his condition to them was an enigma, and the closest they had come to concluding anything was that Titus was experiencing some form of schizophrenia. What had caused the random triggering of it, though, could not be explained, and they all tried to point to the battle against Razmus, but it seemed a poor excuse. Gaians were hardwired for fighting. It was in their blood. It was part of the bargain their ancestors had struck with the Unknown, according to legend. It was part of who they were as a people. The known worlds of the Federation knew that when a Gaian found themselves of a field of battle, the odds of the enemy winning diminished immensely.

"I'm sorry, father, but I don't." Titus shook his head. "I wish I had something more to tell you, but every time I'm in that state, it's like a haze."

Venetor nodded his head though he was still somewhat disappointed. He hoped, secretly, that one day the answer would be different.

Titus opened his mouth then as if to say something, but closed it immediately after. Instead, he reached under his desk, retrieved a spray can and, sprayed its contents over what he had been working on. He then got a sketchbook out from under the papers, got up, walked over to Venetor and handed it to him. "I've run out of room in this. I'm not quite sure what all of its contents possess, but maybe it can shed some light."

Venetor accepted the leather-bound book. It was another part of the scenario which repeated itself. Each time Titus was himself, he would present his father with a filled-up sketchbook. Venetor would then pass it along to his scholars, who would come up with nothing. He didn't have the heart to tell Titus, though, not knowing what the news would do to his son's already manic condition.

"I'll make sure the scholars get it to analyze," he said, stiffly. "And I'll get you another sketchbook."

Venetor then began to turn again to leave, only to hear Titus's voice again. "How much longer do you think I'll have to be down here?"

"I don't know, Titus." Venetor glanced back at him. "It depends how long it takes for our doctors to determine what's going on with you."

A light seemed to go out in Titus's eyes at hearing this. Venetor had wanted to lie at that moment, but he knew better. For all he knew, this was where his son would live out the rest of his days, even if the thought pained him beyond belief.

"Has Puc or Annetta not gotten back to you with anything?" Titus asked. "That was why she was going, wasn't it?"

Venetor inclined his head slightly, running a hand over the leather spine of the sketchpad. "I have not heard anything back from them since."

∞∞

After parting with Titus, Venetor made his way up to his chambers. Night had fallen completely over the castle at this point, and the majority of those inhabiting it had gone to sleep. Entering his room, Venetor sank onto his bed, the sketchpad resting on it beside him. He had been fighting with himself all the way up to his room. Each of the sketchpads had always gone to his scholars and psychologists, he'd never sent a single one to Earth so that Skyris could pass it on to Puc and the elves of Aldamoor.

His pride was like a clenched fist. He had refused to seek the aid of one who had, in his opinion, wronged his family. Each time the elf's name was brought up, he had to relive the shame of what he had done to his sister, how he had seduced her even when he had known that she was a Princess of Gaia. Even now, he worried that the dark-robed and brooding First Mage was trying to win her back while she stayed on Earth. He had been against the whole thing from the start, but Skyris was her own being and her Severio stubbornness on the subject had not let up when he'd tried to stop her. All he could do was hope that his sister would do the right thing by her people. He too had that responsibility to them. He also had one to his son, and it was worth more than his pride.

Venetor rose again and grabbed the book from beside him. He then left the chamber, muttering a silent prayer to the Unknown in hopes of guidance that he was doing the right thing.

Chapter 24

To Annetta's surprise, the next day after the episode with the ash, a familiar face awaited them in the arena at the Lab.

She, Darius, Jason and Sarina all froze at the entrance to see Matthias glaring back at them with arms crossed and a glowering expression. He was dressed in an olive green t-shirt and dark jeans that were half tucked into a pair of combat boots. On his arms, he wore brown leather gauntlets with silver finishing made to look like bear paws, which hid his infamous psychic claws. All in all, he looked more foe than friend.

"Matt?" Sarina broke the silence, taking a few steps in his direction.

The scowl on his face disappeared and lit up with a smile. "Good to see you guys again."

The atmosphere instantly relaxed, and the youth all made their way towards him. They saw that both Xander and Liam were already present, their school days being much shorter now in comparison to their own. The boys were occupied with swinging blunted swords at one another in sets of robotic motions.

"Hope you don't mind, Darius, but these two were bored so I put them to work while they waited for you," Matthias indicated, to which Darius nodded.

"So, any news?" Annetta asked. "Of Amarok or Valdhar?"

Matthias sighed and shook his head. "As much as I'd like the answer to be different, no. I get the feeling, if he is out there, then he's hiding in a different dimension and biding his time. It would be impossible for me to track him down in that case, especially with the ship I was piloting."

"Almost seems like you'd need a veil blade to do so," Sarina stated.

"Veil blade?" Jason asked.

"Apparently it's how angels get around to other worlds, they use a weapon called a veil blade to create a temporary tear between worlds to cross over where they please, and then it reknits itself," she explained.

"Would be handy, but I don't think they sell those on the black market." Matthias ran a hand through his messy hair.

"He's always one damn step ahead of us." Annetta bunched her hands up into fists.

"Nothing we can really do on our end," Jason reminded her.

She glared at him at hearing this. "Yeah, well, we should be able to. Otherwise, what are we good for?"

Jason didn't answer this and moved forward to begin his pre-sparring stretches. Annetta joined shortly after, but she didn't understand their lack of interest in the matter. It was as if they'd all forgotten it had been Amarok who had freed Razmus in the first place. Who knew what he'd unleash next if that were the case.

"For what it's worth, I know what you are thinking." Matthias came up beside her.

Annetta pulled one leg up and held it in place while balancing herself against the wall with her free hand. "Is this the point where you tell me I'm wrong?"

The assassin shook his head. "No, I think you're right, and they don't get it. Amarok is not someone to be underestimated. I made that mistake once, and I won't do it again."

She narrowed her eyes at hearing this, finished her stretch and began the next, watching Jason and Sarina as they also prepared. Darius had gone ahead and taken his place instructing Liam and Xander on the far side of the arena.

"Always a partner short now." She sighed as her mind went back to Link.

"I'd say you have more than enough." Matthias indicated to himself. "Or are you just too afraid to go toe to toe with me finally, Severio?"

A chill washed over her as Annetta regarded the sly and roguish smile Matthias beckoned her with. She realized that it had been a while since she'd sparred with him, and the thought of being able to test everything she had learned from Venetor in her time on Gaia against him excited her in a way she didn't think it possible.

"Bring it." A smile manifested on her face.

Jason's voice rang out somewhere from the side. "Uh… Anne… do you think that's such a good idea?"

Annetta ignored the comment and continued to stare down Matthias.

Matthias's grin widened, and extending a hand, he motioned to an unoccupied portion of the arena.

226

"What's your weapon?" he asked, watching Annetta shed the red leather jacket she wore.

"I think I'll use my hands," she informed him, and tossing the jacket to the side, she got into a fighter's stance.

The assassin raised an eyebrow as he also got into his stance. "Okay, then. No sword?"

It was Annetta's turn to have her smile widen as Venetor's words from one of her first lessons with him came to the forefront of her mind. "Since when has your enemy courteously told you how he intends to kill you?"

Without warning, Annetta then teleported from where she stood and reappeared behind Matthias, ready to collide her leg with the side of his head. Instead, his forearm blocked the attack. All this time, she'd thought him not to be as skilled as the King of Gaia, when the truth had been that he had been holding back. She saw this now in his azure eyes as he measured not as a student, but as a foe.

"Good one," he sarcastically complemented her as she retracted her foot and he his arm. He then spun around to face her. "But I'll call it beginner's luck."

He then faded as his body teleported and Annetta's muscles tensed. An adrenaline fueled thrill filled her. He could be anywhere. As soon as this feeling came over her, however, she composed herself as Venetor had taught her. Where would the next most logical move for the assassin be? Where would she not think to look?

In her mind's eye, she pictured a chessboard as pieces moved over it and created a chaotic mosaic of possibilities of where he could appear, and where she as a piece could move. The question, of course, was which of these options held the lowest probability.

A light breeze from the upper left gave him away, and Annetta rolled out of striking distance, only to see Matthias drop from the sky to where she'd been standing. She teleported and staying suspended in mid-air hovered above her opponent. "It's over, Matt. I have the high ground."

"Oh and what's that supposed to mean?" he scoffed. "I hope you don't mean literally Severio."

"It means you're predictable," Annetta taunted, another technique Venetor had been very adamant on her learning. Distracting your opponent was sometimes all it took.

If Matthias had been bothered by the comment, he didn't show it, and once again teleported. This time, Annetta followed.

Their bodies met once more in midair, arms locking in an array of punches, thrusts and blocks. Each time Matthias swung at Annetta, she blocked and parried with her own vicious counter. They held nothing back, save for the use of weapons, which included Matthias withdrawing his claws. Shields of psychic fire encased their bodies to prevent the hits from causing any real damage, the blue and purple flames licking at their forms from head to toe as they floated above ground.

They were so engaged in their sparring that they didn't notice everyone around them had stopped and had moved to the sidelines where the bleachers were. Their faces varied from stages of excitement to worry.

Among those spectating, another form appeared in the background and watched for a few moments, before deciding to make its presence known.

"The both of you will desist in this childish behaviour!" Puc's voice bellowed.

Instantly, both Annetta and Matthias descended to the ground and their shields dissipated.

"Now what?" Annetta wrinkled her nose.

The First Mage of Aldamoor strode towards her, his dark blue robes trailing behind him like smoke. "Did anything even remotely stay in that thick skull of yours when last I spoke to you, Severio, or are you so keen to play stabscotch with the lives of your friends and family?"

Before Annetta could open her mouth to say anything, Matthias stepped in. "The fault is mine, mage, I got carried away in the heat of the moment. It's been a long time since I've had a decent sparring partner, and I wager if you set Annetta loose, then we'd have ourselves quite the contest from what I just saw."

Puc's pale blue eyes zeroed in on Matthias. "Yes, well, there will be none of that."

As he spoke, a frazzled-looking Skyris peeked through the door, followed in tow by Dexter, who floated behind her like an obedient dog trailing its master. "What's all the commotion in here about?"

"It was just a bit of sparring." Annetta breathed the words heavily, as if she were confessing to having run someone over. At least, that's how it felt to her.

Skyris sighed, folding her arms. "Anne, you know you're not supposed to. At least not until we figure out-"

"Until we figure out what?" Annetta's agitation on the subject simmered over the edge. "If you haven't noticed, I'm not spontaneously combusting and turning into a dragon at random."

"Yes, Annetta, but we do not know what caused the transformation to begin with," Puc stated. "It could have been being in the heat of battle, it could have something to do with your lack of sleep, it could be something completely unrelated. We do not know, and as such, we need to exercise caution. Nothing which could trigger stress in you."

"Lack of not being able to do anything might trigger stress in me. Did you even consider that?" Annetta growled, placing her hands on her hips. "I can assure you if stress were the trigger, then half of Toronto would be levelled right now due to my classes. Look, I get it, there's something wrong with me, but I'm not some... fragile five year old or something. Do you honestly expect me to just sit around while everyone trains?"

Puc, Skyris and the others all looked at Annetta, and the girl felt as though she were placed under a set of spotlights. When no one said anything, she threw her hands up in the air. "You know what? Forget it!"

She then stormed off and out of the arena, oblivious to the sound of her friends calling out her name.

ဆဝဆ

Rain poured from the open heavens while Korangar stood at the mouth of the cave, watching fat drops fall into a small pool forming in a depression just outside the entrance. He had ordered that he and his newly acquired wife leave her homeworld in search of another to destroy, and more importantly, in search of a world that would add to his slowly growing army. His most immediate targets had been the worlds Amarok had suggested to him, the ones that had pledged loyalty to Mislantus and his father Mordred some years ago. Those he would have called kin, Gaian men who should have been his direct descendants, but had been his brother's instead. It seemed that almost every other world he came to, an army of fanatics would flock to his banner, further swelling his ranks.

He pressed a hand against his forehead as a needle-like pain shot up through his skull. It was becoming a more and more frequent occurrence of late. With it also were coming back memories he'd long forgotten, of a life he had once had, of fields filled with gold and green crops and of a woman whose name he had long cast out of his mind. The jolts created confusion within him.

As far as Korangar was concerned, his primary purpose in life was to end it. An insatiable hunger lay beneath his skin to extinguish everything around him. He was well aware he could destroy all worlds with ease on his own, but there was something about watching the frenzy of others as they took life away and then died themselves that could not be replaced by anything else. There was something else, but try as he might, he couldn't remember what it was.

As he dwelled on this, other memories began to slowly bubble to the surface, along with the pain, which not only intensified, but spread like roots at the front of his skull. Unable to contain it any longer, Korangar's knees buckled and he crashed onto them. His hands both pressed against the rough floor of the cave, and he saw something crimson drip into the rainwater. He withdrew one hand and pressed it to his face, pulling it away right after. A line of blood was smeared on it.

Touching his face again, Korangar identified the source as his nose, and wiped it. He then ran his hand under the rainwater outside of the cave. As he did so, he realized how much he liked it and stepped outside, removing his shoes as well. He didn't particularly like those, but he wore them because if he didn't, then others seemed even more uncomfortable around him than they already were. He couldn't afford for his soldiers to be distracted by such trifles.

Once outside, the downpour intensified. Korangar smiled, feeling the droplets trace every inch of his body. He liked how the drops seemed to sting his flesh when they collided with it. He wanted more. He always wanted more.

The rain continued without any indication of stopping. Soon, no grasses could be seen on the plains before him and trees began to bend and break from the amount of water crashing into them. Some of the smaller ones even began to fall, either from being swept up by the current or from the soil having grown so soft that the roots simply fell out. Korangar took it all in, fascinated by the destruction and the beginning of the end.

ജ

Annetta felt the same sensation hit her as always when she meditated, and let her eyes come into focus in the blinding white light.

It was always disorienting when she did this, and she had to be especially careful in order to not forget where she was. The grass materialized around her feet, and she began to walk down the familiar woodsy path searching for him.

"Annetta?" a man's deep voice called out to her from the still somewhat hazy world.

She whipped her head around and squinted, doing her best to remove the fuzzy afterimage of the all-engulfing light. With some concentration, a few seconds later she was able to see the solitary figure which stood at the end of the path. It was a tall man with a greying black beard and short cropped hair. His right hand held onto the wooden shaft of a large double-bladed axe that he used as a walking stick, and a ragged brown cape was clasped to his tunic.

"Grandpa?" she asked, still unsure if it was him.

He smiled and nodded, to which Annetta sighed in relief. At least she was still able to recognize the Lord of the Axe. Relaxed hands shoved in her pockets, she walked over to him.

"It's been a while since you've come to visit." The corners of his eyes crinkled, losing themselves in his laugh lines.

The girl felt a pang of guilt at hearing this, but didn't falter her pace. "There's some stuff that happened, grandpa, stuff I'm not sure I even know how to begin explaining, and I was hoping maybe you knew something about."

"What do you mean?" Orbeyus fell into stride with her once she caught up to him, and the two of them made their way towards the fallen logs they usually met on.

A sigh escaped Annetta as she allowed herself to sink into the log. She then looked out into the now clear surrounding of the woodland area. "Was there ever any history of anyone turning into dragons in our family?"

"Dragons?" Orbeyus raised a bushy eyebrow as he joined her and placed the axe beside him. "Where would you get a notion like that?"

"Since I apparently transformed into one." Annetta glanced at him. "And apparently did some terrible things that no one wants to tell me about."

"Ah, that." Orbeyus nodded. From what Annetta could tell, he already knew, and worse yet, he was keeping something from her. She sensed that whatever it was, it was the same thing that Puc and the others had kept. Finally, he spoke. "They fear you, Anne."

"You think?" the girl growled.

The Lord of the Axe shifted his weight. "I don't need to, I've seen it."

What little strength Annetta was holding onto began slipping. The one person she'd wanted to make proud, the one being she hoped would understand was now siding with everyone else. In his eyes, in the eyes of everyone she had ever known and cared about, she was now an outsider.

"What's happening to me, grandpa?" she asked in a fragile voice that she barely recognized as her own.

Orbeyus turned his head to look at her. "I've been trying to get answers to that myself, Anne. Psychics don't just turn into dragons after using psychic fire, least of all, Gaians. It's not in our genetic structure."

The gears in Annetta's head turned, and she nodded trying to come up with an alternative answer. "Could one of the giants have cursed me?"

Orbeyus shook his head. "No, I doubt Thanestorm would have struggled so much to contain it. This is beyond even his skill."

Annetta sighed, not getting the answer she wanted, and looked down at the worn teal sneakers on her feet. She could begin to see places on them where the fabric was beginning to thin and the more she looked at them, the more she was beginning to feel like them. The sneakers at least, she knew she could replace, the feeling inside of her, not so much. A heavy hand then landed on her shoulder and she found herself looking up again at her grandfather.

"Whatever else may happen, trust that those around you have your best intentions at heart, even if you don't see it at first," he said to her.

"That's easier said than done," she muttered.

"I never said it was easy." Orbeyus chuckled. "A lot of the time, we don't see it until it's too late."

Before Annetta could reply with anything, she was caught off guard by the sound of another voice calling her name in the distance. She rose from her seat and looked around. She couldn't make out who it belonged to other than it was distinctly male and that it wasn't Brakkus, whom she'd seen with her grandfather on previous occasions. Her brain went to the only other logical conclusion.

"Link?" A stunned expression crossed her face as the voice continued to grow closer.

"I don't think that's your friend calling you, Anne." Orbeyus got up as well. "It's someone from the other side. I think it's best you go."

She shook her head. "No, it has to be him, he's here."

She heard the voice call her name once more and turning around, this time she knew it was from the woods. Of course he would call her from there. Without saying anything else, she leapt over the log and took off in its direction.

"Annetta wait!" Orbeyus called after her, but that was all she heard, and it was not enough to stop her.

Crashing into the foliage, Annetta listened for the sound of the voice again and hearing it beckon to her, she began to run in its direction, doing her best not to trip over small shrubs, uneven ground and twisted roots.

"Annetta," the voice whispered on the wind.

"I'm coming, Link!" she called back, pushing branches out of her way and ignoring the scrapes of pine needles and small twigs as they cut into her skin.

She continued on, listening to the voice as it kept calling out her name again and again. She became so focused on it that she soon forgot the world around her, running and moving branches out of her way until everything faded once more into white light.

ʀʒʘ

Annetta gasped for air as a hand gripped her shoulder tightly and everything around her came into focus. She heaved with the effort of breathing and looking to the side, she saw a very disturbed Puc, who'd knelt beside her with a hand on her shoulder. Panic washed over the girl in a chill, and she got up immediately.

The mage rose after her, steadying himself on his staff. His pale eyes fixed themselves on her once he was composed. "You are a medium."

Annoyance followed her hearing the words from him, but those were quickly replaced with curiosity. "I'm a what?"

"A medium," Puc stated again. "One who can visit the lands of the dead. It is the one portal that is forbidden to all other mortals. No one can get through, not physically, at least."

The girl didn't know how to react to what was being said and so she stayed silent.

"How long have you had this ability?" the mage inquired.

"I don't know," Annetta shrugged. "I noticed it after I started meditating, and it just sort of happened at first. After that, I could just kind of go in at will."

"And whom is it that you go see when you go there, if you do not mind me asking?"

Annetta looked down at her feet again to see the same sneakers she had been wearing while there. She felt uncertain about answering Puc's question, but then she thought back to what Orbeyus had just said to her.

"I go visit my grandfather," she replied. "Sometimes Brakkus is there, too."

Puc nodded slightly, his face remaining neutral when she said this. She hated when he did that, now more than ever, since it meant she had no idea what he thought of her.

"It must have happened when I brought you back after you took that blast of psychic fire," Puc stated. "It is often said that a clinical death can unlock such an ability, to be able to walk among the living and the dead."

Annetta thought back to the battle between Amarok and Matthias when she'd been caught in the crossfire. "I did start having those dreams after that, the ones you told me to meditate to get rid of. That's around the same time this started."

Another bout of silence followed, but was soon broken yet again by Puc. "Does anyone else know you can do this? Does Venetor know?"

"No," Annetta replied. "I didn't want anyone to know. I didn't think it was a good idea, and seeing your reaction, I think I was right."

"Indeed you were," the First Mage told her. "Under no circumstances should anyone know you can do this. Especially not someone like Venetor."

"What does my Uncle Venetor have to do with this?" she frowned.

"He would try to use your power for political gain," Puc explained. "Imagine him being able also to say that the White Lioness of Gaia cheated death. That she cannot be killed. So under no circumstances can he know about this, do you understand?"

The girl lowered her head to look down at her feet again, and she considered Puc's words. Though part of her didn't want to admit it because Venetor was blood, the mage was right. In just the span of a few weeks, she had already seen the legend of the White Lioness of

Gaia grow exponentially, turning into a tall tale before her very eyes. In her time on Gaia, Venetor had not hidden her from the world, either. She was Gaia's new symbol of hope. She shuddered at the thought of being made immortal on top of everything that was being added to her falsified life story. She already had a hard time when it came to correcting people on the rumours that existed.

"You don't have to tell me twice." Her mouth twisted into a grimace.

Puc regarded Annetta with a curious look, and then something like a roguish smile began to creep its way onto his mouth.

"Why, Miss Severio, I do believe that is the first time you have agreed with me without even a hint of rebellion in your tone. Either you have grown up, or I am starting to lose my hearing."

Rolling her eyes at the comment, accompanied by an exasperated sigh, Annetta said no more. The two of them then made their way back towards the exit of the biosphere.

Chapter 25

Jason's class finished early for the day thanks to the Teaching Assistant emailing everyone saying she had a case of the stomach flu. He therefore found himself walking lazily through the university hallways while other students zipped by. Sarina had not had any classes that day, and because of that, she was already in the Lab helping to organize and brew potions, since both Puc and Darius were otherwise occupied.

An involuntary smile crept onto his face as he thought about how excited she got whenever she discussed a new project Darius or Puc had given her. There was a certain way that her brown eyes would twinkle when she did. It was as if they held a life of their own, filled with starlight. Or filled with fibre optic cables, if he was to think back to his last class and be less romantic. She'd probably get a kick out of that second one either way, especially once she saw the comparison. It was one of the things he loved about her. She understood his sense of humour.

He'd never thought it possible to feel for someone the way he did for Sarina, and the older the two of them got, the more complex the feelings inside of him grew, like a tree that had its roots deep in the soil, entwined with the earth to a point that it was impossible to pinpoint where it all began. It seemed another lifetime ago to him that he and Annetta had to battle the forces of Mislantus the Threat, and a lifetime ago that he'd first met Sarina as a result.

Once he left the main campus building, he took the path leading towards the two larger parking lots on the southeastern side. Beyond this lay the apartment buildings where they were staying. After some calculations and the want for total privacy, they'd agreed that renting an apartment made more sense than a single room residence.

Jason's mother had fought fiercely against the idea of him and Sarina staying together at first, but as the summer had gone on, she had accepted it. What had changed his mother's mind, he was not sure of, but he thanked the force of nature had been involved nonetheless.

He fumbled for his keys as he stood in front of the door to their rooms. Finally, he opened it and was greeted by the sight of a familiar sweater sprawled out on the couch. A few stacks of books and papers occupied its seats. The small kitchenette was also left in the same state he'd left it, clean. Jason couldn't help but grin at the thought of his mother not yelling at him for leaving a mess.

"Man, I can't wait till this becomes a permanent thing," he said quietly to himself as he locked the door behind him, and not bothering to take off his shoes, went directly for the bedroom.

The room was capable of squeezing in a queen size bed and a desk along with two nightstands. The walls were a pale blue which bordered on white and at the insistence of Jason, almost half the walls were covered in videogame and movie posters. It was, in his mind, the only way to remove some of the sterility from the room.

He set his bag down by the bed and then turned to the mirror that was mounted on the wall beside the entrance. It was roughly the same shape and size as the one Annetta had in her room, but with an ornate wooden frame with antique painted gold accents.

Jason then reached into the pocket of his jeans and pulled out the metallic card key with the phrase Q-16 etched into it. It was strange to think that such a tiny object had changed his life so much.

"Well, home sweet home, here I come," he muttered to himself and as every time before, he slid the card key down the side of the mirror.

ℬℭℜ

After his descent into the Lab, it did not take Jason long to orient himself towards the Lake biosphere. It was usually where he and Sarina would meet up whenever the two of them were busy with one task or another.

His retreat, however, proved to be occupied when he spied Annetta sitting on a log by the lake. While his initial reaction was to turn around and leave, part of him decided it was better to stay. It had been too long since he'd had a chance to speak with his friend without the distraction of anyone else around, and when he realized that, he realized how much he missed it. Before Sarina and before everyone else, Annetta had been his best friend. Yes, Darius had been there, but their friendship was not the same, not like with Annetta. With her, he could have spent hours talking about anything and everything, and they'd never be bored. Their company had been more than enough for one another, along with the understanding that they were both kindred spirits, the misunderstood lovers of fantasy and magic in a world that thought them strange.

Jason saw that she was looking out into the water, watching the tide go in and out. Her mind, he knew, however, was a million miles away and focused on something completely unrelated.

"Mind if I join you?" he asked.

The girl snapped out of it and looking over at him smiled, "Knock yourself out."

"I mean I'd rather not, I like being conscious." He planted himself on the log beside her.

There was silence for a time, not that words were needed. The wind through the trees by the bank of the lake and the thunderous rolling of the waves in and out were words enough.

Jason looked over at his friend, then, and saw just how tired she looked. He'd seen it before, when she'd come back from Gaia and after the battle with Mislantus before that, but the rose-tinted glasses of being around Sarina seemed to dull just what it was that had been going on with her. Now it was plain to see.

"You alright, Anne?" he asked.

The girl looked back at him with the same steely defiance she always had about her. "I'm fine, it's just everyone else who doesn't think I am."

He voiced his thoughts. "You look tired."

Annetta squirmed a little at the assessment, but didn't look away. "It's been hard for me to sleep since I found out. I just keep asking myself why and what it all means. No one can tell me anything, except I killed a lot of people, even turned on the Four Forces."

"You weren't in control, Anne. You were like a werewolf under a full moon."

"Yeah, a very large werewolf with scales who flies and breathes fire." The girl rolled her eyes.

Jason exhaled heavily and looked out into the lake again. He didn't know what else to say to her, and for the first time in his life, this frightened him. Suddenly, he felt it should have been Link who was sitting in his place. Maybe Anne would have listened to him? He looked over at her again, reddish-brown hair falling in her face, and those saddened tired blue eyes.

He remembered his Visium, the vision quest each Ogaien was made to go on, so they could face their internal demons. In Jason's case, it wasn't so much about the demons as it was in realizing just how important he was despite beating himself up and saying he wasn't. He remembered with clarity the alternate world where he hadn't existed and where Richard and his gang of friends had picked relentlessly on an Annetta who didn't have a friend in the world. Jason then did the only thing he could think of, and placed his hand on her arm.

"I'm sorry I got scared, but I want you to know that no matter what happens, you are not a monster," he said to her. "You are my best friend, and she who fights monsters."

Annetta looked over at him, and what ember there was of her former self seemed to spark anew in her eyes. "Thanks. I'll try not to disappoint."

"Not being roasted alive for starters is always good." He grinned.

She returned the smile, but their mirth was short-lived when another pair of feet could be heard crashing through the twigs and long grasses leading down towards the lake.

Their owner appeared a few moments later, Darius dressed in his regular day clothing, which consisted of mainly all things black. He was panting heavily from the run, and his hands were smeared in something red.

Both Jason and Annetta rose at seeing his palms.

"What happened?" She asked.

"It's the Soarin," Darius said through rapid breaths. "Doriden's been wounded."

Jason furrowed his brows. He couldn't imagine what would have driven the Soarin to come to Q-16 seeking aid. "How bad?"

Darius tried to catch a larger breath and spoke rapidly again despite his best efforts not to. "He's lost a wing, and he may lose a whole lot more."

No further words were needed, and they ran for the exit of the biosphere, hoping that they weren't too late.

೫೦೧೪

Annetta, Darius and Jason tore through the last set of corridors together as they rushed towards the infirmary wing of Q-16. Turning the final corner, they found at least a dozen Soarin standing by the door, along with Sarina guarding it.

"What's going on?" Annetta demanded.

Sarina turned to face them. "Skyris and Puc are trying to stabilize Doriden, he's lost a lot of blood though and they're not sure if he's-"

A howl pierced the air from beyond the door, one that clearly wasn't Gaian or elven. The Soarin in the room seemed to grow tenser, the fear for their Alpha written plainly on their faces.

Annetta then noticed that all those gathered also did not look to be in the best of shape, covered in an assortment of nicks and cuts, but none as severe as what she'd heard Doriden was going through.

"So what happened?" Jason broke the silence.

"They came out of nowhere," one of the gathered Soarin with a purple mane spoke. Annetta recognized him past the scratches as Alterin, one of the Soarin who had helped her and her friends during the Eternal Hunt.

Confused by the cryptic words, Annetta inquired further. "Who?"

"Those who we should have called friends," Alterin spoke yet again. "The ones we called allies, the Minotaur."

"What? That's not possible." Jason's eyes widened.

"We didn't want to believe it at first." Alterin shook his head. "And many of us died because of it. A few hundred of us escaped before they took the Trafjan cliffs and put our longhouses to the torch. They did it with others dressed in cloaks bearing the symbol of a seven-headed dragon on them."

Annetta listened but the more she heard, the more she was confused. "There has to be some mistake. The Minotaur are part of the Four Forces, they're our sworn allies."

"Were." Darius corrected her, and his eyes fell to the ground right after. "I'm sorry we didn't tell you sooner, but Puc asked us not to say anything. After you turned on everyone, Snapneck went into a rage of his own and no one has been able to reach him through C.T.S. since."

"The seven-headed dragon was my father's sigil," Sarina chimed in. "This can only mean Amarok is somehow involved."

"Damn it." Annetta gritted her teeth. "No matter how we try, we can't seem to get rid of him, and he's always one step ahead of us."

Just then, the door behind Sarina opened, and Puc emerged from the other end of the room, wiping his hands on a crimson-stained cloth. His dark blue robe had been discarded somewhere, and he remained in what had once been a white linen shirt that wasn't faring much better than the rag in his hands.

"He has been stabilized," the First Mage of Aldamoor announced, and instantly, the tension lessened. "He is, however, not out of the woods just yet, and your Alpha will need to rest."

"Then we will make sure none will disturb him," Alterin said, those gathered agreeing behind him.

Puc nodded. "Very well, though I dare say some of you should return to your camp by Severio Castle to let the others know. They will be anxious for news."

A few of those gathered departed at hearing this. Puc took the opportunity to turn to the gathered youth. "Come with me to my study. We have much to discuss this night."

೫೦೦೩

The room lit up with dozens of red and white candles as soon as Puc strode into the room. The study, or rather the room that had been part of Puc's living quarters while he had been a permanent resident in Q-16, had remained unchanged to Annetta's eyes. Leather-bound books of various sizes and colours lined the farthest wall behind him, along with neatly rolled-up scrolls. A grandfather clock stood at attention in one corner of the room, while the other held a cabinet with potion ingredients, as well as some of the finished product.

In the centre of the room stood the large dark wooden desk that had every square inch of it covered in papers and stacks of more books. A lone green feather quill poked out from among these, along with other odds and ends that she could not identify.

Puc paused behind the large ornate chair that stood behind his desk and leaned his free hand against the back. "I have had long to think on this and how to go about telling you what transpired after the events of the battle on Morwick. The only conclusion that I have managed to come to is to tell you the truth, and so, here it is: The Four Forces as we knew them are no more."

Annetta's eyes widened. "No more?"

"We wanted to tell you sooner, Anne, but Puc wouldn't let us." Jason curled his hands into fists at his side. "He was worried how you'd react when you found out and right after the-"

"I would react the same way I'm reacting now," she snapped at him. "What do you mean the Four Forces as we knew them are no more?"

"I mean exactly what those words say," Puc replied solemnly. "We are the Four Forces no more, but three instead. The Minotaurs have broken off all contact and alliance with us. Lord Snapneck blames us for the chaos that ensued against the giants."

Annetta felt the words hit her with the force of a bag of bricks, and she had to wait a few good moments before she was able to respond.

Her hand went down almost immediately to her C.T.S., and she typed in the numeric combination that went with Snapneck's.

"Anne, we tried contacting him, he wouldn't respond," Sarina reminded her.

"He's been ignoring all communication with us since his initial declaration that he won't have anything more to do with the Four Forces," Darius added.

Jason bobbed his head. "Yeah, apparently he said that he's made a truce with the giants, but I think that's just him trying to intimidate us."

Her friend's words bounced off Annetta as she waited for Snapneck to answer. Her mind wandered to images of him as still a mere child whom they had rescued from Yarmir. This was Snapneck. He knew them and he was their friend.

She was about to give up and close it when the ringing stopped.

"01 here," Annetta announced into the watch.

Again there was silence, and the sound of heavy breathing from a beast of burden could be heard coming through.

"I see that you're awake now, Annetta Severio," the harsh and ragged voice of Snapneck replied. **"That's good to know. You'll be conscious when our armies come for you."**

"Whose armies, Lord Snapneck?" Puc inched closer to Annetta.

There was another brief pause and more harsh breathing before Snapneck spoke again. **"Him that they call The End."**

The communication went dead and static could be heard. Annetta closed the watch and looked around the room dumbfounded at those present. Bubbling anger began to simmer at the edges of her consciousness. Just what could have caused such a reaction in Snapneck?

"I want answers," she demanded. "No more sugar coating or evasions. What happened?"

The three other youth present turned to Puc, who kept his gaze down on the chair, gripping its back firmly with both hands. Had he long nails, Annetta was sure he would have torn the worn leather from the sheer force he seemed to be applying.

"At least a third of the Minotaur forces went down in the fight," the mage said, "Not including the losses from other races. With the Minotaur leaving the alliance, we have about half the warriors we did before."

242

It was then Annetta's turn to look down. Tears threatened to fall, brimming around her eyes out of the frustration that continued to churn inside of her. This was her fault and her fault alone. Worst of all, she had no way of fixing it, and in one battle, she had singlehandedly undone her grandfather's life's work.

"This still doesn't explain why my father's sigil was seen," Sarina interjected. "I know you all say it was Amarok's work, but no matter how cunning Amarok was and is, he wouldn't be able to gather the loyalty of so many so quickly."

Jason shoved his hands into his pockets, feeling uncomfortable at the mention of the assassin. "Well, he managed to free Razmus without so much as batting an eyelash."

"And I'm afraid Razmus may have just been a pawn in the scheme of something much larger." Puc let go of the chair. Walking over to one of the shelves behind him, he selected a large black tome with silver markings on it. Bringing it to the table and laying it flat, Annetta and her friends recoiled to see a mark they recognized. There, engraved in silver on the front cover, was the seven-headed dragon of Mislantus.

"Tell me, how much do any of you know of Korangar?" the mage inquired.

The four youth all looked at one another, trying to read each other's faces to see who would speak.

Feeling the most comfortable on the subject, Sarina took a step forward. "Korangar was once the son of Freius, my ancestor. His soul was broken up into the seven aspects of evil."

Puc shook his head at the last part. "Not broken, not quite at first. Korangar was given up by his father to the Angels to be a host for what they proclaimed to be the root of Khaos. When Freius realized what he had done by making his son hold such evil within him, it was too late, for Korangar was no longer able to discern right from wrong. He was consumed simply with the desire to end everything. Freius, being bound by Gaian law to never harm his direct descendant, was forced to imprison Korangar in fear of what his son would do to the multiverse should he be allowed to walk free."

There was a brief bout of silence before Annetta broke it. "So what you're saying is Amarok somehow managed to free Korangar?"

"All signs are beginning to point to it, I fear," the mage replied, "Including your cousin's illness on Gaia. I am afraid that rather than be ill, he is a prophet."

"Titus is a what?" Annetta wrinkled her nose.

"A prophet," Puc stated. "Many will not know they are born with such a gift in their lifetime, for it will lie dormant and only emerge in the event that something on a divine scale occurs in the multiverse."

"So Titus's fits are just him being able to sense that Korangar is free?" Jason summarized. "Does he know how to beat him at least?"

"I am afraid that prophets do not have such precision of skill, even when they have mastered their abilities, which Titus, from what I hear, is far from doing."

Jason pursed his lips. "I love it when these things don't come with a manual."

"This is far from a game, Kinsman," Puc hissed, "and the sooner you start treating it as such, the better."

"I have to tell Venetor," Annetta said and begun to move towards the door.

"It will do no good, Annetta." Puc's voice made her stop dead in her tracks.

She pivoted on her heel to face him. "I have to try, and besides, my uncle has a right to know what's going on with my cousin. He's the heir to the throne of Gaia. Plus, Gaia is the sister planet of Earth. I'm pretty sure he'll lend us a hand if Korangar tries to show his face here."

"No offense, Anne, but where was he when we were up against Mislantus?" Darius reminded her.

Annetta rolled her eyes. "Being blocked by the Greys who are currently running the Galactic Federation, though if Venetor has his way, then the Gaians are gonna be running it and then nothing is going to stop him from coming."

No one moved to challenge her on this declaration, but she could tell by their faces that they were against this. Annetta left the room without further words, regardless of their thoughts. She would make them see what she saw in the Gaian King.

Chapter 26

Venetor's steps thundered in his ears as he strode through the corridor towards his balcony on the Una Space Station, flanked by Gladius and Atala. The crown atop his brow seemed to weigh a metric ton as he mulled over the course of action he was about to take. His choice of words, tone and actions would be the determining factors of whether or not Gaia would advance past the preliminary elections and whether he had a chance of dethroning the Greys.

His want for exacting revenge was just a minuscule bonus in the scheme of things. Now, with Titus as ill as he was, it was just another task that needed to be carried out to better conditions for his people.

There were also the unsettling reports he'd been paying more and more attention to. Ever since the last meeting, where Galecto Kelper Twenty Three's loss of life had been revealed, the King of Gaia had heavily investigated the event. Life didn't just go extinct on a planet one day, there was always a cause behind such cataclysmic events. Galecto Kelper Twenty Three had been thriving, with no indications of a threat to its life, yet it now floated through space as a mass burial site.

The more Venetor investigated it, the more he grew convinced there was something the Greys weren't telling the rest of the Federation, or there was an event beginning the likes of which Venetor hated to think about. It was the sort of thing Gaian philosophers had long argued about, and the sort of thing that one Gaian not long ago had challenged the monarchy on. A name floated on the tip of his tongue as he thought of it, but he didn't wish to utter it in the event that it would breathe life into a thing that in his long life had, until now, been fiction.

When he reached the end of the tunnel, Venetor waited for the others to catch up, their footfalls creating an echo to his own.

"Ready when you are, yer Majesty," Gladius confirmed.

Venetor glanced back to look upon his old bodyguard and friend. The Hurtz noble was dressed in full plate armour from head to toe, and while a little medieval-looking to many civilizations present, he was nonetheless an impressive sight. Every inch of the dark steel had been polished and buffed until it shone.

To the other side, Atala stood wordlessly, dressed in Beta scale mail and a deep burgundy cloak that was clasped at the side in the Gaian style. Her high black officer's boots were also lacquered and polished, fitted into loose black pants. Venetor knew without a doubt that the Gaian general had spent the better part of the night perfecting her uniform until it was up to her standards.

The Gaian king exhaled as some of the tension managed to escape his shoulders. It was good to know that he had such fierce followers behind him, even if they were but two.

Venetor took a deep breath and strode out onto the platform, his arms loose as they swung back and forth with a warrior's bravado. Though he had been taught to move otherwise for most of his life, as far as Venetor was concerned, here he was a fighter, and the station before him was his battlefield, and enemies occupied it. He would conquer them all one way or another.

The light intensified tenfold as he emerged. Venetor took a quick sweeping glance over the other balconies, filled with representatives from various species from across the multiverse. He then seated himself on one of the benches inside the balcony and waited for the meeting to begin.

Shortly after, a Grey emerged on the podium below and began the opening address. Venetor blotted most of it out of his brain, having heard it a thousand times already before, and focused on what he would need to say instead.

"As per the fifth item on our agenda, the Intergalactic Federation will begin its election process today." Venetor felt himself return to the world of the living upon hearing these words from the Grey.

The alien at the podium continued. "We ask now that those species which will put forth a candidate to press the button or activate the switch device equivalent located at the forefront of their balcony. You may begin now."

Venetor rose instantly and strode over to the large red button that had been placed on the control panel at the front of the balcony. Laying a meaty fist over it, he pushed down, feeling the click creep through his arm when it had connected. He then scanned the balconies again to see if any had lit up to indicate that another species was also competing against him. He needed all the information he could get, and he needed to know his opponents in order to be able to form a battle strategy against them, otherwise, he might as well be a Gaian commoner that had never spent a day training.

Only three other balconies glowed a pale green to signify their candidacy for the seat. The tension in Venetor's neck lessened somewhat, out of the five hundred and sixty-seven species that were part of the Intergalactic Federation, competing against three other planets were not the worst odds. It did mean, however, that these planets meant business, and they had reasons for putting forth their candidacy.

Atala made her way to Venetor's side, hovering slightly over him. "You will need to make this less about vengeance, it seems, and more about what you can bring to the table that they can't."

"That's going to be a tough one to swallow," Venetor muttered in return. Gaia was not at its strongest. Much of its spaceships had been destroyed and many of its warriors were still recovering from the battle against Razmus. It was a hard thing for him to admit, but Venetor knew that Gaia was not in prime fighting shape, no matter its proud warrior heritage.

"The candidates have put forth their names. The Intergalactic Federation recognizes the Verden of Zriz moon, the Rimork of the planet Brion, the Greys of the Zeta Reticuli System for a returning term, and the Gaians of planet Gaia. Should anyone wish to still put forth their planet, you may still do so now."

A silence followed this, and the speaker continued. "Very well. It is made evident that no others wish to cast their candidates. We will begin with the preliminary speeches and introductions."

The arena darkened until only a single spotlight shone on one of the balconies. Venetor recognized the species inside it as the Verden, a stout-looking people with leathery grey skin and small horns protruding from the ridges of their noses. He had always thought they resembled Earth's rhinoceroses.

The tallest of the four on the platform moved forward while the others sat. He wore a set of black hide armour with silver accents that more than likely was a space suit. "I, Kluahk, Prime Ruler of the Verden, Smasher of Comets come here today to put forth my name in the Intergalactic Federation..."

"Did the Verden seriously just put forth their candidacy?" Atala whispered in Venetor's ear.

Venetor pulled himself away from the speech, but still half listening for anything of value. "A setup, more likely. I think the Greys bribed them to make it seem like there were more candidates than just Gaia and the Greys."

Atala's golden eyes narrowed as she looked up to where the spotlight was. "I suppose we can't put it past them, but would they really stoop so low as to ask the Verden?"

"It can mean one of two things," Venetor spoke, crossing his arms as he continued to watch. "The Greys are low on allies, so low that they had to ask the Verden for aid, a nation that is known for having supported Mordred and Mislantus. The other angle is they are trying to throw a curve ball and divert attention from something far greater."

Venetor felt the hairs on his neck stand on end as he contemplated this in his head. Just which of the two was it? The more he thought on it, the more he felt himself being sucked into the quicksand of paranoia that was politics. Though he had been trained since Orbeyus had abandoned his post as heir of Gaia, he didn't have the calm temperament that had come naturally to his brother. In his blood swam the wrath of a second son, a man who had been destined to be a warrior, the general of the Gaian forces. Try as he might, Venetor couldn't deny that which was instinct. In every face that was not part of his retinue on board the Una Space Station, he saw a potential enemy, someone who could and would turn against him in a moment's notice.

"...It is, as was pointed out by the candidate of the planet Gaia, that the Intergalactic Federation's current leadership is hiding important information and glossing over events which we should be paying more attention to. For all we know, the world is unravelling before us and in this, the seed of Khaos thrives."

Venetor felt his hands tighten into fists. "Those words..."

Atala glanced at him again. "They're what Titus keeps repeating in his fits, isn't it? I found them scrawled on his wall the one night."

The king nodded shallowly. Now was not the time for him to think of his son's condition. He needed to keep his face in a steely reserve to not tip any of his competition off. Rumours had begun to emerge for a while now of the prince's absence, but no one had yet dared to voice them before Venetor.

"Thank you, candidate Kluahk, for your speech. Are there any who would refute his claim to running in this election?" the presenter turned to the masses.

No one said anything, and Venetor was well aware of the fact that they wouldn't until it was much further in.

"Let them think they are strong," his father, Balthazar, had told him. "In this is their weakness. Let them feel superior as they build their tower of bones. In the end, one good swing of a club will send it toppling, for there is no solid foundation."

Despite it having been years since he'd heard this, the words had resonated with Venetor and he intended to make full use of them in this race. Folding his arms before him, he continued to observe.

The Grey announcer craned his large head around to get a good look at everyone before speaking again. "If none will refute this, then we shall move onto our next candidate, based on the proximity of the candidate's star system to the Una Space Station."

The lights then intensified on Venetor, who narrowed his eyes. He refused to shield them with his hand, and walked towards the edge of the balcony. He couldn't tell who was where. All he saw in his vision was the bright lights that seemed to be trying to blind him, as though he were being interrogated. The more he thought about it, the more he realized he was, but there was no backing down from it now. Everything he had done in the past few years had led him to this moment.

"My fellow members of the Intergalactic Federation, I come before you today to put forth my candidacy in the upcoming election, or rather, I come to put forth Gaia's candidacy. Though I am but one, Gaia is made of many, and it is those many that I am here today representing. As a king, I have been taught to understand that representing a larger group is not only a responsibility, but a privilege. It is a trust between a people and one person that they will do everything in their power to uphold their way of life and the sanctity of it. During a coronation on Gaia, should a prince not be found suitable with the desire to do so, the people can vote him off and cast him aside for a more favourable candidate. So far, the Severio line has endured and ruled Gaia for over twelve thousand years without fail. The Federation, in my eyes, has always been no different than a planet, we are but a series of continents that come together to discuss rules, laws and government. Of late, however, I feel that this planet, or rather the current government has not been working in the best interest of the people, but in its own. Should you here gathered today seek the change I know I do, then put your strength to mine, and I will see to it that we emerge stronger together as one."

Silence followed, as Venetor had expected. He knew there would be no cheers for him here, not initially, anyway. All members would keep a straight face until the very end, only to descend like wolves to tear apart the candidates they didn't favour. Unless they had seen through his charade and through the fact that Gaia was not what it had once been, he knew they would say nothing at the present time.

"If none will disprove this candidacy, then we shall move onto our next candidate in the proximity of the star system to the Una Space Station," the announcer repeated, and the light faded from Venetor.

A chill crept down the spine of the Gaian king, and looking on into the crowd, he crossed his arms. The initial speech had been passed, but the battle was far from over.

Chapter 27

It was amazing to see how overnight, hundreds of tents had risen around Severio Castle. The announcement of the Minotaur's betrayal of the Four Forces had spread like wildfire after the events that had befallen the Soarin. Annetta and Jason watched from the exit of the portal on the ridge, counting the numbers, while close by, their horses munched happily at some grass they'd found.

"They can't stay out here," Annetta said. "They're far too exposed."

Jason looked down again at the tents. The Soarin had only taken what they were able to carry with them, and it sorely showed. "What can we do, though? It's not like we can all fit them in Q-16."

"You'd actually be surprised," a third voice came from behind.

The duo turned around to see Skyris atop a pure black horse with a long wavy mane and tail. She seemed sober for once, though that was hard to tell, the two of them had learned. She was very good at keeping a steady head, even under the influence.

"The entire base is made of a metamaterial with particular qualities harvested from Beta dragons." Skyris dismounted and walked over to them.

"You mean the creatures who are responsible for the beta scale mail?" Annetta asked.

Skyris nodded. "Their skin can adapt to almost any environment, so it was only natural that early Gaian scientists would experiment with such a creature's raw materials, as un-Gaian as it sounds. They learned how to use it for a lot of different things, like a metal that would expand the size of a room to accommodate more people comfortably."

Jason's eyes widened. "So you're saying that if the Soarin all come into the Lab, then its gonna stretch like playdough?"

Skyris laughed. "In simple terms, yes, it will stretch, but there's more to it than that."

Annetta turned to look down at the tents below again. She hadn't been able to reach Venetor the night before, due to him being away on business with the Intergalactic Federation. Due to the time, Annetta had given up on further pursuits, since she had class early next morning. This was the problem of having to live a double life, there were only so many hours in a day that she could spare before collapsing from exhaustion.

"I need to get in touch with Venetor." She voiced her thoughts and turned to Skyris. "Can you try patching me through again, Aunt Sky?"

The older woman's smile vanished into a neutral expression. "I can, though if he's still at the meeting with the Federation, we won't be able to reach him unless they're taking a break from the session."

"I can't just sit around and wait." Annetta pushed back her bangs as the wind tousled her hair. "If anything Snapneck said is true, then we're all in danger. I need to do something about it, even if it's just a stupid warning."

Skyris glanced over at Jason, who only offered a shrug in reply. Her eyes then wandered back to Annetta. "Alright, no time like the present."

With that, she mounted back up on the horse. "Meet me in the control room."

Veering the horse around, Skyris then brought the beast up and increasing speed, she vanished through the wall of the portal that separated Q-16 from the Eye to All Worlds.

"I know we've been through this before, Anne," Jason said once Skyris was gone, "But I don't trust Venetor. There's something off about him."

"You just don't like him because he beat you that first time." She rolled her eyes. "For the record, he beat me just as bad."

Jason shook his head as he begun to walk over to their horses. "It's not that, there's just… I don't know, it's just a vibe I get. Every time I interacted with the guy, it was all about Gaia and him being its future king. It just rubbed me the wrong way, okay? I know you spent almost the whole summer there, so you probably got to know him better but… I don't think I'm over the fact that he didn't show up when we needed him most against Mislantus."

"So there it is." Annetta followed him. "You think he's not gonna show again? You know that wasn't his fault. I told you-"

Jason spun on his heel abruptly to face her. "Anne, what if he loses the election? We'll be stuck in the same mess as before, with our forces severely reduced. I'm worried if we get too optimistic then we'll be putting our faith in something that only has a small chance of happening. How long do these elections take? How long until his forces come here? It could be all over and done before Venetor even takes power. The way I see it, it's just us against the world."

He then turned back and mounting on his horse, left through the portal.

Annetta stood beside her horse alone. She looked up at the portal, a wall of red and black water swimming horizontally in the sky. She remembered the first time she'd seen it for herself when Brakkus has brought her. It was more proof of the world she had become part of.

Shrugging off the thought, she swung herself into the saddle, her mind still swimming with what Jason had said. What if Venetor didn't win the election and the Greys won again? What then? How long would it take the troops to get to Earth? Doubts began to mingle with the clarity of vision she'd had in her mind before, like the red and black water swirling before her. Then another idea came out of nowhere. A tiny voice that formulated into a single and coherent thought in the back of her mind, pushing against her skull like a dull headache.

Finally, she spoke it under her breath. "No cause is lost if but one fool is left to fight."

ଚରେ

The vast glass screen before Annetta was black, with a beeping that sounded similar to the dialup tone on her internet router they'd had a few years back at home. She stood rooted to the spot behind Skyris, who was seated in a rather large leather office chair with her legs stretched out before her on the table, and her hands folded across her stomach pensively. They'd gone through the same routine the night before, which had ended in disappointment when no one had answered. It seemed that today would be no different.

"Where could he be?" Annetta asked as her stomach started to knot.

Skyris removed her legs from the table and straightened in the seat, her brows creased together in thought. "There is another possibility. He could be at the Una Space Station for a meeting. I could try reaching the balcony console there. Though, if they aren't on break, then there's a good chance he won't answer there, either."

The feeling in her gut slightly lessened as Annetta glanced over at her aunt. "Do it. We don't have anything to lose at this point."

Skyris nodded and cancelled the current call, then began typing in another sequence on the table's touchscreen surface. The screen went black again, and Annetta resumed her standing position with her hands clasped behind her back. Three beeps later, a camera feed flooded the screen with the faces of Venetor, Atala and Gladius. All three seemed to have had little sleep, from the dark circles under their eyes.

"Annetta? Skyris?" Venetor raised an eyebrow. "This isn't the best time for long conversations. We're going to be starting up the platform speeches next, and I've yet to-"

Annetta lowered her head, the feeling of ears flattening against her skull taking over her as she instinctively flex the muscles around her jaw. With her feral form, she now at least knew where the strange reflex came from. This was not what she was here to think about, though, and cut Venetor off before he could continue. "I understand, uncle, and I wouldn't be contacting you if this wasn't serious, but we have a big problem."

The Gaian king narrowed his eyes. "What problem? What are you talking about?"

Skyris exhaled roughly, then gazed up at her brother on the screen. "The Minotaur have broken from the Four Forces and have threatened to come after Earth, and they seem to be working with Amarok Mezorian."

"Broken? How and why?" Atala spoke up.

"It's my fault," Annetta said, the knots returning to her stomach. It felt like someone had jammed a boulder down her throat, and it was slowly making its descent. "I... well... apparently, I turned into a dragon and may have killed almost a third of the Four Forces, mostly Minotaur... I wasn't in control, though. I didn't even know it happened."

"You transformed into a dragon?" Venetor's eyes widened.

"Such a thing is impossible." Gladius shook his head. "Ye can't just turn into a dragon. No Gaian ever has. Why, I can't even think of anyone who had a beta dragon for their feral form in all my years being alive."

"None that we know of." Atala pursed her lips. "There is no registry of feral forms, and never has been. Not unless you count Gaian noble coats of arms."

"Aye, and Annetta's form be a lioness. Ye can't just switch," Gladius argued.

Venetor raised his hand, curling his fingers into a fist to silence them, then turned to the screen. "Annetta is still young, and her form can change. It is very rare, but happens, though what Gladius says is true, no such form has ever been confirmed, and... You said you were not in control, either?"

Annetta lowered her head in shame. "I was like a werewolf. I woke up the next... well, next week with no memory of what happened. I only know because Jason showed me, against Puc's wishes."

Though he didn't show it outwardly, Annetta could see the concern in the corners of Venetor's eyes.

"There's more," she continued, unsure if this was the right course but proceeded regardless. "Puc may know what's wrong with Titus... he said he might be a prophet."

"A prophet?" Venetor furrowed his brows. "What brought this conclusion on?"

Annetta wanted to bite her tongue, but it was too late for that. "Puc believed that Amarok freeing Razmus was just a front while he got ready for his real objective, releasing Korangar."

For a split second, Annetta feared she had said too much, or said the wrong thing. She had not, up until this point, ever felt like she was out of place with what she spoke to Venetor about. Seeing the crown on his head as he looked down at her from the screen in deep thought, however, had her questioning it. Maybe this was what Puc had been trying to warn her about?

Finally, Venetor straightened himself in his seat. "Perhaps then, there is more to Galecto Kelper Twenty Three than is being revealed to us, and if this is the case, then it ought to be investigated."

"But how, my king?" Atala looked over at him.

Venetor folded his hands before him as he spoke. "Galecto Kelper Twenty Three was a nature reserve belonging to the Eolif, who live on a small planet, and yet are part of the Federation. They have rangers posted on planet's surface, and in space stations around it should poachers try to get through. There are strict regulations and permits in place to even get close to Galecto Kelper, and the Eolif guard it with as much ferocity as any Gaian would their keep."

"If there be guards, some would have been on leave with family, only to return and find everything void of life." The gears clicked into place on Gladius's head. "We get a hold of one of the guards..."

"And we have proof of what is going on, thus bolstering other planets to our cause." Venetor nodded and then looked back at the camera. "Annetta, I'm sorry I cannot be of immediate help. Should this election be won, then I'm breaking every rule in the book to come to

Earth. She is our sister planet, and it's every Gaian's duty to see her safe."

Hope, trailed by a sense of failure, sent tingles down Annetta's spine. "I… thank you Uncle Venetor."

"Don't thank me just yet." He shook his head. "There's a long battle ahead. Skyris, keep this one out of any further trouble. I don't think the locals will take too well to any more incidents."

Skyris raised a questioning eyebrow. "What am, I, her mother?"

Venetor barked a laugh. "No, but you might as well be, considering how alike the two of you are."

Skyris rolled her eyes. "I'll see what I can do, brother."

"Thanks, sis." Venetor gave a weary grin and then turned to Annetta. "Hang tight, kid. We'll be there as soon as we can."

Annetta nodded and the screen went black. She looked over at Skyris, who still seemed to be looking as though something would materialize on the glass before them.

Finally, the tension grew too much for Annetta. "Did we do the right thing?"

Skyris got up and stood before the girl. She was a good head taller than Annetta, which made the girl still feel like a child whenever the two of them interacted, though not in a bad way. Despite her many strange behaviours, there was a grace to Skyris that Annetta longed to be able to emulate. She was like the older sister the girl had never had.

"I'm not sure, Anne," the woman spoke. "I know that saying nothing would not have improved our situation, and yet giving Venetor the information we did could help him win the election."

"Why does everyone make this seem like such a bad thing? I don't get it. He's King of Gaia, the people chose him."

"They did, but you know what they say about power corrupting people," Skyris said as they began to leave the room. "Don't get me wrong, Venetor is a good king, and he cares for all of his people, but I'm afraid of what such extra power would do to him."

"You think he'd bend rules in favour of the Gaians, then? Is that what Puc's worried about, too?" Annetta tried piecing it all together in her mind.

The woman looked ahead of them down the steel corridor. "Puc and I only need to look as far as our own example to understand the type of man Venetor is. The Federation, as you know, is made up of much more than just Gaians."

"Wouldn't that be a good thing for Gaia, though?" Annetta asked. "I mean, with what the Greys did about them not being able to help Earth, and all."

"They did abuse their power there, it's true, and these things happen in politics," Skyris stated. "The Greys, however, have had a good reputation for seeing to the good of others, something I'm not sure how capable Venetor would be doing. If it were Orbeyus, on the other hand, I'd be thrilled. He was born for that sort of thing."

Skyris continued to walk in silence for a little until she spoke again. "Although, if I have to choose between the end of the multiverse, as you put it, and Venetor at the head of the Intergalactic Federation, then I suppose I can live with a few years of Venetor in control. Thankfully, it's a Federation, and not a dictatorship."

Annetta nodded and said nothing else. They continued their journey towards the teleporters, knowing that no matter the outcome of the information that was given, there was no point in dwelling on what could have been.

⁗⁖

The transmission having ended, Venetor leaned back from the screen. His mind was flooded with the information he'd just been given. A bead of sweat that had managed to escape from beneath the crown trailed down the side of his jaw, and he caught it with his thumb in an annoyed manner. He turned back to Atala and Gladius, who sat on either side of him with equally brooding looks.

"And?" The word came out sounding hoarser than he'd like.

Gladius's one good ear flattened, his good eye directed at his king. "Our hands be tied, my lord. I don't think there's much we can do at the present time."

Venetor's eyes flared with determination. "Wrong. My hands are tied, yours are not."

He then directed his gaze at Atala. "I need you to return to Gaia. Whatever forces we can spare, prepare them for Earth."

The Gaian general frowned. "But what about the regulations regarding interference with Earth?"

"If we follow regulations, there might not be an Earth, or a Gaia, or any other planet left in this universe if Korangar is left unchecked. I, for one, would rather hold my last stand against the enemy, no matter how hopeless the cause."

Atala nodded. "Spoken like a true Gaian, my king. I will do as you command."

She then got up and made her way down the corridor towards where the ship was docked. Venetor then turned to Gladius, the Hurtz still watching him intently.

"I've another mission for you, as well," Venetor stated. "I need you to do some snooping with the Eolif representatives. See if they are willing to share any points regarding the events on Galecto Kelper Twenty Three. It's clear the Federation had minimal interest in it."

"You think if we show more interest, they might be willing to support Gaia's claim?" Gladius asked.

Venetor bobbed his head. "More than that. They might give us the ammunition we need to show that the Greys are not fit to run. Everyone loves a good story of how the Federation top dogs ignore the smaller planets."

"Aye, that they do, that they do," Gladius agreed. "Though if I can be honest, I don't think I'd be the best candidate for the job."

Venetor placed a hand on Gladius's shoulder. "You're the only candidate for the job. I've trusted you with my life for more years than I can count. What do you think will make me stop now?"

Gladius then stood to his full height of over seven feet, armour creaking as he did so. He made Venetor feel like a little boy each time he did so.

"Then I'll continue to do the same thing I have done all these years, and I'll do my best," the Hurtz said.

He then did the traditional Gaian salute, which included one arm across his chest, a closed fist resting over his heart, and the other behind his back. The symbolic gesture was meant to indicate that he carried his country in his heart while always being vigilant of threats from behind. Venetor smiled remembering this. It was a lesson from his father in a time long ago, before he was meant to be king.

"Onwards, soldier," Venetor said, and watched as the Hurtz left. The King of Gaia then found himself completely alone on the balcony, which still had the metallic shielding over it, enclosing the area into a soundproof pod during break time. He sighed, taking in the makeshift room. It was up to him now to see it through. The alarm signalling the end of the break then sounded, and the wall began to slide away from the lookout. The light of the outside threatening to blind him, Venetor looked down at his hands. Rough, calloused and scarred from more battles than he remembered. Hands in fists, Venetor slammed his knuckles together, then stood, ready for the next round.

Chapter 28

Hideburn gazed into the sky above which was populated by constellations he wasn't familiar with. His mind wandered to that stars in the heavens above Aerim. It was by the power of those stars at night that he'd navigated many a labyrinth at night while patrolling the outskirts of Morwick.

Unable to sleep, he rose from his place by the dying campfire. His eyes scanned the scattered masses of soldiers around him, both Minotaur and giants alike, as well as a host of other races that he'd never heard of. All seemed to be held in the thralls of sleep after the fighting of that day, and on the horizon, only a single solitary figure could be seen upright. He moved towards it.

As he drew nearer, Hideburn was able to see in clarity the outline of his king. Snapneck sat hunched over on a boulder, gazing into a private campfire he'd made. Were it not for the rising and falling of his massive chest, as well as the occasional flaring of his nostrils, Hideburn would have assumed his liege lord to be a corpse. The Minotaur King's face seemed somewhat gaunt, as if his features had grown sharper, and his eyes looked tired. Not since his father's death had Snapneck seemed this way, and even then, he'd been able to reason with the young Minotaur. Now, ever since the battle that had been named the Severing, Snapneck was possessed with a fury that neither Hideburn nor any of the other Minotaur warriors could get past.

"My lord?" Hideburn came to a stop, still maintaining some distance between them.

Snapneck's ears perked up, and the large Minotaur rose to his full height. Even now, Hideburn was amazed at how quickly he'd grown in the last few years. It seemed impossible that he'd once fit into the palm of his hand.

"You should be resting, Hideburn," Snapneck stated. "Korangar was very specific that when he returns, we will march again and onward to Earth."

There was a venom in the king's voice when he said the word Earth, and it made Hideburn shift uncomfortably.

"I understand, my lord, and I think you should do the same," Hideburn replied. "When was the last time you laid down?"

Snapneck didn't answer right away and continued to stare into the flames. "I have slept a thousand years, placated by the idea that a Severio would be our saviour. I will sleep no more."

More venom seeped through the king's teeth, as though he were a cauldron overflowing with it. Hideburn felt the urge to flinch again, but didn't do so this time, not while the king watched him. There was a madness behind the bloodshot blue eyes, eyes that had once belonged to his father, the late Lord Ironhorn. It was hard to even think that the two of them had been related, seeing Snapneck in such a state. Where had the sweet calfling that had ridden on his father's shoulder gone?

"I understood, my lord." Hideburn bobbed his head.

Snapneck nodded back, and turning to the dying embers that had been his fire, he threw in another few logs, watching it come to life anew. "Now, I do suggest you go get some rest if that is all. I've got a lot of things to do."

What Snapneck meant to do other than think, Hideburn wasn't sure, but gave another curt bob and turned to leave. There was a heaviness in his hooves as he did so. None of this felt right, and something in his gut churned for him to do something. Mixed with this was a sense of failure to his king. Not the king that was, but the king that had been, his brother, Ironhorn. It had been a secret well-kept in the event of his brother's untimely death, should there have been no heir to the throne. With Snapneck's birth, he could have come clean about it, but Ironhorn had insisted on keeping it secret.

"I want you to promise me something very important, brother," Ironhorn had said to him before the battle against Razmus, when they were alone. "You will keep my son safe."

In this, without a doubt in his mind, Hideburn had failed.

�⃝�

Away from where his growing army of followers camped, Korangar found himself staring out into the distance. He wore nothing more than a pair of pants that were torn and cut away just below the knees. He never felt cold nor warm, and the clothing he wore was mostly because some part of his mind told him it was proper. What others would have seen as deep contemplation about coming events was a battle far deeper within.

Images flashed across his mind, as they had for days now, though he was unable to pinpoint their origin, which frustrated him to no end. He saw scenes of sunlit fields with golden stalks of wheat blowing in the wind, as a hand, presumably his, reached out to touch them. It would then switch to another field, and before him stood a raven-haired beauty with a full and passionate smile, a smile meant only for him. Her warmth eclipsed the sun that shone on the land surrounding her each time he saw it. The happiness and serene feeling would fade as the same woman was dragged away by multiple men in the rain, screaming, reaching for him and presumably calling out his name, but her voice was muffled. All he had were the images and without any sound, they held little meaning.

Aggravated, Korangar shook his head, trying to get the scenes to spill out of his ears like water. He could feel their importance deep under his skin, and yet none of them made any sense to him. The longer he stayed awake, the more they came to him. They confused him, muddying his purpose for being. He didn't like that, and it stirred a rage within him to destroy even more. His body shook, and he drove off the latest memory.

"My lord?" Tamora then emerged from the tent, holding a blanket of fur wrapped around her.

Korangar glanced sideways to face her, removing any trace of what was bothering him from his features. Beneath the fur of the blanket, she looked small and frail, but he knew otherwise. There was a woman who would set the universe ablaze with him and never look back. He'd first realized a few weeks ago that he could communicate with Tamora while in his state of imprisonment, about the time he had awakened. Trapped in their respective cells, they had quickly formed a bond as one another they confided their darkest secrets, revealing their most primal selves to each other. Despite the short time, it felt to Korangar as though they had known each other a lifetime.

As he reflected on this, the scene with the raven-haired woman appeared once more, her intense blue eyes shining at him as she reached for his hand and then took it, leading him through a sea of golden stalks of wheat. Where they were going didn't matter to him as long as she was there.

His mind snapped back to the present as Tamora wrapped a hand around his arm from under the blanket. He glanced briefly at this, and then turned back to where he had been looking initially.

"I had a dream that woke me, that's all," he said in a voice void of emotion. "It… I think it was of the past. My past, but I can't remember anything like it from before my imprisonment, so it has to be false."

The Fire Elf woman nodded. "I had dreams like that once when your presence first came into my mind."

Korangar shook his head. "This is different. There are hills of green grass and golden wheat… and a woman…"

He furrowed his brows as he tried to recall her face, but it was lost to him, only appearing in the visions. The concentration on his face then turned to anger as he realized he could not summon it at will. "A simple and stupid dream, nothing more."

"A dream, and nothing more," Tamora reiterated and gently pulled on his arm. "Now come and get some rest."

Korangar glanced sideways again, but Tamora had already left and was heading inside the tent. He did not follow and instead tried to think of the images from his dream. He needed to know why they kept reoccurring. None of it made sense to him and the longer he tried to think, the more frustrated he became, because in the end it didn't matter, he would end all life. It was his destiny, he was the Seed of Khaos. As he was about to go, he was hit with another wave of memories, stronger than the ones before. He fell to his knees, gripping his head. He felt himself drowning, swimming in thoughts as though he were being interrogated and immersed in a sea.

Finally, the fit passed, and Korangar rose, remembering everything. Everything about his imprisonment made sense now, and a part of the man that had been in those fields so long ago resurfaced from among the bickering aspects of evil which had clouded his mind until that moment. He now knew his course, a target that needed to be destroyed no matter what it cost him. He wasn't meant to destroy all worlds as the voices in his head since his awakening had told him, but to save them from the one who would continue to cycle.

"Amarok," he growled, to which the shadows on his right shifted. "You have kept track of my father's other offspring all this time I am sure. Tell me, where are they located?"

Amarok's silver mask emerged from the dark as he strode over to Korangar's side. "I have indeed my lord. His descendants were not very fruitful of late, more concerned with starting wars than families. Mislantus Freiuson only had one daughter."

"You are sure there are no others anywhere?" Korangar looked over at him.

"None my lord." Amarok shook his head. "Sarina Freiuson is the last living descendant of your father and she currently resides on the planet Earth."

Korangar closed his eyes as relief passed over him. This would be easy and it would all be over soon. "Prepare the troops to march. The last Freiuson must die."

෧෬෬

Annetta had once enjoyed reading. A trip to her local bookstore always ended with a purchase of some kind, and it had gotten to the point once where she had needed to ban herself from entering it at the mall to save her allowance for other things.

She sighed at the happy memories as she turned the page of her school textbook while sitting in her room at home. If she'd thought her classrooms taught dry material, then the writing in the textbook was the equivalent of dry toast that had been dehydrated further till it was comparable to sand. The more she read, the more confident she became that the textbook material was how they got people to drop out of the course.

Quitting, however, was not in Annetta's nature, and so she used all the focus she could muster while scanning the contents of each page at least twice in order not to omit any crucial information. She had also decided not to waste time on shining her shoes, and behind her hovering over her bed with newspapers spread on it was a single black combat boot, while a pair of brushes attacked it from either side vigorously. She had to make up somehow for lost time in the Lab, and hoped that the Unknown would forgive her for such brash use of her abilities. Her training with Venetor had allowed her to be able to multitask better with her abilities in use as well and if she had the advantage of using it then why not? It was also the only way she could think of keeping her mind off everything that had transpired. If ever she'd reached a breaking point, this was it.

She was so absorbed in her studies that she didn't even hear the thud of feet going up the staircase from the main floor.

"Uhm… Annetta?" her father's voice asked from the doorway.

Shocked and a little embarrassed, the girl whirled in her chair, while the boot and brushes crashed down onto the newspaper, causing it to crinkle.

"Hey, Dad." She grinned sheepishly.

Arieus pointed his finger towards the bed. "Were you just using your abilities to shine your school boots?"

Annetta nodded slowly and waited for the worst. The reaction she got, however, was the opposite, and her father's face lit up.

"Arcanthur and I used to do that with our armour whenever we had our studies, too." He chuckled. "Our fathers would be furious when we did so. They said it took away from the discipline of it. Meanwhile, we just thought we were being efficient with our time."

Annetta relaxed slightly, watching her father come into the room. Moving the papers over slightly, he sat down on the corner of the bed. It was strange to Annetta to know there was a man far younger-looking that lay underneath the enchantment that was attached to his wedding band. It was even stranger to know that one day she too would have to go through the same thing. She sighed, turning back to her books as her mind began to think about Gaia again and the possible impending fight. Her shoulders tensed as she flipped to the next page, attempting to scan its contents.

"Everything alright, Anne?" her father asked.

Annetta glanced back at him again. Part of her knew she shouldn't say anything, and part of her wanted to let it all out. Her brows furrowed as she fought with the decision in her head.

"Your mother and I haven't had a chance to talk to you really since you came back from Gaia, but it's obvious that something has changed, especially in the last few weeks since you were here," Arieus began. "You know we aren't going to pry, it's not our job, but we will worry if something is bothering you, Anne. You're our daughter, and we don't care if we're over three hundred years old and still alive, you will always be our little girl."

The words crept under the armour that was Annetta's resolve, sinking their teeth into her. There was a way her father spoke to her that was able to disarm her completely, and it was never out of malice that he did so, but concern. She felt the tears begin to well up around the edges of her eyes, tears she'd been holding back for weeks now as she did her best to shove aside everything that had transpired.

Her head fell into her hands as she clasped it, fighting against the bleariness that was overtaking her vision.

"I've done some horrible things, Dad," she said through uncontrolled tears. "And I'm not sure I know how to fix them. Not this time."

She did her best then to keep her composure and began telling him all the events that had transpired since she'd returned to Earth, and of everything that had led to her leaving Gaia early. Arieus would nod and occasionally clear his throat, but the entire time his eyes were completely fixed on her. When she had finished, Arieus straightened where he sat and continued to regard her.

Finally, he placed his hand over the top of both of Annetta's, which lay in her lap, clasped together in worry. It made the girl see the small scars and imperfections on his hand in greater clarity when he did this, and she saw just how little her own hands were still compared to his, despite being almost an adult.

"We'll find the answers," he said to her. "Though it might not be easy, we're family, and we'll stick together to the bitter end no matter what. That's what family does for each other."

"Right," she managed to say as she looked into her father's eyes. They were the same shade of blue as that of her grandfather and Venetor, and beyond that, she imagined, many Severio lords and ladies past. She knew what he said to her was right, and she wasn't alone. She could only hope that it would be enough this time.

Chapter 29

Jansen's hands flew across the keyboard as she sat in the coffee shop. Her mind of late had been fueled with inspiration unlike ever before, and she partially admitted to herself that having met Darius had something to do with it. What were the odds someone would share a name with one of her characters?

"Jeez, Jan, you want me to bring a fire extinguisher over?" Travis cleared the table beside her of abandoned Styrofoam coffee cups, wiping it down with a rag.

Jansen paused, and a confused expression formed on her face. It took her a second to come back to Earth fully, but when she did, the joke instantly snapped into place.

"Very funny... Am I that loud?" she blinked a few times as self-consciousness crept in.

"Just a tad, but this ain't no library." Travis gave his signature goofy grin and she rolled her eyes in turn, shaking her head.

He always knew how to get her, and his wit was just as sharp as her own, at least when she was paying attention. More than half the time, he'd catch her off guard as she wrote, which then led to one of their pleasant bantering sessions. She didn't mind the distraction. The conversation gave her a pause when she felt a writer's block coming on, or a fork where ideas would split. More often than not, the interactions were enough to regroup her thoughts and tackle the next lines of the story.

"Sorry." She sighed. "I'm just in a hurry. I'm trying to get my word count in for the day."

"You count words? I thought you just sat down and went like a little automated typewriter. Isn't that how that stuff works?" he squinted an eye at her.

Jansen giggled. "Not on purpose, but I always have a goal of how much I want to write per day, so the story keeps going. And I try not to take breaks so I don't forget where I am. I did that one time, when I went away for two months to England to visit some relatives. Didn't remember anything about the story, and I had to start over when I got back."

"I always thought authors had like little notebooks with all their ideas written down." Travis tossed the coffee cups into the garbage bin.

Jansen saved the file, noting the time, and then looked back up at him. "Some do, depends on their writing style. Some like to have everything plotted out beforehand, but some like to just do things organically and let plots evolve on their own. Some do a bit of both. I like to just sit down and let things happen. I can't really explain it, but it's almost like my characters speak to me, and I record what I see."

"So you listen to the voices in your head," Travis concluded.

"I…" Jansen bit her lip. "I guess you could say that. It's more complicated than that, though. I can see places, feel what they feel at a given moment. It's like I'm in a movie, but I'm acting out all the parts and rolling the camera at the same time."

Before she could elaborate, the front door of the shop opened, signalled by a two-tone chime from the motion detector mounted on the frame. She turned to see Darius standing in the entrance and scanning the room. Dressed in his leather jacket with a black shirt and dark jeans, his pale skin bordered on vampiric in appearance. Jansen had to admit to herself that he looked kind of handsome, in a rugged metalhead sort of way. She raised an arm and waved at him.

He smiled when he noticed her and made his way over. "Hey, how's it going?"

Jansen did her best to prevent herself from beaming at his line while in the corner of her eye, she noticed Travis saunter off to continue clearing other tables. "Hey, not too bad, I'm just getting some writing in."

Darius pointed to the chair beside her to which she nodded and seated himself. "This that story you were telling me about before in the car with the girl who has the same name as my friend Anne?"

"Yep, the one and the same." She bobbed her head. "Just finished a big scene where these creatures come to her and her friends for help. They kinda look like wolf people with wings. I call them Soarin."

Darius's expression remained neutral when Jansen said this and she thought she'd offended him. She felt herself curl into her shell at the reaction.

"Uhm, I'm not into furries, I just thought they looked cool, so I went with it." She blurted out right after.

He raised an eyebrow. "Huh? Oh, sorry, I was just thinking about if I'd remembered to turn off the stove before I left. Actually, I think it's kind of a cool concept myself. Even the name kinda makes you think of flying."

Jansen grinned at him, picking up on the subtle reference in the name.

"So, I guess since we're here, we could grab that coffee I mentioned," Darius offered. "Unless you have somewhere else you need to be. I don't want to keep you in case you have work or something."

It took Jansen a moment to process the words as she worked through her mental calendar. The word count could wait to be completed in the evening, she reasoned with herself.

"Nope, I'm free actually." She beamed.

"Cool." He returned a closed-lipped smile and rose from the seat to go to the counter then paused half way. "Uhm... any preference?"

"Dark roast and black," she replied.

Darius nodded and went over to the counter. A few minutes later, he returned with two ceramic cups, aromatic steam rising from them.

"I got them for here, hope that's okay," he said as he slid back in his seat.

"Yeah, that's fine, thanks," she replied, accepting the cup with a smile, smelling the rich coffee scent wafting from the fumes. Coffee was always good in her books, but coffee she didn't have to pay for was all the better.

Jansen took a small sip from her cup and used the opportunity to study Darius's face with greater clarity than the occasional glance she'd gotten from all of their previous encounters. She was able to see his thin-lipped roguish face with sharp cheekbones, and deep dark brown eyes that seemed to almost border on the side of black were it not for the occasional flecks of amber she saw in them reflected from the light. Darius Silver didn't look half bad, and she actually wouldn't have minded if this had been a date. In fact, she found herself somewhat regretting that it wasn't. She then remembered what her mother had once said to her and that sometimes the best relationships started out in friendships.

Darius pulled his gaze away from her in the midst of the silence and glanced into his cup. "So... uhm, what were we talking about again?"

"Oh, I was just telling you a bit about my book, that's all," she replied, ready to change the subject at a moment's notice. Over the years, Jansen had experienced two types of people when it came to talking about her writing; those that held a genuine interest in her hobby, encouraging her to pursue it, and the people she did her best to avoid, that made Jansen feel as though her writing had little value if it didn't bring in a steady paycheck.

She watched Darius with anticipation for his reaction as the young man brought the cup to his lips while she spoke and then lowered it.

"Right, that's pretty cool that you're writing a book. I've never met an author before."

Jansen could feel herself beaming at the use of the 'A' word in the sentence. "I'm actually just a writer. I don't really consider myself an author, I haven't had anything published yet."

"Oh, well, I still think it's pretty cool, and I'm sure it'll get published." Darius took a sip of his coffee. "So, what inspired you to write this story?"

Jansen paused, thinking on it. "To be honest, I'm not quite sure. It's a story that's been with me for as long as I can remember. The basics anyways. As I've gotten older and learned more I've added to it, making it a whole and complete fantasy world, or… worlds I guess I should say."

"Huh, seems like it's pretty complicated," he said with genuine surprise. "How long have you been writing it?"

"Just a little over a year now. I felt confident enough to give it a try one day, and now I'm in over twenty chapters. Some days writing comes harder than others, of course, and it all depends on what scene I'm doing and how in-depth I planned things. Some days, however… it's like I'm there with them."

Jansen had to stop herself and take another look at Darius to see if his interest was still there. The last thing she wanted was to bore him. She decided, either way, it was time to stop. "Anyways, that's enough about that for now I think. So… you said you were taking Police Foundations with your friend Anne, how's that panning out?"

"A lot more discipline than either of us anticipated," he admitted with a laugh, running a hand through his black hair. "Well, for Anne, anyways. She's always sort of gone to the beat of her own drum. I was kind of surprised when she told me she was thinking of going into it. I think it was mostly because she's always the one who broke up any situations in school that involved bullies."

"She sounds like quite the individual." Jansen nodded, noting the look in Darius's eyes when he spoke about her. Despite both of them agreeing this wasn't a first date, part of her heart seemed to sink.

"Yeah, Anne's a great friend once you get to know her. She's the type of person who will go out of her way to help others," Darius concluded, taking a sip from his cup. "I should introduce you guys one of these days. I bet you'd both hit it off, since you're a fantasy writer and she's a reader."

Hearing the word friend attached to the girl's name, Jansen's spirits lifted a little. "Sure, that sounds great."

"So are you studying anything in school right now?"

Jansen smiled and began the long and winding track that would lead to her current position in life. Throughout all of it, Jansen couldn't help but feel that they were being watched. It was a common enough feeling she got in public, though that she generally dismissed it as her overactive imagination.

"So you dropped out of English because the teaching assistant didn't like your analysis of a poem?" Darius concluded. "Sounds pretty rough."

"Wasn't meant to be." Jansen shrugged, she'd gotten over the fact a while ago. "I dropped out and spent a year doing some soul-searching, working a part-time job and writing. I started my first semester of Library and Information Technician studies in college, and I haven't looked back since."

"Sounds like a mouthful for a course, and here I was thinking Police Foundations was long," Darius mused.

"Oh there are longer ones out there," Jansen said with a smile.

Darius returned the smile, but only briefly. He seemed distracted, as though he needed to be elsewhere. Maybe she'd bored him.

Before Jansen could say anything to begin to draw their meeting to a close, the sound of shattering glass could be heard a few feet away from them. Jansen veered around just in time to see a six-foot humanoid being with platinum blonde hair dressed in mismatched hide clothing jump through the broken window, while the nearest patrons scrambled out of the shop, screaming. Her skin began to prickle, forming into goosebumps, as an abundance of blood flowed into her legs with the need to flee as well. Her mind told her otherwise, and she stayed in her seat, waiting for the moment when it would turn around to face her. She needed to confirm something for her own sanity.

When it finally did, a pair of crimson orbs glared back at her from an angular face, scanning the shop, oblivious to her actual presence.

"Fire elf." She mouthed the word inaudibly in disbelief.

She was snapped out of her thoughts when Darius's hand clasped her upper arm sharply.

"Grab your laptop, we need to get out of here now." The words were more of a command than suggestion coming from him, and all traces of the boy she'd been speaking to seconds before were gone. She understood the change in his demeanour, though, even if she herself seemed dazed.

His words gained further validity when the elf drew his sword and began to make his way towards them.

Jansen didn't need to be told what to do twice, and swiping her bag from the floor, she tossed her laptop and power cord into it. She followed Darius's lead as he began to manoeuvre around the now-abandoned tables and overturned chairs. The elf closed in on them, however, and soon it was evident there would be no escape without a confrontation.

"That sword looks pretty sharp." Jansen swallowed hard.

Something shiny then flashed before her eyes, and Jansen reached out in time to catch a set of car keys. She looked over questioningly at Darius.

"Get out and start the car, I've got this," he ordered her, and as she was about to protest his decision he added, "I'll explain later, just do as I say and don't argue. I don't have time for dealing with heroics!"

The words cut through Jansen in icy strikes, and she didn't need to be told twice. She scrambled past him, catching out of the periphery of her eye as the Fire Elf charged and prayed to whoever would hear her that Darius's words hadn't been empty promises.

Once outside, Jansen scanned the street, looking at all the cars that lined the sides in parallel parking jobs of varying degree of neatness. Using the buttons on Darius's key to unlock the doors, she looked around frantically for a pair of flashing headlights on a black car. It didn't help that about a quarter of the cars parked were all black. She vowed at that moment to never get a car that was a common colour, just for times like this.

Her eyes then caught a shine of lights from the other side of the street. Jansen ran past the parked cars and charged across the street. Her dash was interrupted by a taxi stopping before her and honking, and she apologized to it with frazzled hands. Not bothering to watch it speed off in its fury, she slid into the passenger seat of the car and began to fumble with the keys, trying to get them into the ignition. She succeeded and heard the engine roar to life, causing the entire car to rumble in an angry growl beneath her fingertips. She could see the appeal of the older-looking car to a young man.

Darius then jumped into the seat beside her and slammed the door behind him. Without so much as acknowledging her, he began to reverse out of the parallel parking job and sped away, the engine of the car roaring in full fury as it left the coffee shop.

Jansen felt a sense of paralysis come over her as she clutched her laptop bag to her chest. The image of the Fire Elf was still burned into her eyes, its own crimson orbs glaring back at her with bloodlust and fury. No one had ever looked at her in such contempt, and she hoped that she'd never witness that look again.

Darius then rolled back his left sleeve and popped open a large watch with a silver faceplate to reveal a number keypad on it. He typed something it, keeping one hand on the wheel at all times and waited.

"05 here," a British male voice spoke over the speakers of the car, which caused Jansen to jump slightly.

"This is 117, I've run into some complications," Darius replied. "Fire Elf complications."

"On Earth?" the voice, though mostly dispassionate, had an edge to it now that bordered on concerned.

"Yeah, how, I don't know, but they attacked me and the target. What should I do?"

Jansen felt her arms tense at being called a target, and everything just became that much darker. Of course someone trying to get close to her would use a fictional name of one of her characters. The Fire Elf had to also be part of some bizarre plot to kidnap her. Why, she didn't know, but she had no intention to find out. Her right arm, the one farthest away from Darius's line of sight, began to slink towards a hidden compartment in her bag, the one that held the pepper spray her overly-cautious uncle had given her to carry around for whenever she was out alone.

"Bring her to the Lab. Then meet me in the common room area. 05 out," the transmission ended.

Jansen felt the hair on her arms raise at hearing the voice, a voice she pictured with vivid clarity in her mind each time she sat down to write. Her hand faltered from the spray.

"Thanestorm," she whispered to herself.

"The one and only," Darius answered, having evidently heard her.

"I don't understand how any of this is possible." She shook her head. "I mean how can you..."

"The truth is, I don't know." Darius cut her off. "We were told by the Sisters of Wyrd to find you and bring you to them. I didn't even know I was looking for you until we began talking to one another. I was just told that I would know you when I met you. This whole time I've only been going off a hunch, but the Fire Elf confirmed that something is really going wrong."

Jansen frowned upon hearing this. "So you are going to kidnap me, then?"

Darius continued to drive, putting as much distance as he could between them and the Fire Elf. "I don't think it's kidnapping if I just saved your life."

She pursed her lips as she replayed the scene in her head. "Point taken."

The remaining car ride went on in virtual silence until Darius pulled into the driveway of a small house with a rustic stone finishing. It looked somewhat unkempt, thanks to the amount of moss that had managed to grow in the cracks where the mortar was, making the house look like it had green veins growing around it. The garden beds lay littered with fallen leaves and other natural debris. It looked as though the owners had completely forgotten to do any maintenance.

The engine shut off, making Jansen focus fully on her surroundings. She watched as Darius got out of the car and walked over to the door as though he'd been at the location a thousand times. She could not pinpoint it from any scene she had written, and decided that maybe she didn't know Darius and his friends as well as she thought she did due to her writing. Seeing little alternative, she unbuckled her seatbelt, took her backpack, got out of the car and followed him inside.

She was shocked to find that the interior had little to almost no furnishing in it. It was as though someone had just bought the place and hadn't bothered to move in. On the far wall from the entrance, a great mirror with a gold filigree engraved frame revealed her reflection to her. Its grandeur was overshadowed by something Jansen would again not have thought possible. A device consisting of a platform with a hovering keyboard stood before the mirror.

"It's best to go down one at a time at first," Darius told her, standing beside it. "Though, to be honest, all of us still go down individually. I don't think one really gets used to the feeling."

Jansen's feet moved towards the teleporter. Her shaking hands reached out, touching the smooth metal, checking to make sure it was actually there. It was real. A tingling at the base of her spine confirmed it, and she knew that she was there for a reason.

Not bothering to ask how it worked, she stepped onto the platform and typed in the number one. She then waited for it to begin.

Chapter 30

As soon as the shuttle touched down and opened its doors, Atala strode out onto the walkway connecting the ship with the port. Her purposeful gait as she cleared the hallways was a well-honed march that had been practiced over her lifetime. The crimson cloak she wore fluttered and snapped through the air with each step, trailing behind her like a faithful dog. Though she hadn't been allowed to take her blades into the station, her uniform as general of the Gaian forces had not been denied, and for this she had been grateful. It was a semblance of her old life before Razmus, a thing she'd been denied those few months while on Earth, and she would hide no more.

Atala ordered the first able-bodied guard she could find to bring transportation, and soon found herself mounted on a sabretooth dog resembling a St. Bernard. She travelled down the well-known route to Castrumleo, her mount's claws clicking on the cobblestone road while she planned her next move. She would need to summon the nobles before she could begin rallying forces to stand ready for Earth's aid. She would also need to reach out to Skyris and see if she could activate the cannon they had used to come to Gaia, for their supply of ships was nowhere near ready to bring their full force to Earth. A portal would be much simpler for their purposes.

Once she arrived at her destination and dismounted, Atala took note of how quiet the castle and courtyard seemed, despite it being midday. It was almost too quiet for her liking as she tied the dog to one of the posts outside the main building.

She then made her way over to the two guards by the door. They were both part of the new recruits that had more than likely just graduated, for not a single wrinkle creased their faces, and the young man that stood on the right showed only the faintest trace of reddish facial hair.

"You there." Atala ordered his attention. "Why is it so calm on these grounds at this hour of the day?"

Both guards straightened slightly and saluted her when they noticed the colour of her cloak.

"General Shade." The woman on the left acknowledged her. "The Crown Prince has called together an assembly of the nobles. Whatever illness held him is no more."

Atala squinted somewhat in disbelief. "Titus is better, and no one decided to inform the king?"

"The physician tried calling," the young man answered this time. "Apparently the line at the Una Station was busy, and when they tried again it looked as though the electoral process was back in session."

"It must have happened when Annetta called," Atala muttered to herself. "How long ago was this?"

"Early morning yesterday," the female guard stated. "We're not sure exactly. The last of the nobles just finished arriving. You may be able to catch the meeting as it starts. We can make sure your mount is taken care of."

"See it is so," Atala ordered, her patience running low.

The doors then opened, and she strode inside without another word.

The castle inside was also void of much life. Atala made her way towards the throne room, where she was sure the audience would be held. The nature of it was what worried her most as she recalled Titus's condition before their departure. The once-proud son of Venetor Severio had been reduced to a mess of fits and half coherence. If in his coherence he had ordered a meeting, there was a risk that he would slip into madness midway, and fuel the propaganda of those who remained loyal to Razmus, despite the Lord of the Unfinished Tower having mistreated and enslaved all Gaians in equal measure.

With these thoughts in mind, she wound down the last of the corridors in a near-sprint, and burst into the throne room. The gathered nobles turned to regard her, all dressed in the finery of their ancient and prestigious houses. They looked like a scene from an Earth renaissance painting, rather than nobles from an advanced spacefaring race.

Atala's gaze then fell towards the dais at the far end of the room where Titus stood. He was dressed in a fresh set of clothing, his face shaved clean, save for the sideburns he'd always kept. His silver circlet, a more delicate version of the Gaian monarch's crown, rested on his brow, keeping the hair from falling in his face. What Atala noticed more than any of these minor details were his eyes. Where before in his fits there was a murky quality to them like tainted water, they were now sharp, keen and alive as they regarded her.

"Atala." He called out to her as a smile formed on his face and a faint echo filled the room. "I take it father is back, then?"

"I'm afraid not, my Prince," she answered with an edge of uncertainty. "What is this meeting about?"

The smile faded from Titus's lips, and his countenance was overcome with a sternness that was second only to his father's. "These past few weeks have been a trying period for me. The Unknown has seen fit to restore me that I may better help prepare our people for what is to come."

Atala shifted her weight from one foot to another, and took another glance at those gathered in the room, older lords and ladies mixed with eager youth ready to prove themselves. They were the remnants of those that had not been murdered by Razmus and his horde. The usurper had made a point of disciplining those whose ancestors had once turned on him, and it now showed.

She then turned back to Titus. "And for what are you to help prepare us?"

"For the one thing every Gaian has always been told they must lay ready for." Titus folded his arms behind his back. "To come to the aid of their sister planet in her time of need. More than this, to prepare for the greatest battle yet waged in the Aternaverse, for when Korangar wakes, no one will be safe from his fury.

≈✦≈

Annetta got her hands on the first, best gelding she could find, and took one of the many well-travelled routes by Severio Castle. She kept her profile low beneath the cowl of a long grey cloak she'd managed to obtain while on one of her strolls through the Lab. The atmosphere of the Soarin that were camped around Severio Castle was thankfully not such as to make her need to explain her leaving, for they were all too focused on what was to come.

Annetta halted the horse when she came upon the trail she and Firedancer had always taken. Some feet above her was the all-too-familiar ledge cut from limestone. She got off the horse and tied it in the same fashion as she'd always done with Firedancer, then teleported above.

The mostly smooth plateau of pale stone created by years of erosion had remained unchanged from her last visit. Small tufts of grass and moss sprouted here and there among the cracks where soil had managed to manifest. Above her head, a golden sun rolled on a clear blue sky in what was, to her estimation, a perfect summer day, but she was not here to enjoy that.

An idea had crept upon Annetta in her sleep, one she wished to explore further. She'd not shared it with anyone for fear of being deterred in her quest. This was something she had to do alone, and letting others know would only potentially slow her down.

She lowered herself down into a cross-legged position, shut her eyes, began breathing in and out deeply as Puc had taught her, and cleared her mind.

Her destination this time, however, was not the garden where she met with Orbeyus. It was a place further deep down inside of her, just as she had when trying to find her feral form.

೮೦೧೪

Annetta felt the heat of a roaring fire upon her face as her focus returned, and she found herself looking at the same surroundings she'd been in moments before upon the mountain ledge, but set ablaze. Trees burned below in orange and red like large candle wicks. In the distance behind her, Severio castle had also been set to the torch, its once-pristine cerulean tower heads reduced to a distant memory.

Focused on taking in everything around her, Annetta was knocked off balance by the beating of wings as they passed overhead. She scrambled to her feet and was confronted by a large reptilian head of red scales, with enormous emerald cat-slit eyes. Dagger-like teeth protruded from its mouth and smoke curled out from its nostrils in puffs, enveloping its curved horns. Two powerful bat-like wings folded at its shoulder blades as the creature glared at her with malicious intent. She didn't need to think twice about what it was that stood before her, for Annetta was familiar with the concept of dragons.

"Hey," she managed to say, anticlimactically. "So, you're the thing that's been inside me all this time then?"

The creature didn't answer her. There was an aloofness to its face as it shook its long neck, much in the manner a horse would rid itself of blackflies. Its eyes, however, told a different story entirely. It knew something Annetta didn't, and that was what the girl had hoped for in this encounter.

"I can feel you under the skin," she continued. "Puc says he's placed a seal on you, but I can still feel your presence. I think he can, too, and that's why he asks me not to use my abilities or avoid fighting. He fears you."

The green orbs were now watching at her. An intelligence was present in them when moments before they had been entirely animalistic.

"I'd be lying if I said I didn't fear you, also," she added grimly as an afterthought.

The creature pulled its lips back, revealing multiple rows of razor-sharp teeth. A thrumming growl reverberated from deep within it. Annetta did not so much as flinch at this, reminding herself where she was.

"This isn't real," she breathed quietly. "And I might fear you for the same reasons Puc does, but that fear comes out of misunderstanding. I need to know why you are here, why you are part of me."

Silence followed, and the dragon continued to regard the girl, a massive, scaled tail swishing back and forth much in the way a cat ready to pounce would.

The tension left Annetta's shoulders, and she relaxed a little at seeing this. The creature seemed to sense this, though, and spread its great wings with an earth-shattering screech. Taken unawares, Annetta staggered back and fell. The heated stone burned her fingers where she touched it, and hissing, she scrambled to get up again. She then found herself face to face with it again, mere inches separating her from the draconic maw. The last thing Annetta saw was a thousand teeth and flame.

ഌരെ

Annetta shook herself awake and wiped the sweat from her brow. She sat back and stretched her legs. The sun was still high overhead, meaning she'd not been out long. She squinted against the strength of the rays, and rising to her feet, she dusted off her red leather jacket. Her hand absentmindedly brushed against the lion on her left breast pocket, which caused her to look down at it. She recalled that it had taken time for her to understand what her feral form had been and what she needed it to be in order to beat Razmus. Her gaze then tore away from the jacket, and she looked towards the castle, untouched by fire.

"Well, that didn't go down how I planned it." She frowned.

Disappointed in the lack of answers, she began to walk over to the ledge before teleporting down. While she was none the wiser from the experience, she had learned that the beast could be communicated with.

Better yet, it appeared to have a purpose. All she needed now was time to uncover it.

Chapter 31

Jansen felt queasy the moment she materialized on smooth metal panelling. She'd never been a big fan of wave pools, and they usually left her sick for a few hours. It was the same for rollercoasters, she'd discovered sadly while on a date with her ex-boyfriend who'd bought them a season's pass to Canada's Wonderland. It had been one of the reasons the two were no longer together, and as she lay on the floor reminiscing about how she'd felt, she realized it was probably for the best.

Darius appeared beside her a few seconds later and made a quick recovery, rising to his feet almost instantly. He looked down at her writhing form with a quizzical look. "Uhm... you okay?"

"Just peachy," she groaned. "Can we not have to do that again?"

The sound of large metallic doors screeching could then be heard, followed by feet and something wooden striking the ground. Black boots with the end of a staff then appeared in her line of sight, followed by a large pale hand.

"I believe I may be of some assistance to you, Miss Morrison," a disembodied voice said.

Groggily, Jansen reached up and grabbed the hand, allowing herself to be pulled to her feet. She then found herself looking up into a face she'd only ever pictured while writing. It was pale and angular, with ice-blue eyes and framed in black hair.

"Puc Thanestorm?" she asked.

"What's left of him," the mage said. Reaching into the folds of his robes, he pulled out a small vial that he handed to her.

Jansen accepted it, eyeing the purplish liquid sloshing around with curiosity. Uncorking it, she downed the contents. She regretted the decision right after and found herself doubling over, expelling the contents of both her lunch and the potion. So much for being graceful in the face of adversity.

"Sorry," she managed to say, through coughs.

If Puc was showing any disgust to the situation, he was hiding it, as was Darius, who'd run up to her and put her arm over his shoulder so she could lean on him.

"First one is always the worst," the mage told her, and with a wave of his hand, the mess on the floor vanished. "Though I may advise you take one of the vertigo counteractors before descending next time."

"Does there need to be a next time? That was horrid," she said.

"How else do you expect to come and go?" The mage raised an eyebrow.

"To be honest, with what happened, I didn't think it would be an option," she admitted in a small voice.

"Perhaps not until the Sister of Wyrd have a look at you," he replied, and began to move towards the hallway that lay behind the doors.

Jansen squinted a little at hearing the name. In all of her writing she'd done, she was not familiar with whom the mage was talking about. She was feeling slight better now as she walked, part of her weight carried by Darius as he helped her. "Sisters of Wyrd? Who are they?"

"They will be best adept at explaining their origin. More so that I," Puc answered. "I will tell you, however, that they are highly regarded by my people. Their influence stands in higher regard than that of First Mage."

"That's flattering of you to say, Thanestorm," a voice spoke from some distance before them.

The girl looked away from Puc and focusing ahead, saw three hooded figures in grey cloaks approaching them. The one in the middle dropped its hood in a nonchalant manner to reveal a woman in her early forties with pinned-up golden hair and a long, thin scar that ran from one side of her neck all the way across it and ended on the opposite side of her face just above her cheek. Despite sharing the same cold blue eyes that Puc had, hers were filled with a warmth that Jansen could only describe as the same one would find on a midsummer day.

"Welcome, Jansen." She gave her a genuine smile. "I've been expecting you."

A frown lined Jansen's face at hearing this. Being expected could only go one of two ways, and Jansen could only hope that it was the more positive of the two. As far as she saw now, she was completely powerless, and it frightened her to no end.

The woman seemed to pick up on her uncertainty. "You've nothing to fear from us, young one. I am Lysania Chironkin, founder of the Sisters of Wyrd. You could call us a society of librarians, in the simplest of terms."

"Librarians?" Jansen's brows smoothed out a notch.

Lysania nodded. "Yes, I asked Puc and Darius to find you for us."

"What for? Why should I go with you?" she asked.

The Water Elf woman seemed to search for an answer herself before proceeding to speak again. "We were instructed by the Angels to find the one with the ability to record truth and keep her safe from the path of the End. If we are to have a chance to stand against the storm, then we need to make sure you were safe from his fury."

"Fury?" Jansen was about to inquire further and then stopped herself as her face paled. "You mean… Korangar?"

The girl had scarcely noticed that in the time of her contemplation, Lysania had managed to advance the last few feet that had separated them. The woman's hand draped onto Jansen's shoulder, causing her to snap out of her thoughts.

"Come, and perhaps both of our questions will be answered." The words rolled off her tongue in a warm and inviting manner.

Despite this, there was still some level of hesitation that filled Jansen. What would her mother think if she just took off? She was already more than likely to be grounded from not having come home from the café when she said she would. Worst yet, there was the concept of losing her part-time job, and college… she didn't even want to think about that. These and a thousand other thoughts began to surface in her head like lights in an audience during a ballad at a concert.

"I'd like to go as well," Darius said, interrupting her train of thought. "If it's allowed."

Jansen's eyes darted from Puc to Lysania hopefully. It would be a relief to have someone at least slightly familiar there with her, even if she didn't know Darius that well.

"Very well," Puc intoned. "You may go for now. Have your C.T.S. on standby."

Darius bobbed his head and Jansen caught a twinkle that passed through his eye briefly when he looked in her direction. It could have been a trick of the light.

"We will take our leave then, Thanestorm," Lysania said to him. "If there are no other pressing matters for us to discuss."

"None I know of." He shook his head.

Jansen then watched as Lysania raised the hood of her cloak once more and rejoined the procession with the other two Sisters of Wyrd. Though part of her still wanted to resist and run, she felt overall a sense of peace with what was happening. Submitting to that, she raised one foot in front of the other, and accepted her fate.

හගෙ

Puc stood alone at the round table where he had called the other members of Q-16. Though he was First Mage, he was still pulled to his duties as the advisor of Orbeyus. It had been his calling long before his new post, and try as he might, he could not separate himself from it. In all the years they had known each other, Orbeyus had grown to be more than just the leader of the Four Forces and the Defender of Earth. He had also become his friend. Now, watching everything they had built unravel at the seams made him feel responsible. Like a captain, he would go down with his ship, if that was the will of the Unknown. All he prayed for in return was to be reunited with his long-dead friends.

His mind was torn from further contemplations when an all-too-familiar form entered the room, Skyris. Clad in her usual bomber jacket, her hair tied back in a messy ponytail and with oil smudges on her face, she looked like a mad scientist having been forced to leave work for some menial task which had little meaning in the greater scheme of things.

"Hey," she greeted him. "So, what's this meeting about?"

"I would prefer to wait before I go into any details," he stated. "I have to repeat myself enough in my writing to remember spells. I like to avoid it whenever possible in speech."

"Ah, right, that." Skyris gave a short bob of the head as she folded her arm across her chest. "I guess even you would be tired of it."

"I am getting older, am I not? I think at over five hundred years I am allowed to have my shortcomings when it comes to patience."

Skyris laughed, a sound Puc had not heard in years. It brought back other memories, and the mage smiled faintly.

"Well, lookie there, you didn't completely forget how to smile after all," she teased with a grin.

"No, I suppose I have not," he replied.

Her grin widened, causing Puc to be further flooded with feelings from his past. There was no malice attached to them as there had been when he'd first learned of Skyris's return to Q-16. The few months of her presence in the Lab had given him time to further heal the freshly-slashed wounds of his psyche by her return. He then realized something he'd never dared to ask her before.

"Why did you leave all those years ago?" he asked.

"You told me to," she stated nonchalantly. "It was in the letter you wrote. Don't you remember?"

Before either of them could answer, the sound of sirens and the glow of red and yellow strobes filled their ears and peripheral vision. The bulbous form of Dexter sped into the room where the two of them gathered, his single red eye seeking them out with full fervor.

"Puc Thanestorm and Skyris Severio, your presence is requested in the control room," he announced, before speeding off again. "Alert! Code Omega engaged."

"Code Omega?" Puc's brows furrowed.

Skyris didn't respond right away and only stared off into the distance, where the exit of the room lay, pensive in her own thoughts. She then finally spoke. "The code Orbeyus had me put in place in the event of the one thing he feared most. What he didn't think humanity was ready for... invasion."

ഇ൝൞

After Jason excused himself from tutorial and met with Sarina in their apartment, the pair dashed to the control room as per the requirement of the message that flashed across their C.T.S. watches in crimson lettering.

Once in the Lab, Jason found himself puffing from the effort of the run. His gaze was almost immediately stolen when he looked up to see what looked like video footage of Toronto featuring panicked civilians that appeared to be running from something.

Jason moved closer to the screens and realized that he was watching a Fire Elf rampage through the city with an enormous scimitar that it seemed to be using to hack at whoever got it its way. The shock of the image caused him to look at other screens and examine them. They were recording similar scenarios with not only Fire Elves, but also Minotaurs and other species of aliens that Jason had never seen before.

Jason tore his gaze away to see everyone who had gathered in the room, which included himself, Sarina, Puc, Skyris, Matthias, Annetta and to his surprise, Xander and Liam.

"What's happening?" Jason asked as he took in all of the different smaller screens that were fixed into the large glass displays of the control room setup.

"War is upon us," Puc said, as he leaned on his staff before another set of monitors. "A war I did not expect would ever be fought in your lifetimes, or even mine."

"I don't get it," Jason snapped, gesturing at the nearest screen. "We even attempt to use our psychic powers in public, and we'd have Angels come after us, but an army of Minotaurs and Fire Elves in downtown Toronto is okay with them? Who's in charge of their rules?"

"It would appear that the time has come for the Earth to step into the light," the mage stated.

"Not exactly how I ever saw it going down, to be honest." Matthias furrowed his brows. "Even when I was fighting for Mislantus. I imagined things would have happened a lot swifter."

"What? No bloodbath?" Jason griped.

"I don't think standing around here's the solution to any of it," Annetta finally spoke. "The biggest question now is are we allowed to help these people?"

A silence ensued right after as all eyes went to Puc, who seemed to be at a loss for words. He stood rooted to the spot with his right hand gripping his staff, wrestling with what to say.

"For once, I do not think I have an answer," he said finally. "I will say this, however, I am not of the opinion that any human man, woman or child should suffer the fate they are now being subjected to. Orbeyus had first and foremost crowned himself the Defender of the Earth, and I will leave you with this."

Another bout of silence persisted, but was cut short by the sound of Annetta summoning Severbane. Jason and the others turned to regard her, taking in the etched wording on the sword that said 'Severed Be He Who Forgets.'

"I said I would fight because no one else would." She glowered at those present. "I know you don't think I can because of something swimming around inside my blood, but I'm going to try anyways. Those people need our help. We have to try and save as many as we can."

Typical Anne, Jason thought to himself and took a step forward. "No one doubted you, Anne, and you best not think you're going alone."

"No, most certainly not." Puc nodded in agreement. "I will contact Natane as well as Illiam to mobilize what troops can be spared, as well as speak with Amelia."

"There will be no need to contact me, Thanestorm." The voice of Natane beamed from some distance behind them. "For I and my warriors are already here."

"Great Mother?" The elf's eyes seemed to widen.

The Ogaien woman inclined her head. "Black ash falls from our skies and is no product of any volcanic activity. Tiamet laments for the end of our days."

"Black ash?" Jason furrowed his brows. "We had that too not long ago here. They blamed it on some factory."

"Your human media will do much to cover up the supernatural as the supernatural will do much to conceal itself from other species that do not know of its existence," Puc said, and then turned to Natane. "We are grateful for any aid we can receive."

"And you shall receive everything we can give, for in the Severed One we trust." The reptilian green eyes fell to Annetta, who still held Severbane.

Jason looked over at his friend. He could see by the tense setting of her shoulders that she was heavily contemplating what to say next. It was only he who could tell. He'd known Annetta long enough to be able to see the signs, even under the folds of her leather jacket.

"I'll do everything I can not to disappoint." She slid Severbane into its scabbard at her hip with a faint smile.

To the outside world, that smile was meant to show heroism, but Jason knew it for something else. It was the look Annetta gave each time she was too pained to smile truly, and forced one on because she didn't want others to feel defeated.

While those gathered began to discuss their course of action among each other, Jason found himself bounding towards Annetta and with a firm clasp of the hand, he turned her around.

"You alright, Anne?" he asked.

There was a brief second of shock which appeared in her face before she released herself from his hold.

"J.K., I have to be," she replied. "There's no time to wait for how things could be or could go. We only have each other, even if you all think I'm broken. We said we would protect the Earth. I'm no expert, but I think it needs us now."

"I hear ya, Anne." Jason nodded.

"Regardless of what you plan to do," Puc cut into their conversation, "There are still others who would wish to aid you."

"Yeah, dudes, some of us have a bone to pick," another familiar voice called to them.

Those gathered turned to see Doriden standing in the hallway. The Soarin Alpha, despite his accident, seemed to be in good health, save for his one wing. It looked off in its construction, as if it had been dislocated, but the more Jason looked at it, the more he realized that it was attached to Doriden artificially. Brown leather belts that ran around the side of his chest fastened around where the wing was held in place. Silver gleamed from where the slicing had taken placed and left the rest of the wing in its natural state. Then, to further prove his point, Doriden opened both wings to their full span, the attached wing glittering in the harsh halogen lights.

Annetta's face softened a little. "I can use all the help I can get."

"Our first order of business should be the extraction of as many life forms from the surface as possible," Puc stated. "Jason, Annetta, Matthias and Liam, you shall be responsible for bringing civilians into Q-16."

Matthias raised an eyebrow at hearing this before stating his thoughts. "I'm sorry, you want us to bring people down here?"

Puc's jaw twitched slightly. "Not ideal, but yes."

"You want just four of us to evacuate all of Toronto? Are you nuts?" Jason's eyes widened. "That's like what? Over two million people."

"I never said it was an ideal plan but given our resources it is the best we have got." Puc stated.

"Eight." Another voice came from the hall. Doriden stepped aside to reveal the forms of Talia, Aurora, Arieus and Arcanthur, who was being pushed in a wheelchair by Arieus.

"Dad?" Jason's jaw dropped.

The elder Kinsman looked different than when Jason had last seen him. He was completely clean-shaven, and his brown hair, lined with streaks of grey, had been neatly trimmed short and brushed. His green eyes were focused and didn't dart away when they met Jason's.

"You didn't think I'd let them keep me locked away when the world as we know it was coming to an end, did you?" He smirked and then looked over at Puc. "I believe you have some damaged to undo, mage, so best get cracking, before we have even bigger problems on our hands."

଼ଔ

Skyris's fingers raced across the keyboard as images of various sectors flashed on the glass screens before her. Using infrared cameras that she'd placed into a series of nanobots that had been released into the air, she homed in on the largest clusters of population running around the city as it was slowly being swallowed up by invaders. They would need to wait to focus on everyone who was indoors after the fact, if it came to it.

She adjusted the single small earpiece with a slender microphone while using all of her focus on the screen before her. Dexter floated lazily at her side, observing all of the happenings with his one red bulbous eye, ready to obey any command given.

"The attack seems to begin around Front Street, and pushes out into the city from there," she stated after having analyzed the situation. "You'll need to teleport in there and get those people out of there first."

"This plan sounds great and all, but how do we even get people to trust us?" Jason's voice came through the earbud.

"Tell them you can take them someplace safe. Don't elaborate. Things get complicated if you do," she told him as she adjusted the brightness of the screen. "Now, remember: Follow the coordinates I sent to your C.T.S. watches. They'll tell you where to find people if you don't see them immediately. Only teleport down when you have a group of at least thirty if not more, when possible. Puc wants you to avoid using too many potions, since we only have so many made."

"Seems easy enough, in theory," Annetta's voice came through. "How hard can it be to find and teleport thirty people down?"

"Uh, with Fire Elves, Minotaurs and all this other stuff out to get you?" Jason paused dramatically for effect. "Sounds pretty hard."

"Which is why you have teams of Water Elves, Soarin and Ogaien with each of you for backup," Skyris reminded them. "The one good thing about being in a metropolis is open warfare against large groups is not a possibility. Even if they destroyed every building around, they'd still be forced to fight around the ruins."

"Let's hope that's the case," Jason muttered.

"The medical wing is prepared to run at full capacity," Sarina reported from another line. "I've got every available healer and medic here with me to treat anyone who comes in."

"Sounds good on this end. Let's hope that we don't really need them." Skyris nodded and clicked a few buttons, switching to a GPS-like screen where little greens dots moved across the map of downtown Toronto.

The communications then went silent. Skyris was left with only the suspense of the screen. She then reached into the coat pocket of her jacket and produced a flask from it, which she shook to listen for the sound of sloshing liquid. Satisfied to find its contents full, she was about to open it when she paused. She ran her fingers over the aged and cured leather, which wrapped around the stainless steel. On it was embossed the rampant lion of Gaia with a pair of wings, resembling the version of the heraldic symbol that had been on her father's crown and was now present on Venetor's. The flask had been a gift she'd received on her birthday from some lord or lady, which one, she didn't remember. The flask had lain in one of her drawers for years, and she didn't think she'd ever use it. It was only recently that it had become a permanent part of her ensemble. Skyris tore her gaze away from it and placed the flask on the desk before her, pushing it back with a single finger. She then resumed her wait, reflecting on better times.

Chapter 32

The world Annetta teleported into didn't resemble the Toronto of her childhood. Crashed and abandoned vehicles lined the streets, creating a maze to walk through. The girl tread cautiously through the scene, her crimson cape decorated in the white lioness emblem billowing on the wind behind her. She'd chosen to wear her Gaian armour specifically, hoping it would make people more inclined to trust her, since, in her mind, it made her look like how a superhero would dress.

Her shoes crushed broken glass into more shards as she walked through the abandoned streets. The smell of burning gasoline accompanied by the blaring of distant sirens confused and dazed her senses. This was not her first battlefield, and yet she felt more out of place here than ever before. Her everyday life combined with the world she knew beyond was a bit much even for her to comprehend.

"What should we do now?" the voice of Natane broke through her train of thought.

Annetta pivoted on her heel to see the Great Mother mounted up on her Aiethon, surrounded by five other Ogaien. Beside them stood six Water Elf mages, as well as six Soarin. The girl took a ragged breath through rattled nerves as she tapped into her feral form abilities and focused on amplifying her hearing. She closed her eyes and allowed the sense to overpower all others until she heard what she wanted. Voices.

"In that direction." She pointed to her right and began sprinting, her hand firmly gripping the hilt of Severbane at her side and her shield in the other all while keeping her senses heightened.

It took mere moments before the group encountered the first group of humans surrounded by alien forces and quickly set to action. This time, Annetta did not lead the charge, and instead turned her attention to the small group of people that were huddled into a bus stop. Two of the men in front used a torn-off car door as a shield to block the opening. She lowered her shield arm and released the grip on her sword hilt.

"It's alright, we're here to help," she said, the words sounding awkward as they came out.

The people in the bus stop continued to look at her with contempt and tension. She could tell they were nowhere near trusting her. Her shoulders slumped as she sighed. Maybe the Gaian armour wasn't such a great idea after all. She probably looked like a fool to everyone there.

Before she could say anything else, the car door barricade lowered and out came the eight people that had been sardined into the stop. They were visibly shaken, unable to trust anything around them. Annetta had had time to adjust to the various races she interacted with, but to these people everything they saw that didn't resemble human beings was a monster, and Annetta's armour certainly didn't fit the bill of normal. She shifted somewhat uneasily as they all pooled around her.

"You with the RCMP?" A larger old woman pointed a ringed finger at her.

Annetta moved back another few paces, while attempting not to lower her shoulders or posture. One could retreat, but not do this, Venetor had stated that to her time and time again.

"No, I'm not," she told them. "But did you honestly think the RCMP would be here with everything going down this quickly?"

Her words had been a last resort, a desperate throw across the finish line and Annetta hoped that they had hit home. She knew how stubborn some human beings could be, and she didn't discount it for a second as she locked eyes with each one of them. She didn't know how else to tell them the dire situation they were in.

"Government ain't never done anything good for me." The woman who had spoken before shrugged and walked towards Annetta. "About time some people took things into their own hands. Why didn't ya'll show up any sooner?"

The others followed wordlessly and it then became clear to Annetta that the woman she was addressing was their appointed leader.

"Let's just say we were being kept under lock and chain," the girl replied.

The forces Annetta had with her came back, having driven off the intruders. The group before her recoiled a little into the shelter. Seeing their reaction, she waved a hand.

"They're on our side," she told them. "They're with me."

"And how are we supposed to tell them apart from the other things running around?" A tall young man with a backwards baseball cap dressed in a leather jacket pointed at them.

"The ones on our side are all the same species you see here," Annetta indicated. "Now, I don't have time for any more questions. We need to find other people. Get in line behind me and don't leave the circle of soldiers."

The group obeyed with little opposition, although the stares of fascination and fear remained. Annetta ignored this and continued listening to the sounds of voices that were nearby. Already it was shaping up to be a long day.

೫೦೧೩

Arieus trudged down the streets of Toronto with a grim look on his face. The longsword at his side was half-drawn, while Arcanthur trailed closely behind. He'd ordered the squad of soldiers to go ahead and scout for people. The elder Severio was dressed in chainmail armour with the red tabard of his father displaying a black rampant lion on it. Though he'd sworn never to lift a sword in battle again, fate had made him wear the mantle, and despite better judgement, Arieus didn't mind it. This was where he belonged, the life that he'd been born into and the life his father had given him.

Puc had undone the binding that was placed on Arcanthur and allowed Skyris to fit him with a prosthetic foot so he could walk on his own, but he had not allowed the elder Kinsman to bring people down to the Lab on his own. Though the scars of the fight from over ten years ago had mostly healed, they hadn't closed fully. Neither Arieus nor Puc trusted the man enough not to do something which could bring harm to the ones they were currently trying to save.

"I never thought I would see the day," Arcanthur spoke as he took in another deep breath. "The day when both worlds we knew of would come together as one, and it isn't even my doing."

Arieus turned to regard his friend, who was in a state of euphoria as he looked at the decimated buildings, burning vehicles and heard the sounds of blaring sirens in the distance. All of this seemed music to Arcanthur's ears, and he couldn't understand why. Perhaps having released him and given him his psychic abilities back hadn't been the smartest gamble. Despite this, Arieus did his best to believe that there was something left of his old companion beyond the veil of madness.

"This isn't how we imagined it would play out," Arieus reminded him and began to walk forward, feeling the leather as he clutched the sword hilt firmly.

Arcanthur rolled his eyes and trailed behind Arieus, hobbling awkwardly on his newly gained foot. "I never said it was. I'm but merely making an observation. The Unknown and the Angels tried so hard to shelter this world from the rest of the multiverse, and to what end? If it weren't for us, this world couldn't even defend itself against what's coming. Hell, I don't even know if we can this time."

"So why bother agreeing to come with me if you think we're all doomed?" Arieus questioned him while listening intently for any signs of people.

"Isn't it obvious? If I'm to die, I'd rather go down fighting than pumped full of drugs." Arcanthur grinned, his crooked nose more prominent in the smile.

Arieus shook his head at this, then stopped as a sense of déjà vu came over him. There was something oddly familiar about the way in which the buildings came together over the patch of sky overhead and the curve of the streets before him as they merged into other side roads, ushered by neatly planted maple trees and streetlights.

"Hey! There it is!" Arcanthur pointed to a lonely tavern sign that seemed out of place among all of the modern buildings around it.

It then clicked and Arieus shifted uneasily a step back. The last time he'd been here with Arcanthur, it had cost him their friendship, and nearly cost them both their lives. He'd avoided the place like the plague since. He was about to say something to Arcanthur when a female Soarin descended before him, her great wings causing the dust and smaller debris to rise.

"We found a group," she reported.

"How many and where?" Arieus inquired.

"Fifteen at least," she replied. "We were unable to get a clear count due to the fighting. It's just around the corner in that artificial cave filled with machines."

Arieus looked where she pointed, to realize she meant a levelled parking lot. His gaze then turned to his friend, still lost in his reminiscing and nostalgia. He grabbed him by the shoulder firmly, causing Arcanthur to snap out of it and look over at him.

"Stay close to me and… watch my back," Arieus told him, hesitant in the last part of the sentence.

Drawing his sword free of the scabbard with a sharp metallic ring, Arieus charged and was met by two otherworldly creatures who bore the grey tabards with a black seven-headed dragon. Arieus parried their assaults with a series of sword strokes, while the pair mindlessly threw themselves at him with their weapons. He immediately recognized their actions as religious fervour, a devotion without rational thought.

Fanatics. Onwards and onward they pressed him, the larger of the pair Arieus recognized as a Verden through the haze of fighting gaining significant ground with his great sword that he swung like a butcher would a cleaver. The other on Arieus's heel was a smaller creature that was humanoid in form with deep blue skin, yellow eyes and matching spiky hair. He didn't recognize it from his battles against Mordred in his youth, nor from the limited space travel he'd done with his father on the few occasions they'd gone to visit Gaia. It was mad, this much he knew, as it continued to attempt to assail him with a pair of scimitars which had little effect against Arieus's chosen bastard sword.

Finally seeing an opening, Arieus dashed and drove his weapon through the gut of the Verden. He then retracted it in time to make a clean sweep through the neck of the other creature. Staggering back a pace, Arieus processed the amount of carnage he'd just dealt. His contemplation didn't last long when another enraged Verden charged for him, this one wielding a warhammer that was twice the size of his head. He jumped out of the way just before the mallet would have collided with him.

Arieus braced his hands with psychic energy and grounded his sword to himself, making it an extension of his arm. He didn't wait for the Verden to realize what he was doing and sliced with an upper cut, shattering the hilt of the hammer which dropped to the floor with a clang.

The Verden's eyes widened at the attack and then narrowed completely lunging for Arieus with both beefy arms extended. The creature didn't seem to care if it were hit by the blade or not. Arieus quickly bested it and watched as the creature dropped to the floor.

"Why are they acting this way?" he muttered under his breath, panting from the effort of the fight.

His answer came in the form of a shock to the system as Arieus was hit in the back and flew several feet through the air. He collided against the side of a parked car and hissed, grabbing his side, which now sported a cracked rib if not more. Flexing his fingers, he realized the sword he'd been carrying was now lost and he was unarmed. Panic surged through him as he looked around frantically for the weapon. Worst yet, fear trickled through as Arieus spotted his assailant.

At first, all he could hear was the flaring of great nostrils as air was inhaled and exhaled, which prompted him to look up. Their owner was a large Minotaur wielding a club with raised metallic spikes that had hastily been driven through it. It lacked the elegance of a Minotaur weapon and this made Arieus frown, even if for but a split second. His eyes then landed on where the sword had fallen.

Before Arieus could even think about recalling the sword to himself, he watched as the creature before him went fully into its rage, raising the club over its head.

A crunching thud broke the moment and the beast fell to its knees as a film formed over its eyes and it fell face first into the pavement. When the dust cleared, Arieus looked up to see Arcanthur standing before him, his mace bloodied. There was a sharp clarity in the green eyes that looked back at him. Arieus never thought he would see it again.

"What?" Arcanthur grunted, seeing his friend's expression. He then extended his hand to him.

Arieus licked his lips nervously and summoned the sword back into his grasp, clasping his fist around it tightly before accepting Arcanthur's hand as he rose to his feet.

Arcanthur cocked his head to the side as he regarded his friend, seeing how uptight Arieus was. "Uhm… you okay?"

A tightness overtook his neck, but despite this, Arieus managed to give a single brief nod. His mind, however, had gone back to a far darker moment in his life as he recalled another battle with the man who stood before him, the one he had called his friend.

A great sigh escaped Arcanthur as he glanced back in the direction of the sign they had passed. "Look, I get it. It's not easy to forgive what I did. At times, I can't forgive myself for the time I missed out on with my boys. There's a part of me that wants to take it all back, but it's not possible. The only thing we can do is move forward. I've had over a decade to think on it, and I forgive you for what you did. The question is if you can you forgive me and if we can we fight as brothers once again, even if it's just one last time?"

Arieus looked into Arcanthur's green eyes. Reaching out his free hand, the duo clasped forearms. Turning towards where the Soarin had pointed out the civilians, they ran.

ဆာလ

Jason and his team of Soarin, Water Elves and Ogaien scanned the area for civilians as they sprinted through the desolated scenery. They'd already managed to pick up a small group that had barricaded themselves in a convenience store when the attack happened. Jason had only found them due to tapping into his feral form's heightened hearing. It didn't always work, since he didn't have enough training with it, it but he'd been lucky this time around. The group had agreed to follow Jason's lead without much hesitation, anything in their minds being better than staying in the convenience store and waiting for another wave of creatures to come for them. This was not to say they were very trusting of the Soarin, Ogaien and Water Elves which surrounded them, herding them like sheep. Jason didn't blame them, in fact he would have been the first person to object were he part of their group. Now was not the time for it, however, and he needed to get as many people out as he could and fast.

Breathing in and out to calm his nerves, he decided to check in on the others. *'Liam, you doing okay, buddy?'*

'J.K.? Uhm, yeah, we got a group of fifty people out of one of the malls. I'm collecting my second group now.' His brother's voice came through his head.

Jason nodded, despite knowing his brother couldn't see him. *'Okay, I'll check in on you in a bit.'*

His thoughts then turned to another. *'Anne? Everything good on your end?'*

A wave of silence passed. Jason feared the worst and briefly scanned the skies above for anything that resembled the winged creature he'd witnessed back at the battle around Morwick.

'Yeah, I'm here.' Annetta's voice finally came through in his mind. *'Everything's fine. Why? Did you run into trouble?'*

'Huh? Oh, no. I was just checking in with everybody,' he replied.

'Oh, I see,' Anne replied. *'Well, everything's good here. Don't check in too often, though. As little as it does drain, telepathy also takes a toll on psychic abilities. You may wanna conserve your energy.'*

Jason cringed. He hadn't even thought about that. *'Uh... right. I'll see you later, then?'*

'At some point, yeah,' she said, and the connection was gone instantly from his mind.

He was suddenly conscious of everything around him tenfold, as if waking from a dream, and he inhaled deeply to catch his breath. He looked down to Helbringer. The mace seemed to weigh double in his hands, and he pressed his fingers tighter into the leather grip while looking at the lion-head-shaped blades. If Anne had no problem with this, then he couldn't, either.

His ears then picked up something faint from the far right. It sounded like the snorting of a bull and as soon as he recognized it as such, he pivoted in that direction with his mace raised before him.

"Minotaur!" he shouted as the rest of his party sprung to engage, blocking the civilians behind them. The creature burst forth from the alley on the right, followed by a score of Fire Elves and other smaller aliens. Jason charged at the head of the group, and with an uppercut powered by psychic force, he thrust his mace's blades into the Minotaur's stomach, before retracting it and cutting the beast across the heel ligaments on his right leg. Unable to keep his balance, the Minotaur toppled, to be picked off by one of the Water Elves.

Jason then turned his attention to the approaching Fire Elf with a raised scimitar and raised his mace to parry the blow, catching the blade of his opponent's weapon between the teeth of the lion head. Using additional force, he snapped it in two and was about to land the final blow on his opponent when an explosion from the wall of the building beside him threw him to the floor. Shaking off the shock, Jason's eyes widened at the sight of not one but four additional Minotaur that had come to pick at his group. Rising to his wobbly feet, he raised the mace before him and went for the closest of the four, aiming for the legs of the giant creature.

The Minotaur scoffed at seeing this and with a backhanded swipe of his shield arm, Jason was thrown to the floor, his only saving grace being the armour he'd decided at the last minute to wear. When he came to a halt on his back, he felt like a beached turtle and only then realized how much energy he'd drained. Perhaps he should have listened to Annetta's warning about using psychic energy.

"Damn," he muttered under his breath, and braced himself for the worst.

No sharp pain through any part of his body came, however, as seconds later another crashing of hooves and feet occurred. With an adrenaline rush, Jason scurried to his feet to see something he'd not expected to witness in this battle. A third group of two other Minotaur had emerged from out of nowhere and were attacking the one that Jason had been fighting. His opponent fell seconds later and Jason was forced to look at the two newcomers, whom he recognized almost instantly.

"Hideburn? Bonebreak?" His eyes widened.

"The one and the same," Bonebreak assured him.

"Though not here under the circumstances we would have liked," Hideburn added. "In any lifetime."

"Yeah, tell me about it." Jason sighed, taking another glance around and looked to the terrified civilians who stood behind the tight line of Ogaien, elves and Soarin.

"We do not follow the orders of Lord Snapneck," Hideburn stated. "Our king has fallen ill, been poisoned by words of malcontent. That seven-headed snake of a flat-footer has been putting things into his head that have turned his thinking away from everything we have stood for, for thousands of years."

Reluctantly, Jason lowered his guard slightly. "How do I know I can trust you and you're not just going to take me and the others out when we let our guard down?"

The great nostrils on Hideburn's face contracted and expanded as he regarded the boy with his intelligent amber eyes. "I have nothing to offer you but my word, Jason Kinsman. Once, this would have been enough."

Jason sighed as he weighed his options. His gaze went back and lingered on the terrified group of humans, guarded by their otherworldly keepers. Mere hours ago, they had all been oblivious to the world he'd been made part of over two years ago. Now, their entire lives were unravelling before them, and it was up to him and his friends to make sure they would survive the oncoming storm, a storm that he and Annetta didn't have the resources to stop. They needed every advantage they could get, even if the risk was great. He focused once more on Hideburn and Bonebreak.

"Where are these others you speak of, and can we get in contact with them somehow?" he asked.

Relief flooded Hideburn's face. "They are scattered among the other soldiers. It would be easiest if I and Bonebreak were to split up and show that we have defected to the others."

Jason nodded hearing this. "Yeah, that doesn't sound like such a bad plan, and I have just the way to do that."

೮೦೧೩

Annetta gasped after her latest trip down to the Lab and coughed as she let go of the people who had been holding onto her. It was now her fifth time down in a row, and her knees were beginning to feel weak from the exhaustion. Murmurs of shock, fear and excitement came from behind her as each of the forty individuals she had just brought down expressed their feelings on having been transported into Q-16.

On cue, one of the several Dexter units Skyris had made floated into the room and analyzed the group with a single red bulbous eye. No matter how many times Annetta saw the thing, it still unnerved her to know there was an A.I. that was prowling the depths of the Lab at all hours of the day.

"Hello, I am Dexter, or Digital Escort X-droid and Technical Exploration Robot," he said to them in a sing-song voice. "Welcome to Q-16. You must all be wondering where you are. Please follow me as I explain this to you and answer any questions."

The group shuffled along obediently as though they were tourists, but a few shot worried glances in Annetta's direction. She would have done the same were she in their shoes.

She ran a hand down the side of her face to have it come away covered in sweat swirled with grime. Her whole body, including her cloak and armour were stained from the grit of fighting wave after wave of would-be attackers. Once everyone was out of sight, she slid down against the closest wall, continuing to breathe heavily. Every muscle in her body seemed to be on fire and her lungs felt as though they were lined with lead. She wanted to keep going, but her body refused.

When she looked up again, a vial of dark blue liquid floated before her face which she snatched before realizing it had been attached to a hand. Glancing further up, she found herself staring into Sarina's brown almond-shaped eyes.

"Oh, it's just you," she said quietly, hesitantly examining the potion. She then uncorked the mixture and downed it with a grimace.

"You look like you've seen better days," the girl observed.

"I feel like I've had better days," Annetta grunted in response and rose to her feet.

Annetta turned around at hearing displaced voices to behold another group of people being escorted by a Dexter clone. Though some of those present managed to look mesmerized by the Lab, there was a clear underlying fear in their faces as they analyzed their surroundings.

Annetta straightened a little as she felt her energy return, but the stiffness in her muscles from both fighting and teleporting remained. There was also something else she noticed that she'd not been conscious of before, a thrumming in her veins. It was as though something was trying to get out, and Annetta knew full well what it was.

Pressing her thumb and forefinger to either side of her temples, she turned away from Sarina, masking the feeling by making it appear as a headache. She closed her eyes and felt overwhelmed by the thrumming. It began to sound more and more like great wings beating.

"Not now, whatever you are," she hissed under her breath.

"Anne, you okay?" Sarina's voice came from a few paces closer than it had been before.

Annetta opened her eyes and shuffled away from her. "I… I don't know what's going on."

When she looked back at Sarina again, the girl's face was lined with worry, and it made Annetta guilty for having done anything. She swallowed hard and tried to drown out the noise by thinking about what needed to be done. They needed her, her city needed her. It was the one place she'd sworn to protect and up until just now, she'd never been made to make good on the words she'd said to the Angels all those years ago.

"I need to get back up there," she said through gritted teeth. "I have to keep going no matter what it takes. Those people need us."

"Before you do Anne, there's something you need to see."

Chapter 33

The boat slid easily onto the sandy shore, and before she knew it, Jansen found herself at the entrance to the residence of the Sisters of Wyrd. Her mouth hung open as she took in the polished brass chandeliers and shelves upon shelves of large leather-bound books and scrolls. The wood of the shelves was cut intricately, featuring various designs that Jansen swore resembled those of the Victorian era as she had seen it portrayed in Jane Austen movies.

"This is like a bookworm's dream," she managed to say as she continued to look around.

"There's a lot more where this came from, trust me." Darius smiled as he tapped her on the shoulder, motioning her to move forward.

Jansen blushed at his touch, embarrassed by the way she was behaving, but at the same time being unable to stop herself. It was all real, Annetta, Jason, Puc, Aldamoor. Just this morning she'd awoken with the dull notion of having to go into her day job, and by the time the afternoon hit, she was in another world. She would probably lose said job for giving the excuse of 'I travelled into another dimension,' but it seemed a miniscule price to pay in the scheme of things.

Shaking off the thought, she continued to follow Darius and the woman who had introduced herself as Lysania, their other companion who had been referred to as Sister Nadja having wandered off into another hall to perform other tasks.

They soon stopped before a massive wooden door that was so intricately sculpted, it seemed to spring to life before her. The scene depicted a couple standing back to back while mists swirled around them. In the mist, or clouds, as Jansen thought them to be, were other scenes depicting the pair from the middle, some of which were more pleasant than others.

"The door was created for mine and my brother's five hundredth birthday," Lysania spoke as she ran a hand down the wood. "Feels like only yesterday instead of five millennia ago."

Jansen's eyes widened at the number. The woman before her didn't look older than her early forties, but from the moment she'd seen Lysania, there had been something about her light blue eyes that had been unsettling, like they were far older than the skin they inhabited. It then hit her.

"You're Lysania Chironkin," she gasped. "You're the sister of Chiron the Creator. The first Water Elves."

A faint smile lined Lysania's lips. "I am, but we were not the first. Chiron's title came not from being the first Water Elf in existence. He was the first to attempt to have our people settle. In our days, there were no great cities like Aldamoor. We were a nomadic people with no ties to any land, but only to the seas. Anywhere close to water was home for us, and we wandered like the currents of a river. It was Chiron who created us a home in Aldamoor. It was also he who left years later, and disappeared."

"I thought Chiron died of old age." Darius frowned.

"No, Chiron didn't die, at least not to my knowledge. He could very well still be out there somewhere. Alas, if Chiron wished to be found, he would allow it. He was as good at disappearing as he was at building." Lysania seemed to space out for a moment, then sighed and shook her head as her brows furrowed. "Forgive me for reminiscing. Though I may not look it, sometimes my head begins to swim in the past. Now, onto the reason we came here."

With a push, the doors crept open. Inside was a large rectangular table set with a few candleholders and the odd pieces of papers. The walls beyond it were lined with books, and had Jansen not known better, she would have thought them to be a wallpaper. Towards the back of the table she then noticed a group of women ranging from their mid-thirties to late sixties, all of them with the same feral blue eyes. Their gazes fell on her in a predatory manner. Glancing sideways, she saw Darius standing by the door, as she was led further in by Lysania, and a part of her silently begged that he would go in with her.

"Now Miss Jansen, I, believe my colleagues and I have some questions for you."

∞∞

What Sarina led her to caused Annetta to stop. Among a crowd of people, two towering Minotaurs with bull heads stood. Thick, coarse hair sprouted wherever the joints of armour or mail didn't cover it, and there was an intelligence in their eyes which made them seem sentient despite their otherwise bovine appearance.

Ice followed by fire began filled her veins as Annetta plotted her next course of action if the attackers saw her. She didn't need this right now, there couldn't have been a worst timing. Suddenly, something landed on her shoulder. Jumping from the shock, she turned to see

Jason beside her and Sarina. His own face and clothing didn't appear much better than her own, and he seemed to have a patch of crusted blood that streaked down the side of his face. She only hoped it wasn't his own.

"Relax, Anne," he said.

"Relax?" she fumed. "Are you blind?"

Jason's face turned into a scowl. "No, Anne, and you shouldn't be so quick to jump to conclusions."

As if on cue, the two Minotaur began to make their way towards them. Annetta tensed as she readied herself to draw Severbane from its scabbard. It was only when she recognized who they were and that they had no weapons that she let her guard down slightly.

"Hideburn? Bonebreak?" she inquired the as the two former guards of the Morwick gates came to a halt before them.

"Lady Severio." Hideburn included his head. "Forgive us for the intrusion, but Lord Jason thought it best if we come down and explain ourselves."

Annetta crossed her arms. "Well, make it short, because I've got people to get down here."

"Lord Snapneck has gone mad," Bonebreak stated. "He's not the sovereign we once served, and certainly not the king his father had meant him to be. The one he follows now, this Korangar, has twisted him, made him believe the cause of all our woes has been the Four Forces, and that he will unite both Minotaurs and giants. All we have seen so far is his endless quest, the goal of which doesn't seem certain, but could lead to the end."

Hideburn took this as his cue to step in. "There are others like us who feel the same way, but they fear going against the king."

"What makes you so different?" Annetta eyed them skeptically, her hand still on the sword hilt.

"It is a secret I have long carried, but now I fear it makes little difference if kept." Hideburn exhaled. "I was the brother of Ironhorn."

Her brows furrowed as Annetta digested what she'd heard. "He never mentioned having a brother at any point."

"It was a secret to be taken to my grave." Hideburn sighed. "One I would have been happy keeping, were it not for how poisoned Snapneck's mind has become. It is not uncommon for Minotaur kings to keep their sibling a secret should an assassination attempt be made by the giants on those of royal blood. This way, at least part of the bloodline endures."

"It's strange, but it's also really clever," Jason added.

Annetta weighed it all in her mind and analyzed it. "I'm still not certain how this information will help us if no one knows you're Snapneck's uncle."

Hideburn then reached into his armour and pulled out a small circular medallion that hung on a chain. The disc was dark, ebony in colouring and had writing chiseled into it which glowed blue. As soon as he took the medallion off and handed it to Annetta to examine, the glowing stopped.

"My father had that pendant commissioned upon my birth," Hideburn explained. "It will only glow when held by his direct descendant, and one who could potentially wear the crown."

The girl pursed her lips and finally nodded, handing it back to him. "As good of an explanation as I can get, given everything happening right now. I'm not one for threats, but if you do betray us, know that I won't hold back."

It was the first time she'd used such words on anyone who was or had been part of the Four Forces. She felt dirty doing it, and she had to remind herself that she didn't have much choice but to assert herself before those who could potentially harm her friends and family.

Hideburn seemed to sense this as he met her gaze. "I understand."

Annetta nodded and then looked over at Jason. "Take Bonebreak with you and I'll take Hideburn. The moment we get more Minotaur, we'll meet here to disperse them among the other psychic teams."

"Good a plan as any," Jason agreed.

Taking hold of Hideburn's forearm, Annetta inhaled deeply, trying to quell the headache as she teleported.

ⅮⅯ

Sparks flew around the barrel of the pistol as Xander's hand jerked back in violent recoil. The Minotaur that had been rushing to attack him toppled in a heap some ten feet away and didn't get up again. Though relief flooded his body from the immediate threat being eliminated, he knew it was far from over and pivoting on his heel, he aimed the gun again. His next target was a Fire Elf berserker who'd managed to make its way towards him through the maze of abandoned cars that flooded the street. Some were still on, and the fumes which rose from their exhausts made Xander's nostrils burn. He never wanted to live in downtown Toronto, if that was all he could smell.

The creature grinned viciously with crimson eyes set on him, and brandished the short sword and hand axe it carried. Xander felt the finger around the trigger begin to pull back.

A ball of flame then hit the approaching elf and caused it to turn tail, screaming. Xander turned around him just in time to see Liam land on the hood of the nearest car.

"That was…" Xander began to say but paused mid-sentence.

"Awesome?" Liam grinned.

Xander sighed. "My shot."

Liam rolled his eyes as he slid off the car. "Yeah, well, you were taking too long, and we need to find more people."

He nodded, knowing his friend was right and then checked on the slew of at least ten people who were shielded by an escort of three mounted Ogaien warriors, four Water Elf mages and four Soarin. It was tough to find people where they were, especially since so many of those they found barred the doors of their hiding place and didn't want to let them in. Xander felt it had something to do with their age. No one would listen to a teenager, even if the world was under attack by an alien force.

"How do heroes face rejection from those who they're supposed to save in the comics?" Xander mused.

Liam's lips pursed in concentration as he struggled to come up with an answer. "You know, I don't think I've ever read anything like that before. Most of them just kind of swoop in and save the day no matter what people think of them."

"Then we're doing a really crappy job of swooping in." Xander motioned to their group. "We're supposed to bring these people to safety, and we've just been dragging them around downtown Toronto."

"Yeah, but we're only supposed to go down if we have a certain amount of people," Liam reminded him.

Xander frowned and looked towards the twisted maze of tall buildings that lay to their right. They'd kept so close to the main road that they hadn't gone down any of the side streets to investigate.

"Change of plans," he said to Liam, then turned to the others. "We'll go down here to the right. People could be stuck in the side streets and not know where to go."

The plan sounded good to him, adult, and he could see from the way the soldiers and civilians nodded their heads that his assumption wasn't far off. His faith somewhat restored in himself, Xander and Liam led the party.

Xander swerved past the cars that blocked their way and stepped into the shadow of the first alley. Despite all the times his parents had ever told him not to go down them, it didn't seem all that bad. He could clearly see everything around him. Maybe it was only after dark that the rules applied?

A silhouette then appeared at the other way of the alley. Xander smiled and puffed out his chest as he hurried in. His valiant effort to remain heroic in his mind's eye, however, failed when his foot collided with a discarded beer bottle that clinked and then flew ahead of him, spinning in a tempest of green light. Cocking its head to the side, the figure paused, looking directly at him.

"It's okay, we're here to help!" Xander called and waved.

He regretted his words right after as the shadow from the other side drew a sword and gave a signal of attack, then charged. Other shapes burst through the light at the end of the tunnel, drawing their own weapons. Xander drew his gun in response, aimed, then fired.

The blinding beam of light pierced the first of the attackers and sliced through their midsection. Sparks coursing around his body, they collapsed midway through the alley, creating an obstacle for its comrades. The others didn't stop at this, only more frenzied by the drawing of first blood.

A car flew overhead, crashing into the forms of the second wave of attackers with the sound of breaking glass and bending metal. Xander turned to and saw Liam readying the next vehicle, levitating it into the air as he prepared to hurl it.

"I hope these guys have insurance," Liam said with a smirk, and seeing the next wave of fighters cross over the destroyed car, he flung another.

"That'll be the least of their worries," Xander replied as he took aim at another creature, this one looking much like a human being with red eyes and platinum hair. Sparks blaring from the barrel of his gun, he watched as it met his end.

The screech of bending metal then overpowered everything else around them as the overturned cars moved. Taking a step back to stand beside Liam, Xander watched in both fascination and horror as a single

Minotaur raised them, and a torrent of smaller foes poured through the bottom like water through a dam. It then pushed the cars aside to reveal not one, but three Minotaurs, who bared their teeth and gripped large twin-bladed axes.

"Liam, get those people down now!" Xander ordered as he fired at the nearest enemy.

"What? I can't leave you!" Liam protested as he threw another car.

Behind them, the retinue of their soldiers mobilized to enter the fray, leaving the civilians they had been guarding exposed. Xander gritted his teeth at his friend's reluctance.

"It will only be for a few seconds, alright? Just go!" he bellowed and took aim at another fighter.

Xander watched out of the corner of his eye as Liam gathered up the people they'd managed to rescue, instructing them quickly to link hands. They then vanished. He then felt a sharp pain across his forearm and turned to see one of the red eyed humans, this one a woman, attempting to cut deeper into his arm with a saber with a grin of pure glee on her face. Horrified, he whipped his other pistol around and shot straight into her midsection, watching her get blasted some few paces away, then fall to the ground from where she didn't move. He then clutched his arm as he attempted to stop the bleeding while using it to aim and look for anyone else who would be close by. Maybe he should have worn thicker armour when told to. It was getting harder to hold the gun firmly as his palms began to sweat more and more and his muscles strained from the effort of holding his arm at a straight angle.

"I'm gone for like five seconds and you already get injured?" Liam's familiar voice beamed from behind.

Xander exhaled and just as he turned around, he saw a Minotaur heading straight for them. The massive hooves of the creature pounded the ground at a speed he wouldn't have expected from the behemoth wearing full plate armour and carrying a two-handed mace. His hand shot up on instinct and he pulled the trigger once more.

A blast did come from the gun, but it was nowhere near the brilliance of the others he'd done. The shot only stunned the beast. He then remembered what Darius had mentioned to him about needing to replenish his energy, and looked around frantically in his pockets for the potions he'd been given. Xander's eyes widened as the Minotaur gained ground, Liam only now just beginning to react and ready another vehicle from nearby to throw. Finally locating a vial, he ripped his hand from the pocket and did his best to uncork it with fumbling, sweat-slicked hands.

Liam whipped the car at the creature and to his surprise, watched as the Minotaur braced itself against the attack then pushed the car back in the other direction. It then grinned viciously under its helmet.

"A psychic." Liam whispered.

They'd been told that psychic warriors could occur in any race, Xander remembered. It was different to be told something, however, then it was to experience it. Xander felt a panic take over his body that almost made his face go numb with shock.

"Liam, watch out!" he called as he downed the foul-tasting concoction and aimed again.

He pulled the trigger, but with no response as Minotaur rushed at them. The smell of greased metal mixed with sweat filled his nostrils as he summoned every bit of energy he had in him, only to have sparks fly from his gun and nothing more. Beside him, Liam called on debris, unable to lift a car any longer with his abilities, and threw them at the creature as a way to deter it. He too fumbled for a vial in his pocket. Cursing, Xander fired again as a small blast hit the Minotaur causing him to stagger. The Minotaur shook off the shock and then lifted the mace into the air, aiming for Liam, who was distracted by downing a vial he'd located in his pocket. A flash of white brilliant wings then blinded Xander's vision, and the events which followed were a blur.

Chapter 34

The destruction surrounding Korangar was a beautiful thing. When Amarok had told him where the descendant of Freiuson could be, he'd wasted no time in lengthy preparations, and instead had chosen to go as soon as his troops had mobilized. He'd been in such a hurry that he'd only donned a cloak and breeches, having forgotten to put his shoes on. Not that he needed them, since he felt none of the dire effects of cold or heat that plagued most mortals. Now, he walked the streets barefoot, the soles of his feet touching the warm asphalt as he passed by abandoned cars and skyscrapers that greeted him like a slew of villagers hailing the returning hero.

A discarded stuffed brown bear that looked to have one eye missing made Korangar pause, and looking up, he found himself gazing at a tall, pointed structure with an oval that sat about two-thirds of the way up from the top. It appeared to be an observation deck on a tower. Its design and structure looked completely out of place among the other rectangular buildings. It bothered him.

"You are certain that it is in this city she's hiding?" Korangar uttered in his rich voice and turned to his right, where Amarok and Tamora stood a mere few paces from him.

"Yes, it is the last place that I remember her being," Amarok stated. "She'd befriended the descendants of the Severio clan."

Korangar wrinkled his nose at the name, as more memories surfaced in his mind's eye. His expression then faded into a malicious grin. "How fortunate it is that the descendants of the prophet who did this to me have all settled on this backwards world. I'll just have to kill them, too. It'll be a poetic ending, don't you think?"

"It will, indeed." Amarok nodded thoughtfully, placing his hands behind his back.

"With your permission," Tamora chimed in. "I humbly ask to be able to take the life of the one named Puc Thanestorm. He and I have some unfinished business."

Korangar cocked his head to the side, his gaze focused on the pale woman with crimson eyes. She wore the traditional patchwork leather garb of her people, and carried a scimitar at her side that she eagerly clutched as she spoke. He also sensed something else about her, though he wasn't quite sure how he knew.

"Under normal circumstances," he began. "I should refuse you, given the state you are in, but because I have heard you tossing and turning in the night, murmuring this Thanestorm's name, I shall allow it."

Tamora's eyes widened and her free hand went instantly to her lower abdomen. She then looked back up at him. "You mean…"

"The heir to the dragon's empire grows within you," he confirmed. "Be cautious in your dealings."

A wide grin formed on her face and reaching out, she took Korangar's hand and kissed it, before taking off with a maddening laugh and drawing her blade as a slew of Fire Elves emerged from among the wreckage to follow her lead.

"Was that wise to let her go on her own, my lord?" Amarok asked.

Korangar stood unmoving, watching her disappear into the maze of buildings. "Her life is her own. It was just her army I needed. The cycle must end, and I must be the one to do so."

∞∞

The meeting with the nobles to mobilize Gaia's forces having come to an end, the last of the gathered left the throne room, and Atala watched as Titus slouched where he sat. Despite doing his best to maintain a regal air, evidence of his past sickness still clung to him. The dark circles under his eyes and the gauntness in his cheeks turned his face into a semblance of a skull beneath the sharp lights, as he lowered his head to remove the coronet from his brow.

"You did well." The general commended him as she strode up the dais. "Your father would be proud of you."

Titus rose from the throne, his backside cramping, visible from his twisted expression. "Right, well, there's still a lot to do, and from what I hear, he won't be around in time when we move out."

"Not if the Federation has its way, with all of their pomp and ceremony." Atala sighed and crossed her arms behind her back. "There's also the issue of us not having enough ships to get to Earth. Our spaceports are still in the process of rebuilding all of the ones Razmus ordered destroyed when he took power. We don't have a single Drake to take to the skies in."

Titus wiped the clammy skin that had been hidden beneath the circlet, attempting to free plastered strands of hair. "True, I hadn't thought of that bit. Our psychics can't possibly teleport us all the way to Earth, can they?"

"I'm afraid not." The general shook her head. "We could attempt tapping into a CCTV feed from Earth, but who knows if they have cameras in the area we are trying to reach. It could be a tricky situation if they are unable to see or picture where they are to teleport."

"I feel like this is a job for Aunt Skyris." The youth furrowed his brows and then his eyes widened. "Is that cannon she made still there?"

Stumped, Atala searched her memory, trying to recall what had become of the machine that Skyris had created. "Now that you mention it, I think it may still be in the Lab. It would be risky to use it a second time to bring an army through, though."

The gears in Titus's head then began to turn. "We could use that to at least get the psychics through, so they could see where to teleport. Could they then bring the rest of our forces to the surface? It's a bit of a backwards plan, but it's the best I can think of to get them there."

"Given the resources we have, I think it's our best option," she replied.

Before Titus could say anything more, two guards wearing scale mail with short red side cloaks burst into the room carrying spears.

"General Shade, Prince Titus, we apologize for the intrusion, but we have a situation on our hands," the first of them spoke.

"Is it the rebels?" her eyes narrowed.

The second shook his head. "No, General. It's... well... it's complicated to explain."

An exasperated sigh escaped Atala as she strode down the dais, her cape billowing behind her. Titus followed, replacing the coronet on his head. Atala noted this and gave a small, approving smile. It would do them good to see the rumors had been false of his illness, even if for a time they had been true.

To her surprise, they were taken to the quarters where Annetta had stayed. The large door of her room appeared to be ajar, and at least five other guards blocked its entrance, pointing their spears at something within it. Atala strode towards the crowd and paused as soon as she peeked inside.

On the four-post bed, or rather, what had been the four-post bed, a large, sabretooth dog lay sprawled out. Thick, shaggy black and tan fur covered every inch of the creature, complete with a set of tan eyebrows that sat above its large, intelligent amber eyes. Its sentience was only betrayed by the large pink tongue which lolled sideways from its open maw, and gave the illusion that the creature was, in fact, brainless.

"How did it get in here?" she demanded of the closest guard.

"Window, we assume," he replied, stiffly. "Though the jump should have been impossible, even for a sabretooth dog, not to mention it getting past the city gates. We've tried to coax it out with food, but the thing won't budge, and attacks anyone who comes near it. Two guards are already in the infirmary because of minor bites."

As Atala listened to the guards, she kept an eye on Titus, who had caught up to her and was inching forward, passing each guard with minimal movements to not alarm them. When he'd gotten around the last of them, she turned her attention fully away from what she was doing. "My Prince, be careful. For all we know, the thing could be rabid."

"I highly doubt it," Titus stated, then outstretched his hand towards it.

"My Prince, I insist you stop right where you are," Atala spat out sharply as every muscle in her body coiled, preparing to strike.

Titus ignored the warning and stretching out his hand more, watching as the creature rose from where it lay. It studied him, before deciding to inch closer. Atala saw that there was a hesitation that took hold of Titus for a few seconds, but the prince didn't falter in his actions. His actions were rewarded when the creature pressed its muzzle against his hand. The initial contact made, Titus moved in closer, rubbing the creature's neck and losing his hand in the sea of fur.

"Hey you. Are you the one Annetta was always visiting beyond the walls?" He scratched the giant canine behind its ears.

"Wait, you know about this thing?" Atala pointed at it.

"On a rainy day, it's hard not to notice your cousin smelling like wet dog after she escaped the castle walls for a few hours, and you know her mount was a horse." He grinned. "Especially when you find out she'd been sneaking food from the kitchen, too."

"So what now, my Prince?" Atala allowed her shoulders to relax.

Titus took a step back from the beast and turned to face those gathered. "As far as I'm concerned, nothing has changed. In fact, we might just have won ourselves an additional fighter."

›‹

Sparks flew as Skyris put the last touches on her masterpiece. Satisfied, she lifted the visor of her welding mask the way a smith would toss a hammer after having completed their latest work of art. She gazed down at the fine metal sheets, and pleased with what she saw, took the mask off completely, shaking her head from side to side as sticky hair came loose from her skin.

"It's done." She sighed as the muscles in her neck relaxed.

She was about to reach for her flask, which rested in her back pocket, when she heard a familiar humming not too far behind her. Her hand lowered and she pivoted to see Dexter hovering. The A.I. had its usual vacant look of a single red eyeball as it observed her with continuous vigilance.

"Yes?" she asked, crossing her arms.

"Your presence has been requested by Sarina Freiuson. I am to escort you to her," the A.I. replied, the gentle hum of its engine filling the room with white noise.

"My presence." Skyris raised an eyebrow. "For what?"

Dexter didn't answer, and only swiveled around to exit the room. Skyris rolled her eyes as she reminded herself of some of the glitches in his programming she would need to address, if the A.I. allowed her to do so, and followed.

Clearing a number of hallways, Skyris came into a large hall where hundreds of humans, to her understanding of what she saw, were being held captive and at bay by soldiers from the Four Forces. In the midst of all of this, she could see the tension that emanated from the humans, the feral way in which they regarded their captives, ready to revolt if given even the slightest chance.

Skyris looked sideways briefly to see Sarina approaching. Dark rings around the girl's eyes made it look like she hadn't slept in over a week, even though it had only been a few hours since the crisis had begun. She worried what a few days would bring for her if this was the case.

"You asked for me?" Skyris inclined her head politely. In truth, she would have rather been back at her workbench or checking the camera feeds in order to help the others that were out in the city. Her lack of psychic abilities had always been a hindrance to her, but what Skyris didn't possess with that, she made up for in intellect and ingenuity.

"We have a problem," Sarina said, and tilted her head to the side, where behind her, a Soarin worked to contain a large human male who seemed to be trying to fight with it.

Skyris cocked her head slightly and watched for a few seconds as the man struggled against the Soarin. Tapping into her feral form, a thing she rarely did, she allowed herself to eavesdrop form a distance.

"They're keeping us here for some sick experiment!" he shouted. "They'll be sticking tubes in us the moment we least expect it."

She rolled her eyes at the man's ignorance and took that as her cue to step in. "You know, if I didn't know any better, I'd say you were one of those doomsday preppers I've read so much about."

Strolling in his direction, she did her best to give off the same aura of command Venetor did when he strode into a room with chest forward and shoulders back. She was also aware that she probably looked very silly, dressed in a black tank top with grime all over her arms and face, but it was too late now, and there was no one else in the Lab she could count on but herself. She halted before him and planted her fists on her hips, glaring at the man with all the ferocity she could muster.

"I'm no prepper," he snapped. "But I've read and watched enough to know where this is going. You guys can't fool me."

Skyris felt another wave of eye-rolling coming on, but she did her best to suppress it. Instead, she gave a closed-lipped smile. "Oh really? Care to enlighten me about what's going to happen next? I'm all ears."

The man was stunned. Try as he might, he could not find anything to say, and Skyris continued to glare at him intensely. He then hesitated in his gaze and looking down, he melted back into the crowd of people.

Skyris sighed and saw the masses of people had turned their attention to her. They were from all races, ages and genders. What united them, however, was the look in their eyes. It was the look of hopelessness and fear in a situation that was far out of their hands. It was a look Skyris was all too familiar with in her people after the takeover of Gaia by Razmus.

This would be the point that Venetor or Orbeyus would have said something. It would be something that would make the hearts of those present stir, but the problem was that Skyris was neither of them, nor was she the White Lioness of Gaia. She was, at best, she realized an inventor, pilot and a drunk. Still, she had to try. Her hand reached for her back pocket where her flask lay and then hesitated, pulling away from it.

She straightened her posture. "Whatever fears you have about being here, please know that we're not going to harm you. Yes, many here aren't human. In fact, I'm not human, either, but that doesn't mean we're going to experiment on you or whatever it is people like the man who spoke up think we do."

This first part seemed to get the attention of all those present, and so she continued. "Despite what you may think, we're here to help. I come from a planet called Gaia in another solar system, and we're pledged by oath to protect the Earth."

"Doing a damn fine job then!" someone shouted from the crowd.

Skyris turned to the source of the voice. "I never said we were perfect, did I? Get your ears checked. I heard that's covered by insurance in your country." She paused for a moment, before taking a breath, and starting over.

"People of Canada, people of Earth. You aren't alone. You have never been, as your little blue planet travelled around the sun. There are people out there who are fighting for you, even if you refuse to see it that way. So you can hate us if you want, make monsters of us if you want, but the truth is that we're fighting things that are even more monstrous than we appear to be, and we do it because if we don't, then no one else will."

A level of venom had risen to her voice now, filling her like an overflowing cup. "So think on that before you jump to conclusions."

Skyris then pivoted on her heel and began to leave. To her surprise, her exit was given applause as a few voices lifted in cheer. A slight blush overtook her, but she took her leave nonetheless without looking back.

Sarina waited for her close to the entrance with a wonder-filled look. "How did you do that?"

The woman paused and glanced down at the girl. "I don't know, but I think I was just being honest with them."

Chapter 35

Venetor pressed a hand to his forehead and squeezed his temples, hoping to rid himself of the sleep deprivation headache that had begun. What he wouldn't do for a cup of green coffee or an energy potion to pick him back up again. He wasn't sure how many hours had passed since he'd been sitting in the small compartment with Gladius, but he was sure it was beginning to reach the twenty-hour mark, and it was more than his Gaian body could take without actual rest. His mind was also able to focus less and less on the speeches given. It wandered more and more to what could be potentially happening on Earth.

"Korangar." He muttered the name.

Ever since he was a boy, he'd heard the legends from his father, but they were nothing more than that. He realized, though, that the same could be said for Razmus and the White Lion (or Lioness) of Gaia. It was strange to know that he was alive in a time where legends were emerging from their crypts to walk among the living. It was also terrifying if even a tenth of the power Korangar possessed was true. He was the embodiment of the seven aspects of evil, the seed of Khaos. Could the Gaian forces, as they were, even hope to put a dent in his might?

Venetor closed his eyes and pushed the doubt from his mind. If Gaia didn't make a stand for Earth, then everything they stood for would be for nought. His eyelids opened slowly to be flooded once more with the light of the chamber, blinding him with their intensity. He then looked over at Gladius, who also looked worse for wear. A redness had begun to fill the white of the Hurtz's single eye, which could only be attributed to lack of sleep. Despite this, it was focused and at attention as it met his gaze.

"What are we doing here, old friend?" Venetor shook his head finally. "We're not politicians, we're warriors."

"Doing what needs to be done," Gladius stated. "Ain't that what you said?"

"I did, didn't I?" he replied and then turned his attention back to the happenings before them.

"We will now turn to the candidate from Gaia, King Venetor Severio, to give his final speech before we break and then begin the voting process," the Grey at the front said and looked in Venetor's general direction.

The lights dimmed around him, and Venetor's balcony became the sole focus of the auditorium. The King of Gaia rose in acceptance of the challenge, and donning his crown once more, he stepped into the light.

He then took a deep breath and looked around at the tiny forms which stirred on their respective balconies. They looked small and insignificant to him in the larger scheme of things, knowing that the end of the universe and perhaps also the multiverse had begun.

"Fellow members of the Intergalactic Federation…" His train of thought cut him off. He could no longer ignore it despite everything he had done to get there. "I regret to inform you that I must leave. I have said everything I could and everything I have felt is relevant. The universe is unravelling right now as we sit here and discuss who better to lead us instead of attempting to prevent it. Well, I for one won't sit by idly as the sister planet of Gaia is destroyed by the seed of Khaos. The Reaping has reached Earth, and soon it will spread to other worlds, as it already has happened on Galecto Kelper Twenty-Three. It's only a matter of time, so you can sit here and debate all you want, but I know my place. I abandoned the Earth once when Mislantus threatened to take it by storm, obeying laws made by ignorant leaders who do not actually care for the preservation of life, and it is a shame which I will take with me to the grave. I cannot abandon them again. The Unknown made Gaia a warrior race. We are the peacekeepers of the universe, the defenders of those who cannot defend themselves, and that it is exactly what I intend to do until my last breath."

He didn't wait to hear the reaction of the room. With a whirl of his cape, he strode from the balcony with Gladius in tow back to his shuttle.

ഇൻഗ്ര

Xander didn't know what hit him. At first, it was faint flashes of images in a world that seemed to all go in slow motion. It was only after the winged creature had picked him up and whisked him away, did everything return to real time for him.

Shock pulsing through him, he shouted the only word that made sense. "Liam!"

The great beating of the wings above him dulled the sound of the name, making it inaudible against the wind. Xander shouted repeatedly, searching for any sign of his friend as the ground below him grew smaller and smaller.

"Relax, I've got you," the Soarin carrying him said as his grip on Xander intensified.

Not long after, they landed in an area that looked to be a park, or had been before everything was trampled. As soon as Xander felt his feet touch the ground, he began to dash in the direction from which he'd come from, only to be blocked by a pair of Ogaien on horseback.

"Stay here, young one, where we can keep an eye on you," the one on the right said.

"My friend is out there and he needs help." Xander protested and removed the gun from its holster. "Move or I'll fire!"

"You'll do no such thing," an angry and yet quivering voice spoke.

Xander's face softened as he turned around it see its source. Standing but a mere few feet behind him was Talia. Her eyes were rimmed red and her jaw was clenched firm, causing her face to look strained. She looked ready to collapse, and yet she stood unmoving, glaring at him with all the ferocity only a mother could muster.

"Is he…" Xander trailed off, unable to finish.

A second wave of wings touching down could be then heard and a female Soarin landed beside Xander.

Talia sized up the new arrival. "Report."

The Soarin's ears immediately flattened. "I'm sorry, but we couldn't get the other one out. It was too late."

Xander felt a wave of ice pass through him, his skin going numb at hearing the words. His legs buckling beneath him, he sat on the ground. He'd just seen Liam mere moments ago, the two of them had been fighting shoulder to shoulder. He couldn't just be gone.

"No," he said in a small voice. "No, he must have gotten away."

The female Soarin looked over at the male who'd carried Xander away. She then turned to him. "I'm sorry, but we had a confirmed visual."

Talia began to weep in the background again, a hand shielding her eyes as if to cover the shame of her tears. The sound of her sobs made Xander's own eyes water as well. Liam had been his oldest friend, and even though they hadn't always been the closest, he'd still always been there as one of the great constants in his life.

"He's stubborn, like his father." Talia's voice sounded deflated as she spoke. "Then again, so is Jason, it's a Kinsman trait."

Xander's eyes clouded over with a veil of water as the reality of it sank in. He looked down in order to prevent others from seeing it, only to see tears fall to the ground and create splatters in the dusty pavement. He then felt a hand on his shoulder, and looking over it, he saw that it was Talia's.

"Come, there's nothing else to do here,." she said, and with that, they teleported.

ഌരൄ

Annetta and Jason both teleported into the Lab with their slew of refugees in tow. Leaving them to the care of Dexter, the duo pushed past the growing clutter of people towards their destination.

After sliding through the throngs of bodies, they burst through into the command centre, where Skyris, along with Talia, Sarina and Xander all stood. They turned to the duo with solemn looks on their faces, unable to say anything.

Jason felt himself inflate with frustration. "Well? Where's Liam."

Out of the whole group, it was Xander who spoke. "He didn't make it."

"What do you mean he didn't make it?" Anger seeped through his voice. "Did you lose him in Toronto? Is my brother out there alone right now?"

Xander cowered back at his reaction, and Skyris stepped in. "He's dead, Jason. Don't you think someone would be out there looking for him if it were otherwise?"

Jason's legs collapsed beneath him in an instant. The words came down on him like a bag of concrete and his only saving grace was the pair of strong arms that caught him as he crumpled to the floor. He looked over, half conscious, to see Annetta holding him up as best as she could.

"No, no, no." He shook his head as Annetta carried him over to the nearest chair. He felt himself being placed down, but couldn't comprehend much else. His head spun as he tried to ground himself in what was being said. No matter what thread he tried to grasp, however, everything seemed to slip through his fingers.

Somewhere through the haze of it all, Jason saw the shape of his mother come towards him and embrace him, while Sarina knelt beside him, holding his hand. Out of the corner of his eye, he could make out Annetta standing over him like a watchful bodyguard.

It was a long few moments before feeling re-entered his body and he was certain that he was once again in control. He removed himself from his mother's embrace to stand up.

"I'm going to kill them," he announced with a tear streaked face. "Every last one of them, I'm going to kill them for what they did."

He felt a hand grip his shoulder just as he was about to exit the room. He turned around and saw that it was Annetta, no longer in the motionless sentinel stance she'd been in. There was a look in her eyes that Jason didn't recognize ever seeing before.

"I won't stop you," she said. "But I want you first to think hard on what we promised the Angels when we met them and how charging in there blindly will void that promise. I also want you to consider that doing so won't bring him back. Do you think Liam would want you to die as well? What about everyone else you'd leave behind here?"

Jason looked around the room, first at his mother, then Sarina, then Skyris and Xander until he finally came full circle on Annetta. His eyelids fluttered far more than they normally would as he tried to rid himself of the tears. Caving, he ran the back of his fist over his eyes and looking back up, he gazed back at his best friend. They'd been through a lot together the last three years, and he scarcely recognized the rugged warrior before him. She looked more like the sketches she'd once drawn than the girl who had read fantasy books and stood up to school bullies. Despite this, he could still see a faint trace of that girl, lurking in the corners of her visage. She'd never let him fall, and more importantly, she'd never let him break like he was starting to now.

"You're right." He sighed in defeat, even though his whole being felt the opposite of those words at that moment. "And we made a promise to be the defenders of the Earth."

"Then let's go and do that."

∞CR

Once Annetta, Jason and the others had left, Skyris scanned the various channels in the control room, doing her best to keep an eye on the civilians, while trying also to let the others know where people were still present in the city. This had taken additional effort on her part, for not every area was monitored by a camera and so there were many dead zones. A few drones she'd managed to fix on short notice had also been deployed, but it was all not enough for a city as large as Toronto.

Zones had also been prepared in the Lab for psychics to teleport in, and were cleared of people almost immediately once they did to prevent jams. These, too, she tried to monitor. The effort was making her feel strained, and she dearly wished for extra hands. The problem was that no one else knew how to work the equipment, not well, at least.

"If only I'd had more time," she groaned, pulling a loose strand of hair back behind the wireless headset she wore.

One of the Dexter units then dashed into the room, its bulbous red eye fixed on Skyris. "A possible security threat has been detected outside of the Canadian border."

Skyris furrowed her eyebrows regarding the A.I., "A threat outside the border? Do I need to tighten a screw on you?"

Dexter ignored the comment, its red eye turning to the screen to showing multiple feeds, some of which were coming through pixilated computer cameras as well as two CCTV cameras that were present in the room. Skyris didn't recognize any of the men or women in the room, but what she did recognize was the bald eagle on the seal that was on one of the banners in the room. She then noticed footage playing in the background on a large television monitor from Toronto, and began picking things up from the heated discussion going on.

"Oh, this can't be good," she said as the blood drained from her face the longer she listened in and realized things had just gotten a lot more complicated.

ഇറ

Matthias's claws tore through armour and skin in his latest battle. The Verden he'd been fighting collapsed in a heap before him, and didn't move. A blast of green light shot past him a few feet away, causing him to glance over to its origin point. Puc was not holding anything back, and if the spells were not indicator enough, then the fact that he had drawn Tempest from its sheath was. The folded metal of the sword seemed to move like ripples of water each time the mage swung it.

"That was the last of them!" Matthias called to Puc, and made the claws from his gauntlets retract back into their resting place.

The mage bounded over to him in sweeping strides as he sheathed the sword beneath the layers of his robes, which billowed like a storm of dark clouds around him. "For now. How many are we up to?"

Matthias turned to where a small group of Soarin, Ogaien and Water Elves guarded an unsure group of humans who were huddled closely together. "I'd say about twenty. I lost track after the last building."

Puc's face glazed over in distraction as he looked up, and coming within range, he put his hand on Matthias's shoulder, causing him to look up as well. The assassin obliged and saw smoke as it rose into the sky.

"Fire." He narrowed his eyes.

"Let us go." Puc dashed ahead.

It didn't take them long to get to the source. Crossing the labyrinth of buildings, they came to their target. The four-story apartment building was blazing fully beside one that had already been burned, and beneath them, a firetruck with lights still flashing stood, but the firefighters were nowhere in sight. Matthias caught the glimpse of a fire helm which lay some distance away, and made the connection instantly as to what their fate had been. Checking around, he saw no sign of those who could have been responsible and moving closer, he saw the front door of the second building had been barricaded with what looked like an overturned car.

Eyes fixed on the building, Matthias made an inspection of the blaze. His training as an assassin had taught him at what point anyone in a fire would be beyond rescue, and looking upwards now, he still saw a small window of hope.

"I'm going in," he announced. "Get that hose going, or a spell."

He didn't wait for a response, nor did he care. He didn't have time to waste. Nostalgia floated to the surface of his mind as he was reminded of his time working for Mislantus. They were far less complicated days, ones where all he had to do was complete a mission, and everything else around him didn't matter. It was a feeling he sorely missed, and seeing the fire had ignited the memories. He'd never had to rescue anyone from a burning building, it was true, but he'd had to make sure plenty of people had been trapped in order to make their removal look like an accident.

The car from the entrance skidded to the side awkwardly as Matthias moved it with his mind. Instantly, at least a dozen people poured out, coughing and spluttering around him.

"Everyone please stay calm, we are here to help you!" Puc called out, vying to get their attention.

Most seemed to turn their head when he did this, Matthias noticed, but he was unable to pay attention when a woman collided with him. Thin and covered in soot, she fell onto both his arms with a wild look in her eyes.

"My boy," she pleaded. "Please, we couldn't get to him, the beams fell and blocked the door. He's on the third floor. Apartment three-o-six. Please save my boy."

Everything in Matthias's body wanted to shove her away, tell her that he would do no such thing. He realized right after that this was not who he was anymore.

All feelings of nostalgia faded as he placed his bloodied and filth-caked hands on her wrists gently.

"I'll do what I can," he said and moved past her into the building. Covering himself with a protective layer of psychic fire from both the flames and smoke, he located the stairs and darted up them.

When he came to the third floor, he located the apartment number mentioned by the woman, and kicked down the door, causing sparks and ash to fly in his face. Matthias saw the beams which had collapsed and moved them with ease using his psychic abilities. He then strode into the room. To his dismay, there by the window was an unconscious little boy on the floor clutching, in all irony, a toy firetruck. He noted the faintest of heartbeats when he checked for a pulse, and scooping him up into his arms, he turned to see a Fire Elf behind him. The creature looked half crazed as it lifted a crude scimitar and readied itself for an attack.

His only route of escape blocked, Matthias did the only thing he could think of, and ran at the elf with a deafening roar.

Confused, the enemy fighter faltered in his attack, and that was all it took to create an opening as Matthias slammed a hand with extended gauntlets through the elf's midsection, before teleporting behind him. The thud of flesh on the floor was all Matthias heard as he moved briskly to the exit, dodging the decaying timbers in the fire.

Running outside, he exhaled deeply, ridding himself of the psychic fire shield, but catching a whiff of the smoke behind, he coughed regardless. The child, he noted, lay limp in his arms.

The woman he'd spoken with broke through the ranks of soldiers protecting civilians and dived for the child with a tear-streaked face. She clutched him, sobbing uncontrollably.

Matthias stared at the scene in loss, unable to find anything to say to the woman. He felt himself get shoved aside as Puc emerged before him.

"May I?" he asked the woman, who was lost in hysterics and pulled away even further. Puc exhaled deeply. "Please, if I can just see the boy, I may be able to help. The longer you wait, the more there is a chance that irreversible brain damage has occurred."

The last sentence made the woman stop and she held the child out. Puc accepted, and setting the boy on the ground, he began to check for vital signs.

Matthias watched events unfold from a distance. There was an eerie similarity to the time when Annetta had been caught in psychic fire intended for him. Anger heated his face at the memory, and he crossed his arms.

Stupid girl shouldn't have gotten in the way was all he could think.

His attention was drawn back to Puc. The mage raised a hand, pressed it to the boy's chest, and uttered an incantation. The area around his hand glowed a light blue, creating a pattern over the child's chest, almost like veins. The effect lasted a few seconds before dissipating. The boy then heaved as black smoke spewed from his mouth and he coughed, brought back into the world of the living.

The mother urgently rushed to his side and scooped the child up into her embrace.

"Thank you," she said to Puc, who had already taken a step back to give them space.

"We are going to take you to a safe place now. You will need to grab hold of this man, here or the hand of someone who is holding onto him already." Puc indicated to Matthias.

Matthias's muscles flexed as he braced himself for the onslaught of physical contact which was about to occur. Arms of nervous and frightened civilians grabbed hold of him, threatening to tear off a limb or two in the process. He then looked over at Puc for confirmation of everyone holding on, and the mage nodded. Matthias sighed and teleported to the area he'd mapped out in his mind.

He didn't bother to wait until Dexter would pick up the humans, and instead teleported back to the surface immediately. Uncorking a potion, he downed it and smashed the vial on the concrete floor. Of all the things Matthias had ever thought he would have to do in his life, being a transportation device for an underdeveloped species was not one of them.

His eyes then fell back to Puc, who had not moved from where he stood. He appeared to be in a conversation on his C.T.S., and a very heated one at that, judging by the strained expression on his face.

"…How close can you get us?" were the first set of coherent words Matthias could hear from Puc as he came closer.

"I have CCTV feed that you can use, you'll need to teleport back to the Lab to get it. Oh, and I don't suggest going in alone," Skyris said over the C.T.S.

"I'll bring a squad of elves. I don't think it would be a good idea for anything else," Puc replied. "I'll meet you in the Control Room shortly. 05 out."

Puc then closed his C.T.S. and looked over at him. Matthias was still not sure what to make of what he'd just heard, but from the look on Puc's face, he knew it was only a matter of moments before he would know.

The words that came next from Puc confirmed his thoughts. "We have a very serious problem."

Chapter 36

Miles away from the happenings in Ontario, in the capital of the United States, a group of men and women sat in a boardroom in the White House. They analyzed everything they were seeing from the live footage from Toronto. On it, a helicopter was recording the carnage as hundreds of creatures poured through the streets, slaughtering anyone they could get their hands on. There were also other groups of creatures, these usually led by a single human, which strived to collect as many of the people as they could before disappearing with them and reappearing on their own to begin the cycle again.

"It's like a science experiment gone wrong," someone from the back of the table finally said. "Who's to say this isn't Canada testing some biological weapon on a grand scale?"

"Canada? Are you out of your mind?" A man closer to the chair at the far end huffed. " You expect me to believe that they've been hiding a weapon of this scale from us all this time? No, this is definitely a terrorist attack."

A gruff-looking man at the head of the table dressed in a crisp suit sat with his lips pursed as he analyzed everything that was presented on the screen before him. His greying brown hair was combed to the side, and the longer bangs fell partially into his eyes, obscuring his expression.

"I think the most important thing we need to ask ourselves what do we do in the event that Toronto falls?" he finally asked, leaning back in his chair.

"That is a valid point Mr. President. They are close to the border and if they fall, the States are next," a younger woman in thick-rimmed glasses began as she looked down at the stacks of papers before her.

A man in his fifties with white hair looked away from a telephone in the corner of the room. "I've been trying to reach the Prime Minister, but the line is dead. Whoever was in Parliament has gone to ground."

"Cowards." The President huffed. "Well, try the other lines. I want answers, and I want them now. Miss. Hart, anything from the NSA on this?"

A wiry woman with blonde hair that had the definite beginnings of greying in it shook her head, her short ponytail swishing back and forth as she did so. "Mr. President, I'm afraid that we don't have any additional information. Some analysts have found evidence which ties these events to biblical accounts of the Second Coming."

"I've got no time for superstition." The President snorted. "I want facts, and I want them now."

"I've got the Prime Minister on the line!" the white-haired man called out. "Shall I patch him through?"

"Have I not been asking for this the whole time?" The President growled. "Do it."

The in-wall speakers screeched as the call was transferred and the sound was replaced with the frantic breathing of a man over what sounded like a short wave radio. "Hello? Are you still there?"

"Prime Minister." The President spoke the name without a note of hesitancy in his voice. "This is the President of the United States. I'm addressing you from a safe location, can you hear me?"

A sigh of relief followed the address. "Yes, loud and, clear Mr. President."

"Good, I'm seeing the happenings from Toronto right now. Can you convey any information to us based on what we're seeing? Is this a terrorist attack?"

"To be honest, none of us know," the Prime Minister stated. "We were in a meeting when the sirens went off, and everyone was taken to bunkers by security. I have just as much information as you do. Our armed forces have been dispatched as well, though they're overrun. The one thing we've managed to determine is that these invaders aren't from this world."

"Aliens?" the President squinted in disbelief. He then looked back at the screen, where a pair of creatures resembling Minotaurs were busy destroying an eighteen-wheeler, the tires exploding each time their weapons found them. He shook his head. "Maybe it's North Korea?"

Those gathered in the room turned skeptically to regard the President. He, in turn, raised an eyebrow and shrugged. "What? Who's to say some of these other nations haven't been experimenting with genetic manipulation. I, for one, don't put it past Russia."

This made everyone in the room nod in agreement, though there was still some uncertainty on the faces of a few of those gathered. The President was among those hesitant. Something didn't feel right to him.

"It still seems far-fetched," the Prime Minister added, finally. "These things didn't come in with machine guns swinging. Instead, they're using medieval weaponry. You'd think if it were another country, then they would at least invest in equipping them in more modern means of defence."

Again, everyone in the room nodded. As they did so, a young girl's form filled the left-hand corner of the screen of one of the drones floating in the air. She couldn't have been more than eighteen years old, with reddish-brown hair that was tied in a loose ponytail and thick bangs that blew freely in the wind. She was dressed in a sort of black skin-tight armour with a pair of jeans thrown over top of the lower half of it. A crimson cape with a rampant white lioness embroidered on it snapped back and forth on the wind. She was utterly oblivious to the drone, and instead focused her eyes on the two creatures below. The girl clasped her hands before her as though she were holding onto an invisible ball. A ball of blue and purple flame then formed between her palms. The girl struggled to control it as it expanded, and once it reached the size of a soccer ball, she let it loose, hurtling it towards the unsuspecting creatures.

Gasps of horror and shock followed as the truck and the creatures were engulfed in an explosion. The girl turned her head away, shielding her eyes, and then noticed the drone. Intelligent, ice-blue eyes stared back into the screen for a few seconds in confusion and shock of their own. She poked the drone with a finger, causing it to wobble and create an unsteady stream of images. Before anyone present could analyze her further, she drew a sword, and the screen went blank.

"I think that's all the proof we need to say these things aren't from this world." The President folded his hands before him. "Nor are they friendly in any way, shape or form, if what happened to the drone just now was any indication."

"What do we do?" The Prime Minister asked over the phone.

"You don't do a damn thing," the President informed him. "You let us handle this."

He whirled around to the white-haired man. "Get ready to launch the FOAB."

The man's eyes widened at hearing this. "You... sir, are you sure you want to proceed with that? There are still civilians there, and we haven't even sent in the military to aid-"

At this comment, the President rose from his seat and stood directly in front of the screen, then pointed to it. "Did you not see what just happened? I don't think our military will be able to do a whole hell

330

of a lot against powers like that, unless there is anything else any of you would like to share with me."

The room was silent, and the President stood a little straighter at seeing his point proven. He then watched in further satisfaction as the white-haired man dialled the number he'd requested.

The Prime Minister's panicked voice then came through the speakers. "Wait! You can't just launch a nuclear bomb into the heart of Toronto! Under what authority do you think-"

"The authority to make sure the rest of the human race survives." The President cut him off. "And the FOAB isn't nuclear. I'm not an idiot. You'll just need to rebuild that tower of yours, and a few stadiums."

"And the people?" The anger rose in the Prime Minister's voice.

All eyes fell yet again on the President, but he wasn't listening. A blanket of silent fear had covered his eyes. All he could see was the girl glaring back at the camera after she'd let loose the blast from her hands. Somewhere in the back of his mind, something egged him forward to proceed, as the questions piled on in his thoughts. How could his army even hope to stand against something of that magnitude? Did no one else see it?

Lowering his gaze, he took a moment to stare at the gnarled-looking hands before him, hands he no longer recognized as his own. He sat back down in his chair, contemplating his next words, and the burden he would need to carry for the rest of his natural life, words that would most likely be his legacy.

"Casualties of war, I'm afraid," he stated and then turned to the white-haired man. "Fire when ready."

Unrest followed as the Prime Minister began to utter threats about trade treaties and the United Nations getting involved. There was perhaps even some mention of a third World War, but the President couldn't make it out among the commotion.

He was about to rise again to say something when he noticed the strangest thing. His surroundings began to slow down around him at a rapid rate, and shaking his head, he struggled to see if perhaps he was having a stroke. Before he could get a word out, however, the doors at the far end of the room burst open. In poured a score of men and women dressed in long robes, with chainmail beneath them. A large staff was carried by each of them, and they all wore an oval-shaped helm which had half a gear on either side made to look like a pair of wings. Getting to the far end of the table, they then stood at attention with their weapons at their side.

The President blinked as sweat began to form at the base of his neck and began threatening to cover his whole scalp. His eyes darted from side to side at the new arrivals, and finally settled on the door at the far end where another two figures entered, walking with gaits that suggested they were in charge.

The taller of the two wore a long navy-blue robe piped in gold, and carried a large, gnarled wooden staff, the head of which was covered in moss. A sharp-featured face with pale blue eyes and black shoulder-length hair finished off his look, and had he not known any better, the President would have guessed that he'd stepped right out of one of the comic book conventions that were so popular with his kids.

The other wore a sleeveless green turtleneck, jeans, combat boots and gauntlets on his hands that covered the length of his forearm and were decorated in silver plates which resembled the paws of a bear. Messy brown hair, a goatee with no moustache and a scowl that put many drill sergeants to shame decorated his face, and if that wasn't enough to make people realize he was the muscle, then his powerful build did.

The younger of the two stopped and scanned the room with azure eyes, much in the way a bodyguard would make sure an area was secure, while his counterpart continued towards the President.

The man with the staff stopped a few feet from him and looked down. "Now, Mr. President, I believe you, and I have some things to discuss before you make a truly terrible mistake."

"Mistake?" He cleared his throat. "I don't know what you're talking about. I... how is no one moving in this room right now except you?"

"I have placed a spell on the room to slow time to a standstill, and targeted everyone but you. It was the safest option given what needed to be done," the man before him said.

"Needed to be done?" Panic set into the President's voice, despite his best efforts to mask it.

"We didn't kill anyone, if that's what you're worried about," the second one spoke as he strode over to join his companion. "We just needed to sneak in, is all."

The President raised an eyebrow at him, and then turned to the first one he'd been speaking to. "Who are you people? What do you want with me? If it's the codes you want, you can try to get them from me, but they won't do you any good alone. There are procedures in place for that sort of thing."

The duo looked confused at this, to which he became more confused.

"I am not certain exactly what is it you speak of, but I can assure you we are not here for these codes," the dark-haired one replied.

"Then what do you want?" the President swallowed hard and dabbed his now sweaty forehead with his hand, causing his hair to stick to his forehead even more.

"To prevent any weapons or armies from being deployed into Toronto," he said again, and then paused as if remembering something. "Where are my manners, forgive me, but in times like these, I will forget myself. I am Puc Thanestorm, First Mage of Aldamoor."

"Matthias Teron, no fancy titles," the second one chimed in. "I just kill a lot of people."

"I am the President of the United States of America," he answered in a shaky tone.

The man named Puc nodded. "Yes, we are aware of your title, which is why we are here to speak with you. Right now, Toronto is being overrun by alien forces that are led by a creature named Korangar. His motives are unknown, the only thing that is certain is his path of destruction will not stop with the Earth."

"And you don't want me to send any bombs to Toronto?" the President gazed at him sceptically. "If he plans to destroy all life, then that means the United States as well. Someone needs to take a stand against such a monster."

"Someone is." Puc cut him off; the man's blue eyes seemed to penetrate right through him.

The President frowned. "Really? Judging by what I was seeing, you're in much need. I saw what that girl did to the drone, cleaved it right in half with a sword after destroying two of those Minotaur creatures. Besides, it's too late, I've already called for a FOAB to be dispatched."

"You what?" Matthias burst out in rage as he glared at him.

The President felt his entire face flush at the display. "Look, we didn't know what else to do after seeing that. We don't have the technology to defend against that kind of power if it gets into the United States."

Puc sighed as he looked down at his feet and then back up at him. "Did you even consider for just a moment that the one you were condemning was the one who was trying to save you?"

O'Connor stared blankly at the men before him. He'd never, in all of his life, felt as powerless as he did now. His mind raced through the scene of the girl as she turned to face the drone. Thinking back on it, there had been a quality of innocence to her, as though she genuinely didn't understand what she'd been looking at. He also remembered malice etched onto her face as she shot the blast at the creatures below, creatures that had been destroying the vehicle, and who on other news feeds had been seen chasing after civilians.

Piecing it all together in his mind, he stared at the duo before him with his mouth agape.

"What can I do to fix this?" he asked.

ॐ

Jason roared in fury as he swung Helbringer at the Verden warrior before him. There was a raw quality to his attacks as his mind kept reminding him over and over again that his brother was no longer alive. A permanent tightness had taken over his chest in the wake of his initial shock. It was a pain unlike any he'd ever known, and part of his mind wondered if this was anything like what Annetta had felt when learning about Link's death. The mace swung harder and harder with each thought until the giant Verden could take no more and succumbed to Jason's attacks.

The youth then veered around and slammed into the shield of another enemy fighter, this one not of a race he knew, and collided with him in a full frontal attack.

From some few paces away, Jason's ears picked up with the sound of Annetta's growls and grunts as Severbane sang in her hands with the impact of colliding on enemy weapons. He could think of no sweeter music to accompany his rage.

When his latest foe collapsed to the floor, Jason staggered back from the impact of the newest blow and breathed heavily. The muscles in his arms grew heavy as the rush of adrenaline left him. He gripped the large mace with two hands, much like a baseball player would hold a bat.

Jason took a good look around at the desolation, and his mind peeked to the surface again through the red haze of his grief. His arms slackened, causing the mace to slump down to the floor. Another thought then filled him just as he heard the fighting stop where Annetta had been.

"I'm sorry, Anne," he managed to say when he heard feet move towards him.

"For what?" she asked.

"For not having reached out more when you were on Gaia," he said. "For not having tried harder to understand what you were going through. I knew, we all did, but I just…"

Tears of fury began to stream down his cheeks involuntarily, and using the back of his right hand, he wiped them away as best as he could. He looked down, trying to get the water building up in his eyes under control.

The sound of feet scratching against the pavement as they came to a stop then signalled that Annetta was right beside him. She then sighed. "You can't know until you find yourself in the same situation."

Jason grimaced at this. "But even when Brakkus died I didn't feel anything as strong as-"

"You did, you just don't remember," she reminded him. "We all did."

Silence passed between them before Annetta spoke again. "Look, I don't know what you want me to say, because I know no matter what I do, it won't help. Not now, anyway. But I'll ask you one thing. I'm going to ask you to stay alive. Not just for my sake, but for the sake of Sarina and your parents. Imagine how they'd feel if they lost you, too."

This clicked with Jason on some deeper level, and for all of a second, the pain was gone, before returning. Despite it, he now anchored himself to Annetta's words.

"Did it work for you?" He looked at her.

No immediate response came, and the girl looked away, out across the desolated and abandoned roads of Toronto, while their teams of warriors scoured the buildings, searching for survivors. She seemed older at that moment, as though all traces of the girl he'd befriended years ago in Elementary School had faded away.

"No." The word fell solidly from her mouth. "But every day, I keep telling myself that, and somehow, the pain lessens just a little, until one day, maybe the feeling will only be a memory."

The pounding of Jason's pulse in his ears seemed to lessen as he spoke to her. He'd never noticed the slightly haunted look in her eyes before, and now it stared him blatantly in the face. It was a reflection on his grief, just buried behind a wall of the very thing she had just told him to do, keep moving. He was about to voice his thoughts when he heard the frantic beeping of his C.T.S. going off. Jason rolled up the sleeve of his hooded sweatshirt, then lifted the faceplate of the beeping device.

"02 here," he answered.

"05, and we have a very serious problem." Puc's voice came through the watch.

"Great, what else could possibly go wrong?" Jason rolled his eyes, feeling Annetta inch closer to him to listen in.

"Jason, this is not the time for prattle," the mage continued. **"I need you to concentrate."**

Jason glanced over at Annetta, who merely shrugged in return. He then faced the watch on his wrist. "What is it?"

There was no pause between question and answer from Puc. **"The United States of America has launched the Father of All Bombs, and it is heading your way."**

The words took a moment to register in Jason's grief-torn brain, but when they did his eyes widened. "What?"

"They sent a bomb?" Annetta's jaw dropped.

"I have already contacted Skyris. She is working on sending you the coordinates as we speak," Puc replied.

On cue, Annetta's C.T.S. began to beep. As soon as she opened the faceplate, a small hologram projection appeared, with two dots across a map that she recognized as part of Toronto. Farther away, a blinking dot was heading towards their location at high speeds. Jason's hair stood on end as he saw how quickly the gap between the dots was closing.

"What do we do?" he asked as a hollowness formed in the pit of his already-churning stomach.

"You will need to alter the course of the weapon away from the city and prevent it from colliding with anything which could cause it to explode," Puc instructed. **"Your best course of action would be to get it into outer space. Once there, it can cause no damage, and the engines will die."**

"We'll get it done. 01 and 02 out," Annetta interjected before Jason could reply, shut the lid of his C.T.S. and then turned to him. "How are your flying lessons?"

"I can hold my own." He swallowed hard.

Jason then felt the ground around him vibrate. Seconds later, Annetta was in the air, rising upwards faster and faster, as though someone had strapped a jetpack onto her. She did it with such ease that Jason almost wanted to take back what he'd said just moments before. Instead, only a disgruntled sigh escaped as he focused on the technique Venetor had taught them months before, and that Jason had neglected to practice as much as he should have.

He situated himself in the air as quickly as possible, and followed Annetta's lead without any complaints.

"So, any idea what we do once we find this thing?" he called to her over the sound of rushing wind.

"We'll do what Puc says," she shouted back. "If I'm right, then it'll take both of us to get it done."

Jason furrowed his brows at the comment. "What do ya mean?"

They heard it before they saw it. A thunderous roar so loud it shook the core of Jason's being even without being grounded, and for an instant, he forgot who and where he was.

"J.K.!" Annetta's voice was barely audible as she screamed at the top of her lungs right beside him.

A split second later, the projectile appeared before him out of nowhere, and he was about to teleport when he noticed something. The bomb had stopped in midair, and wasn't moving.

'This is where you come in.' Annetta's voice echoed in his head.

He looked over in confusion at her. *'I don't understand, what do you mean I come in?'*

'You need to push the bomb upwards and out of the atmosphere.'

Jason raised an eyebrow at this. *'Couldn't you just do that on your own?'*

'Can you swat a fly in midair? Not likely,' Annetta replied. *'One of us needed to slow the bomb down while the other pushed, otherwise there was a good chance we would miss the window of opportunity needed to get it away safely.'*

Jason nodded, but when he turned to the floating projectile, he froze. Sleek, with its black metal paint shimmering in the sun, it was an impressive sight. The sharp tip of the missile was mere inches away, and he could feel the heat of it on his skin, which threatened to sear off his face. He could only guess at the firepower the bomb had and the devastation it could cause. Worst of all, there was a possibility it would not destroy Korangar, just his city.

Though he knew better from the countless lessons he'd received with Puc, Jason put his hands out before him and pushed with his mind. The gesture gave him a sense of comfort in the crisis, and he wasn't about to turn down any help he could get with his concentration. Slowly but surely, the bomb began to budge, floating strangely, as though suspended in space instead of struggling to travel over a thousand kilometres an hour.

He was slightly disappointed with his need to use his hands when he saw Annetta appear from the other side of the weapon. She floated in the air calmly, with her arms crossed and the wind causing her cape to flutter around her.

'Show-off,' he muttered in his mind to her.

Annetta didn't seem to hear the comment. She was completely focused on the task at hand. Small beads of sweat had begun to form around her temples and forehead, despite the cold air and her calm exterior. Jason wondered when the last time she'd taken a potion to replenish her energy was. He also wondered how many of the vials they had left back in the Lab. He knew Sarina had been helping Puc and Darius prepare as many as possible, but they seemed to be downing them at a speed far faster than in any fight they'd ever been in.

'On my mark, let it go.' Annetta's strained voice came through.

Jason's gaze fell to Annetta's face, and he watched for any change. Her bangs were matted against her forehead now, and other loose strands of hair framed the edges of her face, creating a swirling design around it. The reflection of the bomb's flames danced in sapphire of her irises, lending them further intensity. She finally nodded after what seemed like the longest pause. Without flinching, Jason let go and was blown back by the power of the rocket's blast going full force.

He was thankfully not flustered enough to fall from losing his concentration, but he couldn't say the same for Annetta. Jason watched for a split second before springing into action, and dove after the girl, her cape enveloping her completely like a blanket as she fell towards the Earth.

"Gotcha!" Jason snatched her hand and wrapping his arm around her, he then floated both of them to the ground safely.

He then plunged a fist into his pocket and rummaged around until he found a vial of the energy potion. Jason uncorked it, and handed it to Annetta, who was still partially conscious.

"I shouldn't," was all she managed to murmur as she begun to pull away from him slowly.

"Anne, this isn't the time for heroics," he said, waving the vial in front of her face. "You need to take this. You're barely able to stand on your feet."

A larger grimace formed on Annetta's face as she crawled back. "I shouldn't take any more J.K., what if the thing inside me gets triggered?"

Jason frowned. "What do you mean triggered? From taking energy potions? It's never happened to anyone else."

"Listen," she hissed as she clutched her forehead. "What if the... let's call it what it is... the dragon came out because of some weird Gaian stress thing from using up my psychic energy and then replenishing it really quickly."

"How many of the things have you taken?" he asked.

"I took one before I remembered that," she confessed. "Right after I did too, I felt it, like it was trying to get out of me or something. It's... I don't know how else to describe it."

His eyes widened. "No wonder you look so ragged. I've taken like three or four already. How are you still functioning?"

"Adrenaline, I guess," she said. "Venetor had me using my abilities daily for training. There weren't any potions, so my tolerance got pretty high."

Despite what he'd just heard, Jason still held out the vial towards her. Annetta's blue eyes locked with the potion, her face still grim as she studied it. "Did you hear anything I just said?"

"I did, and I also know that Puc put a seal on whatever it is. Now, are you gonna help me save this city or are you gonna fail it?"

The words pressed just the right buttons in her, and Annetta snatched the vial from his hands. She didn't raise it to her lips right away, however, and looked up at him again. "J.K., if I lose control... I need you to promise me something."

Jason bit his lip, knowing exactly where the conversation was going. "You can't ask something like that of me. I won't do it."

Annetta glared at him as an exasperated sigh escaped her. "If I'm a threat to the city, how does that make me any better than Korangar?"

"I can't do it, ask someone else," he protested.

"Then I can't take this potion." She handed the vial back to him.

Jason was practically smouldering inside as he snatched it back. "Damn it, Anne. You didn't actually think I'd agree to kill you?"

"You seemed content enough to do it after Brakkus's death."

The words from her cut like knives as images of the fight down in the Lab surfaced. Though it was almost two years ago, Jason had blocked it from his mind completely, embarrassed by how he'd acted. It had been childish, blaming Annetta when in truth all she was guilty of was being at the wrong place and at the wrong time.

"I was angry, and I was just a dumb kid." He glowered. "I'm not that person anymore, and that's why I can't do it. You're my best friend, Anne. I don't care what you think you have inside of you, dragon, wyvern, werewolf or whatever. What I can promise you though is that I'll make sure you don't hurt any people."

Another wave of silence passed between them, and neither budged. Finally, it was Annetta who outstretched her hand. Jason handed her the vial, and she wrapped her fingers around the glass.

"That's a promise I can accept." A small smile formed on her face, and she downed the contents.

Chapter 37

After all her marvelling at the arrival in the cave of the Sisters of Wyrd, Jansen could only think about being able to go home if her tests didn't show anything unnatural about her. True, she'd never cared before, but the longer the proceedings took, the less desire she had to spend time behind the long rectangular table while the women before her asked series of questions that reminded Jansen of the time she'd been sent to a psychologist when she'd had trouble sleeping.

"Where did you come up with the ideas for your story?" a woman seated to Lysania's right with short cropped grey hair and a wiry frame asked from behind a pair of half-moon spectacles.

Jansen took a deep breath. She was certain she'd been asked this before already at the beginning, but the questions were all starting to blend with each consecutive answer she gave. "I don't know to be exact, they just sort of came to me. I spend a lot of time in my head since I'm an introvert and to entertain myself I just started coming up with these stories of Annetta and her friends."

The woman jotted down some notes on the stack of parchment before her using an elaborate blue feather quill. "Is it specifically only things Annetta does that you write about?"

"Well I mean the story is from her perspective but I also know about the other characters, uh… I mean people in her life. I mean I knew about Puc and Skyris and Venetor."

"But your protagonist, as one would put it, in the stories you write is Annetta?"

"Yes." Her answer was firm on this, but her sureness dissolved when she saw the woman jot down more notes. "Why is this all so important? More importantly how is any of this true?"

"That is the mystery we are trying to solve." Lysania said. "As I said, the Angels told us to keep you safe but as to why, we were not privileged to such information. Though my theory is this does have something to do with the Saga."

"The Saga?"

"The Saga are a group of special beings who are chosen by the Unknown to write the life story of one individual, recording their life. The Citadel of the Unknown is said to be where they reside. Your ability closely resembles that of a Saga and yet you are not one."

"So like the Fates in Greek mythology?" Jansen mused.

"Yes, exactly like them though on a much larger scale." Lysania closed the hefty tome that she'd been recording her notes in and rose from her seat. "I think it's best we take a short break to convene our thoughts, and I'm sure you'd like to rest as well. I can't even begin to imagine how draining this must be. We have a room prepared for you should you like, and we can have quarters arranged for Darius as well."

"Actually." Jansen pursed her lips as she looked around. "Would it be okay if I look through the library? I mean, unless there's like books that are forbidden or something."

Lysania smiled at this. "Please, feel free. The knowledge the Sisters of Wyrd hold is for all, but I must warn you that much of it is in Elvish, so you may not be able to read it."

"Aren't we speaking English, though?" Jansen narrowed her eyes.

"Yes and no. What you hear as English, we hear as Elvish and vice versa, though our Elvish is quite similar to your Latin, I hear."

"I can help with that," Darius offered as he got up at the back and stretched. "I was taught to be able to read both. The benefits of having to attend school on Earth."

The other women in the room had already begun to disperse despite the conversation, leaving Lysania as the only one paying any attention. Her smile deepened ever so slightly, forming creases on the corners of her mouth. "Very well. You may both look through the library as you please, though I do encourage you to get some rest. I will see the rooms are both ready."

Jansen was both shocked and somewhat apprehensive about the ease with which Lysania had left both her and Darius alone without any supervision. Something like that would never do in Toronto, and she couldn't help but wonder if maybe it was because Darius was in on the whole thing. It didn't matter, though, since Jansen didn't plan to torch the place. She just needed answers, and she hoped that whatever she was looking for was in here. Jansen got up and stretched her sore back muscles as the room emptied. She then went to the wall furthest in the place and stood before it with her hands planted on her hips.

"So, do you actually know what you're looking for?" Darius's voice surprised her from behind.

Pivoting, Jansen found herself right in front of him and had to shift back a pace, feeling she was in his personal space. She could see the dark golden-brown hues of his eyes, and if that didn't count as being too close, then she wasn't sure what did.

"Honestly, not really," she admitted. "A lot of this seems to be based on gut instinct, and I felt like I needed to look through these, so I'm rolling with it."

Darius's mouth hung open for a split second before he closed it. "So, you just feel the need to look through these books, but you don't even know why?"

"Yep," she replied. "Shoot me, I have no clue, and the longer I'm here, the less anything makes sense. You sure this isn't Wonderland? I mean, we went down a hole and everything."

Darius laughed. The sound was deep and honest, and Jansen couldn't help but notice the way his nose scrunched up. There was a twinkle in his eyes and a sureness to the gesture that she'd seldom seen from others she interacted with. He hid nothing from her, and for perhaps the first time in her life, Jansen felt she didn't have to, either.

She turned away instantly when she caught herself staring at him, and that was when she saw it. Her eyes narrowed as she walked towards the bookshelf. She couldn't make out the words entirely at first, but the closer she got, the more she was able to confirm that she wasn't seeing things. Her small hand reached out for the spine of the book, and touching it, she felt the smooth and worn leather under her fingertips sag a little as she pressed into it. She slid the tome out, and resting the back of it on her forearm, she studied the cover.

"A History of Gaia as recorded by Chiron." Darius read the title. "Do you think they mean Chiron the Firstborn?"

"I don't know, but I thought the Water Elves didn't encounters the Gaians until Orbeyus came to Aldamoor," she said.

"No, the Water Elves helped in building the Eye to All Worlds," Darius stated. "They were the ones responsible for much of the magic in the castle and in helping pinpoint where new portals were created. Alternate worlds are as much a part of our existence as water itself. From what I remember in my history lessons, the Water Elves always knew a descendant of Severio would come again to make alliances with them, they just didn't know when, and they certainly didn't expect Lord Orbeyus to appear to them when he was a teenager."

Jansen lugged the book over to the nearest desk and placed it down with a hollow thud that caused some dust from between the pages to flutter up into the air. Her eyes watered with the effort of withholding a sneeze. She took a step back, smelling the mustiness coming from the volume and began second-guessing her decision to look through it.

What if she tore a corner accidentally, or the moment she opened the book, it turned to dust in her hands? Questions danced in her mind's eye as she read the words on the cover, embossed and painted over in gold lettering on the faded green leather.

The sneeze stifled in its tracks, she shook off her worries and carefully opened it. The first page contained an intricate hand-drawn map on it that folded out. She opened that and studied the lines and contours etched in black pen on parchment.

"How old do you think this book is?" Jansen traced the page delicately with a finger.

"If it's Chiron the Firstborn, then this book could be well over two thousand years old." Darius leaned in over her shoulder and studied the map. "It wasn't written recently, though. I don't recognize any of those cities, if that's supposed to be Gaia, and the city of Pangaia looks like a little village compared to the behemoth it is now."

He studied it further. Jansen glanced sideways briefly, and he looked as though he were analyzing each quill stroke on the page with utter reverence. When he finished scanning it, he took a step back. His expression was a blend of seriousness, consternation and confusion.

"I don't get it. The Severio coat of arms isn't present at all, and they've ruled Gaia for generations, from what I remember Puc telling me."

"A map from before the time the Severio family ruled Gaia." Jansen's brows furrowed as she folded the map back up and turned to the first page after the front matter, glancing only briefly at the table of contents.

To her surprise, the words were written in English, and she had no trouble reading the neat print. Had she not known better, she would have guessed it had come from a printing press instead of being handwritten. She began speed reading through the contents, unsure of how long the so-called break they had would be. She also knew full well that she and Darius would both need rest before further questioning by the Sisters were to take place, and she didn't want to spend all of her time in the library, even if she wanted to. Her body would pay for it later. The faster she went, however, the less productive she felt her absorption of the material was, and she slowed back down to an average pace after a few pages.

"There's no kingdom," she stated. "The author mentions tribes and villages with nobles or... well, I guess war chiefs would be more appropriate… no… that doesn't quite work either… war kings? Earls like the Vikings had… man, I wish I'd paid more attention in history class. Anyways, they were the ones who oversaw the villages and protected their people from attacks from others."

"So this is talking about Gaia before they even had a king." Darius whistled and ran a hand through his hair. "I bet Puc and even Venetor would get a kick out of this."

"Somehow I don't think the Gaian king would care much for reading this," Jansen admitted, knowing full well about Annetta's uncle and the now present ruler of Gaia.

"I guess you're right. He doesn't strike me as the reading type. What else is in there?"

Jansen flipped back to the table of contents and scanned it. She paused when she got to a name she recognized instantly.

"The rise of Korangar," she read, and flipped the page.

She felt Darius hover over her. Finding the section she wanted, Jansen sped read through until she came upon a passage of interest.

"And it was foretold by the great prophet, Avitus Severio the brother of the explorer Adeamus Severio, that born was to be a Gaian who would hold all the aspects of evil within him. A father would give up his untainted son in thinking he is committing the ultimate sacrifice, only to bring about the creation of the greatest evil. The innocent known as Korangar, the son of Freius would take up this mantel without knowing its full costs and blindingly trusting his father to fulfil the task bestowed upon him. Awoken with his new power, the fury of Korangar would threaten to set all worlds onto the path of their end. As all sin wishes, his will would from henceforth be to destroy all worlds."

Darius ran a finger down his chin pensively. "So Korangar was sacrificed by his old man because he was pure of heart and could hold all the evil of the world inside of him? Doesn't make much sense, considering the state of things in all worlds, but okay."

"Tell me about it." Jansen rolled her eyes and glanced back at the page. She scanned for a little more before continuing. "Hrm… something here about… hang on."

She pressed her head closer to the page as she did her best to read. It was as if someone had spilt onto and then wiped it off, leaving only thin, scratched lines on the parchment that was barely visible in certain angles of the light. Jansen didn't envy medieval scribes in the least due to what they had to deal with to even write a single page.

Her face contorted as she tried to make out the words. "Something about… I want to say dragons, if that makes any sense."

She pulled away from the chair and stood, letting Darius slide into her place. His face drooped over the book as he analyzed the contents. Any closer and Jansen would have had a good chuckle at watching his nose press against the page. He pulled away almost as quickly as he'd sat down.

"We need to get back to Anne and the others." He stood up. "I do, at least. You should probably stay here. Korangar won't think to come here until he has his way with Earth, if his target is who I think it is."

"What are you talking about?" Jansen frowned. "And don't think for a second that I'm going to stay here, Mr. Imaginary Character from my Book I was Writing."

"Jansen, this isn't a discussion. I've made my decision, and you're going to stay here. My friends need me, and they need this information if they are going to be facing Korangar. It's safer here for you."

Her jaw tightened at hearing this as she struggled to come up with a counter-argument. "No place is going to be safe now that he's free. You didn't think I knew about him when I was writing? I mean, sure, he was just a name that got thrown around, but I was aware. Besides, I bet you I know things you even don't, and they could come in handy."

Darius looked as though he was struggling to say something, but nothing came. It was only after a long pause that he found his thoughts and let out a frustrated sigh. "Look, I'm not explaining to Lysania why you disappeared suddenly. The last thing I need on my back now is the Sisters of Wyrd."

"But you won't have them on your back," Lysania's voice answered from the door.

The duo turned and saw Lysania, flanked by two other Sisters. There was no malice on her face, in fact, it was the opposite, like that of a concerned mother.

"You are both free to go," she said. "You have seen what was intended to be seen, and you may leave now if you wish. Take the book to show Thanestorm. I do ask, however, that when the dust of this fight settles, that Jansen returns here with the tome. There's still a lot we'd like to learn."

"I guess I can do that." Jansen ran a hand through her hair and scratched her neck.

"It's settled then." Lysania motioned for her followers to make room for them to leave. "Go now, the fate of all worlds may depend on your words."

Chapter 38

Annetta and Jason pushed further into the city. They'd decided not to split up in the wake of Liam's death, both for Jason's mental state and safety. There was also the question of Annetta's dark passenger she feared would come loose, despite Puc's seal on her. The two of them fought back to back as a blurred cyclone of sword and mace with the odd interlude of Annetta's shield. Mechanical and yet fluid all at once, their actions were the result of hours of training.

Jason cleaved into the nearest Fire Elf, landing a blow in his chest that sent him flying across the road and into an abandoned SUV. "I'm starting to feel like I'm in a hack and slash game with no enemy spawn limit."

"Tell me about it." Annetta wiped her matted bangs away from her forehead as an Imap warrior charged her with with a scimitar and axe.

The longer they fought, the more apparent it became to Annetta that they were sorely outnumbered. She glanced back briefly at their extraction team to confirm this, seeing each of them with their hands full, and cursed under her breath. They were on the losing side. The year in between the battle against Mislantus and then on Gaia against Razmus had severely depleted their army, and the final blow had come at Snapneck's declaration to leave the Four Forces after the supposed betrayal at Annetta's hands.

Betrayal. Despite her best effort not to, the word caused Annetta's blood to boil, and she drove Severbane forward with more fury than she'd dared to all day. She could feel the bloodlust rushing to her head, pounding at her temples, and for a single instant she lost herself in it. Images flashed through her mind as she remembered when they'd first come to Morwick and rescued him from being sacrificed by the giant Yarmir. The time they'd come to visit his father's court during the Crossing of the Sun, the equivalent of the Minotaur New Year. These and many more memories welled up inside of her. Her eyes fogged involuntarily with tears that she pushed back. She was not a traitor. Her sword lodged in the chest of a fighter she didn't recognize the race of and she pulled it out, staggering back.

"He doesn't know what betrayal is." Her breaths were slow and ragged as she blinked and expelled the excess water out of the corners of her eyes. A wild cry escaped her lungs as she charged again for the mass of soldiers, with Severbane gripped firmly and her shield before her.

A force she couldn't identify then flung Annetta back. She sailed through the air until she landed and skidded across the pavement. Were it not for her Beta Dragon scale mail, she was sure she'd have broken more than one bone, but thankfully it wouldn't end in anything more than bruises if she survived the next assault.

Her eyes adjusted, and she saw her assailant clear as daylight. From far away, he would have blended in with the others, but up close she couldn't deny who it was. Snapneck stalked towards Annetta slowly. Any kindness that would have been present in the Minotaur's blue eyes was absent, and had been replaced with malice. In one steel-clad hand he carried Fearseeker, while in the other, a club dangled loosely.

"I have wanted to do that for a long time now." He inched closer. "Ever since I understood the magnitude of what you'd done. My father and countless others died for your cause. In fact, he died carrying these two weapons on him. It's only fitting then that you meet your end at their hands."

Annetta stared at the club he held as memories of the battle of Gaia flooded her. She was there all over again, watching helplessly from a distance as Razmus Severio killed Lord Ironhorn with an ease that was criminal. Her mind then wandered onto Link, to the grave they had laid out for him on Gaia, and the knowing she would never see him again.

"We all lost someone on Gaia." Annetta rose to her feet, cringing as she felt the impact aftermath on her body intensify. "I never asked your father to come with me. He offered to help. I simply said I was going."

"He was blinded by your supposed chosen one status." Spit frothed and flew from Snapneck's mouth.

"Chosen one?" She raised an eyebrow. "Since when have I ever called myself the chosen one? I fight because no one else will. If I don't take a stand, there is no one else left."

"To fight whom exactly?" He brandished his weapons.

"The bullies like you." Annetta gritted her teeth.

Snapneck needed no more provocation than that. Instantly, Fearseeker swung towards Annetta, who raised her shield. A metallic thud followed as the blade bounced off the enchanted Calanite diamond surface and was followed by Snapneck raising the arm with his club skyward.

"Annetta!" Jason's voice called out to her from somewhere nearby.

Just as the club came down, Annetta teleported behind Snapneck and kicked the Minotaur's knee. Snapneck stumbled with a grunt, losing his balance for only a mere second. He pivoted on his good leg to face her. Fearseeker came towards her, the pitch-black blade with gold edges aiming to find its mark, only to be met with Severbane. The metal of the two blades shrieked as they collided and parried blow for blow.

Annetta then found an opening and drove Severbane forward, piercing Snapneck's armour where his forearm joined with his bicep. Snapneck howled and retracted the limb, but not before Annetta dug deeper with the blade. For all she knew, it would be the only chance she'd get in this fight.

She managed to jump away at the last second with her shield raised as the club collided with the space that had been her head seconds before. Her face heated with the fury of the fight, she raised the shield further up, pointing her sword towards him as though she were a phalanx armed with a spear.

"You think that toothpick of a blade will be enough to stop me?" Snapneck growled as he tested his damaged arm.

Annetta didn't respond to the taunt. She didn't even move, and only watched as the Minotaur came at her with both weapons raised. Her shield came first, taking the brunt of the attack from the club and pushing it aside. Severbane then locked with Fearseeker, causing sparks to fly. The sight did nothing to deter Annetta from her position. The muscles in her legs and arms strained as she faced Snapneck, and it was only the added strength of her feral form abilities that allowed her to hold equal ground, a last resort on her part.

"You're holding back." The Minotaur King's bovine face contorted in rage.

"With good reason. You don't know what I'm trying to hold back here," she said through gritted teeth. Her grip on Severbane began to shake as it struggled against Fearseeker, and she knew there was little time left before she would need to tap into her psychic abilities. A lion could only hold off a beast like the Minotaur for so long.

"It is an insult to hold back against your enemy," Snapneck spat while taking a step back. "You as a Severio should know this. You are a Gaian after all, aren't you?"

"Raised on Earth, or did you forget that part?" Annetta lowered her weapons and felt the blood flow through her arms freely in a rush that caused them to tingle.

A howl of rage escaped Snapneck next, and he launched himself at Annetta with full power. The club dropped from his hands mid-sprint and was replaced with an axe from his belt. Annetta drew up her shield.

Were the shield made of anything but Calanite diamond, Annetta was sure it would have shattered. Instead, it bounced back awkwardly from the impact, causing the girl to stumble. She regained her footing almost instantly, being no stranger to such attacks, and pointed her sword forward in the same position as before.

Snapneck watched her with his blue eyes, which were worn and rimmed red with the lack of sleep. The more Annetta looked into them, the more she saw the same eyes that had belonged to Lord Ironhorn. The father's had held none of the venom that now leaked from the son's.

"This will end here and now, Severio." His nostrils flared as he sucked in great gusts of air.

Annetta found herself looking sideways, over to where Jason and some of her soldiers fought on. She locked eyes with her best friend for a split second before she glared back at Snapneck.

"It doesn't have to," she said. "We don't have to fight. Your ancestors and my grandfather were allies once. Your father believed you and I could be, too."

"The time for that has passed. My father erred in believing that a young girl from another world could be the salvation of our people, the force that would unite us with the giants and end all wars. He was wrong. I see that now. We should have always counted on ourselves."

He then seemed to wait for her to say something. The gears in Annetta's head turned, and she felt the leather texture of the sword hilt come into the forefront of her mind. The blade had always felt good, right in her hands, but it was not until that moment that she realized why. The leather was soft, worn down by years of use, by the number of times that her grandfather's or father's hands had gripped and hoisted the blade into the air as the symbol of the Four Forces. Now, it seemed to stand for nothing but a dream of what could have been.

"You're right. Your father did fail in placing his trust in me." Annetta felt herself deflate as she exhaled. "Just as I placed my trust in you."

Shield raised before her and Severbane tucked tightly at her side, Annetta charged with a battle cry that picked up momentum until it became a blurred blood-curdling scream erupting from her lungs.

Snapneck ran at her as well. The sound of his heavy armour clanging together resonated in the air much like the clanging of weapons on shields. He lowered his head forward with horns pointed in her direction, hoping to skewer her before the fighting even began.

A dark blur suddenly appeared from the corner of Annetta's eye and then rammed into Snapneck, throwing him off balance. The large Minotaur skidded across the road and landed on a grey sedan, crushing the front and setting off the vehicle's alarm. The girl halted in her tracks, her chest rising and falling heavily from the sprint. She squinted against the midday sun and turned to the new arrival.

Hideburn stood before her, clutching a war trident. The shaft of the weapon was easily as thick as a small tree, and wrapped around the middle in blackened hide. The three prongs curved slightly inward, finished off with barbs.

"Remind me never to piss you off," Jason called as he ran over to Annetta's side.

"I'll say." The girl nodded.

The Minotaur didn't reply, and there was a tense air to his body language. He wasn't enjoying what he was doing.

"Hideburn?" Snapneck rose with a groan. "You'd dare to attack your liege lord? What's the meaning of this?"

"I cannot allow you to continue with this mad quest. Korangar has poisoned your mind."

Snapneck's thick bovine brow furrowed. "I have not been poisoned. I am the only one who's not poisoned!"

Before he could continue his rant, Annetta saw other Minotaurs come into view around them. She grew uneasy at this, and readjusted her grip on Severbane. A glance in Jason's direction also indicated that his feelings reflected her own.

Hideburn slammed the butt of the trident into the ground. "I am not the only one that thinks their king has gone mad. Look around you."

"Kill him!" Snapneck roared, with Fearseeker outstretched. When none of the Minotaurs moved, his bloodlust-glazed eyes sobered some.

"So, this is where we stand, then? Traitors, the lot of you! You will all burn for this, mark my words. Just as soon as I finish with him."

"Lady Severio and Lord Kinsman," Hideburn addressed them. "There are still civilians in need of aid. Go and see to them. I'll take care of matters here."

There was a finality to how Hideburn spoke. Annetta wanted to stop him, to say she wouldn't allow him to be left unaided, but realized that if she did, then she'd be casting herself in the role that Snapneck already saw her in, the glorified chosen one. This was no longer her fight.

Annetta nodded lightly at Hideburn and then turned to Jason. "Come on, J.K."

The duo and their ragtag retinue then began to move past the two Minotaurs.

"You can't just leave! This isn't over, Severio!" Snapneck roared.

Before Annetta or Jason could respond, Snapneck bolted from where he stood and raised Fearseeker. The fury in his eyes was replaced by that of shock mere seconds later, and his body jolted before the Minotaur King dropped to his knees, the light fading from his eyes. Towering above and behind him was Hideburn, with the trident still raised and the pendant he'd shown Annetta and Jason dangling from the same hand that clutched the shaft of the weapon. His face held a pained expression.

"I am sorry nephew," The words came out of Hideburn with a tremble and the trident moved forward.

Snapneck turned and looked at him for a split second as realization dawned on him. His body jerked when it made contact with the trident before toppling over.

Despite her better judgement, hot tears welled up in Annetta's eyes. Memories of a younger, happier Snapneck clouded her mind. Whatever chance there could have been of redeeming him from Korangar's hold was lost.

"It shouldn't have ended like this," she whispered to herself.

Jason placed a hand on her shoulder. "There's nothing we can do here. We need to keep moving."

Annetta said nothing and sheathed Severbane as she began beside him. She adjusted the straps of her shield in hand, glanced over her shoulder, and stole one last look at where the Minotaur King had fallen.

∞○≈

Korangar took in the sight of one of the charred buildings before him. Embers still danced on the edges of flame-devoured timbers, flickering in the dying light. Further beyond was more desolation in the forms of upturned and burning cars. A smashed bus stop grinned at him in a jagged smile of glass shards hanging from the metal frame, while a newspaper fluttering on the wind took shelter in its embrace. Though Korangar didn't fully understand what these things were when he saw them, he took pleasure in seeing them destroyed. This alone, however, didn't fully satisfy him and served as a distraction from his true mission.

He paused briefly enough for Amarok, who shadowed him from behind, to come within hearing distance. "I grow tired of this game of hide and seek. You said she would be here. Where is the girl?"

Amarok's broken mask glinted in the cloud-covered grey light. "My lord, I said she was in this city. I didn't say I knew exactly where she would be located."

Before he could continue, Korangar threw an arm up to stop him. "I grow tired of your excuses, and your advice has served me ill. No matter, though, I'll level the whole city to the ground with this rabble you told me to gather."

"But you will need an army," Amarok interjected.

"I have an army," he snapped, and looked back at him. "An army of me."

Korangar allowed for no further exchanges and strode into an alley, disappearing between the jungle of buildings.

Chapter 39

Puc and Matthias wasted no time returning to Toronto to help its civilians once the situation with the States had been handled. They soon located a building that they'd identified as a school. Upon venturing inside, they found that all of the classrooms had been placed on lockdown and were filled with both teachers and students, terrified of what the outside world held.

"We are here to help." Puc recited the line over and over again to closed doors until they reached the door to where the Principal and the secretary were hiding.

The mage sighed, trying to come up with something more he could say. Puc understood the fear these men, women and children were experiencing. It was the same he'd felt as a child when the Fire Elves had attacked Aldamoor, the day he'd been left an orphan. For all his knowledge, however, he had nothing to offer them to ease their suspicions except his sincerity, and hoped it would be enough. At the same time, turmoil roiled inside him, knowing that each minute counted, and that he had no time to waste. This conflict of feelings manifested itself in him by his grip tightening on his staff, causing his knuckles to turn an even paler shade of white.

The door where the Principal was opened a smidge. "Are you with the police or the fire department?"

Puc exhaled. "We are not, but we are here to help take you to a safe place."

The door crept open a little more to reveal the side of an older woman's face, rimmed with dishevelled blonde graying hair that was cut to about shoulder length. Thin wire-framed glasses rested on the ridge of her nose as she regarded Puc with an air of mistrust, but also an air of desperation.

Puc did his best to keep a calm resolve. "Please, you must believe me when I say I am here to help. We do not have much time until the real enemy gets here, and mark my words, they will not take time to speak with you as I am now."

The door then shut before Puc's face.

"I take it we'll need to do this the hard way." Matthias cocked his head slightly to the side as he began sizing up the door.

Before he could make any move, a crackling sound came through the speakers, along with a high-pitched wail as though someone was adjusting a microphone.

"Your attention please." The voice of the woman Puc had just spoken to came through. "This is Mrs. Weaver, your Principal. We will be evacuating the premises of the school. All teachers have students take their coats and bags, then line up in twos. We will begin with junior and senior kindergarten classes, and then move up through the grades. Announcements will be made when the next set of classes is to proceed."

The speakers then went silent, and a few seconds later, the door before Puc opened, and out peered the woman he now knew as Mrs. Weaver.

She took two steps forward until she was gone from the safety of retreat into her office at a moment's notice. "Now you'll need to tell me where exactly it is you'll be taking everyone. I didn't do this lightly, but if what I'm seeing on the news is true, then I don't really have any options."

Puc veered around to Matthias, who had decided to retract his claws into his gauntlets, making him look slightly less menacing than he had beforehand. The mage began calculating a plan in his head. "How many can you bring down at once, and how many trips before you need to take another potion?"

"I can take two classes down at a time," Matthias informed him. "And I can make about five trips total before I need to take one right now, I think. Ten after that."

"It will have to do. Make sure the exits of the school are secured and we will proceed," Puc commanded Matthias, who bounded off to see to the task. The mage then turned to Mrs. Weaver, who stood patiently with a skeptical look on her face. "You may begin calling the classrooms out two at a time. There is not much time for me to explain the rest. You have my word we are trying to lead you to safety."

"It doesn't look like the O.P.P. or the Fire Department are going to show up any time soon." Mrs. Weaver bobbed her head and went back inside the room.

An exhale mixed with a sigh of relief escaped Puc when he heard this, and out of the corner of his eye, he saw a group of young children being escorted down the hall by two adults. The youngsters seemed oblivious to the danger they were in as they clutched bags or stuffed animals to themselves, walking along quietly in twos. A few would stare at Puc as they passed him by, in a mix of awe and fright.

"This isn't going to be easy." Matthias interrupted his stream of thought. "Just how exactly do I explain to four year olds they're going to be teleported to a base under the ocean? More importantly, how do I get these adults to agree?"

"Tell them to close their eyes and think of a safe place," Puc instructed him. "Once they are in the Lab, it will not matter, and Skyris has Dexter explaining to each new arrival where they are. We, unfortunately, do not have that privilege. As much as I disagree with frightening these children and the adults with them, we do not have a choice if we wish to preserve their lives."

Matthias nodded at this, and went to meet the group that had formed in the middle of the hallway.

Puc watched from a distance as the former assassin explained to the group what he wanted them to do. After some resistance from the adults, he got them to comply and teleported them all before anyone could utter a sound.

☙❧

Skyris noted that the Lab was becoming more and more populated as her eyes flickered from screen to screen at her station in the control room. Her attention was then diverted to the latest group of new arrivals that had been brought down by Matthias, who teleported from sight almost right after, leaving a frightened group of children with a few adults.

Luckily, another Dexter unit was nearby, and quickly gathered the attention of the newcomers. Her fingers raced over the touchpad on the glass surface before her as she adjusted the unit's manner of speaking to match with the mind of a child. She watched through Dexter's camera as the expressions of the children began to relax, the stress on their little faces decreasing with each word uttered by the A.I.

"Not a people person at all, are you, Teron?" An uneasy chuckle escaped her. It was a poor attempt to diffuse the tension in the air, but Skyris didn't see the harm in trying, especially if she was the only one in the room.

She was about to begin her routine check-in on all of those out in the city when she heard the beeping of her C.T.S. She looked over at the watch and had a moment of dread, but quickly shook off the dark thoughts as she lifted the lid.

"037 here," she answered in a steely tone.

"010 here." Sarina's voice came through the watch. **"I need your help. We appear to... well.... We may have an uninvited guest, if I can call him that..."**

Skyris's brows furrowed at the wording. "I'll be over there in a few once I lock onto your coordinates. 037 out."

Skyris disconnected, but kept the lid of the C.T.S. open. She then changed the settings over to the GPS she'd built into the device. The hologram of a map appeared before her and honed in on the location of the C.T.S. Sarina was wearing. Reading over the coordinates, Skyris closed the device and made her way over.

The familiar humming of an engine thrummed in her ears from one of the numerous corridors she passed and joined her in tow. Dexter's presence had become part of the normal sounds in the Lab, especially since she had activated the other units. The robots used a single hive mentality, allowing for Dexter to be all places at once, which made him incredibly useful in the given circumstances. Despite being sure that she was capable of cloning herself, Skyris was not about to perform such a feat in order to keep an eye on thousands of humans as they poured into the Lab.

"How are they doing?" She broke the silence while walking.

"Many having become restless," the A.I. answered nonchalantly. "There have been some complaints of bodily needs, but I have addressed those as needed by providing facilities and resources."

Skyris nodded. "Have there been many injured coming down?"

"Yes. Sarina and some of those who claimed to be doctors, nurses or paramedics have been seeing to the injured. So far we have not had any casualties within Q-16."

There was a pause from Dexter. Skyris could practically feel his red glowing eye on her and turned to face him. "But?"

"This, of course, does not account for the thousands dead in the city."

The words stung at Skyris's pride. She knew they were all doing everything they could to bring people to safety, but it was not enough. They were not enough. If only she had the backing of the Gaian army now, if only they had more able bodies to help. She gritted her teeth in frustration as she tried to come up with something more they could do, but nothing came. She was running out of solutions, just as they were running out of time.

"I detect a change in your breathing and heart rate. You are upset. Is there anything I can do to help you?" the A.I. chimed in again.

Skyris reached absentmindedly for the flask still in her coat pocket, but paused and let her hand drop. "No. I'll be fine, Dexter. Thank you."

Skyris came out of the corridor, and her senses were flooded with the sights and sound of bodies. Men, women and children of all ages and nationalities stood, sat or lay around the common room area, making use of the many chairs that just days ago had been pushed to the sides of the walls, having been unused for years. Most paid her little mind, their attention fixed on Dexter, who hovered just a few feet behind her. A wave of empathy rushed over her as she took in everything, and it was only then that she understood what the meaning behind a sister planet was. In the faces of these people, she saw her own.

Her revelation was interrupted by the urgent cadence of incoming feet. Skyris looked up and saw Sarina rushing towards her. The girl's clothing was stained with blood and grit, as though she'd been fighting on the surface with the others.

"Thank the Unknown you're here." Sarina sighed as she caught up her.

"You run short on doctors?" Skyris raised an eyebrow. "Because I should warn you, I'm no good with a scalpel."

Confusion flooded Sarina's face for a split second, and then she shook her head. "No, we're fine on that front. But we have-"

A blood-curdling shriek filled the room before Sarina could finish her sentence.

Skyris grasped at the space beside her hips where she'd wear her swords, and cursed herself for not having armed herself. Had she Venetor's foresight, she would have been in full armour since the whole ordeal started, but alas, despite being a Gaian, she was only a warrior part-time, and the rest of her time was dedicated to science.

"If I survive this, I'm going to have to change that mindset," she muttered to herself, and strode forward with the same conviction as before, only this time, she was thinking of how to diffuse whatever was going on.

"Whats is all these peoples so close to Fefj's master arts!" A furious, high-pitched voice bellowed.

"It's another monster!" Someone cried out as a score of people ran from the voice's direction.

Others began to rise and panic with this declaration, and Skyris knew all too well what that meant if left unchecked.

"Secure the area, Dexter," she commanded the A.I. "And get other units here. Activate the rest if necessary. There should be another fifty shells that are not in use."

"Of course, at once, Skyris." The A.I. hovered away from her and to the nearest group of citizens to quell their fears.

Skyris, with Sarina in tow, pushed past the fleeing and dispersing humans. They stopped when the source of the panic came into view.

The creature was unlike any Skyris had ever seen in her many travels. The thing's face seemed to consist entirely of wrinkles and folds of fat. The more she looked at it, the more uncertain she became as to where its head or neck began. A patch of shaggy brown hair sprouted from its pudgy head that became lost in the folds of the creature's rumpled leathery skin which all seemed to originate at the creature's large and unnatural grin.

"Ruins it! All ruinsed." The thing flailed its tiny, spindly arms, which seemed completely out of proportion with the rest of its grotesquely obese body. "Humans folk no appreciate beauty of master arts. Too simple in their tastes for somphistimicated cultures."

Skyris looked down at Sarina, who stood mortified on the spot. "So, this the thing you called me about," Skyris said.

"I heard a commotion happening." Sarina glanced up at the woman. "But this... well, this doesn't make any sense, if this is the troll J.K. told me about..."

The thing noticed Skyris and Sarina looking in its direction, and glowered with its beady eyes. "So, you's heard of Fefj greatness?"

"I heard you were turned to stone in a cave," Sarina bluntly stated.

"Fefj?" Skyris stroked her chin for a second. "My brother mentioned something about a creature like that, said it had been killed in a cave with a rock."

"Pfft! Nots possible! Fefj has plots arm-amour." The thing scoffed and waved a hand. "Knows Unknowns fella. Him got Fefj's back."

Skyris wanted to turn away more than anything to retrieve her weapons, but found it impossible. A slowly-growing crowd of curious onlookers, mostly young men, had begun to watch the scene unfold from a distance. She was instead forced to carry on the conversation. "So, how exactly did you get here?"

360

"Heres? I always been heres. This Fefj home." The thing grinned in oblivious glee.

"I find that unlikely, but alright." The woman shrugged, feeling more and more uncomfortable.

The wrinkled flabby head bobbed at this, and then furrowing its bushy eyebrows, it glared at her. "So, business talks. Whats you gotsum for Fefj in exchange for invadsin loverly home?"

Skyris felt the wind knocked out of her lungs at the notion, and then turned to Sarina, to see the girl going through similar emotions.

"Nots alls in one line." Fefj waved a hand with spindly digits. "Fefj no sends the dark ones rights away. I is feeling genemarous todays.... Yes."

He leered at Skyris and ran a large purplish tongue over yellowed teeth, at which Skyris did her best not to recoil, though Sarina took two steps back. Fefj seemed to delight in her reaction, and was about to advance towards the girl, when Skyris moved before her, blocking his path, which caused him to yelp.

"Cut to the chase." Skyris crossed her arms.

"Nasty talls flat-footer." Fefj grimaced and wiped a little drool that had come loose from his mouth while he spoke. "Impatience and rudes."

"Cry me a river, build me a bridge and get over it." Skyris huffed.

Fefj ignored the comment and instead turned back into the dimly lit hall of the Lab. "Oje!"

"What does master want of Oje?" Yellow eyes glittered from the dark area.

Skyris felt her muscles coil with the need to strike, but relaxed as the second creature emerged. The one was significantly shorter, standing at maybe two feet, with a large, pointed nose and a thin, nearly-hairless tail, tipped lightly in coarse fur. A drooping cap lay between large ears, with hair sprouting from within and around them.

Fefj outstretched a hand towards it and cleared his throat as though he were expecting something. When nothing happened for several seconds, he glared at the shorter creature with disdain. "Where Oje has it?"

While the unlikely duo was distracted, Sarina took the opportunity to move closer to Skyris. "What do we do?"

Skyris continued to face them, but her eyes drifted to Sarina. "If only I had something I could use as a weapon, this might end much quicker. We don't have time for this right now. There's an apocalypse happening above us."

Sarina nodded, and no longer being the object of anyone's attention, she darted away. Skyris took this as her cue to distract the creature.

The little creature, Oje as he was called, had managed in the meantime to slink into the shadows and re-emerge with a large rolled-up patchwork parchment. The parchment was so large that Oje had to drag most of it on the floor, and when he finally got to Fefj, he struggled to lift it over his head to hand to his master.

Fefj sneered and snatched it, seeing as Oje could not reach up all the way. He then dismissed the creature with a wave of his hand. Exaggeratedly clearing this throat, Fefj then unrolled it and let it roll out to its full length. That was when Skyris realized she had not been looking at parchment at all.

"You write on rags?" she raised an eyebrow.

"Infuriatsing, isn't it?" Fefj's Cheshire cat grin widened and he cleared his throat yet again several times.

"I suppose." Skyris eyed the crudely-patched-together material and realized there was a pattern. "Are those... all single socks?"

"All singles, pairs so overrated." Fefj showed off the patchwork cloth triumphantly, and then narrowed his eyes until they seemed non-existent in the sea of wrinkles that were his face. "Now for demands most fair."

Fefj cleared his throat once more for emphasis, and glanced at the top of the supposed list he'd created. Silence followed, and Skyris noted the frustration on the troll's face as he tried to decipher just what had been scrawled out on the fabric. He glanced up for a second to see her glaring at him and shuddered, muttering something under his breath.

Another hacking sound from his throat followed, and then he began. "Firsts, all peoples shall bows to Fefj and ackernowledges his superiors intermalect."

Skyris shot a quick glance back at those gathered to see everyone dumbfounded by the demand. She, however, had suspected something in that vein, and stood unmoving.

"Seconds, all shall pays tributes of one third of mens, womens, child population to be Fefj's slaves. I be merciful and allows for picking." The troll looked up at this last part with a gleeful smile.

People in the background began to mutter among themselves. A few shouts of outrage occurred, and were Skyris not standing before them, she was certain the mob would have descended on the troll in a locust-like wave to tear the creature limb from limb.

"Anything else?" She continued to stand dispassionately before him.

"I onlys just beginnings," Fefj sneered at her, his irritation apparent with the pronounced hiss at the end of the sentence. "Thirds, all lands on surface and in loverly cave will be claimed to belong to-"

Fefj seized up mid-sentence, his eyes bugging out to be as large as Skyris's fist before closing. The troll then fell with a thud on the floor without any warning. Floating behind him, with a gleaming crimson eye, was Dexter.

Skryis didn't want to acknowledge any of the science fiction stories Annetta had told her about artificial intelligence on Earth, and dismissed them without any sort of gravity. But staring into Dexter's single bulbous red eye, she was beginning to rethink that. Perhaps there was something on Earth that corrupted all A.I. into murderous machines. "Well, thank the Unknown the Federation will never give a seat of power to artificial intelligence."

"I apologize for my rash actions." Dexter broke through her thoughts with his usual pleasant cadence. "But according to my calculations and scenario analysis, the troll known as Fefj could not be reasoned with in any capacity. It was then best to dispose of him as quickly as possible. What shall I do with the body?"

Skryis gazed down at the crumpled mass of the troll in a perplexed manner. She barely heard the approach of feet as Sarina broke through with her swords in tow, and froze beside her.

"I…uhm." Skryis snatched the swords absentmindedly as she took a few steps forward, fastening the straps around her hips. "Do whatever is most efficient and will not disturb the other people in the Lab."

With that, Skyris turned on her heel to look at those gathered. "Nothing to see here. Everyone just please remain calm, and if anyone has any needs that have not been seen to then speak with one of the Dexter droids and they will make sure you're taken care of."

She didn't wait to hear if anyone would speak up after her address, and continued walking, her hand once again wandering to where the flask was hidden in her pocket. Once she was away from the crowd, she reached to grab the flask, and uncorking it, she took a drink form it.

"Are you sure that was the best idea back there?" Sarina's voice trailed behind her.

Annoyance flooded Skyris's mind, but she continued walking. "I did what had to be done. At this point, some traumatized humans are the least of our worries."

"Still, it could have been handled another way."

The muscles in Skyris's face went rigid and she veered around to glare at the girl. "When I was your age, I was put in an examination where I was in charge of a crew of military cadets onboard a Drake-class spaceship. We needed to rescue another ship from invaders, and the task was said to be impossible. In fact, originally, there was no ship at all, but a smuggling ship that was being chased by pirates hacked the signal and made us think the signal was coming from them. Mind you, I didn't know the latter part of this until much later. Despite these supposed impossible odds, I devised a way in which to rescue the ship and destroy the enemy. Forgive me for being blunt in this case, but I think I have a good grasp on how to handle these situations. Experience has taught me that at times the dreams of idealists are not the answers that are needed, but harsh and grounded reality is."

She didn't bother to wait and hear what Sarina would say. Skyris had long ago abandoned notions of what could be done better or handled another way. She'd tried that and been burned one too many times. Her hand still clutching the flask, Skyris reverted once more to her original path and didn't look back.

Chapter 40

Arieus cut through the foe before him and removing his blade, watched the body of the Verden warrior fall at his feet. His breathing was beginning to feel raspy from the strain of fighting, and he debated taking one of the potions Puc had supplied him with, but decided against it.

To his right, Arcanthur was engaged in a bout with a large Fire Elf. The elf's twin sabres locked with Arcanthur's mace. The gritting of steel on steel could be heard from where Arieus stood as Arcanthur and his foe struggled for control.

Arieus's attention was taken from the fight as another enemy came at him, a lithe-looking Minotaur whom he assumed was a female by the shape of her armour. She wielded a great spear that was crafted completely of metal from spearhead to shaft.

He regretted not taking the potion when he thought he had an opening, but stood his ground nonetheless. The female charged at him with spear thrust forward at a speed many would have not thought possible of a Minotaur. Arieus knew better and rolled out of the way at the last second to watch her amble past him and attempt to stop. She pivoted around and with her great bovine nostrils flaring, she charged yet again.

Arieus raised his sword before him, meeting the eyes of the Minotaur as he charged to meet her. She responded with a battle cry and rushed at him as well.

Arieus then used the last reserves of his energy and teleported just as the tip of the spear nearly hit his shoulder. The Minotaur stopped and confusion clouded her face. Seconds later, Arieus reappeared above her and slammed his sword down. The Minotaur moaned and collapsed.

The blade slid out with difficulty and Arieus staggered back in exhaustion once he dislodged the sword. A beeping coming from his C.T.S. then caught his attention, and he flipped open the device.

"This is 05 here." Puc's voice came through, mixed with radio static. "I and 09 are trapped within a school at the coordinates being sent out. We are surrounded by enemy forces, and have not evacuated all of the students yet. I have shields in place, but we require aid, for I do not know how long they will hold. Whoever is closest, please contact me."

The transmission went dead. Arieus's brows furrowed at the message, and he closed the lid of the watch.

"You got that too, eh?" Arcanthur walked towards him with an uneven gait. He was still not used to the prosthetic leg he'd been fixed with. Arieus suspected that he was using a fair bit of psychic energy to keep himself upright, and how it was not draining him was an even bigger mystery.

"I did." He nodded.

Arcanthur did a quick scan of the area to see if there were no enemies around, and flipped open his C.T.S. to type something into it. He then watched as a hologram of a map emerged and studied it intently. "This is three blocks from here."

Arieus looked around at the soldiers of the Four Forces they had with them. They were a ragtag group that was being worn thinner with each wave of enemies that came their way.

"I'm not sure how many more hits we can take." Arieus placed his sword in his scabbard and rummaged through the pouch at his belt for a potion.

"The hell is that supposed to mean?" Arcanthur placed his hands on his hips. "You realize everyone else is probably in the same boat as us, right?"

"I do." The words came out thick, as though someone was glueing Arieus's jaws together.

"Then you understand that it doesn't matter who goes to help?" Arcanthur halted mere inches from Arieus's face. "If you don't want to go, that's fine. I can see exactly why Annetta and my son had to take matters into their own hands. It's because there were no adults to stand up and do the right thing."

The blood coursing through him felt as though it turned to ice as Arieus glared at Arcanthur. "You know, for one who speaks so bold, need I remind you of the reason you weren't around."

Arcanthur moved his gaze and turned away. "My transgressions came much later, and you know it. Now, are you coming with me, or do you want to explain to Thanestorm why you left me unsupervised?"

Arieus's mind raced back to when he and Arcanthur had been just boys under their father's wings. Now, more than ever, Arieus saw the younger version of Arcanthur, the one that had wanted to take on the world and didn't believe in going down without a fight. He smiled to himself as he recalled their last conversation.

"Welcome back, brother."

ഇന്ദ്ര

Jason and Annetta's legs pounded with all the ferocity they could muster, flanked by the soldiers they had with them. The duo had just finished another round of teleporting to and from the Lab, when their C.T.S. watches had both gone off and recited the message from Puc. The school had been some distance away, but through the use of some teleportation, they had managed to cut that distance down to almost nothing. Their initial decision made them hesitate for much of the journey, until the outline of the school came into view past the slowly decreasing jungle of buildings.

"We're almost there." Annetta forced the words out through laboured breaths and glanced back at their entourage, who were doing their best to keep up, despite their exhaustion.

Jason paused beside her and pushed back hair plastered in sweat from his forehead. "I just hope Puc and Matt can hold on long enough."

Annetta nodded at this, but before she could say anything back, Natane approached them. She had long since lost her Aiethon to one of the enemy fighters, and the Ogaien Great Mother now fought on foot, in which she proved no less lethal than on horseback.

"Lady Annetta." Natane planted the butt of her spear in the ground. "There is another entrance to the underground tunnel we just passed, the subway as you called it. One of the Soarin scouts tells me he could hear humans hiding in it."

Annetta and Jason glanced at one another, the pull in their bodies splitting as to where to go. Neither of them said a word, not until Annetta exhaled and gripped the hilt of Severbane with a grime-covered hand.

"You go towards the school. I'll make this run and catch up," she told him, and adjusting the straps of the tower shield on her back, she veered around to head back.

"Anne, wait! You can't go alone!" he called after her.

"Trust me on this!" she yelled as she continued jogging. "You're going to need all the help you can get."

"If I didn't know any better, I'd say she was insulting me," he grumbled.

"Revel in knowing that she is not." Natane placed a hand on his shoulder. "Now come, Thanestorm and Teron need our aid."

ഇന്ദ്ര

A blast of green energy shot forth from Puc's staff, cut through the barrier which encapsulated the school, and hit one of the Fire Elves on the other side. He then went into a neutral stance and picked out his next target with what little focus he could spare. His energy was going wholly into maintaining the shield to keep those of his allies he had with him safe from a full out assault by forces on the outside. A blast of psychic energy rushed past his head and felled another of the denizens who lurked outside.

The mage turned to see Matthias a few feet away. "I told you to conserve energy and finish getting everyone down!"

"It was one blast," he growled. "Besides, I'm waiting on the next group of students. They're bringing out the classes in pairs."

Puc cursed silently under his breath, and locking eyes with a Verden in thick hide armour, he readied another attack. A golden fireball erupted from the staff's end and burned the Verden, along with the few other fighters who were right beside him. He retracted the staff into an upright position. Shifting the weight from one leg to the other, he noticed a slight throbbing in his chest. Touching his collar bone, he confirmed it as a sign of low magical energy and reached into the folds of his robes. Feeling around one of the hidden pockets, he withdrew a potion and once he uncorked it, downed the contents.

He was unsure how many more of the vials lay hidden away in the folds of his robes. The truth was that he'd lost count in the endless sea of enemy fighters. He tucked the empty vial into his pocket and felt the cold wave of liquid wash over his insides, instantly removing the signs of fatigue. Out of the corner of his eye, he noted the students being brought out by the teachers who led them, panic visible on the eyes of the adults in the task they had to carry out.

Matthias, who stood in the same spot as before didn't give the man and woman leading the two rows of children much of an explanation. He reached his hands towards them and instructed each adult to do the same to the closest child, and for them to do the same with their classmates. There was usually little resistance in the matter, and those gathered complied. The older the students got, however, the more difficult it came for Matthias to manage them. Some refused to hold hands with whoever was in front of them, and after an unfortunate trip where half the class was left behind, Matthias needed to check multiple times to ensure everyone was brought down.

"Now everyone, and I mean everyone, hold hands together." Matthias barked the order through a raw throat.

Puc pulled himself away from the sights and shook his mass of black, tangled hair in an attempt to free it from snarls. He glanced sideways and noted the fatigue in the faces of his comrades; the few worn-down Soarin firing their bows without pause, the few mages that fired alongside him, as well as the four Ogaien and two Minotaurs who had formed a circle in the middle of the room where the students and their teachers gathered. They were on their last limbs, and if the barrier he'd placed collapsed, then it would more than likely be over very quickly.

Puc had always been prepared for the possibility of death in battle, having been trained in the Academy first as a fighter and then a mage. Despite this and the long life he'd lived, he found himself with one lingering regret in the sea of everything around him, and that was of not having fought harder when it had come to her. It was too late for thoughts of that now, and the only thing that remained was to channel his underlying grief into rage against the enemy who threatened to end him and everyone around him.

Matthias reappeared in the centre of the ring of soldiers. "How many more we got left?"

Puc frowned at the question and sent another blast of energy from his staff. "I do not know, ask the principal."

The statement resulted in a rolling of eyes from the assassin, who strut over to where the principal and her staff were hiding.

The split second that Puc looked over in his direction cost him the attention he'd needed to keep the shield going. His gaze moved back towards his target, and he was horrified to see a Fire Elf burst through the barrier. It charged towards him with a raised crude poleaxe.

"No! We need more time!" Puc's eyes widened, and he refocused himself on the barrier spell.

Two of his fellow mages blocked the enemy fighter's path and dispatched of him quickly with a few close-range spells. Puc's jaw clenched tighter as he steeled himself to pour more energy into the shield.

Behind him, the sound of shoes and heels on the tiles of the school floor squeaked as they ran towards him. Puc half-heartedly turned his head for only a brief moment to see the principal with her entourage in tow behind Matthias.

"Four more classes remain," the assassin said to him. "I'm going to try bringing everyone down to the Lab at once, although…"

"Although what?" Puc's voice sounded more vicious and strained than he had intended, but he was unable to focus on apologizing just now.

"I may not be able to return for a few minutes," the assassin confessed. "My reserves are low."

A heave escaped Puc's lungs as cool resignation gripped him. He watched as the rest of the classrooms rushed towards Matthias. His pale eyes turned to the assassin, and he nodded. "Do what must be done."

Matthias bobbed his head and gripped hold of the principal's hand, as well as one of the other teachers. In a voice that was authoritative, but that Puc could not hear among the commotion, he watched as others linked hands, and then once everyone was holding on, vanished altogether.

He felt his teeth clench in a final resolution, and he redoubled his efforts on keeping the enemy occupied. Puc's mind was clear, and a single thought continued to fight for dominance in the forefront of all others, the thought that this very well could be his last stand. Despite the despair that formed in the pit of his stomach, the First Mage of Aldamoor continued to fight, remembering what a girl he had followed into battle not so long ago had told him.

"I fight because no one else does." He whispered the words through gritted teeth and shot another blast of energy into the mass of soldiers swarming around the door.

Another of the warriors burst through. This time it was a Minotaur, who charged at full speed once the barrier cast its weight off of him. Hot, foaming drool escaped from the corners of his mouth, frothing as though he were mad, with twin axes raised overheat. A lesser combatant would have run, but Puc would not. Drawing Tempest from its hiding place, he braced himself for the oncoming fight.

Two bodies teleported before him seconds before the collision, and Puc watched as a man of copper hair appeared on the creature's back, gripping the horn closest to him with a firm hand. He then slammed his sword into where the shoulder and neck of beast met, and leapt off gracefully as the creature collapsed behind him, sliding forward a few feet from the momentum he'd accrued.

"Thought you could use a hand, Thanestorm." The voice of Arcanthur came from the other figure as he spun around to face him.

The man's broken nose accentuated his smile into a caricature of whom he had once been, the young boy that Puc had once watched over and taught. Puc found a measure of peace in seeing his former student come to his aid. Perhaps, despite the turmoil of the last decade or so, there was hope for the elder Kinsman.

"I've soldiers on the outside cutting at the ranks," Arieus told Puc, cleaning his blade on the tabard of the fallen Minotaur before sliding it into his scabbard. "Are you still waiting for anyone here, or should we teleport you out?"

It took a moment for Puc to formulate his plan before he responded. "Matthias will reappear soon. He was taking down the last of the students and staff."

There was not a word of complaint or conflict from either man on the subject. Instead, they turned their attention to the masses gathered outside, and began to create balls of psychic fire in their palms.

Something resembling the faintest of smiles flashed across Puc's face as he watched them fall into a natural rhythm with him and the fellow soldiers around. For a split second, it was like having Orbeyus there again. Scenes of past battles flashed before the elf's eyes as he caught glimpses of them in his peripheral vision. Arieus and Arcanthur let loose a flurry of psychic fire, the balls of blue and purple flames crashing into the enemy on the other end of the barrier. Though they looked worn and grizzled, underneath those exteriors lay the youth he'd once taught.

The time they spent there seemed to stretch into eternity for Puc. It was as though time had slowed down. He could practically hear the minute hand of the clock on the far wall of the hallway ticking away.

"Damn it, Teron, where are you?" The mage gritted his teeth.

Two more soldiers came through the barrier, a pair of Fire Elves, one waving a scimitar in the air, while the other held a trident close to his side. Before Arieus and Arcanthur could get to them, however, they were swarmed by the other fighters on their team, who no longer had to worry about protecting travelling students.

Four more beings teleported into the room. All were from different species that Puc had never seen in his long life. His grip tightened on Tempest as he glared at the one closest to him, a man with scales protruding on random parts of his body, as though a lizard were trying to come out of a human husk. Yellow eyes leered back at him with menacing contempt as the creature raised his hand before him, filling it with psychic fire.

"Looks like Korangar also has some psychics on his team," Puc called over to Arieus and Arcanthur.

"Nothing we can't handle." Arcanthur shifted his weight from one foot to the other as he sized up all four opponents. "Which one you want, Airy? I think I'll take the giant orange satyr."

"Doesn't matter to me," Arieus answered curtly.

Arcanthur smirked and nonchalantly dodged the ball of psychic fire that rushed past his head and collided with a door on the other side, setting it ablaze. "Boy, I sure hope this place has insurance."

"I don't think any insurance on Earth covers psychic fire." Arieus threw his volley of fire back at two of the fighters that had been closest to him, the reptilian man and a woman with green skin and a tattooed face.

"We missed out on a potential business opportunity then, I say," Arcanthur called over the chaos, and saying no more, he fully engaged with his foe in a series of teleportation and psychic fire blasts, mixed in with swings of his mace.

Puc rolled his eyes at hearing conversation. He continued to fire blasts past the barrier, though his efforts seemed in vain, as more and more soldiers surrounded the building, their faces a swollen mass against the windows and doorways. Even if they teleported outside, there was a good chance now that they would be overrun. Worst, the door that had caught fire was beginning to spread at a rapid pace.

"We took too long." The thought formed into words before he could stop it from doing so.

As if on cue, Matthias teleported back into the room and sidestepped out of the way just in time to see a blast of psychic fire sail past him.

"Throwing a party in here without me? That's a bit rude." The assassin extended the hidden claws from his gauntlets.

The fourth psychic in the group, a creature with smooth purple skin that looked much like a large Grey alien with an oblong-shaped head raised a gangly hand with four long fingers. Sparks encircled its arms as a ball of flame formed on its palm, and it aimed for Matthias once more.

Matthias glared at the creature, the dark circles under his azure eyes making them appear far more sinister with his wind-whipped hair.

An aura of uncertainty crossed the creature's completely black eyes after he stared it down for a few seconds.

"Go ahead. I dare you." The assassin grinned wickedly.

The alien leapt towards him, threw the ball of flame and teleported. Matthias dodged the blast, pivoted on his heel, curled his hands into fists, and stabbed the claws into the air before him. It was not until seconds later that they were covered in a blue, blood-like substance. The creature materialized with both of Matthias's clawed gauntlets piercing just under his ribcage. The assassin retracted them and watched his vanquished foe fall to the ground.

"Matthias," Puc called. "We need to leave."

Puc saw the recognition on Matthias's face of the fact that the building was now half on fire. Orange flames licked at the doors and wooden finishing in the school.

"And here I just thought it was the heat of the battle." Matthias retracted his claws and motioned to the other soldiers to come close to him. He then linked hands with them and Puc, but stopped at seeing Arieus and Arcanthur still fighting the other psychics. "What about them?"

Puc's eyes began to water from the smoke as he caught glimpses of Arieus slaying the reptile skinned man.

"Arieus! Arcanthur!" he shouted.

"We're right behind you," Arieus confirmed as he finished another of the fighters off.

Hesitation lined the face of the mage, but an anxious look from Matthias caved his resolve. "Very well, let us get these people down and then come back up do deal with this rabble that has gathered outside."

Matthias nodded, and saying no more, he teleported them out of the building.

∞≪

By the time Jason arrived, the building he'd been told to go to was up in a blaze. He had no time to contemplate the meaning of it when he and the group of soldiers with him were slammed with a wave of enemy fighters, which had presumably been waiting around the school where Puc had raised the shield.

Amidst the torrent of parries and blows in a sea of enemies, Jason could only hope that those inside had managed to escape.

His fears were set to rest when a familiar blast of green lightning flew past his cheek and tore through one of the oncoming enemy fighters. Jason looked sideways to see Puc and Matthias, along with another score of soldiers join in and take on the enemy they had encountered.

"A little late to our call for help but good to see you're still alive and kicking." Matthias's voice came from the right as the assassin flanked him.

"I could say the same thing about you," Jason replied and focused on the enemy fighter before him, an Imap wielding two short swords.

Their attention was suddenly diverted when, with a loud boom, the school building came down, crumbling to nothing more than its foundation, causing the fighters they'd been dealing with to retreat with screams of terror.

Their hands free momentarily, Jason and Matthias looked in the direction of the collapsed heap. The shuffle of feet rushing towards them soon announced Puc, who came up on Jason's left side.

"By the grace of the Unknown, I hope they managed to escape in time," the elf said quietly.

"Who?" Jason furrowed his brows.

Puc turned his gaze to the boy, and was about to speak, but before he could utter a word, two figures teleported before them. A worse for wear Arieus held Arcanthur's arm slung over his shoulder. The elder Kinsman held his side with his free hand, a dark stain forming around it.

"Dad!" Jason's eyes widened, and he bolted towards them.

Arcanthur removed his arm from around Arieus, and when his companion attempted to assist him, he waved a hand in dismissal. He staggered a little, his face pale and breathing heavy, but he remained upright as he looked over at his son. They were almost on the same level now, Jason having started his growth spurt over the last year.

"It's good to see you again, son," Arcanthur spoke through gritted teeth. He was about to take another step forward when his foot gave out beneath him, and he fell to one knee. He hissed and looked down at his bloodstained hand.

Puc strode forward, and kneeling beside him, he began to examine the wound. "You have lost a lot of blood, Kinsman, even if I heal this over, then you will still be weak. We will need to get you down to the Lab."

374

"Do what you gotta do, Thanestorm." Arcanthur gave his signature closed-mouth smile that accentuated the break in his nose.

Suddenly, Arcanthur's body jerked violently and was thrown slightly forward. He looked down with wide eyes, where a large arrowhead protruded from the front of his chest.

"Dad! No!" Jason screamed.

Everyone gathered turned their attention to see a pack of enemy soldiers, predominantly Fire Elves, swarm towards them. At their centre stood a figure with a large bow that had not originally belonged to it.

"I was doing you all a favour, you know." The figure that strode closer into view was Tamora. "Injured beasts should be put out of their misery."

Jason could scarcely hear her. He was holding onto his father, cradling the man's head in his arms. Despite not having known him very well, tears had formed in the corners of his eyes, blurring his vision.

Arcanthur's hands wrapped around his son's arms in a vice-like grip, as though he were clinging onto life itself. "It'll be okay, son. It's all going to be okay."

"No, no it won't." Jason shook his head.

The older Kinsman wheezed, freeing one of his hands and running it down the side of Jason's face, as if trying to commit his features to memory through touch. "It is, and it has to. Why isn't it? Because we don't get a happy ending riding off into the sunset as father and son?"

Jason blinked out the tears, his chest heaving almost as much as that of his father's. "I just lost Liam. I can't lose you too, Dad."

Arcanthur shook his head. "You never lost me, because you never had me to begin with, but I… I got to see you become… the son I… always knew you would be."

With those words, the older Kinsman breathed his last, and his body went limp in Jason's embrace.

Chapter 41

Annetta heard the echo of every step descending down the staircase to the subway station. Once inside, the halls were virtually indistinguishable from one another, with the red, sleek tiling that was used in many a subway station in Toronto. Lights flickered, as though someone had damaged the breaker panel they were all connected to, which only further added to her disorientation. She paused at the map beside the payment booth, examining it thoroughly for a minute or two. She hoped it was enough time to commit it to memory, and then continued downwards. If anyone was hiding out here, she had no doubt that they would go to the lowest level.

Winding around the next set of corridors, she came across another set of stairs that led down. With one hand on the railing and the other gripping the handle of Severbane, she took step after tentative step down, aware of any noises on all sides. The further she went, the darker it was, and the flickering lights soon changed over to pitch black. She gripped her sword tighter at this, feeling the wound leather compress.

Her feet soon touched the floor and, sure she had no more stairs to go, she let go of the railing. Save for her breathing, Annetta heard nothing down here, as though all sound from the world had been drained along with the light. She did not take another step forward and instead focused on creating psychic fire. In her mind's eye, she pictured the flames exiting from her body not in a single concentrated place, but from everywhere, coming off of every part of her body. The technique was one Venetor had shown her to shield her body from physical attacks, but she thought at present it could also have another use. Her entire body then lit up, the protective layering of psychic fire covering her from head to toe. In the dim light created by the flame, she saw at least fifty faces cowering. They were a mix of people of various ages and races. What bound them together was the fear in their eyes.

Annetta felt ashamed for causing, it and then realized the look in their eyes had been the same she had gotten from her friends when she had awoken after her supposed transformation.

"Please, you don't need to be afraid." She sheathed her sword and raised a hand before her.

This had the opposite effect of what Annetta wanted, as a few those gathered tried to push back further against the walls. She sighed in frustration, looking down at the ground and then back up.

"Look, if I had wanted to hurt you I wouldn't have come alone, okay? I would have had an army of those things that are running around the city, and I certainly wouldn't take the time to talk to you like I am now, okay? I don't know how else to say it, but I'm here to help. I'm one of the good guys. I grew up on Cassandra Boulevard here in Toronto. I graduated from Silver Birch High School and I'm in school studying Police Foundations."

"You're studying to be a cop?" The voice of a gruff man called from among the sea of faces.

Annetta turned in the general direction of the voice. "Yeah, I wanted to be a police officer so I could help people. I don't want to see them get hurt."

She felt naked admitting those words in front of everyone, and worse yet, she had a feeling they wouldn't do anything to change their minds to have them follow her. She was about to turn away when she heard the shuffling of bodies and the sound of boots. Her eyes opened when she recognized the man walking towards her. He was the instructor she'd had for her Introduction to Health and Wellness course.

On instinct, she stood at attention, feeling his steel grey eyes bore into her.

"At ease, soldier," he told her. It was then that she noticed he, too, was wearing a uniform. "Now, you tell me what you want me to do, and I'll help you get these people out of here."

Dumbfounded for a second, she nodded before turning around to where the faint light from the upper platforms was coming. "We should get everyone out of the dark first. It's best for me to see everyone if I'm going to get them out."

"I'm not sure I follow what you mean to do exactly, Severio, but I'm guessing it has something to do with your fancy light show." He ran his fingers through his stubbly beard.

"Yeah, you'll just need to trust me on this, sir," she replied.

The group of underground dwellers was moving in seconds. Annetta felt a wave of relief wash over her at seeing how smoothly everything was going, and she doused the flames that enveloped her.

"I take it this is why you were late to class all those times." Her instructor spoke again. "Saving the world and such?"

"Uh… yeah, sort of." She ran a hand through her tangled bangs sheepishly.

Her instructor was about to say something else when a scream could be heard from the entrance where the people had begun to gather. Annetta ascended the stairs and drew Severbane from its scabbard once nearing the top and called the shield to her other hand telekinetically. She could teleport, she knew, but with all of the bodies that were now likely there, she ran the chance of potentially teleporting on top of someone. Those few seconds would be precious if someone were attacking them. The closer she got, the more she felt as though her lungs had caught fire. Holding the blade close to her, the tangy scent of oil mixed with the air she was breathing, further adding to the mechanical smells around her.

Four Fire Elves had managed to get down the steps and were making their way towards the civilians with flashing sabres and axes. A few of those in the front had already been injured, and were being pulled back by the others.

Anger flared through Annetta, and she bolted forward with renewed stamina. Running, she tapped into her feral form and let out a war cry, amplified with the lion's roar from within. The elves were stunned from the sound and had scarcely enough time to react as Severbane came rushing towards them.

Annetta managed to cut two of them down while they were in shock, before the other two fell upon her. They were both females, one wielding two axes and the other brandishing a sabre and a jewelled dagger that Annetta was certain had been plundered during another battle they'd been in. The pair circled her with animalistic grins, and Annetta heard the sound of more fighters descending into the station. She didn't have much time, and so she sprang into action. Bracing her shield, she used it to smash into the Fire Elf with two axes, and swung at the one with the jewelled dagger.

The enemy fighter parried with her sabre and thrust forward with the dagger, causing Annetta to attempt jumping back. She was unable to move , and the blade sliced open the pant leg over top her armour to reveal the black scale mail beneath. Glancing sideways to see why she couldn't move, she spotted one of the other fighter's axes hanging over the top of the shield, grappling onto it. Another bout of rage surged through Annetta at the action, and she summoned her feral form once more. The lioness's strength filled her arms, and raising her shield arm up, she flung the fiend clinging to it into the other one before her.

For a split second, she felt the other beast within her as it tried to surface, like an enraged animal rattling against its cage. She shook her head briefly to banish the image, but the pounding in her head remained.

When she saw the two had been knocked out, she turned to those gathered. "Everyone follow behind me. If anyone has anything they can use as a weapon, follow directly behind me, even if it's just a piece of wood."

She didn't wait for any comments or concerns. She didn't have time, they didn't have time, and who knew how many Fire Elves had been in the horde that had just descended on them, or if any more were anywhere in the tunnels. Annetta knew little of the Fire Elves and the other races that made up this invading army, so it was hard for her to determine just how they would strike. Everything she did now was based on pure instinct and the need to keep the people with her alive. The Lab would be the safest place for them, she knew, but to get them there, she would need to be able to see the people teleporting, even if for a split second.

When her feet touched the top step, and she peered over the edge, Annetta knew she would not even get that split second. Before her, outside and in the open, a host of at least thirty Fire Elves awaited. Their hostile laughter and hooting filled her ears as she stood before them at the foot of the entrance. She dared not advance further, not allowing any of the people below her pass.

"Stay behind me," she commanded them, not averting her eyes for even a split second from the horde.

"You can't save them all!" one from the nameless mass called to her, causing a wall of laughter and taunts.

Annetta exhaled deeply, attempting to relax her muscles, and despite her better judgement, she glanced back at the sea of faces which stood on the stairs behind her. Their eyes were filled with fear in varying degrees, and even rage in some cases, but what feeling was most prominent was hope. These people, these strangers, despite all odds, were placing their trust in her. She looked back once more at the foe.

"Watch me." The words came out as a snarl.

Then, just as Annetta was about to rush them, a shadow passed over her head. A blur then crashed into the concrete floor before her. The impact shook Annetta off-balance, and she heard a few people below panic at also having felt it. Annetta watched as the hunched form rose before her to become that of a man, a crimson cape draped from one shoulder, fluttering on the wind.

Despite the short, stocky stature of the figure, she didn't believe who it was until she heard his voice. "Didn't they ever teach you to fight fair? Thirty to one is hardly even odds, but I suppose I could help with that."

As if on cue, a band of Hurtz and Gaian soldiers teleported in and clashed instantly with the unsuspecting Fire Elves

"Uncle Venetor?" The question tumbled out of Annetta amidst the newly ignited chaos. "I thought you were running in the election for the Federation."

Venetor pivoted on his heel to face her. Stubble and dark circles decorated his grim face, but his eyes held the same vigour in them as when she had first met him. "I was, but you didn't think I would abandon Earth a second time, did you?"

Before she could reply, Venetor strode past her, and looking down into the entrance to the subway station, he took note of all the people huddled together. He then glanced back at Annetta questioningly.

"I was trying to get these people down to the Lab where they'd be safe," she explained. "I couldn't see everyone, so I was trying to get them out of the station, where it would be easier."

He nodded thoughtfully and then pulled out his hand towards her. "I may need to be caught up on things here if I am to be of any real help."

Annetta glanced down at his hand in confusion, and then realizing what he meant, she took it. Calloused and warm, Venetor's hand reminded her of her own father's, and a feeling of security washed over her for the briefest of seconds. She told herself, however, that this battle was far from over. She then began the process of projecting everything that had happened into his mind, leading up to the present since the attack on Toronto.

Venetor, while a trained king and politician, had a hard time keeping his face neutral as scenes of what Annetta had gone through flashed before his mind's eye. His brows would narrow and nose scrunch up into a snarl at odd points, while his eyes would move from side to side as though he were speed-reading. When it was done, he took a step back and looked at her.

He then put his hand on her shoulder, squeezing it as he did so. "We will do what we can to help these people. They are, after all, our brothers and sisters."

With that, Venetor turned his attention to the rattled group of civilians. "People of Earth, you have nothing to fear. For too long have you all thought you travel this universe alone. The truth is that you do not, and while many would see to ending your existence, there are also those who would aid and protect it."

He took a step forward with his hand outstretched, and those on the stairs shifted back. Venetor looked over to Annetta, somewhat confused.

The girl sighed and took a step forward with him. "He's my uncle. He's just… not from Earth."

The tension on their faces lessened, and Annetta, along with Venetor began the process of evacuation to the Lab.

§OR

Elsewhere on the field, a blast of golden light ripped through a Minotaur and with a bovine moan, the creature fell to the destroyed pavement. Titus lowered the pistol he held, confident that his target was down. His plan to use the cannon to bring the forces through had succeeded, and he now witnessed around him the Gaian and Hurtz troops teaming up with the battle-worn remnants of the Four Forces. He'd not understood why the Minotaurs were attacking at first, but when one of the Water Elves had filled him in, it made sense. Still, he couldn't understand what would have driven them to think Annetta had betrayed them. He would need to ask his cousin when he next ran into her. Somehow, he didn't think it was something careless that she'd done.

He then looked around and realized that somewhere along the way, he'd lost most of the fighters that had been with him when he'd first come out of the Lab.

"Father won't be pleased," he mused to himself, and then a chill passed by him. While it was fall, and he knew cooler weather was to be expected on Earth, the breeze that had just passed by him was pure ice. He replaced the gun in its holster, but kept his hand on it nonetheless, and moved in the direction of where the wind came from.

He wasn't sure why, but the draft carried him down one of the alleyways among the urban forest of skyscrapers that surrounded him.

He paused at the entrance to the darkened crevice between buildings, and that was when he noticed it on the other side.

Beyond the shades and outlines of the darkened parts of the alley, a Gaian male strode forward. Titus watched him for a few moments with his hands on the triggers of the guns in their holsters. The target stalked onward barefoot, with little attention to what he might step on. The air of obliviousness and confidence that oozed with each step he took was unlike anyone Titus had ever seen before in. Proud shoulders thrown back revealed well-muscled physique that was only covered by a cloak which contained his arms. An absentminded façade clouded his vision as he moved.

Titus then realized who it was, and nearly let his guns fire. His rage was, however, quelled by reason. He would take the shot, he knew, but it would not be in this time and place. He had no idea if his guns would work on the one they called Korangar but he had to try.

Moulding himself in with the shadows, Titus began his pursuit that had only one outcome possible for either side.

Chapter 42

The scene before Puc's eyes unfolded at a slowed pace. It was as though his own heart was ceasing to beat along with Arcanthur's as the Gaian man's life force left the world of the living. All Puc could think was how another one was gone. Yet again he had outlived a friend, and there was nothing he could have done to prevent it. The arrow shot had been swift, and Arcanthur had only been holding on by a thread before that. Rage continued to build silently within him as he looked mere paces away to where Jason knelt, cradling his father's body. Was it not a few years ago that Arcanthur had been that age? Though Puc had never fathered children of his own, Arieus and Arcanthur had filled that void in him, and now it felt as though a hole had been torn through his very soul.

Motion returning to normal in his mind's eye, Puc looked around at the desolated streets. Most of the forces that had been surrounding the school had now dispersed to cause chaos elsewhere, seeing as their target had been destroyed and those inside presumably dead. He remembered Toronto only looking like that once before, when Arieus and Arcanthur had fought shortly after Orbeyus's death. It had been that fight which had placed Arcanthur in a mental institution with his abilities blocked off. The irony of his death hurt even more at that moment.

Laughter cut through his thoughts, and his pale blue eyes leered at Tamora, who stood with what he now recognized as a Soarin bow at her side. Behind her, a group of fighters stood leering at the scene and awaiting her command to strike like a pack of hungry dogs.

"Arieus," Puc uttered the name through clenched teeth.

The man, standing a few feet away, still in shock, glanced at him. "Yes?"

"Take Jason and Arcanthur out of here along with the others that were with me to be treated. Bring them all back to the Lab. Skyris will know what to do with the body."

Arieus shifted his weight from one foot to the other, a sign Puc recognized from his youth as stalling. "Thanestorm, I can't just leave you alone surrounded-"

"You will do exactly as I say," the mage snapped. "You will do so completely and without any questioning of my orders. Do you understand?"

Scurrying was heard a few seconds later behind him. Puc didn't bother looking, his gaze remaining fixed on Tamora.

"You want me down there with them as well?" Matthias's voice came from directly behind him.

Puc thought long and hard on the subject as he measured each of the other gathered fighters around Tamora. "No, you should still be well-rested from the potion. I need you to do something else."

He pivoted on his heel to Matthias. The sweat-slicked ash mixed with blood on his face made the assassin's azure eyes appear even sharper. "I want you to live up to your title, the one Mislantus bestowed upon you. Do what you will to them, except Tamora. We have a score to settle, her and I."

Matthias gave a shallow nod and teleported from sight. Seconds later, the surrounding ranks of Fire Elves were filled with screaming, and the sound of weapons clashing interlaced the chaotic melody.

Puc then veered his attention back to Tamora, who held the same mad grin. He reached into the folds of his robe, and his fingers wrapped around a familiar wire-bound hilt. Tempest sang as he drew it from its sheath. The blade's blue metallic surface gleamed with ripples all along it like raging ocean waves. It had belonged to his father and his father's father before him. He only used the sword when he'd no other choice and knew the conflict could only end in death.

Tamora mock-bowed to him in response as another gleeful grin spread across her face. She tossed aside the bow she'd been holding and drew two sabres that sat at her hips. The glinting light of the sun caught both blades as she whirled them around in her hands, and then without warning, she dove directly for Puc.

Puc composed himself as best as he could, despite his mounting rage. Tempest hummed as it countered the oncoming blades of his opponent. The metallic clanging of swords filled his ears as Tamora shot at him again and again with wild, arcing swings meant to take off one of his limbs.

There was a cost to such movement, Puc knew, and soon, Tamora was panting heavily from the effort. Puc, on the other hand, barely felt winded at all.

"Is this your way now, Thanestorm? Knowing that you can't win, so you bide your time till the opposition tires and murder them cold blood?"

"It is not murder if you laid a hand on your weapon first." He deflected another blow and went into a defensive stance.

"Oh, you're not still hung up on that Arcanthur fellow, are you?" She laughed. "I told you, I was doing him a favour. He had no place in the things that are to come for this world. He's better off where he is now. I did that for him."

Puc was out of anything remotely resembling reason, and slammed the full weight of Tempest against her sabres. "Better? How is it better when a man is separated from his son his whole life, only to die in his arms? Arcanthur Kinsman may have deserved to end up where he did for the crimes he committed in his youth, but he did not deserve to be shot in the back and die in his son's arms."

He withdrew and struck again with the same force of power. Tamora's whole body shook as he did so, but he saw none of that. He did, however, see the shocked expression on her face, not from what he said, but from the power of his strike. It was a look he recognized from his childhood on the streets. He'd met Tamora there as a boy with Iliam. The three of them had been inseparable, and it pained him now to be on the other side. Though this nostalgia threatened to surface, he pushed it down with the grief that tore his heart over Arcanthur's death.

His one-track mind soon cost him his advantage as Tamora dropped one of her sabres. Quickly reaching into her boot, she sliced at his midsection with a knife. Puc jumped back, feeling the knife tear through the fabric of his robe and graze him. He pressed a hand to the wound, and found it smeared lightly with blood. His nose wrinkled at the superficial wound, and he yet again heard Tamora's shrill laughter.

"Bit by bit, I'll cut you up." She spun the single scimitar in her hand effortlessly. "It doesn't matter if you struggle or not. Korangar has awakened to bring justice to all worlds, to make them clean, and together, he and I will rule over the ashes with our child."

"Child?" Puc raised an eyebrow.

Tamora said nothing more and only grinned as another laugh threatened to erupt from behind her row of white teeth. She then lashed out again, feinting with her scimitar before attempting to slash at him again.

Puc half-turned and allowed the dagger to become trapped in the fabric of his sleeve. He then elbowed Tamora between the eyes. The Fire Elf woman staggered back, clutching her face with her free hand and leering at him through her fingers.

"When my husband learns that you've struck me in such a state, there will be no end to the torment he'll put you through, Thanestorm." She withdrew her hand and raised her sabre repeatedly. "Starting with making you watch as he slowly kills those Severio and Kinsman whelps."

The words barely registered with Puc. He took the opening and lunged towards her. Before he could reach her to do any damage, he felt a stinging in his shoulder. He hissed as he noticed Tamora's sabre piercing it. He withdrew just as quickly as he'd attacked, his hand clutching the fresh wound.

"I told you that I'd get you bit by bit." Tamora watched as the blood from the tip of her sword travelled down its length. "I think I'll have you watch while we torture that Gaian woman you were so fond of."

Puc flexed the hand of his injured arm. It was harder to move his fingers, and every shifting of the muscles burned.

"Yes, I think the Sky woman will be the last to go before he ends you." She continued to muse on the subject, tapping the flat of the blade's tip to her right cheek, leaving a red mark. "Make you both beg for a mercy that will not come."

His next move was pure reflex, and neither Puc himself nor Tamora could have seen it coming. Tempest in his good hand then shot up with lightning speed, and stopped when it struck something in its path. A metallic clang then followed it. Puc shook himself awake from the rage-blinded attack and saw Tamora standing before him with Tempest piercing her midsection, wide-eyed with shock, her sabre on the floor.

"I am sorry, old friend, but you will get no such privilege from me." Puc retracted the blade from her.

Tamora continued to look longingly at Puc with her red eyes as she fell to her knees. Her lips trembled, and she was about to say something else, but instead, she breathed out one last time before collapsing to the floor.

Puc exhaled roughly, as though a great weight had been thrown from his shoulders, only to be hit fully with the pain of the wound. He hadn't realized how severe the cut had been, and soon found his legs buckling beneath him.

"I gotcha." Matthias's voice came from behind as his arms clasped both of Puc's shoulders. "I think you'll need a trip down for repairs."

The mage winced at his injured shoulder being held, but didn't protest. His eyes still lingered on the crumpled form of Tamora on the floor, her dreadlocks pooling around her on the black asphalt. Despite her having been a thorn in his side over the past few months, she had still once been his friend. He realized then that he'd never truly let that friendship go until that very last moment. He slowly nodded and allowed Matthias to teleport them down to the Lab.

ଚଚ୍ଚ

Jansen stumbled out of the saddle and nearly tipped over from her lack of balance after being subjected to riding the great beast back to the stables in Q-16. She was sure she would have faceplanted into the hay-covered cobblestone floor, were it not for Darius having caught her in the nick of time.

"Thanks." The word came muffled from her as she attempted to dust off her rumpled plaid shirt. Blurred shapes catching her eye, she looked up to see a score of Gaian troops rush past them.

"Judging by the soldiers rolling in, we missed a fair bit." Darius allowed his own eyes to follow the new arrivals as they stormed into the Lab in an orderly military run.

"I'm guessing they're coming through that portal we saw." Jansen ran a hand through her hair. Her mind's eye flashed back to the large circular wall of a portal they had passed by, which looked as though someone had torn a chunk of the sky from another world and sewn it onto the one they found themselves in. It was hard for her to comprehend the notion, and she would not have been able to do so herself had she not seen it.

"It was from the miniaturized version of the Pessumire Skyris made to help us get to Gaia so we could help liberate it from Razmus," Darius confirmed as he adjusted the satchel he had across his back, containing the book Lysania had told them to take.

"Right." Jansen nodded.

"We should get to Skyris. She's probably monitoring everyone's moves on Earth."

Jansen didn't respond to the comment and followed Darius while ignoring her throbbing rump. She'd never look at horseback riding in the same light ever again. Why on Earth did people romanticize it so much?

She clutched her bag to her chest as they moved down winding steel corridors. Some of the larger ones were filled with people trying to find a corner for themselves in the wake of having been torn from their lives due to Korangar's invasion. Heartbreak pulled at her as she walked past the countless faces, both young and old, who were left without a home and whose future now rested in the hands of a few teenagers and a score of aliens. Jansen was surprised that she was coping with it all as well as she was, but perhaps it had something to do with one of the people she had thought to be a figment of her imagination walking in front of her and navigating down the maze of hallways.

She was so engrossed in her thoughts that she nearly slammed into Darius, who'd stopped. Her shoes created an awkward squeak on the metallic flooring as she stopped herself from walking into him. Jansen cringed, then looked over his shoulder and saw that he'd stopped in front of a door. She peered over Darius's shoulder to see they had wandered into the emergency wing. Dozens of small hospital cots sat in rows against the walls, and patients with various degrees of wounds occupied more than half. There were also people running around and assisting.

"They must be doctors and nurses that got brought down here," she said more to herself than to Darius.

The blurred figures Darius had been staring at then came into focus, and Jansen instantly recognized them. She let Darius move first and followed.

Puc sat on a stool with his cloak discarded, applying pressure to a wound in his shoulder. The First Mage of Aldamoor looked more miserable than usual.

"Darius? Jansen? What are you doing here?" His stern face melted partially into concern.

Darius didn't miss a beat and took another step towards his old mentor. "We need to find Annetta. Is she down here with you?"

"No. I am afraid not." Puc winced as he tried to rise, and readjusted the cloth he held. "She was separated from Jason when she went to rescue some civilians inside of a subway station."

"So she'll be coming back down to the Lab at any moment?" Jansen looked at Puc with urgency, and then back to Darius, hoping for some confirmation.

"If all goes well, then yes," he hissed, removing the bandage to check his wound. Looking over at the stainless steel table a few feet away from him, he picked up one of the vials. He uncorked it and poured it onto the cloth, then doused the wound. When he pulled it away again, the wound had scabbed over and was well on the way to healing.

Jansen's eyes widened. "That's incredible."

She forced herself to refocus on what they were talking about. "We found information while we were with the Sisters of Wyrd. We have a good idea of how to defeat Korangar, but we need to tell Annetta."

Puc's eyes narrowed, and he then turned his gaze towards Darius. "Is this true?"

"From what we comprehended, yes." Darius nodded. "We may have found the reason behind Annetta's recent transformation, and it has to do with Korangar being broken out of his prison."

Darius them remembered what he carried with him, and removing the book from the satchel, he flipped to the pages they had been looking at. He then placed the large book on the table closest to them. "It's in here."

The First Mage fell silent at seeing the book, and examined his wound. It was evident that this was just to distract himself temporarily while he thought things over. Satisfied with what he saw, he grabbed the discarded cloak on the back of his chair and threw it over his shoulders. He then walked over to the book and began scanning its contents. He flipped the pages with vigour, his eyes taking in every detail on them.

When he reached the end, he paused and looked up at them with his mouth slightly open. "Unknown's bane. I may have doomed us all."

The tone of his words sent a chill down Jansen's spine. "What do you mean?"

Puc looked up from the text. "Annetta's transformation was to be the catalyst for the change in others to combat Korangar. By placing the seal on her, I have prevented her and the others who would potentially awaken from changing."

Darius ran a hand through his hair. "But wait, one thing I don't understand in all of this. Why dragons?"

Puc lifted his staff and leaned on it. "Isn't it obvious by now? Korangar is no mere man."

∞∞∞

The black, rocky surface burned beneath Korangar's feet as he walked down the road. All around him, human vehicles stood abandoned. His army had had its way with some of them, and in their places sat charred metallic skeletons. Where once this would have brought him joy, now it didn't matter. His awakening to the truth of it all had suppressed the other aspects of his rage. Though they still swam beneath the surface, they were muffled by his need to end the cycle. He needed to find the girl, no matter what it took. The seed of Freius had to be extinguished, and only then would all worlds be safe.

The biggest question, however, was where in the jungle of tall buildings she resided. Korangar's fist curled in frustration as he looked up at the skyscrapers obstructing his view. He hated tall structures that made him feel small.

We can fix that problem, you know. One of the voices in his mind egged him on.

"Not now. Not yet." Korangar muttered under his breath to himself. "I need to know that she's here."

The voices huffed in disappointment, and Korangar continued walking. He was half-considering their offer, but then stopped in his tracks. The flash of a crimson cape with an emblem he vaguely recognized zipped past ahead of him, into one of the large intersections. He smiled. The tall buildings would get their fate handed to them soon enough.

Chapter 43

Annetta ran through the streets toward the buildings coming into view on the horizon. She'd split up with Venetor after having caught him up on events. He'd gone on to lead the troops he'd brought in order to get as many people out as possible and also to push back enemy forces. With the Gaians in the fight, they had psychic warriors to spare, and could set off in teams instead of individually to rescue civilians. Her newest target was City Hall, where according to Skyris's GPS, she detected a large group of human beings hiding in the lower levels.

As she ran, she kept her senses on high, tapping into her feral form's abilities to better hear her surroundings. People could hide anywhere, and with everything going on, she couldn't blame most of them for not wanting to trust her or her companions. In some cases, it had proven to be a losing battle when people rejected her help flat out. Those were the hardest times to teleport down, and she almost felt like taking those people by force, but she knew that if she did, she'd be no better than Korangar or any of his mob. It was their choice.

She then spotted a group of Fire Elves with a few Verden and Minotaur around the building. The large glass windows and doors were almost completely shattered, with bits of furniture and the odd potted plant thrown around outside, as though someone had had a tantrum. Their current target, most likely for no apparent reason but their entertainment, were the large arches which overhung the ice rink at Nathan Phillips Square. The Minotaur and the Verden were making a sport of jumping on one of the arches and attempting to bring it down, while the Fire Elves shot arrows at the light bulbs on the underside, laughing and hooting each time one of them exploded on contact and fell into the water of the melted ice rink below.

Annetta hid behind one of a group of discarded TTC buses, and beckoned for those with her to do the same. The four new additions to her team came closest, one Hurtz with a feline face, a grim-looking psychic warrior with a clean-shaven head and red beard, as well as two Gaian fighters armed with swords and shields. Beyond them, the familiar faces of the Soarin, Ogaien, Water Elves and Minotaur looked out at her.

"We should split up here and take them by surprise. A small group should go ahead and begin scouting the building to make sure there is no one on the upper levels." She motioned towards City Hall's two curved towers, which arched in towards one another. "But don't go too far. If there is a force occupying the upper levels inside, we don't want needless casualties."

Her words seemed sound to her, and she felt rather impressed with her logical thinking, given the stress of the whole situation.

"Lady Severio, if I didn't know any better, I'd think you were lecturing militia." The psychic's bushy beard shifted to indicate the grin beneath.

Annetta's eyes narrowed as she glanced sideways at the man. "Any better ideas?"

The Gaian man, Othor, shook his head. "None, my lady. I think we can manage your plan."

"Good, then you're going in the building first," she replied, and watched as the soldiers organized themselves. Before she knew it, they were off, and Annetta drew her sword to join the fray of soldiers attacking the group of enemy fighters by the melted ice rink. She stopped mid-track, however, feeling the presence of eyes boring into her back.

Some distance behind, the figure of a man watched her. At first, she thought he might have been a Gaian soldier, come to aid her and her companions, but the closer he came, the more Annetta could see there was something not quite right about him. The muscles in her arms and legs coiled, unsure whether they would be needed for fight or flight.

The man's face was not one she would have quickly picked out in a crowd, with short blonde hair and stubble to match framing his square jaw. No, it was something about the way his deep blue eyes took her in across the pavement. As she sized up her potential foe, Annetta noticed even more strange things, such as his bare feet and the fact that he wore little more than a cloak to cover his back, along with tattered pants. Beneath it, she could make out the faint outline of a powerfully-built torso, but not a weapon in sight.

Her suspicions about the man were confirmed when behind her she heard a crash and turning around, she saw the various cars and buses in the area stacked up neatly like bricks in a wall.

"Psychic." The word escaped from between her teeth quietly.

The man continued to observe her, as if drinking in the essence of her soul before he would devour her in the frenzy of the fight. It unsettled Annetta, and the grip on Severbane tightened further.

He seemed to note this change, and crossed his arms before him. "Are you the heir?"

Annetta frowned at hearing this, slightly confused, as she had never been referred to in quite that way. "Depends who's asking."

"I have no time for games. Are you or are you not the heir?" His voice sent a chill down her spine. This was someone important in Korangar's ranks, or he wouldn't be addressing her quite like that.

It was her turn to straighten up, and a brave but grim smile lined her mouth. "Yeah, you've found her."

The seconds the last syllable left her lips, the man charged with frightening speed. Annetta had mere moments to decide where to teleport before he was in striking distance. She reappeared just above him and slammed the heel of her boot into his lower back. Venetor would have been proud of that kick, and yet the man below seemed to wince barcly. He pivoted on his heel and grabbed hold of Annetta's ankle, then threw her towards the wall of vehicles.

Airborne, Annetta forced herself to stop just before she collided with the twisted exhaust of what had once been a bus. The momentum drove her forward too much, however, and her knees buckled, causing her to drop to them. She quickly scrambled to get up and teleported yet again, just before a fist collided with her face.

Once on the other side of the wall, Annetta found herself gasping for air. He was fast, so much faster than any of the psychics she'd faced in Mislantus's army. It was like he knew her every move before she did it.

She slid Severbane back into its scabbard. The blade would do her no good right now. She slowed her breathing and centred herself, remembering her lessons with Venetor. Yes, perhaps he could see her every move before she did it, but she could see his every reaction to that move if she paid attention.

The wall exploded. Annetta shielded her eyes as bits of metal shards flew everywhere.

"It's impolite to make others wait." The man walked out from the debris, his cape swirling around him on the wind. "Or so I've been told that is a custom on this planet."

"Yeah? Well, it's also impolite to invade cities." She gritted her teeth.

"Touché." The man laughed as he moved across the area of broken asphalt towards her.

Annetta widened her stance, moving her feet till they were equal with her shoulders, but otherwise remained still. She stared down her opponent, but stayed aware of the fact that his confrontation with her could just be a ruse to get her guard down. The muscles in her legs remained taunt with adrenaline, knowing that at any second they would be required to act.

The man noticed this and stopped a few feet away from her. "I didn't know the heir would be so well-trained. It seems almost a pity for me to have to kill you, but for there to be any hope for a future without the cycle repeating itself, it is necessary."

"Cycles repeat only because people neglect to read history," Annetta retorted.

At this, the man laughed. "You are just full of wisdom, aren't you? How old are you? Have you even seen twenty summers yet?"

Annetta clenched her teeth, not allowing so much as a murmur pass through.

The man chuckled a little more. "Sensitive about your age, I take it? Not to worry, you won't ever look a day older after today."

He vanished. Annetta raised her right arm and pivoted on her heel as psychic fire flared up around her. The man's calf collided with her forearm. Were it not for the fact that Annetta was using the fire to strengthen her body, she knew there would be more than one broken bone. He teleported once more and reappeared before her, slamming an elbow into her gut.

Winded, Annetta staggered back, and realizing her error, she teleported into one of the alleys she'd passed on her way there. She slid down the concrete wall while clutching at her throbbing midsection. She had to think, and she had to do it fast. Worst of all, it was getting harder and harder to block out the beast in her mind. Since the fight began, it had started clawing at her like a frantic, caged animal. She sucked in a blast of cold air through her nostrils, inadvertently picking up the stench of garbage from the bins across from her.

"You can hide all you want, heir." The man's voice boomed from the main street. "I will find you, even if I have to level this world to the ground, and mark my words, I'm not afraid to do it."

The last part of his threat caused a chill to go down Annetta's spine. His tone made her believe it, and seeing his psychic prowess, she was almost willing to bet that if pushed, he would make good on the threat. She knew all too well what her own abilities could do if given a chance to wreak havoc.

Opening the hand that had been gripping her gut, she noted how filthy her palm was, caked in a layer of blood and dirt. She closed it again, formulating a plan in her head, and then opened the hand once more. Part of her feared what the consequences of her actions would mean, but given the circumstances, she didn't see much of a choice.

More psychic fire burst to life from the centre of it. The blue and purple flames rose up in her hand and grew with every ounce of emotion she fed to it, and she didn't lack the fuel needed. Annetta then threw the blast across from where she was hiding and teleported to the fire escape on the very top. Seeing a discarded bed sheet that had been left to dry on it, she wrapped herself in them, waiting.

Shortly after, the man she'd been fighting emerged from the mouth of the alley and strode in. His cape swirled and billowed around him as he stood unmoving at the centre of it. Annetta caught a glimpse of something tattooed on his back, but she couldn't make out what it was. It wouldn't matter soon, she reminded herself as her sword hand wandered to Severbane's hilt.

Annetta teleported from underneath the sheets and drew the sword. She was right above him, descending at inhuman speed. She raised the blade over her head and brought it down with her entire being.

The man didn't flinch. He seemed to know precisely where Annetta was coming from and raised his forearm to shield his face from the glint of steel. The sword collided with it and the world around Annetta filled with white light.

&)(&

Jason sat hunched over outside the infirmary in the Lab with his back resting against one of the steel walls. His brown hair obscured his face as his head hung low. Everything was changing in his life in the blink of an eye, and it seemed much more than he'd ever been able to take. The news of his brother's death he had still been able to deny in the wake of things, but his father…

The light sound of feet coming towards him didn't so much as to cause him to move. He sat twisted in his spiral of emotions, doing everything he could to prevent it from escaping in the form of tears. Out of his peripheral vision, he saw Sarina's familiar form crouch down. She stayed there, watching him for a few moments before she placed a hand on his arm. The gesture seemed distant and numb to

Jason. It was only when she melted into holding him in an embrace that he finally surrendered to paying attention to her, his own arms slipping around her.

"I'm so sorry, this is all my fault," she whispered.

Jason turned to her, the defeat he felt making his muscles feel leaden. "What are you talking about?"

It was Sarina's turn to look down. "If I wasn't here, then maybe Korangar wouldn't be here. If my father had never come to Earth, then none of this would be happening."

"You can't think like that. Someone else sooner or later would have shown up in his place." Jason sat up straighter against the wall as he pulled away and looked at her. "Besides, we wouldn't have met if we didn't."

"But your brother and your father would still be alive." Her deep brown eyes held a slight hint of tears in the corners.

Jason sighed. "Maybe, but the truth is I could never blame you for that. I love you."

The last three words seemed to escape his lips at a slower pace, and he could tell from Sarina's softening face that she felt just as he did.

He took her hand in his and squeezed it. "It's going to hurt, but I hope with you there, maybe it won't be so bad."

The door of the infirmary then opened. Out came Puc and Matthias, and to Jason's surprise, Darius and Jansen.

"Hey, you guys came back," he said, rising to his feet.

"We need to find Annetta. Any idea where she could be?" Puc asked.

"No, I mean she could be anywhere." Jason ran a hand through his ruffled hair.

Disappointment filled the mage's face along with the others that were with him.

"I can take you guys to where I left her," Jason offered after having thought it over himself. "She couldn't have gone far, even with teleporting. It's not like we have the entire city mapped out in our heads."

"He's got a point." Matthias crossed his arms. "And knowing Anne, she's trying to save everyone she can find, so it's going to take her that much longer to get anywhere."

"It is not ideal, but I suppose it is our best option." Puc then turned his gaze towards Darius. "You should arm yourself before we go up, and I suggest that Jansen do the same."

"Uhm… excuse me?" Jansen raised an eyebrow. "Arm myself? I mean… I don't know how to fight with weapons."

"Let us best hope it does not come to that. Sometimes the illusion is enough to steer unwanted attention away," Puc stated.

A frown creased Jansen's face at this, but she said nothing and only nodded in reply. She then followed Darius, while dodging a few of the many humans who now wandered the halls.

"What's so important that you need to find Anne all of a sudden?" Jason turned his attention back fully to Puc and Matthias. "I mean, why not just contact her with a C.T.S. to see where she is?"

"I have tried but I cannot reach her, she may be in the middle of a skirmish." Puc motioned for them to get moving and away from the entrance of the infirmary. "I need to break the seal placed on her."

Both Jason and Sarina stopped in their tracks and nearly bumped into a team of humans running past them with a gurney that held someone on it.

"You can't be serious." Sarina took one additional step forward. "You saw what Annetta did when she-"

"Which is exactly why we need her." Matthias folded his arms across his chest.

"She can't control it, though." Jason also stepped forward to join Sarina. "She's a loose cannon in that form. Remember what happened on Aerim."

Puc then also moved towards them, resting both hands on the leather grip of the staff. "What if I told you that the only way to defeat Korangar was through Annetta's new ability?"

Jason couldn't believe what he was hearing. "I'm sorry… You wanna exploit this thing that's inside my friend that almost killed all of us?"

"Not exploit, use for the purpose it was put there." Puc motioned for them to get moving once more so that they could clear the hallway. "Sarina, you know the myth of Korangar correct?"

It then clicked in Jason's mind what Puc was trying to get at when he remembered what Sarina had told him about Korangar not too long ago. "Dragons are needed to defeat Korangar. One of the legends stated that for Korangar to be defeated, you needed someone who could turn into a dragon."

"While your name is not Sarina, that is correct." Puc continued to lead them through the maze of people until they reached a clearing, only to be swarmed yet again by bodies going back and forth. "Unknown's bane, I forgot how much I hate crowds."

The mage then turned his attention to them yet again once he was confident that he would not bump into anyone, and no one would do the same to him. "Korangar himself is no mere mortal being. He is a manifestation of the seven aspects. Think where else this is a symbolism of seven?"

It was Sarina's turn to freeze and gasp. "A seven-headed dragon. The Freiuson coat of arms is a seven-headed dragon."

Before anything further could be said, Darius and Jansen ran back towards them, dodging people as they got in their way. Darius was now dressed in dark robes, near-identical to that of Puc. Beside him, Jansen looked completely out of place dressed in chainmail with a red Gaian tabard sporting a white lion on it. It was clear as daylight that the girl had never worn armour, given the way she was walking awkwardly to avoid causing her scabbard to bounce against her thigh too much, or for the rest of her chainmail to clink.

"We're ready to go," Darius announced.

"Good, because we are running out of time." Puc placed a hand on Jason's shoulder, and was followed by the others.

Jason noticed Sarina's hand among those touching him, and he glanced directly at her. "Aren't you staying in the Lab?"

She shook her head with some reluctance. "I need to see this through."

"But you don't have any weapons."

Sarina then tapped at the hilt of a sabre, which Jason had failed to see in the commotion. He'd also failed to notice that underneath Sarina's regular attire, she wore Gaian scale mail.

"I'm armed well enough." She winked.

Jason nodded and cleared his mind as best as he could, focusing on where he'd last left his best friend.

Chapter 44

Arieus came out of the infirmary not long after he saw Puc, Matthias, Darius and another girl leave. His feet felt like lead as they fell on the steel floor, and the blue-tinted halogen lights seemed brighter, as if they were interrogating him. He had ensured that Arcanthur would be prepared to be buried in the crypts by Severio Castle, and unable to do more for his friend, he left him in the care of the Water Elf medics who were tending to the dead and wounded. He didn't want to be present any more than he had to be. It was hard enough as it was.

The familiar aroma of tobacco wafted around the corner, and turning, Arieus found himself but a few feet away from Talia. Gone was any trace of the bright-eyed young woman Arcanthur had fallen madly in love with and pledged the world to. Her brown hair had been tied back into a ponytail, but it had half fallen out, and now obscured her face, hiding the tired green eyes that lay beyond the wall. A half-burned-out cigarette hung from her right hand, while her left arm lay across her chest. He could scarcely begin to imagine what was going through the woman's head right now.

"I don't think you'll be doing Jason any favours by putting yourself in an early grave." His eyes wandered from her hand to her face.

As if to spite him, she lifted the cigarette to her lips and took a drag, letting the smoke swirl around her. "What does it matter? Is the evidence of everything crumbling around us not enough for you? This war will take everything."

Arieus shook his head. "You can't think like that. We're still here. Jason is still here."

"I should have forbidden him from coming here." Fumes escaped her nostrils. "From the start, I knew, I knew exactly where this was going, and I did nothing to stop it. I should have barred your girl from ever becoming friends with him. I should have melted that damn card the moment I saw him come in with it, and I should have forced the mage to bind his powers for good."

"It wouldn't have fixed anything, Talia. Korangar would have still come, Mislantus would have had his way with Earth after taking control of the Eye to All Worlds. Don't you see that?"

A snarl escaped Talia's lips as she threw down the butt of the cigarette and stomped on it with her boot. She then turned to face

Arieus again, the whites of her eyes an irritated pink from the tears she'd shed.

"I don't care to see," she spat. "And you wouldn't either, if you were to lose Aurora or either of your children."

She was about to leave when Arieus gripped her shoulder and turned her to face him. "This war is far from over, and there is a very good chance that it could happen, but I'm trying not to think about that. Do you think it doesn't pain me to know that when this is all over, I have to bury my best friend?"

"A best friend you agreed to commit to an institution because some so-called angels told you to?" Talia broke away with a violent jerk. "And for years, you didn't visit. Do you know what it was like raising two boys on my own? The explanations I had to come up with as to where their father was? The explanations for why you didn't visit Arcanthur whenever I went to see him? For years, you've run from your problems, while I had to stand in the heart of every one of mine."

Tears of frustration welled up in Talia's eyes, and the hands at her side had curled into shaking fists. Arieus took another tentative step towards her.

"I'm through with this fight." Talia shifted back. "Let the others play heroes for all I care."

She then stormed down the hallway and nearly knocked into Aurora, who had been on her way to meet them. She glanced back to watch Talia merge into the sea of people that occupied the Lab, and turned back to her husband questioningly.

Arieus sighed and shook his head. "She needs time, and in all honesty, who can blame her?"

"I don't think any spouse or parent can," Aurora replied.

Arieus took in his wife. Like him, she wore chain mail and a tabard with the rampant black lion on a red field, as they had when they'd both fought for the Four Forces. It was there that they had met, and despite Aurora's insistence that he find someone else due to her rank, he had fallen in love. His mind then wandered to what Talia had said to him. He had been fortunate over the years, there was no denying it.

"How's Xander doing?" he asked, trying to push aside the thoughts from his previous conversation.

Aurora folded her arms across her chest. "One of the mages gave him a mild sedative to help calm him down. I don't think he fully

400

understands what's happened. It's going to take some time for him before it sinks in. I made sure he's also not going back up."

"They shouldn't have been going up in the first place." Arieus's moustache furrowed along with his brows.

Something lightly brushed Arieus's hand, and he gazed down to see Aurora's fingers entwining with his own.

"They shouldn't have, it's true." She squeezed his hand. "But we didn't do our job, and these are the consequences. We were supposed to keep the Earth safe, and instead, it fell to Annetta, Jason, Liam and Xander, because we quit."

Another reminder of what Talia had said to him. He had run from his responsibilities to the Lab, but it had been to protect Annetta and Xander from the same fate which had befallen his father. The Severio clan's history was filled with premature death due to war. He was no stranger to this. The longer he reflected, the more Arieus realized what his ultimate reason had been, and the thing he had been running from since he and his father had uncovered what the prophecy had meant.

"I didn't want to see them die before us," he uttered in a small voice so only she could hear.

"I know, and they won't, as long as we are there to fight with them." Aurora gave his hand another squeeze and then broke away. "Now come on, Severio. Our daughter needs us."

ොශ

Amidst the torn-up asphalt and overturned cars, Annetta lay staring up into the clouded skies, barely conscious of the fact that she was no longer in the alley. At first, she could see and hear nothing except the buzzing in her ears, and then it, as well as the white haze, began to clear. Despite this, she found she couldn't move. Not well, at least. It felt as though she'd fallen into a pile of bricks that pinned down every inch of her.

As she further came out of the bout of shock, her sword hand reached for the handle of Severbane, which she saw out of the corner of her eye. When she finally managed to grip the leather hilt of the blade, she lifted it. The sword had always felt light in her grip, and so it came as no shock when she lifted it to feel as though she were only lifting her hand, until she saw it. The great blade of her grandfather, Severbane, forged from the remnants of the sword of Adeamus Severio was no more.

A single jagged piece of the sword had remained intact with the hilt. The beginnings of the word 'Severed' that had been etched into the blade were reduced to just 'Sever' on the remnants. A tiny part of Annetta wanted to laugh at the irony, but it was overpowered by shock.

She had no time to contemplate this as a hand descended and grabbed her by the cape she wore. The man's grim visage came into view as he lifted her to eye level. Annetta found herself so close to him that she could see her reflection in his eyes; a dishevelled looking young girl with a dirt-stained face.

The man's gaze studied her for a few minutes, the pools that were his blue eyes taking in every inch of her with calculated thought.

"You are not the heir, are you?" he declared finally, and dropped her to the floor with an unceremonious thud.

Annetta winced and scrambled to her feet as quickly as she could. "I am the heir. The heir of Orbeyus Severio."

The man chuckled at this, a fake and hollow sound that rumbled through his entire being. "Foolish girl. I don't care about the heir of some farmer from the north. I'm talking about the spawn of Freius, my father."

It then dawned on Annetta who she was facing. She could only begin to imagine the amount of trouble she was in, and worse yet, how difficult the one named Korangar would be to defeat. She dared another glance at the broken form of Severbane in her right hand, reaffirming her sense of doom.

When her eyes moved back towards him, Korangar was smiling again. "But if you so wish to join the others, I can make that happen."

He advanced, waiting for no invitation. Korangar raised a hand towards her, with his fingers outstretched. The sound of thunder then boomed through the air as it was about to reach her. He scowled as he retracted his hand, the skin broken along his knuckles.

Annetta's gaze shifted sideways, to where she thought she heard the point of origin. There, standing in the middle of an alley with feet spread shoulder-width apart, and the barrel of a smoking gun pointed forward, was Titus. Her cousin looked thinner and paler than she remembered him, with dark circles around his eyes, but sure enough, it was him.

Their eyes met for only a split second, and it looked as though Titus was about to say something when his whole body flew back, thrown into the alley from whence he came.

"Enough! I tire of this quest to find the heir!" Korangar roared as he threw down his cloak. "If you will not give them up, that's fine by me. The same fate awaits this whole planet, anyways. It doesn't matter to me how your apocalypse comes."

Horror filled Annetta's eyes as she watched the man's back begin to ripple and twist. His hands outstretched before him, he threw his head back and welcomed what came next. Six serpentine heads rose from his shoulders, their draconic tongues flickering as they tested the air around her.

Korangar's eyes opened anew, and he zeroed in on Annetta. "Welcome to the end, heir of Orbeyus Severio."

80CR

Skyris's fingers flew across the touchscreen keyboard before her as she typed in various latitudes and longitudes, attempting to find any camera which could have caught a glimpse of where Annetta was. The call from Puc had been an unexpected one, and the tone of urgency in his voice made it apparent just how crucial it was to find her niece if they were to stand any chance in this fight.

She'd already exhausted most of the internet-connected cameras available, which were far and few compared to the complex security systems which spanned much of the city of Pangaia. Maybe when things ran faster, humans would be more willing to add more of the devices to watch their city, should trouble arise.

Through some digging and hacking a few more private networks, she was able to get into another small sector of cameras, this one belonging to some corporate buildings. She skimmed through the streams of interior shots, and paused when she got to the outdoor cameras at the front of the building.

"What in the Unknown's bane?" Her eyes squinted when she picked something up in the corner.

She zoomed in on the blurred part of the image and magnified it as best as she could with a few more typed commands, cursing quietly each time she missed a key. While primitive, a mechanical keyboard was her tool of choice, and the satisfying clicks, much like the turning of a wheel in a ship, helped her ensure she had typed precisely what she'd meant to.

When Skyris confirmed what she thought she had been seeing, she paused the screen. A small figure in a billowing, torn cape, whom she presumed to be Annetta, stood looking up at what Skyris could only describe as a hydra that was at least over sixty feet tall with giant bat wings and seven heads, each with a different number of horns. The creature's heads loomed around its body, all focused on the girl. There was no one else with her, as far as Skyris could tell.

"Damn it, Titus, you were supposed to bring backup." She gritted her teeth. "Where is the Gaian army? They should have been here by now."

Though Skyris didn't know Annetta nearly as well as she'd like due to being absent for most of her life, the few conversations they'd had were enough to fill the void. There was a great deal of Orbeyus in her, even if Annetta herself didn't see it, which further endeared her to Skyris. It was nice to have at least a part of her brother there in some form. She was apparently in trouble now, and Skyris couldn't stand by to watch it. An idea then flickered in the back of Skyris's mind. At first, it had no concrete shape, and it wasn't until she began to think about it more and more that it came into the forefront of her mind.

"Dexter, you there, buddy?" Skyris asked and almost instantly, she heard the mechanical eye of one of the A.I. stir.

"I am always here when you need me, Skyris," the steady and melodic computerized voice chimed in as the A.I. circled to face her.

"Connect to all units and find me a mage, someone who can conjure up a portal inside the base. I'm going to need a big one," she instructed.

Dexter's red eye shifted curiously. "Might I inquire as to what for, so that I may notify whoever will take up the request?"

Skyris turned her attention fully to the robot. "In the simplest of terms, I think it's time to test out the new project I've been working on, and I have just the perfect target for it, too."

Chapter 45

While the city of Toronto fell around him, Amarok Mezorian strode through the abandoned streets. He'd often wondered what fate would have befallen Earth if Mislantus had succeeded in taking control of the Eye to All Worlds. The cracked asphalt, broken street lights and abandoned cars gave him a window into what could have been.

"If only you could see this now, old friend," he muttered inaudibly from beneath his broken mask and smiled lightly. "This is the fight you should have been in. This is how you should have staked your claim on the Aternaverse."

There was no answer to what he'd said, and Amarok would have been taken aback if there was. A deafening roar pierced the skies seconds later, as if to answer his original statement. He shuddered at the haunting beauty of it, and looking up at the nearest building, he teleported up it and then teleported to an even higher area. When his feet softly touched the tar-lined roof, Amarok stared out into the vast skyline of Toronto, and saw it.

The seven draconic heads rose up from among the sea of buildings, fork tongues flickering as they looked down at one particular area. Amarok could only presume that whatever the object of Korangar's wrath was now, it most certainly wouldn't live to see another day, nor would anything else on this planet. It was all over for Earth.

"A pity in some ways," he mused out loud, and prepared to teleport himself in another direction.

A thought nagged the elder assassin like an itch that was unable to escape the surface of his skin. His thoughts were focused on Q-16, and the many things in there that would be destroyed along with the Earth. There was one thing Amarok had regretted not taking with him the last time he'd gone down, and when he had tried earlier to teleport, it had seemed like something barred him from getting into the base. He could only assume that shields preventing unauthorized teleporting had been put up. Orbeyus's sister Skyris was most likely the one behind it. The woman was ever a thorn in his side when it came to technology. It was moments like this that he wished he had eliminated the others from the line of Severio to prevent future obstacles. Yet, when all was said and done, Amarok relished the challenge. He enjoyed it like a puzzle only he was meant to solve, and in turn, he provided ones for them.

The realization then hit him, and a jagged smile formed on his lips. There was one possible way in.

Amarok looked down and saw a hoodie, as well as some other clothing hung up to dry on a clothing line on one of the balconies, fluttering in the wind much in the way pennants would upon castle walls. He teleported himself down and snatched some of the clothing.

ɞɔʗᴙ

Annetta's eyes froze over in horror as she watched the form of the dragon grow, change and warp in front of her. The great shadow of the beast engulfed her completely as it towered over many of the surrounding buildings. Never in her life had she felt as small as when she looked up at the seven-headed black behemoth that loomed over her. Her grip tightened on the handle of what remained of Severbane, finding some slight comfort in the presence of the broken blade. Despite it, the feeling of dread and helplessness continued to rise.

Her legs shifted beneath her on the cracked asphalt as her shoes creaked on loose rocks beneath them, imploring her to run, but the rest of her body didn't want to comply. She'd made a promise that she couldn't break. Now it seemed truly apparent that this was what that promise entailed.

Her brows knotted together as she summoned up the courage to look up at her foe. The dragon's heads watched her with a dispassionate gaze, each serpentine face differing from the other in its design.

"Give it up girl," a multi-toned voice spoke. "Give it up and let me cloak you in darkness. I can end your suffering, and let the healing begin."

Though the voice was jarring to hear, it somehow calmed Annetta, and for a split second, she considered the offer. The grip on the soft leather of Severbane's hilt began to slip, and she nearly let go before it tightened again. Her visits with Orbeyus had prepared her for death, and because of them, she didn't feel so frightened. She looked at her surroundings in confirmation that she was alone.

Her posture then straightened. "No."

"No?" the heads of the dragon laughed at this. "You would defy him that is The End?"

"I would defy anyone who threatens to hurt my home," she growled. "I would oppose anyone who even thinks of abusing it and hurting the people in it."

Annetta felt her whole body begin to burn. She could practically feel as though someone were putting her in a large cast-iron pot and beginning to boil her alive. The creature, the beast living within her was thrashing hard against the remains of the shield Puc had placed. She wasn't sure what to expect of it if it got through, except that it would rage like the last time. Looking at the monstrous thing before her, she realized that perhaps that wasn't the worst thing in the world.

One of the dragon's heads that was already lowered to the ground then lashed out, its serpentine neck coming at her at full speed. Annetta teleported mid-jump. The creature's maw collided with one of the vehicles that had been behind her, crushing it between rows of sword-like teeth. The girl reappeared a few feet away, her heart pounding in her ribcage. Without putting much thought into it, her hand dove into the pouch at her waist which contained the energy potions, and uncorking one, she downed it. Another of the heads shot for her and she dodged again. Bits of asphalt flew when it collided with the spot she'd been standing in seconds before.

A thought then occurred to her as she felt the effects of the potions begin to take hold. What if she took more? They were constantly worried about not having enough energy to use their abilities and having to replenish. Puc had also warned her that the use of the potions could free the beast within her again if she used too many of them. If all bets were off the table, then what did it matter?

Her hand dove back into the bag as she pulled out another. A dark shape veered in towards her from the corner of her eye, and she teleported yet again.

"Hold still, you runt! This will go down easier if you do," Korangar snarled.

Annetta barely heard the comment, and uncorking the second vial, she shot back the contents. Nothing happened. She didn't even feel the tingling she normally did when the potion began to work. She frowned, disappointed in the experiment, and began contemplating her next move. Then it happened.

The sensation began with a warm feeling in the lower part of her spine. Annetta had experienced something similar when she'd accidentally hit the seat warmer button once in her mother's car. It wasn't unpleasant, but she didn't particularly like it. Then, it came in full force. Her body surged with heat, more than she'd experienced when the beast had tried to come out. She began sweating almost instantly, and without missing a beat, she began to put her plan into motion. Psychic fire engulfed her, surrounding her body in a protective layer. The first task complete, her attention then turned to the remainder of the sword in her hand. The word 'Sever' glinted back at her on the jagged remainder of the blade attached to the hilt.

Drawing on the reserved of energy within her, she pictured the blade as it had been in her mind's eye. Every nick and scratch flashed before her eyes as she thought of it. She'd used no other sword since obtaining it. It had been an extension of her right hand.

Psychic flames formed in place of the missing blade, creating its outline and filling in the missing pieces. Were it regular fire, Annetta was certain the remainder of Severbane would have melted, but psychic fire was different. It was a product of her mind, and she controlled it to act as she wished. Now, more than anything, she needed a weapon, and the fire did as she commanded.

With her shield gripped firmly in her other hand, Annetta launched herself into the air. Another of the dragon's heads came at her, rows of razor sharp teeth gleaming. The girl teleported above it and slashed at one of the creature's horns, which came clean off. Korangar howled in rage as another of the heads pursued her with jaws snapping.

Annetta didn't miss a beat, and waiting until the last moment, she darted away, teleporting as the head collided with the neck of one of the other heads, its fangs digging into it. The other heads seemed to coil in the throes of pain.

Alight with the energy coursing through her, Annetta didn't wait to see how things would play out, and took her opening. Pushing herself further into the sky, she then allowed gravity to take its course as she rode it down, positioning herself over one of the massive serpentine necks. The sword of flame grew and extended, until it was as long as the neck was wide. Reaching its goal, the blade sliced through its intended target.

Annetta landed not too far away, and heard the meaty thud of the head. More screams followed as Korangar thrashed uncontrollably. A small smile spread across her weary lips as the hope that she'd found a weakness filled her. She prepared to send a message to Jason as well as Venetor through telepathy, calling on them for their aid. There were still six more heads, and she would need all the help she could get.

The head which she'd cut off fizzled and changed to the texture of old coals on a fire, white crust with a glowing orange inside. The head then turned to ash and dissipated on the wind. Annetta looked up, and to her horror, the head she'd cut off had grown back.

"Foolish girl," Korangar's voice boomed. "Did you think that you could best me with psychic fire?"

Before Annetta could even contemplate what to say back, Korangar's tail collided with her. The blow threw her back, causing her to collide with the brick wall of a large building. The wall shattered, and Annetta found herself on the other side of it, buried in debris. She did her best to shake off the shock, checking to see if anything was broken. Her body felt as though it were set on fire. Every inch of her burned and ached as though she'd run a marathon.

"Well, at least I know I don't need to hold anything back." She coughed weakly, thinking out loud to herself.

Pain and exhaustion created a temporarily paralysis which overtook Annetta's body. Somewhere in the wreckage, she managed to pull the broken hilt of Severbane out, and lifted her other arm which still had her shield strapped to it. This was, however, the extent of what she could do. Outside, she heard the rumbling growls of Korangar's seven heads.

Annetta coughed a little, inhaling the dusty air. She could do no more. The thought angered her beyond belief, but she could no longer deny it. Stripped of Severbane and her psychic abilities, she was, no matter what any prophecy claimed or however many titles were given to her, just a teenage girl.

The sound of a roaring engine then overpowered anything she could have thought or heard. Annetta did her best to push past the exhaustion she felt and rummaged around in her pouch to find one more potion vial. She examined the colour in the dim light to confirm its use, and downed its contents, just as she had with the others. Immediately, some of the exhaustion lifted, though she could still feel every ache and sore all over her body.

Each foot dragged as she moved across the expanse of rubble. She manoeuvered her way to the opening, and then saw it.

"A mech?" Annetta blinked a few times, trying to get any dust out of her eyes, but there was no denying what she saw.

The giant being which now stood before Korangar easily measured up to him. Humanoid in shape, it was made up of various large plates of metal that had been painted white with blue and red accents. Large jets, the source of the noise she'd heard in the building, came out of the thing's calves. They were in a standby mode of sorts, this much Annetta could tell by the lack of flames and the presence of rippling air around them. The robot held two large swords made out a controlled plasma laser, and Annetta couldn't help but smile in knowing who, most likely, sat in the cockpit.

∞∞

Contained. That was what Skyris's mind told her about her current situation, but what her body refused to acknowledge as it surged with adrenaline. The cockpit of the mech she'd built had enough room for her to stand and maneuver, but nothing else past that. Currently, she stood with the virtual reality headset strapped to her, a controller in each hand. The headset allowed her to see through the mech's eyes without taking her out of the space of the cabin. The control sticks with their command buttons gave her the ability to use her weapons, and under her regular clothing she wore a virtual reality suit that allowed her to control the mech itself. Never in her life had she thought this whimsical project of pure fantasy would find purpose in her lifetime. She had simply made it because she could, to prove that she was capable of creating a machine such as the ones she'd seen in the television program she'd stumbled upon.

A war cry erupted from Skyris's lungs as she forced the mech forward, the twin swords raised in attack. The seven-headed dragon coiled its many necks in anticipation, and lashed out. Skyris expected as much, and with a quick reversal move, she pulled back inches from the snapping jaws. She then leapt into the air, spun over the beast, and brought both blades down in a scissor move, removing all the heads with one swift movement.

She landed the mech just beyond the creature, hearing the distinct thud of heads on the ground. For a split second after, she thought she heard someone screaming in protest of what she'd done, but dismissed it as nothing but a figment of her imagination. Clicking one of the buttons, she forced the mech to rise to its full height, and turn around to face the dragon's remains.

The body of the thing had not collapsed, however, as Skyris had thought it would, and remained upright. Her hands gripped the controllers tighter as she scanned the area around her.

'*Skyris? Aunt Skyris! Can you hear me?*' The voice of Annetta echoed in her head.

Skyris flipped over her C.T.S. and typed in the code for Annetta. The beeping ceased almost immediately.

"Aunt Skyris?" The frazzled voice of the girl came through.

"I head ya loud and clear, kid," she spoke back.

"Aunt Skyris, you need to get out of there," Annetta informed her. **"Korangar's heads don't mean anything."**

"What do you mean they don't mean anything?" She frowned.

"I don't know, but when I tried to cut one off, it just grew back," Annetta answered.

"Unknown's bane," Skyris muttered under her breath.

Before she could question the girl anymore, Korangar's heads began to regrow, the severed heads before him disappearing in a pile of ash. Skyris clicked a few buttons on the control sticks she held, and the thrum of engines could be heard below her. She launched the mech skyward just in time to see one of the many maws of Korangar try to chomp down on where her right arm had been. Airborne, Skyris watched as the seven-headed beast spread its bat-like wings, and took off after her into the air.

Skyris clicked a few more buttons, the laser swords retracting into their scabbards as projectile weapons came out of the robot's forearms. She aimed them and opened fire at Korangar. She didn't wait to see the outcome when the dust had settled, and instead, she soared higher still.

The flap of leathery wings then followed, and a massive shape rose into the air from her periphery. Checking her rear view, she saw Korangar closing the distance between them with each powerful stroke of his wings. Skryis gritted her teeth as she supressed a curse, and instead used the energy to continued flying the mech. The cabin around her rattled. Skyris sucked in a breath, and watched one of the creature's heads bite down on the mech's leg.

"Great, just what I need." The words came out with a simmering malice.

She pushed the thrusters further ahead, only to feel the pressure of the one leg being slowed down by the clamped dragon's maw. The grinding of mechanical parts followed. Skyris could practically feel the tugging on the leg with her own body, and it wasn't pleasant. Once, when she'd been a girl, she'd pulled her arm free of her socket in a training exercise with her father, and it had been the most excruciating thing she'd ever gone through.

Skyris sucked in a deep breath as she refocused her energy on surviving. If she managed to do that, then maybe there was hope for what she planned to do in order to ever-so-slightly injure the threat they faced. Skyris was not that naïve enough to think she alone stood a chance against Korangar. Yet she dared to, even in some small capacity.

She gritted her teeth as she felt the cables in the snatched-up leg begin to weaken and tear. Hundreds of hours wasted in trying to complete the machine flashed before her eyes, and her blood began to boil anew in knowing how much was being lost with the pull of every single fibre. She wanted to get out and scream at Korangar for the work that was being destroyed, but she knew all her efforts would fall on deaf ears. Such was the fury and frustration that came with being a scientist.

Engrossed in her rage, Skyris barely noticed the behemoth structure that was quickly closing in on them. A red "incoming object" sign flashed across her screen, and turning her head, she saw the CN Tower. Its strange, pointed design with a flattened oval through the middle had always intrigued Skyris whenever she saw it, its architecture amiss in the city of rectangular buildings. A thought then occurred to her, one which gave birth to a plan.

"You wanna fight? I'll give you one." The words came out in a growl as Skyris thrust the engines into full speed, on a collision course with the tower. She was sure that anyone who would be watching would think she planned to collide with it, and Korangar didn't seem the least bit bothered as he clung to the leg, calling her bluff. She'd counted on just such a reaction.

Only meters away. Skyris whipped the engine to a hovering standstill. Korangar's body swung around, and the moment it was before her, Skyris sliced through the neck of the beast. Korangar's other heads roared in pain as they crashed into the tower, and struggled to remain upright in flight. The debris of the tower tangled with his massive bat-like wings.

The mech's arm then folded and transformed into a projectile weapon that she fired into him, sparks of purple light dancing all around it.

A smug grin formed on her face as Skyris watched the dragon crash into the ground. The blood rush a Gaian experienced in a fight coursed through her head, forcing her reaction, she herself not being one to condone violence on any level. She knew her species had a love for fighting at a primal level, no matter their stance on the act itself, and so she allowed it, but kept her cool.

Her eyes narrowed when she heard the flap of Korangar's wings coming through the debris cloud of the collapsed structure. Seconds later, his shadow appeared and then burst through it, the power of his wings causing the clouds to part before him. Seven sets of jaws reached out towards her like desperate hands, and Skyris drew the two laser swords from the mecha's belt.

Korangar's seven maw's tore into the metal of the mech at seven different points, their teeth shredding metal and cable alike. Sparks flew from each point. Warning signals strobed red all throughout her cabin. She then gritted her teeth as she considered her next course of action, limited as it was.

∞≪

Annetta had followed the fight as far as she could, watching the mech and Korangar duel it out. She felt as though she'd stepped into one of those Kaiju movies her father was fond of watching whenever they reran them on television. Her heart ached a little as she watched the CN Tower crumble before her eyes. Images of the vision the Angels had shown her when she'd received her cardkey into Q-16 flashed before her eyes. Her Visium also came to mind, and goosebumps formed all along her arms, despite being in beta dragon scale mail. She'd done everything that had been asked of her, and despite this, her world was literally crumbling around her.

Her heart sank further as she glanced down at the broken sword she clutched in her hands.

∞≪

Skyris cursed loudly as the walls in the cabin around her began to crush inwards. She tore off her visor and tossed the controllers to the ground. Running to the manual escape keypad, she typed in a series of commands.

The hiss of pressurized air filled her ears and the jolt of the cabin coming loose from the rest of the mech followed. Skyris held onto a set of metal bars and braced herself for impact. The cabin crashed into the pavement and skidded a few feet before coming to a halt. Her legs pumping, Skyris ran for the exit and opened the hatch. In a half leap and half tumble, she bolted from the cabin. Her objective was clear, and it was to run as far away as possible from the beast that was now tearing the mech to shreds.

413

One of the mech's limbs fell to the ground before her. Her feet tangled in the confusion and Skyris fell, bracing herself with her hands on the asphalt. The immediate sting of broken skin on her palms followed, and she cringed. A draconic screech pierced the air, and Skyris rolled over onto her back. Her bleeding palms raised before her face, she closed her eyes and prepared for whatever came next. To Skyris, death was no stranger, and she'd been prepared to die the moment she had left the Lab. She had no regrets in the life, except maybe one, but it had been from long ago. Air filled her lungs to capacity as she thought on it, the last words she'd said to Puc before leaving for Gaia all those years ago, words that her brother and father had forced her to say.

"Unknown forgive me, for those words were not of my own free will," she whispered to herself and armed herself in solace, knowing she would see Orbeyus again.

A great shadow passed over her, and nothing. Skyris frowned and cracked an eye open to see a blurred, dark shape above her. She worried it was Korangar waiting for her to look up so he could take his vengeance on her, but when nothing happened, she opened them more. A familiar pair of pale blue eyes gazed down at her, framed with thick black hair.

"Thanestorm?" Skyris's eyes widened to their full capacity as she took in the form of the mage shielding her body with his own. Looking over his shoulder, she saw a dome of energy cover them. Beyond it, one of Korangar's maws continued to slam down into it with no avail.

Puc hushed her, one of his hands cupping her face gently. "I am sorry."

Her brows furrowed. "Sorry? For what?"

"That I did not come sooner." His fingers ran through her hair, which had come loose from its braid. "I should have been here at your side, perhaps then we would have had more time."

"Time for what?"

The mage's thin lips parted and remained hanging open for a split second. His face then contorted in pain and Skyris saw that his other hand had his staff pointed skyward, creating the shield that was around them, while Korangar attempted to penetrate it.

"I do not know how much longer this spell will last." His calm returned. "But if I had to choose who to spend my last moments with,

414

I would have chosen no one else, because the truth is, Skyris Severio, that I am still very much in love with you."

Skyris's eyes began to water at hearing this. They were the words she'd wanted to hear when they were in the cave, the words she'd wanted to hear each time they'd been alone in a room. She'd given up hope that what they'd once had could be renewed, and yet here, standing at death's door was where her wish had finally come true. A muffled sob escaped her, and reaching up with a shaking hand, she touched his face, while looking into Puc's tormented eyes. Drawing him closer still, she kissed him, allowing the gathered tears to flow freely.

She felt Puc reciprocate and then draw back. He was about to say more, when the pounding from Korangar stopped. Puc turned away and looked up, squinting into the air. Skryis followed his lead, and tapping into her feral form abilities, allowed her sight to magnify. A glowing figure surrounded by blue and purple flames held the dragon's attention, while pelting it with blasts of psychic fire. A second figure soon after joined the fray. Had Annetta recovered already from her ordeal?

Her jaw dropped slightly when she realized who it was. "Arieus."

𝔰𝔬𝔠𝔯

Annetta watched from behind an overturned TTC bus as Korangar attempted to break the barrier where Puc and Skyris were. She was still clutching the broken handle of Severbane in one hand, and her shield in the other. She'd been formulating a plan, something, anything to try and distract him, but nothing had come quick enough. She got ready to summon what little energy she had into a ball of psychic fire, when a blast of blue and purple energy slammed into the dragon's head.

Korangar reeled back, howling in fury and turning its attention to something in the sky.

Her eyes narrowing to a squint, and harnessing her feral form abilities, Annetta saw the unmistakable form of a man wreathed in psychic fire. At first, she'd been certain it was Venetor, but the longer she looked, the more she began to see that the man was much taller than her uncle. Held tightly in his right fist was a sword.

"Dad?" The word came out as a whisper.

Though she knew he couldn't hear her, Annetta saw the man turn in her direction. He looked younger than she remembered him. and then she realized that his ring was most likely off. All traces of the man that she had known to be her father had been melted away through the reversal of time, time which she knew had not really passed for him. She then made out another faint shape, a little further in the distance like the flickering of a candle. It was a woman also surrounded by psychic fire, and Annetta knew the deep chestnut hair.

"Mom." Her eyes widened with fear.

The sound of feet coming towards her overtook Annetta, and she saw both Puc and Skyris rushing towards her.

"Annetta, thank the Unknown you're alive." Skyris gave her a quick embrace and then looked over to where she had been focusing.

"Yeah... uh... why are my mom and dad..." she tried to formulate a sentence, too distracted by the great seven headed dragon before her and the sight of both her parents wreathed in psychic fire mid-air.

'Annetta.' Her father's voice boomed in her head.

Annetta took a step back, pressing her hands to her temples. *'Dad? Is it really you up there?'*

'Yes, I'm here with your mother.' His voice came through, strong and clear again.

'Dad, please, you need to get out. Korangar can't be beaten by psychic fire. I tried and it didn't work.' Annetta focused all of her energy into projecting her thoughts into words.

'We know, Annie, but we have an idea, and we need to try.' This time it was Aurora's voice that came through. Annetta's eyes widened as she didn't think her mother could hear her.

Tears began to well up in the corners of Annetta's eyes as she took a step forward silently. *'Please mom, dad, get back to Q-16.'*

'I'm sorry, Anne, but we can't.' Her father shook his head. *'For too long have I let you take on my responsibility, along with everyone else around me. I can't run from this any longer.'*

The blood in Annetta's veins began to boil, and clenching the shield tighter she drew forward, only to have a set of hands land on her shoulders. She turned around to see both Puc and Skyris holding her, a hand on either shoulder. Annetta then looked up to where her mother and father were.

'Dad, please, there has to be another way.' The girl squinted as she looked towards him, then shifted her eyes towards her mother. *'Right, mom?'*

Though she couldn't see, Annetta was certain that her mother hadn't made eye contact with her, and this made her shoulders slump even more under the weight of both Skyris and Puc's hands.

'Annie, you have a chance to beat this monster.' Her mother's voice echoed in her head seconds later. *'But you need to get away now, as far away as you can. Puc can help you.'*

Annetta's muscles tightened at hearing what her mother had said. She then watched as the flames around her parents intensified. They began to move faster and faster in a set of blurred motions that Annetta could only describe as random and yet coordinated all at once. Blasts of psychic fire rained down at Korangar, while the pair dodged his many snapping heads with little effort. The longer she looked, the more she realized that, like she was now, they had been psychic warriors, and fully trained at that.

"We should leave now, Annetta." Puc tugged at her shoulder. "I need to remove the seal from you."

"The seal?" She glanced back to look at him. "I thought the point was that it needed to stay on."

"I cannot explain now, it would take too long." The mage's brow furrowed. "What you need to know is I made a grave and terrible mistake, and-"

Annetta's vision filled with a blinding light. She tore her gaze away from the mage just in time to see a beam of white lightning shoot from all seven of Korangar's maws in different directions. Her immediate reaction was to try contacting her parents through telepathy.

'Mom? Dad? Can you hear me?' She sent the message out.

There was nothing, and she tried once more, as dread gathered in her gut. She'd just seen them seconds before. They had just been there.

'Guys... please... answer me.' Her eyes rimmed with tears as she searched the sky.

Again, silence filled her mind, and Annetta could do nothing more than fear the worst.

Her entire body jerked to move forward despite the pain she was in, but felt both Puc and Skyris restraining her.

Her face contorted in rage as she turned to face them with tear filled eyes. "Let me go!"

"Annetta, you need to trust us." Puc wrapped her arm tighter around her. "It may not seem like it now, but please."

The words sent a column of fury down Annetta's spine as she struggled to break free, but the more she attempted, the tighter the grip around her became. A wave of pain shot through her chest just then, and she doubled over. The beast within flashed before her mind's eye, angrier than ever before. Her body shook and an instant sweat covered her, while her vision blurred into incoherence.

Chapter 46

Skyris watched as Puc knelt before Annetta. Lifting the girl's chin slightly, he examined her eyes. They were fully dilated, and beads of sweat were forming rapidly on her forehead.

"What's wrong with her?"

Puc rose, having completed his analysis. "She has gone into shock, and the seal is deteriorating. I need to get her someplace where I can remove it, and fast. I dare say she will not be able to teleport."

Skyris nodded. Too weary from the adrenaline rush to carry the girl, she placed an arm around Annetta's back, and helped lift the girl to her feet with Puc. Korangar had, for the moment, forgotten them, and was content with destroying the nearest skyscrapers. The structures came apart under him in a frenzy of pounding and shredding, with debris flying in all directions. Skyris had never seen such a force in all of her life, and she liked to think that she'd travelled a fair chunk of the universe. It was not the act of destroying itself that sent chills down her spine, but the delight the creature took in tearing the buildings apart.

When they were certain that they had managed to secure Annetta, they began walking towards one of the nearby buildings. The process was tedious, as the girl's legs refused to work, so Skyris and Puc would need to place their own foot from time to time behind her knee to get it to bend. It reminded Skyris of having to move a robot which had shut down and needed to be repaired. Had she not known any better, Skyris would have thought Annetta had died then and there on the spot. The only indication that she was still alive was her shallow breathing and blank stare.

"Hang in there, Anne, we'll get you out of this." Skyris whispered encouragingly to her, though the words were more for her own benefit than the girl's.

෨෨ඣ

Matthias had teleported separately from Puc and the others into the Lab, after explaining to the First Mage of Aldamoor that there were still people in need of aid. There had been no argument in this, and Matthias had been left to his own devices. Once on the surface, he'd managed to assimilate himself into a team of Gaians, Hurtz, Soarin, Ogaien and Minotaur soldiers that had been in the thicket of a skirmish.

Now, the ragtag team waited for him to return to them. They'd found another group of humans that had been hiding inside a food court in a mall, and Matthias had offered to teleport them down, knowing the way better than the two other Gaian psychic warriors that were part of the group. Having three psychics who were able to teleport would help lessen the burden on his own already spent body. Though the potions worked to replenish energy, a dull strain remained behind, like sore muscles after a hard day's work. The sensation was becoming more and more pronounced with each potion. As much as he didn't want to admit it, he wasn't sure how much longer he would last at this pace. He pulled out his last potion from the pouch at his belt, and examined the dark blue contents under one of the halogen lights before downing it.

The sensation of liquid going down his throat filled him, and he felt his energy stores renewed once more. He looked down at the empty vial in his gauntlet-clad hands, examining the blue filmy tint that had begun to run down and congeal on the side of the bottle that lay flat on his palm. He would need more, despite his body telling him no.

He pocketed the vial wordlessly and began to make his way to where he knew the reserves of the potions had been kept.

"Really hope there's something left," he muttered to himself. "I didn't exactly plan to die during the apocalypse."

The newly-added populace of the Lab had thankfully stayed close to where they had been deposited, and didn't wander farther out so Matthias didn't have any trouble navigating to where the larger potion stores had been kept by Puc and Sarina.

He moved down one set of metallic corridors, and coming into a wider section, he stopped. There was something about the space which seemed familiar to him. The space was not nearly as large as either the work area that Skyris had occupied, or the common area where all of the couches had been. Still, it was big and it wasn't random. His eyes passed over the left side of the room to see a large metal tactical table. He moved closer towards it, and that's when he realized where he recognized the design from. His mind lost itself in the many memories of himself, Mislantus, Amarok and a handful of the tyrant's closest advisors hunched over a table such as this. He reached under it, found a button, and pressed it. A deep tone followed, and a holographic map appeared on the table. From the layout, he presumed it to be the Eye to All Worlds.

A tight-lipped smile crept onto his face as he loomed over it, taking in every tree, hilltop, and the castle itself. "Oh, what Mislantus wouldn't have done to have a copy of you."

His eyes then swept sideways, where a slew of upright glass screens with control panels before them stood, with tarps half-covering them. Edging closer to the nearest one, he raised a hand to pull down the tarp, when the glint of something metallic caught the corner of his eye.

Tentacles of silver shot past the screens, upturning the table in the process, and sending sparks flying. Matthias teleported back and then dodged to the left when the spikes found him anew. His own claws extended from his gauntlets and blocked the next set of strikes.

"Amarok." The name emerged from him laced with venom.

The spikes retracted, slithering back to their origin point, and a figure in a torn hooded sweatshirt emerged. The hood lowered to reveal a mane of thick white hair, and a face that was covered by a silver mask with five points, which had been damaged on one side. There was no indication of threat in his posture, and this was what caused Matthias to tense even more. His old master was not someone you could let your guard down around.

"I would have expected no less of you, Matthias." The older assassin continued to walk forward and then began circling him. "I had a reason when I asked Mislantus to allow me the privilege to mold you in my image."

Matthias rolled his eyes. "Right, I'm sure it had nothing to do with the fact that my parents had the location to Korangar's prison. That just happened to be a happy coincidence."

A dry laugh that reminded Matthias of parchment being torn came from Amarok's lungs. "I would have expected no other answer from you. Yes, your parents did indeed play a role in why you were left alive, but it was I who asked for Mislantus to allow me to train you. I could see the raw potential in you. The killer drive that would lead you to becoming who you are today."

"Because I didn't know any better." Matthias's hands bunched up into fists. "You took a child and turned it into a weapon."

The light caught Amarok's mask in a way which appeared to make it smile. "Is it no different than what Thanestorm and that Hurtz did for Annetta Severio and Jason Kinsman?"

Fury boiled through Matthias's veins at this suggestion. "They didn't have their families murdered and they weren't made to believe they were being saved."

"Yet still they are being raised to be killers." Amarok pointed a finger, moving it up and down to emphasize his point. "Or was it not Annetta Severio that massacred most of her own army?"

Matthias wanted to smash the man's face in then and there. The only thing that kept him from doing so was knowing he could possibly get more information out of him if he held his cool. "Whatever you may have heard, Annetta wasn't in control of that and how did you get down here anyways?"

"It's surprising what a psychic can miss when they are teleporting over thirty humans into Q-16. All it takes is some human clothing."

Amarok retorted with something else in addition to this, but Matthias didn't catch it. His eyes had wandered to Amarok's hand, in which he held some kind of vial. A dark crimson liquid sloshed around in it, the colour and consistency of which was more than familiar to Matthias.

His legs began to slide, until they were a shoulder-width apart. Almost instantly, Amarok's vambraces sprung to life again. The liquid steel tentacles lashed out from the holes created in the hooded sweatshirt, further tearing it to ribbons.

Matthias dodged the onslaught, teleporting left and right without any pattern. When the tentacles ceased to follow, he stopped on the other side of the room and mentally warned himself not to use all of his energy. He had no vials left, and was still some distance away from the storage space where they were kept.

Amarok fully retracted the spikes into a dormant state, and brushed off some of the dust from his sleeve. "You can think what you like, but the one thing I have learned about Gaians in all my years is that you are a destructive lot. Khaos's children, really, even if you see yourselves as the chosen warriors of the Unknown."

Matthias's fists remained curled as he sized up his old mentor. "Look, I may be a Gaian, but as far as I'm concerned, I don't really share anything with them, except that one time I changed into a bear. I'm still not quite sure how I did."

"Instinct." Amarok opened his arms as if pointing out the Lab around him. "The lifeblood of everything that is. The thing that drives the Aternaverse to continue without any help from the Unknown. The thing which drives us, the thing which makes us strive to keep going no matter the odds, and what makes every living organism in all worlds want to push forward, no matter the cost."

422

The vial in Amarok's hand became visible, and Matthias could see something scribbled onto it. He squinted, trying to make out the words while Amarok ranted, to get even just a clue of what he was doing. The mistake cost him his perception, and seconds later, one of the tentacles lashed towards him. Matthias pivoted out of its path as a sharp pain tore through the skin on the right side of his face. His hand immediately went to the source, only to be wet with what Matthias guessed to be his blood. He glared at Amarok with his good eye.

"I'm sorry, boy, but I can't let you know what comes next." The silver mask of the assassin glinted in halogen lights and vanished.

෧෬

Jason, Sarina, Jansen and Darius had managed to stay together in the wake of Puc's vanishing. The mage had taken off towards the mech battling with the seven-headed dragon without so much as a word of warning. Jason could only compare the sight to one of the old monster movies he and Annetta had watched.

Once-proud skyscrapers looked down at him in ruins, with shattered windows and steel beams that poked through the crumbling architecture. He'd played a few games with such scenery, but never had he expected to walk under such skeletal remains of the city he once called home. A lump formed in the back of his throat as in the distance, he saw a jagged stump sticking out of the ground where the CN Tower had been.

"It's gone." The words were hard to say.

He felt something entwine his hand, and looking over, he saw Sarina standing beside him.

"It can be rebuilt," she reassured him.

He nodded, and out of the corner of his eye, he saw Darius and Jansen catch up to them.

"I guess follow the trail of destruction until we get to Anne and Korangar?" Darius inclined his head towards the ruins.

"You know Anne." Jason broke his hand away from Sarina's and took a step back to stand beside him. "Wouldn't be a show if she wasn't involved in some way."

The group then continued through the almost artistic chaos of overturned and crushed vehicles mixed with crumbling buildings. If the city had ever teemed with life before, no one would have known it. It looked to have been abandoned for ages.

The more Jason saw, the more anger filled him. How could someone bring so much destruction to people who weren't even aware such monsters existed? Seeing a discarded pop bottle a few feet in front of him, he curled his leg back and kicked it as hard as it would go. The bottle sailed through the air and landed in a pile of rubble off to the side with a clink. Jason then saw something move in it.

Faster than they could think, the trio surrounded Jansen. Jason summoned Helbringer, while Sarina drew her sabre and Darius's fingertips crackled with the makings of a spell.

The mound before them shifted further until finally, a figure rose and emerged. Jason then dropped his guard at seeing who it was

"Titus?" He moved towards him.

The Gaian prince looked worse for wear. He'd lost a significant amount of body mass since their last encounter, and had dark rings under his eyes. Were it not for the carefully-trimmed sideburns, Jason would have thought him to be someone else. The guns strapped to his hips also helped.

"Kinsman." The surname came out as a groan as he swiped his hair back, moving unruly strands from his face.

"Last I checked." Jason sent Helbringer back to its dormant state, and grabbed Titus's shoulder just before he tipped over. "You okay? What happened to you?"

"Too long a story to tell right now," the Gaian prince stated as he regained his footing and moved away from Jason's touch. "Where's Annetta?"

"That's the same thing we're trying to figure out," Sarina said, sheathing her blade. "Any ideas?"

Titus rubbed his temples, clearly still woozy from whatever had caused him to collapse in the first place. "There was... a man... Korangar and..."

"See, I told you she'd find Korangar." Jason smiled turning to the group sarcastically. "And then what?"

"We'll all be in a lot of trouble if she can't transform." Jansen blurted out.

The others turned to face her, confused. She shrunk back for a split second, regretting having said anything.

"What are you talking about?" Jason inquired.

Jansen took a deep breath, fanning out her hands before her as though clearing the air before proceeding. "Okay, so if things are playing out like they are in the story I wrote in my head, then Annetta can't transform into the red dragon because Puc blocked her."

"That's exactly what he did!" Jason exclaimed as he took a step towards her. "Wait... isn't mind reading like... illegal? Shouldn't a whole storm of angels show up to like... I don't know... smite you or something?"

Jansen looked like she wanted to say something, but wasn't quite sure how to articulate it. She withdrew into herself and stayed that way before Darius slapped a hand down on her shoulder.

"Which is exactly part of the reason why we need to find her," he stated.

Titus nodded and withdrew one of the pistols at his side from its holster. "Precisely why we must."

Chapter 47

The world spun before Annetta's eyes. She wasn't sure where she was now, nor who the disembodied voices calling her name out in the background were. Something propelled the thing that was her body forward, but it was all irrelevant. The world had stopped when two-thirds of her immediate family had died before her eyes.

Her final conversation with her parents played in her head over and over again like a tide going in and out. She'd warned them, tried to warn them of the dangers in trying to face Korangar. He was too strong. His heads grew back when they were cut off, and he had managed to shatter Severbane like it had been made of glass. There was no winning, not this time around. But with her parents dead, would that be such a bad thing?

The force that propelled her then began lowering her to the ground. Annetta sank to her knees. The voices came around her again. There were two at least. Part of her was certain that it was Puc and Skyris who had been there moments before the blur had happened, but the rest of her wasn't sure. For all she knew, days had passed.

A dark shape appeared before her. It grabbed her shoulders as if holding her for support. A second such shape appeared beside it, and spoke something muffled to the first one.

"Annetta, can you hear me?" Puc's voice called from somewhere in the distance.

The words triggered the rest of her senses from their dormancy. It was as if she'd just emerged from diving into a lake and was resurfacing for air. Annetta's lungs sucked in as much as they could take, and a shudder passed down her spine. The full capacity of what had happened then hit her and tears instantly filled her eyes.

"They're gone." The words came out small and inaudible.

Puc's usually stern face was creased with sadness at having heard her. "I am sorry, Annetta."

Though she knew better, the tears continued to fall from her eyes as thoughts of all the things she could have still done and said overwhelmed her. She would never again wake up to her father making breakfast, or her mother rushing to get last-minute groceries because there was a sale going on. There would be no one to tell her to fold her laundry when it was dry, and no one she could confide in when she had a problem with friends or at school. In this, Annetta and, she realized, her brother Xander would now be alone.

A pair of strong but soft arms encircled Annetta, and she soon found herself burying her head into Skyris's shoulder.

"Let it out Anne. It'll be okay," her aunt whispered in her ear.

"Okay?" Annetta retracted herself from the embrace and wiped away tears with the back of her hand. "How is any of this going to be okay? People are dead, people are dying, and I can't save them all."

Puc rose, dusting off the debris from his cloak. "No, you are right, Annetta, you cannot save them all, but that is life. There is no such thing as a battle where everyone lives."

Though the words were true, Annetta couldn't help but feel something akin to a coiled spring tightening in the pit of her stomach. She wanted to retaliate, she wanted to say he was wrong, but it felt as though the fire had all gone out in her. Her eyes turned down, and tears began to well up.

"Then what the hell is the point of it all?"

A hand landed on Annetta's shoulder, and glancing sideways, she saw Skyris standing beside her. "The point is to try and save as many as you can."

"There is a way that we can still turn the tide of all of this." Puc crossed the small gap that had been between them. "We can still save the great many who are hidden within Q-16."

Annetta huffed and rolled her eyes. "And how do you plan to do that?"

A reluctance filled what Puc said next. "We need to remove the seal on you."

The girl's eyes widened. "You're kidding me, right? You saw yourself that I couldn't control it. The dragon doesn't distinguish friend from foe, and the Four Forces are already hurting for numbers."

"It is, unfortunately, the only way to vanquish Korangar once and for all," Puc stated.

An annoyed laugh filled Annetta. "You hear yourself say this, right? You're going to free the thing which basically destroyed the Four Forces and hope that it'll fight Korangar."

"We don't have to wonder," Skyris interjected. "You've felt it want to escape in you ever since you laid eyes on Korangar, haven't you?"

Silence filled Annetta as she thought about it. "I guess… but how does that tie into it?"

Before anyone could answer, a thunderous sound filled the air. It was as though airplane jets were just outside the brick walls that shielded them.

"The Air Force?" Annetta couldn't help but wonder.

She stepped around the massive piles of debris and stopped at the entrance. At first, Annetta couldn't make out what was going on outside. The sun glowed with an intensity that blinded everything in pure white, until her eyes began to adjust to it. A figure dressed in white armour with a flowing pearl cape stood on top of an overturned bus. A longsword and a shield were held firmly in its grip, and there was something familiar to how the tall and broad-shouldered being stood.

Annetta made her way outside the walls and hid beside a car that had been partially crushed. Her feet accidentally crunched some glass from the windshield that had fallen to the floor, and she cursed herself silently, preparing to use psychic fire to attack. The pair of grey eyes that turned to look at her halted any action from happening.

A name she had thought would never again be spoken to its owner came out. "Link?"

He no longer had the crescent moon scar across his eye, and most of his face was hidden behind a scraggly, not-fully-developed beard. Despite this, Annetta knew the face. For a split second, the pain of her parents passing diminished, and she was about to run towards him. She hesitated, though, at seeing his distant and cold expression. It was as if he saw her, but was also looking through her at the same time.

"Annetta?" He inquired, narrowing his eyes to see her better from where he stood.

It was deeper than she recalled, but not unfriendly. Remembering herself, she looked down at the tatters of her Gaian armour, and then felt around for the brooch that pinned her cloak. The once-brilliant red cloak with an embroidered white lion on it was stained with blood and dirt, causing it to resemble something close to burgundy. It was not the way she wanted to present herself, and she could only guess that her face looked no better. Severbane was gone, and the only thing even close to a weapon on her was her father's shield, which she summoned into her hand from where it had been strapped on her back. There was no point in hiding, and she took another lead-filled step forward, but didn't advance any further, only enough for him to be able to see her.

"What's left of her," she half-whispered.

As soon as she emerged, Link's grey eyes lit up for only a split second before fading back into their neutral gaze. Annetta's shoulders sagged a little at seeing the change. She'd gotten excited too soon, and for all she knew, this wasn't Link.

The man slid his sword back in a white leather scabbard at his side. "That's not the Annetta Severio I remember."

Annetta couldn't help but smile despite the pain, and looking up, she saw a dozen or more white lights streaking across the sky and landing in different parts of the city, just as he had. She then refocused her attention back on him. "Things have changed since you left."

"As I would have expected them to," he replied, adjusting the shield on his other arm. "I was technically gone for thirty years of training."

Annetta's face began to crinkle with a million questions at the last sentence, but she was promptly cut off by the sound of feet as they approached from behind.

"Anne! There you are!" Jason's exasperated voice called out, catching his breath from running.

She turned around to see Jason, Sarina, Darius, Jansen and to her biggest surprise, Titus, all standing behind her. Seconds later, Puc and Skyris emerged from the building to join them.

"Lincerious?" Puc squinted against the sun as he joined Annetta's side, with Skyris in tow.

"That is my name." the figure confirmed. "I did also once go by the name of Link, but I do not anymore. Nicknames are part of what is shed to become a White Knight."

"He's a White Knight." Skyris's eyes widened and then she whispered into Annetta's ear. "Trained for thirty years, who knows how much of his personality is left intact at this point. Watch what you say to him."

The warning in the older woman's tone came as strange to her, but she understood what she was getting at. Thirty years was a long time, enough to forget the friendships and bonds once held. As far as they were all concerned, all they saw was a vessel that looked like Link, but didn't retain any of his personality or memories. Despite this, Annetta wished it wasn't true, and she searched his eyes for any spark of remembrance that could have been present in them.

Link turned his attention to Puc. "Did you bind Annetta, Jason, Sarina or Matthias with any spell that could be impeding any of their abilities, aside from the spell to block the art of mind reading in Annetta and Jason?"

"There was a binding spell placed on Annetta not too long ago," the mage confirmed.

Annetta felt Link's gaze pierce her yet again with calculation. "Then she is the catalyst, the key."

"Key? What key?" Jason furrowed his brows. "This some chosen one crap?"

"Not exactly." Link shook his head. "All Gaians carry the predisposition in their genes to be the catalyst, the one who brings on the change. Annetta just happened to be in the right place at the right time."

It was Annetta's turn to furrow her brows. She looked over first at Puc, then Skyris, and finally back at Link. "You mean the beast, don't you?"

There was a pause of silence among the group. The answer, however, was obvious as much as those gathered were terrified of the prospect of setting the creature free again.

Titus was the one to finally break the silence, recalling words he'd recited in fits of fever for weeks before. "While peace restored and violence quell, darkness breaks a forgotten spell. The end times awake, and make all worlds quake. Abandon hope and end lives, in this the seed of chaos thrives. Black beast of seven minds and crowned in ten, the catalyst of its end living in man's kinsmen. In the prison among the stars it waits, raging to govern all fates."

Annetta felt a lump grow in her throat. On top of everything else that had transpired, now prophecy had crept in. She wanted to scream and beat her hands until they were sore against the pavement if it meant she didn't have to be part of it. She'd never cared for prophecy, and now more than ever, she wanted nothing more to do with it. As far as she was concerned, prophecy had gotten her into the mess she was in now. She was no war hero of legend, no White Lioness of Gaia as they called her. True, her feral form was that, but it had all been luck, hadn't it? Everything she'd ever done that lined up with prophecy had been luck of the draw, decisions made on instinct.

"I can't," she muttered through partially-closed lips, glancing down again at her ruined attire. "The dragon can't be controlled. You all saw what it did on Aerim attacking everyone. It's too late, anyways…"

Link leaped off the bus he'd been standing on and made his way towards the group. "We can fix this, Annetta, but we will need your help. The dragon most likely attacked because it sensed Korangar being awakened but it didn't have the target it was seeking."

"How do you know?" Jason crossed his arms. "I don't think you know what we're dealing with here if I can be honest."

An exasperated sigh escaped Link. "You need to trust me on this. The White Knights have taken a special interest in knowing everything there is to know about Korangar."

Anger mixed with the not yet fully expressed sorrow of having lost her parents ruptured through. "I haven't been able to accomplish anything here. My parents are dead, so are many, many other people. What makes you think my changing into a dragon will make a difference?"

Another bout of silence followed. Annetta did her best to suppress the tears which escaped at the corners of her eyes, but losing the fight, she wrinkled her nose and turned away from those around her. The tightness in her chest and throat returned with a vengeance that she was certain would end with her not being able to breathe. Perhaps it wasn't the worst way to go, given the circumstances, and at least she knew where she would be going after.

Link's voice then cut through her thoughts. "The same thing that allows anyone in a moment of darkness try to defy it. Hope."

She blinked through drenched lashes and looked around at the broken-down faces of her friends. Regardless of where they'd come from, they had all become family. It was with this, she realized, that there were still people she had to fight for, and any thoughts of despair from the moments before vanished.

The shield dropped from her arm and fell to the floor with a metallic clatter. She then looked at Puc. "Whatever has to be done, do it before I change my mind."

The mage made his way towards her. Unsure of what she needed to do, Annetta knelt before him. She felt a pair of hands that were neither warm nor cool touch her temples. Foreign words were then uttered, and though she couldn't understand what was being said, Annetta could feel the weight of them on her mind. It was as though someone had placed shackles on her whole body, and with the click of a single key, each chain began to drop and slither down until it lay in a pile on the floor. As the last chains fell, her eyes turned to see the great seven-headed dragon tearing through another set of skyscrapers in the Toronto skyline. A surge of heat flowed through her, and then Annetta Severio's world went dark.

Chapter 48

Jason and his companions backed up and watched in a daze as the form Annetta grew and melted away into the dragon then took off. For the split second it had looked at him, Jason felt its wrath sear his skin, rubbing off on him as though he'd put his hands too close to a radiator. It wasn't blind rage, either, unlike what he'd thought the dragon had been like on Aerim. No, this anger was focused, and the fury was clearly directed at the one it sought. Korangar.

"Do you think she has a chance?" Sarina took his hand.

Jason looked down, curling his own fist around hers. "Honestly, I haven't got a clue. I mean, Korangar has at least twenty feet on her and I don't just mean the six extra heads."

Darius stepped closer to them. "That's never stopped Anne in a fight before, and you know it."

Jansen squinted her eyes at the horizon where Annetta had flown off. "It'll take more than one, regardless."

"What do you mean?" Jason turned to her.

He watched her shrink in for a moment and felt bad for having spoken in such a gruff tone, but Jansen quickly regained her composure. "This'll sound a bit crazy, and I'm not sure how accurate it is, but when I was writing the story, Korangar wasn't going to be defeated by just one dragon."

His eyes widened and Jason almost started laughing at what she'd said, but he caught sight of Darius's face and stopped. "I'm sorry... did you say writing the story?"

"It's complicated." Jansen sucked in some air and shrugged her shoulders. "I don't know if this mess is my fault, or if I'm just able to-"

"The Sisters of Wyrd think Jansen may be some kind of prophet who can records things as they happen, sometimes faster than they do," Puc filled in. "This was why Darius was charged with finding her and why we couldn't be given much information about her in the event that she would record us going to look for her."

Darius raised an eyebrow. "Well, I guess now that makes sense. How did you find out?"

"A perk of being First Mage," he replied.

"Why isn't anyone else changing if more than one is needed?" Titus scanned the horizon. "Is there something else we are missing?"

Puc glanced at the ground, holding his chin in thought. "If legend is to be believed, then no, it should have been the first few Gaians to come into contact with Annetta in whom the change should have been triggered."

"Then I, Skyris, Jason and Sarina should have been the first to be hit." Titus ran a hand through tangled hair as he looked over to where Annetta had flown. "Though, I could be exempt, because I am, as you suggested, a prophet, but that doesn't explain anyone else."

⊱◈⊰

While the group weighed in on the subject, Jansen did some contemplation of her own. She remembered the scene of Annetta transforming in her head, how the dragon had reigned fire down on the two armies. Why had she written that scene? It had come to her, it was true, but why and how? Most importantly, how was everything that she had written true?

A roar then came from the distance, which caused everyone to look up. Annetta's dragon soared towards Korangar alone. No others at her side.

Jansen bit her lip as the gears of thought continued to whirl in her head. "If I can influence events, like Puc suggests…"

She broke away from the group and pulling open her backpack, she found a relatively flat surface on the hood of a car. Booting up the laptop she had with her, she sighed in relief to see there was still a little battery life left. Opening her writing program, she then selected the file with her story, and began to write.

⊱◈⊰

Elsewhere in the city, Venetor led his troops into the heart of the siege. The moment he'd seen Korangar transform he knew their time was running out. He wanted to go after the beast himself but his soldiers needed their king to lead them. He'd managed to locate where the enemy forces were conglomerating, and had sent messages to every able-bodied psychic to move their units towards him. They'd evacuated as many people as possible into Q-16, and now, as he saw it, the real work began.

Soaring through the air with his arms outstretched, Venetor let out a war cry before descending into a slew of enemies. The Gaian king grabbed a polearm that was flying towards him and lifted it, along with the opponent wielding it into the air, before sending it flying into another group of soldiers. Not since his fight against Razmus had

Venetor felt so charged with adrenaline and in his element. His fists pumped furiously in a series of jabs, punches and counters too fast to be seen by the naked eye.

Beside him, a beast clad in armour from head to toe swung a sword almost as wide as Venetor's waist and thick enough to cleave it in two. Since his boyhood, whatever battle he faced, Gladius was only a few steps behind. The Hurtz warrior tore through enemy ranks with large arcing swings of the blade, that while not elegant, were always deadly accurate, leaving many soldiers before him cowering in their final moments.

"Yer Khaos god won't save ye now!" the Hurtz bellowed as he continued to administer his reign of terror.

Venetor couldn't help but crack an adrenaline-fueled grin at hearing this. Clear of any enemies, he shot into the air for another hammer-like attack. They were going to win this, Earth would be saved, and he could feel the cheers of victory in his ears as clear as the sounds of battle in the present. His joy faded, however, when he realized how outnumbered the combined Four Forces along with the Gaians still were.

"It's still not enough." His eyes took in the broken-down buildings and swarms of fighters from both sides.

He was not about to give up, though. Gaians were not raised to do so, it was unheard of. They was a warrior people, and would rather die fighting than on their knees no matter the cost. Sucking in another lung full of the charred and polluted air around him, Venetor pulled his fist back. His eyes targeted a particularly concentrated patch of soldiers near the middle of the fray. He was about to plunge down with full force when something silver glistened in the corner of his eye. Venetor almost paid it no mind, thinking it simply the reflection of a weapon, but then the size of it made him pause.

Hundreds of silver glistening lights began to hail down from the heavens above him. Venetor dodged from side to side, watching in horror as they struck the Earth in an illuminated display as intense as the sun. He was eventually forced to retreat to the top of one of the larger still standing buildings and shield his eyes. Though temporarily blinded, he tapped into his feral form abilities, increasing his range of hearing. If death was upon his warriors, he wished to be the first to know, in order to avenge them with all the fury his psychic fire could

435

muster. He didn't hear death throes, however, but the cheering and charge of an army.

Venetor rubbed his eyes to remove the sunspots in his vision and peered down over the ledge. Below, the Four Forces and the Gaians were joined by yet another host of soldiers. Dressed in white cloaks and shimmering pearl plate armour, the White Knights of the Unknown charged alongside them. Their iridescent weapons were raised skyward, the knights appeared to be the crest of a wave of warriors that rushed towards Korangar's ranks, crashing into them.

The Gaian king sighed in relief at the turn of the tide. Shooting himself up into the air, he focused in on a new target, then sent himself projecting towards it at full speed. A feral roar ripped through his throat as he cracked through the defenses of the disoriented troops. Wreathed in psychic fire, he hurled his fist forward, colliding with the jaw of the closest enemy fighter. The foe flew back before hurtling into an overturned vehicle, which then burst into flames. Venetor reeled himself around, ignoring the carnage he'd caused and focused on a new target, a very portly Verden wielding a crude two-handed club with rusted shards of metal spiked through it.

The club swung towards him like a pendulum. Venetor ducked the strike and countered with his own, an uppercut to the Verden's meaty midsection. The creature bellowed in pain before toppling over from the impact.

Venetor didn't have time to celebrate when he felt something sharp pierce his shoulder. His hand reached back and he pulled a crossbow bolt from his shoulder, gritting his teeth as he scanned the horizon, trying to pick out whom the weapon belonged to. His eyes then landed on wiry man with tattoos all over his face that wore a white scarf around his neck. He tried to identify the species, but was forced to dodge another bolt as the projectile almost hit his left cheek. Chilled air stung his face where the weapon had grazed him, and he felt a wet spot form around the wound.

His blood boiled and he pushed away all thoughts of the pain searing from his shoulder. Venetor used the back of his fist to wipe his face and retracting it, saw it was stained red. The sound of the projectile firing again caused him to roll out of the way and then teleport from the man's line of sight.

He reappeared just behind him and was about to slam his fist into the unsuspecting foe's spine when he heard another projectile weapon coming towards him. Venetor pivoted out of the way just in time to see an arrow strike the man, killing him instantly.

Venetor turned around and saw a hooded White Knight standing twenty paces away with a longbow notched and ready to fire anew. The knight lowered it upon seeing that the man who had been firing was no more.

There was something about the fully plate-clad knight with a white cowl that struck Venetor as familiar. He couldn't pin point what it was exactly, but he recognized the stance the fighter had used just seconds ago when holding the loaded bow. A flash of reddish hair from under the hood further raised those suspicions.

"Do I know you?" He narrowed his eyes.

The figure didn't reply, and instead turned its attention to another foe that had been closing in behind it.

Venetor didn't bother waiting for an answer, and with renewed hope in winning the fight, he threw himself into the fray. Psychic fire surrounded his form, singeing any who came too close to him and burning those who were in his way. The Gaian king had spent countless hours training both his body and abilities to be able to use them for extended periods of time, and wasn't about to back down.

An intense gust of wind suddenly began to blow through the ranks. Venetor's cloak snapped back and forth from the invisible force as small pieces of paper, plastic bags and leaves danced through the air. The latter made Venetor feel revulsion at how the humans had littered their planet. The practice had been illegal on Gaia for well over three centuries now. A shadow then passed by the corner of his eye, and grew so intense that Venetor had no choice but to look up.

A dragon of crimson scales flew above the armies. Its powerful bat-like wings knocked many unwary soldiers from their feet. Many stopped to look up at the beast as it soared above them with its long serpentine neck and horned draconic head focused ahead. Focused at Korangar.

A wave of cheers came from the remaining Ogaien warriors, and soon the rest of what remained of the Four Forces also raised their voices. It was then that Venetor realized what it was that he was witnessing.

The Gaian king's jaw slacked a little. "Well I'll be damned."

The sound of feet running made him glance sideways, and he saw Atala bounding up towards him.

"Is that what I think it is?" she asked in between strained breaths.

"If you're seeing another dragon heading towards Korangar, then yes. You aren't hallucinating."

Another larger form strode towards Venetor. Gladius's once pristine silver armour now bore the markings of countless foes slain on the battlefield.

"I think ye'll be wanting to ask yer niece some questions." The Hurtz warrior lifted his visor to get a better view.

He was about to reply to Gladius with a quip when a sudden pounding in his head brought Venetor to his knees. The last thing he saw was were the forms of his Gaian soldiers warping and changing into dragons. A haze clouded over his mind, causing all the noise around him to dim.

ഇരുന്ന

Jansen pulled away from the screen just in time to see Jason fall to his knees. His form melted away along with his clothing into a small green dragon, which then began to grow in size. Soon after, Sarina and Skyris followed, their bodies warping and shifting. In their places then stood a black and a sapphire dragon. The trio took off without any indication that they'd seen those around them.

Her mouth hung slightly agape as she took in the sight of the three dragons flying on the Toronto skyline, towards a creature that was now laying waste to her city just as she'd envisioned it. "It's working."

"Darius!" Puc called to the younger mage.

Jansen saved what she'd written on her computer and closing it, she watched Darius clutching his head as though he'd hit it on something. Puc hovered over his shoulder with a hand stretched out towards him, ready to assist, but his efforts were thwarted when Darius swatted his hand away. He said something inaudible and then collapsed, his form rippling and changing into what was unmistakably a grey dragon. The creature roared, shook its ridged mane of silver locks, and launched itself into the air, still growing to its full size mid-flight. It soon faded onto the horizon with the other three. Two more joined them some minutes later from further ahead, and the flock continued its journey towards Korangar.

Once her laptop was secured in her bag, Jansen rushed over to where Puc, Titus and Link still stood.

"I don't understand, why Darius?" Puc's brows furrowed. "He's not a Gaian."

"Perhaps there's a loophole in the prophecy," Titus offered. "The Water Folk can also be seen as Earth's kinsmen. Their history is heavily interlaced with that of what I believe was once the ancient Roman Empire, was it not?"

"Roman and Greek, but yes." Puc corrected him. "The portal they used to enter this world was once located where Atlantis would have been, and where now Q-16 lies beneath the ocean."

"Okay, so there you have it." Titus clasped his hands together as if to emphasize his point.

"As interesting as all of this history is, we should be pressing on," Link interjected. "This battle is far from over."

Titus's eyes then met with those of Jansen. "What about this one?"

Puc then turned his attention to her. "Human, though she has some abilities that the Sisters of Wyrd are finding most peculiar, as am I."

Jansen felt herself begin to withdraw into her own world, which seemed rather barren of late, since most of her daydreams had become her reality in a little less than twenty-four hours. She didn't like being the centre of attention, even on a good day. She clutched her bag self-consciously to her body, and waited until Puc's feral blue eyes wandered back to Titus.

"We'll keep her close then until we can find a psychic to teleport her down into the safety of Q-16," Link stated.

"And who says I want to go back down?"

The trio turned to Jansen, who stood with her arms folded across her chest. She didn't appreciate the way in which they had just spoken about her, despite the fact that all of it was true.

"You could get seriously hurt," Puc pointed out. "And then I would be forced to explain to Lysania why you have been injured, or worse yet, killed."

"Look, I'm sure that being surrounded by the three of you I'm going to be fine. I mean, of course, unless you aren't Puc Thanestorm, the First Mage of Aldamoor, Titus Severio, the Crown Prince of Gaia and Lincerious Heallaws, the White Knight."

"That is not the point." Puc strode towards her, which made Jansen recoil slightly.

"Well I just wrote down that Jason, Sarina, Skyris and Darius all transformed in my notebook and they did. If you're that worried maybe I should also write that I don't die." Jansen stood unmoving from the spot and glared at him.

Puc raised an eyebrow, unsure how to take what the girl had said. He was growing more curious by the minute of her abilities.

"Thanestorm, if she's that insistent, then let her go," Titus interjected. "She's got a sword on her, so it's not like she isn't armed."

Puc then turned to Jansen. "I doubt you will actually know how to use that, but…"

Jansen rolled her eyes and unsheathed the sword at her hip. "I believe the quote is that the first rule is to stick them with the pointy end."

Chapter 49

The whoosh of wind and flapping of massive bat wings filled Annetta's ears. She was surprised to be present, albeit not in control of the draconic body. She had expected to fade away or black out completely again, but it seemed that this aspect of herself didn't want her to entirely go away this time. Instead of panicking due to her lack of control, Annetta pictured herself flying on top of the dragon, a passenger not truly capable of dealing any damage, but still there nonetheless. Their target was that of Korangar.

Despite Annetta's dragon body being the size of a large plane, Korangar's seven-headed form still towered well over her own as he hurled his bulk in blind rage at the skyscraper closest to him. One of the maws shot blasts of green flame while another froze parts of the building with ice breath. The draconic part of her mind didn't seem the least bit intimidated at this display of destructive fury. It was a confidence Annetta found hard to share after her previous encounter with Korangar. Her mind then went back to her parents' death, and a blood-curdling roar erupted from her as she closed in.

To her surprise, she was answered by more dragon cries from behind. Whipping her serpentine neck to either side, she saw that six other dragons of various colours had joined her; blue, green, grey, white, purple and golden-yellow. Each looked different from the next, with various combinations of manes and horns, but were all roughly the same size as Annetta.

Perhaps the odds are in our favour after all, she thought to herself, and heard the dragon give a low rumble back in approval.

The approaching mass of dragons finally caught Korangar's attention, as all seven heads perked up and roared back. Annetta and her companions screeched back and dove towards their prey.

What came next was a blur to Annetta. Claws scratched, and jaws snapped as the dragons split apart, each taking on one of the heads. Korangar had a hard time keeping up with the smaller dragons as they dove and withdrew with each attack. The massive jaws on all seven heads curled back into a snarl, revealing rows upon rows of jagged sword-like teeth. His cat-slit pupil eyes darted back and forth while they continued to come at him. That was when Annetta realized the flaw.

As soon as the white dragon came towards him, another one of Korangar's heads came in from the side, intercepting the dragon and clamping down on it. Shaking it from side to side, Korangar then tossed the dragon into one of the buildings and watched at it collapsed.

No! Annetta screamed in the silent confines of the dragon's mind. *No, no, no, there has to be something else we can do, this can't be the end.*

She hadn't expected anything remotely resembling a confirmation of her thoughts, much less an agreement, when she heard the low rumbling of the dragon yet again. *Be the catalyst.*

Korangar's jaws came towards her at that moment, and Annetta spun out of the way, climbing higher into the sky until she was out of reach. Catalyst, Titus had used that word when he'd said the lines of prophecy, hadn't he? The problem was, Annetta hadn't the faintest clue how to be the catalyst. Even when she had supposedly taken on the shape of the white lioness, it had been a simple blind blunder into what she thought maybe could work.

It's not much different now, the voice spoke again.

I really don't like it when you do that, read my mind. She frowned.

It's also my mind, the dragon rumbled. *Now go and do what needs to be done.*

Annetta wanted to protest again, but it was clear the dragon wasn't interested in hearing it. Her nostrils flared as she inhaled the scent of burned debris, and other smells associated with the carnage of battle. Beyond those, she found she could smell the individual races, the humans that had walked the streets before, and the scores of other species which had come to Earth. It was strange and overwhelming to be able to pick up so much detail with just her nose alone. The few times she'd transformed into her feral form, she'd never had a chance to linger on such things, and even now, time was not on her side.

With a few powerful flaps of her wings, Annetta settled herself on the closest building. She watched as the other dragons attacked Korangar, the white one rejoining the fray despite having already once been caught in the maws of the seven-headed beast. She knew she needed to head back to them, to keep fighting. They needed her, but they also needed more help.

Annetta's serpentine neck curled back as the dragon's massive lungs expanded to their full capacity. The sound of shattering glass could be heard beyond the draconic screech that had erupted from her. She roared with every fibre, and in her human form, she imagined it would have equated a cry for help.

442

A beam of ice then hurled towards her. Panic gripped Annetta as she realized what was coming her way. She launched herself from the building just in time to watch it crystalize beneath her claws. An ice attack was the last thing she had expected from the seven headed dragon. Rising skywards, she let loose a torrent of flame in retaliation and dove towards Korangar.

The targeted head of the beast shook off the fire that had hit it and began to open its jaws, ready to crunch down on Annetta. The girl didn't miss a beat and lodged one arm on the upper jaw and one on the lower before spewing more fire directly inside. The head snapped back, withering in pain as it caught fire from the inside. The trail of fire then continued, the chain reaction from the one head passing it to the others.

A meaty clawed hand then pushed Annetta to the side, causing her wings to tangle and lose balance. She landed in a heap of rubble with a crash. Annetta then tried to get up but found she was unable to lift her battered wings. Worst yet, she felt exhausted.

A sound then began to fill her head, starting with a light whoosh like that of a windmill in the distance. As it grew louder, however, it began to sound more and more like a flock of great birds. Shaking off the shock of the fall, Annetta peered up to see the sky filled with the silhouettes of not six other dragons, but dozens. They were of different colours and designs, a rainbow of scales against the ashen horizon.

The dragons plowed into Korangar, swarming him like multi-coloured locus. Korangar's draconic heads wailed as he tried to shake them off, all to no avail. There were simply too many, each clawing and biting.

Annetta watched from below, feeling herself growing more and more tired by the second. She wanted to do more, to fight more, but found she had no strength left. She focused on the dragons above, seeing they had everything well in hand despite the absence of the one that was supposed to be the catalyst.

Maybe this is one of those times where it isn't about being the sole hero, but one of many, was her final thought as she closed her eyes and drifted off to sleep.

∞∞∞

Venetor gasped, waking in a pile of rubble. Every muscle in his body was ablaze with stiffness, and sitting up he rotated his shoulders, hoping to loosen them. It all seemed like a bad dream, but when he looked up, there was no sign of Korangar anywhere.

"Did we win?" he muttered to himself as he got up and glanced down to see that his armour and cape were still intact, despite the transformation. He'd never heard of a feral form change where one kept their clothing. This was partially why beta scale mail was so prized on Gaia.

"Father?" A voice called to him from behind.

Venetor turned to see Titus standing some distance away. Further behind him still, he could make out the forms of Puc, Skyris, Gladius, Jason, Sarina and another girl that Venetor didn't recognize. Dusting off his armour, he picked his way through the rubble, but growing tired mid-way, he teleported himself to level ground just in time from for the others to approach.

"Now be truthful with me." Venetor regarded them gravely. "Am I dead?"

"That state will need to be left for another day," Puc stated. "You are still very much alive, and king of Gaia."

"And here I was hoping for early retirement." Venetor groaned as he worked out a knot from his shoulder.

Looking down, he noticed that Skyris's hand was entwined with that of the mage. When their eyes met for a split second, she let go which caused Puc also to retract his.

Venetor sighed and shook his head. He walked up towards them, and grabbing hold of Skyris's wrist, he placed her hand gently in Puc's, locking the two with his own. He then looked up at Skyris. "In times like these, we need to grab hold of happiness where we can find it. Besides, I think the nobles of Gaia had their fair run for the hand of the Princess of Gaia."

She smiled at him in a silent thank you, and he then turned his attention to Puc. "I know we've had our differences, and in my youth, I misjudged you. A young Gaian's pride bleeds as red as the blood in our veins and runs just as fast. When we were in our dragon forms, our minds were somehow linked and I saw what you did when that machine failed. Perhaps you elves aren't as different from us as I thought. Take care of my sister."

He clapped Puc on the shoulder and then turned away to scan the horizon. "Are we all that's left?"

"The Gaians are still recovering from their transformations, but the battle, as far as we can tell, is pretty much over," Jason chimed in.

As if on cue, another hand rose from the rubble not far from where everyone was standing. Darius emerged from among the ruins, gasping for air. His clothing was a little worse for wear, but otherwise, he looked intact, aside from the gash on his right shoulder.

He took in his surroundings with a dazed stupor before he spotted the others and waved with his good arm. "Hey, guys!"

The group headed towards him at a hurried pace. Venetor was distracted, however, when he noticed another unconscious form begin to stir, and rushed over to it instead.

Atala groaned as she sat up and rubbed her eyes with the back of her hand. "Remind me never to shoot any Star Water with the soldiers before deployment."

"I don't think you did." Venetor extended a hand to her, which she grabbed with some reluctance.

"Really? You'd have thought with the end of the world so close at hand that I'd have at least snuck something in." She chuckled weakly as she stretched sore legs.

"Not this time, soldier." Venetor smiled back and then noticed the gashes in her scale mail. He then remembered Korangar having gotten hold of one of the dragons. He rummaged through the pouch at his hip, but found no healing potions.

Venetor frowned and looked up just in time to see Atala begin to sway, and wrapped an arm around her waist, steadying her. "I've got you."

He then steered her towards the group.

Elsewhere, Annetta stirred from where she lay. She remembered everything this time, from the moment she had transformed to when she had fallen asleep. The presence of the dragon that had been clawing at her mind for the past few days had vanished like a headache, and Annetta wondered if she would ever see the great beast again. Somehow she doubted it was an ability she could call on, like that of her feral form.

She opened her eyes reluctantly, and took in the grey clouded heavens above. She wanted to get up and move, but found that just like before she had fallen asleep, her body wasn't willing to follow any commands. Her energy had been spent on flight and flying. She had nothing else to give of herself, and so she resorted to having to stare at the sky instead.

The crunch of footwear on gravel filled her ears not long after. She half expected it to be an enemy soldier having found her, and she closed her eyes. Perhaps she could fool it into thinking she was dead to make it lose interest. If it didn't, then maybe she would be reunited with her parents much sooner than she thought it would be. Both options had their pros and cons.

Seconds passed, and she heard no more footsteps. There wasn't even the sound of a weapon being drawn, which she found peculiar. Instead, she felt a pair of arms wrap around her and lift her.

When she opened her eyes, she found, to her astonishment, that it was Link who was carrying her out of the wreckage. The silver sword he'd held was back in its sheath, and it slapped against his thigh in a manner that reminded Annetta of when they had been together in Q-16. Back then, Link had always carried his father's sword on him, which now marked his supposed grave on Gaia. She wondered if he'd want it back now.

She studied his face, still finding it odd that he no longer had the scar across his eye, and even stranger yet was the presence of his thin beard. He looked so much older with it, and less like the Link she had known. An echo of Skyris's words then rang in her ears, and she became conscious of their meaning.

She cleared her throat, causing him to pause. "I'm awake. You can put me down."

Link obliged, letting her slide down out of his grip, but remained firm on her shoulder with an air of protectiveness.

"I guess I can't be expected anything else, considering I was a giant fire-breathing lizard with bat wings." She groaned as she shook her head.

"A body that big takes a lot of energy to get around," Link answered.

"Makes sense." Annetta let go and steadied herself on feet that felt very much like lead.

Taking a few steps forward to get sore muscles moving, she looked around at the overturned and crushed vehicles, as well as the partially demolished buildings and twisted lamp posts. Signs of battle were visible in every corner.

"Things are going to change now, aren't they?" She glanced back at Link.

Link shifted his feet, trying to find a better centre of balance before he strode over to her side again, his white cape billowing as he did so. "Yes, things will change, though not all of them, and it's for the Angels and the Unknown to decide what does and what doesn't. I can say one thing for sure, it's going to be a massive cleanup either way."

"Tell me about it. And how are humans going to deal with the existence of alien races?"

Link remained the silent sentinel at her side, which caused the girl to sigh. "Well, I guess it really isn't my problem now, is it?"

"But you are one of the defenders of Earth, aren't you? The Angels charged you with it, like your father before you." Link's eyebrows furrowed as he looked at her.

At the mention of her father, Annetta felt hot tears well up in her eyes, and she quickly turned away from him.

"Yeah, it's who I was supposed to be," she managed to say, wiping away tears from the corners of her eyes. "Great job I'm doing at that, I got my home city destroyed and a whole lot of people killed."

"You also saved many," he interjected. "Thousands are alive because of your actions in rallying together the Four Forces, as well as the Gaians. Were it not for the fact that you tried, many more would be dead. You might not realize it, but I do know what Korangar held in store for all worlds, and what happened here in Toronto is very small in comparison to what he did to entire planets."

Despite his optimism, Annetta didn't see it. She had let people down, and she had failed her city. Her gaze shifted from her feet back at Link, only now having time to take in his gleaming silver chainmail with a white tabard on which a blue tree was embroidered beneath a white-hooded cape with silver trim. He looked very much the part of a knight such as in the books she'd enjoyed reading what seemed like centuries ago now. It suited him, she thought, and then she looked down again.

"Do you…" she cleared her throat. "Do you remember anything from before?"

"It's a little hazy, I admit. Thirty years of training will do that." His face creased into a smile. "But it's not like I forgot everything."

"Do you remember what we talked about then the last time we…" Annetta trailed off.

It was Link's turn to look down. A sigh escaped him, which caused the pauldrons on his shoulders to sag. "I do. I don't remember the exact words, but I remember…"

He lifted a mailed hand and touched two fingers to his lips. His grey eyes then found Annetta. "I'm sorry Anne, but even if I wanted to, a White Knight is bound in service to the Unknown. We can't be in relationships, and all our ties are severed upon being taken in as one."

Annetta felt the back of her neck heat up at hearing this, and the sensation of her ears flattening as if she were an animal came upon her. "Oh, I see."

She wasn't sure what else to say, and before she could even think of anything, Link was already within arm's reach. Annetta's body then collided with his, their lips finding each other in a kiss. The sudden and unexpected jolt caused her body to melt into it soon after, only to find Link pulling away.

"I remember that I did have feelings for you, Annetta. In fact, I was in love with you," he said. "But what was has to remain in the past. Consider that kiss our closure, and know you will always hold a special place in my heart as the first and only girl I ever loved."

The feeling of his rough whiskers hadn't yet dissipated from her skin, and Annetta found herself raising a hand to her face, trying to process what had just transpired. It had felt wonderful, and for a split second, Annetta thought that perhaps, despite the darkness, there was still some light she could hold onto. She was about to say something more when she felt a cape brush by her legs, and a white blur pass her. Link was gone, and Annetta was left alone.

Annetta then flipped open the C.T.S. and typed in the numbers needed to reach Jason.

ഔ

The faint beeping of the C.T.S. on Jason's wrist caught him off guard, and he jumped nearly a foot into the air when he realized what it was that was going on. He flipped open the faceplate to see Annetta's number displaying, and answered it. "02 here. What's your status, 01?"

"Alive, though part of me wishes I wasn't." Annetta's gravelly voice came through. **"Where are you guys?"**

"Honestly, Anne, I haven't got a clue, everything here is pretty much rubble. I don't even see any street signs to tell you." Jason scratched the back of his neck with his free hand.

At that moment, Skyris walked by behind him, and reaching over his shoulder, she pressed a button on the keypad of the watch. A GPS hologram sprung to life before Jason, which caused him to jump, and Sarina, who was standing beside him, to giggle.

"037 here. 01, if you press the green button on the side, it will bring up a holographic projection of your whereabouts. Press zero after that, and it will create a map leading to us that you can keep open even after this transmission is finished," The older woman instructed.

"I really wish these things had instructions," Jason grumbled. "How come you knew about that?"

"Because I built them." Skyris rolled her eyes.

"I think I have it working. I'm not far, so I'll see you guys in a few minutes. 01 out." Another beep signalized the end of the conversation, and Jason shut the faceplate.

He then turned around and looked at Skyris. "I was serious about that instruction manual, by the way."

"You don't need one," Sarina interjected. "He'd never use it."

"I would, too." Jason's eyes widened.

Sarina suppressed a smile. "Sure, like with the toaster oven at our residence."

Jason was about to retort, and then pressed his lips together. "Point taken."

The trio then turned their attention back to the rest of the group. Venetor sat on some ruins, speaking with Titus and Atala, while Puc finished mending Darius's shoulder with a spell. Off to the other side, Jansen had huddled beside an overturned dumpster bin and was feverishly typing away on her computer, which Jason was surprised still had any power.

"Good as new," Puc proclaimed, and took a step back to allow Darius to test out his shoulder.

"Wish spells like this didn't take so long to cast." Darius flexed his fingers. "The results always turn out better than the potions."

"How ya feeling, man?" Jason grinned and feinted a slap on Darius's back, stopping in the last second.

Darius flinched, which elicited a chuckle from Jason. "I've been better, but I'll live."

"We are still left with one mystery, and that is why Darius transformed, and none of the other elves did." Puc stroked his chin, as if attempting to rid himself of some of the grit of battle that had gathered on his face.

The clicking of keys stopped, and Jansen shut her laptop, then stood up. "Oh… right I forget that I might know more than you guys. I just thought that would be obvious by now, wouldn't it? Darius isn't fully elven."

"What do you mean not fully elven?" Puc's eyebrows furrowed.

"It's true, he would have to be… well, Gaian to transform," Titus interjected. "The prophecy specifies it."

All eyes then fell to Darius, who shrunk back.

"But I can't be Gaian. That's not possible." He frowned.

"It is very possible." Atala turned around to face them. Her powerful arms crossed across her chest. Her attention then turned to Skyris. "I am sorry my lady, I should have told you sooner, but I was under orders from your father. Even now, I am bound to this secret."

It was Skyris's turn to narrow her eyes, and out of the corner, she saw Venetor do the same. "What are you talking about?"

Atala's face twisted in concentration as she chose her words. "The child you gave birth to. It didn't die. I was charged with taking the child back to Aldamoor, into the care of an orphanage. Your father didn't want it on Gaia. He felt it would deter Skyris from finding a suitable match among the Gaian nobility, and he would not kill one whom he saw as his kin. It's against Gaian law, one even a king dares not break."

A silence fell on those gathered, and finally, it was Venetor who spoke. "You mean to tell us that my father ordered you to fake the child's death all because of his petty pride?"

"A pride you also share, my king." Atala glared at him coolly. "Was it not you trying to pair Skyris with various potential matches?"

Venetor's grit-covered face reddened with rage as he shot up from where he sat. "I thought the child dead and Thanestorm long out of the picture. As for my pride, I have always set it aside for family. I was willing to accept this child born out of wedlock, even if I had no love for the sire that fathered it. I watched my sister weep for years, and as a brother, believe me, that was not an easy thing. I should have you executed for this, this is by all rights treason."

Atala, despite her injuries, tensed and her hands curled into fists. Puc then strode before Atala, blocking her from Venetor. "I think we have seen enough bloodshed this day, would you not agree?"

Venetor's fists dropped to the side. Titus touched his arm, which further deterred the Gaian king from any sort of actions. "I suppose I can forgive this, but only if Skyris does as well."

෩ඥ

Annetta followed the path laid out by the C.T.S., and was so entranced by the blinking hologram that she almost didn't notice the dark form which limped some distance ahead of her. There was something familiar about it, which gave Annetta pause from her original destination.

Her eyes narrowed. "It can't be."

Taking the shield down from her back and placing a hand on the broken blade of Severbane, she inched after it to investigate.

෩ඥ

As the debate played out, Darius was far from listening. His eyes were locked with the woman he had come to know in the past few months as Annetta's aunt, the sister of the renowned Lord Orbeyus of the Axe. A thousand thoughts ran through his head as Darius tried to process what he'd just heard from Atala, and what his origin was. As a child, he'd always imagined his parents to have been warriors that had been killed in the Great War against Mordred the Conqueror. Never in a million years would he have thought to be anything other than a Water Elf, and yet, perhaps now certain things in his life made just a little more sense.

His whole world was spinning before him, but Darius's lips finally parted in a single word. "Mom?"

In an instant, Skyris cleared the distance between them and was upon him. She embraced him in the gentle and powerful ferocity that he imagined only a mother could give, and for an instant, a wave of safety washed over him. Somewhat reluctant, Darius hugged her back, and was surprised to feel someone else join them. When he broke away from the hug, he found both Skyris and Puc standing side by side before him.

Darius straightened himself. Even if Puc was his father, he was and always would be his old teacher first, as well as the First Mage of Aldamoor.

A rare thing then happened, as a worn smile appeared on Puc's face usually stern face. "I would have thought Venetor's blessing a miracle on its own, but to find out I have a living and breathing son

451

who has been right under my very nose this entire time. That is more good than any being deserves on this dark day."

It was Puc's turn then to reach out and wrap his arms around Darius. It was not the first time that Puc had embraced him, but it felt different now. The tension between master and student was gone, and was instead replaced with something Darius couldn't describe. Puc had always been the closest thing he'd had to a father figure, but to find out they were related was a thing that had never crossed his mind.

The reunion was cut short when Darius heard a cry of agony coming from behind them. He veered around to see a bare-chested man wearing a tattered cape looming over Titus with outstretched hands. From those hands came tendrils of green light that latched onto Titus, causing him to writhe in agony.

"Nobody move!" The man's bloodshot eyes took in everyone around him the way a wild animal would. "Lift a finger to save him, and I shall end his life. If you want him to live, you will do exactly as I command!"

Darius then caught a glimpse of the massive black dragon tattoo on his back. "Korangar."

He sneered. "Do not test me this day! I will end the line of Freiuson, and I'll get that Severio woman right after. So hand over the heir, and if you want this one to live, I suggest you find Severio as well."

"Don't listen to him, he's-" Titus hissed in pain as he clasped his head in both hands.

"You'd best keep quiet too if you want to live." Korangar bared his teeth. "And I suggest the rest of you do as I say before I change my mind and reduce this filthy planet to cinders like I wanted to."

Something didn't seem right to Darius about the whole scene, but before he could voice his opinion, Sarina strode forward.

"Sarina, don't!" Jason reached out to stop her.

She paused a few paces before Titus, who was kneeling in pain and glaring at Korangar. She unsheathed her sabre. "If you want the heir, than here I am. So, what are you waiting for?"

A flash of white teeth signalled his pleasure at having won. Korangar opened his mouth as if to speak, when a look of horror filled his face. His eyes then trailed down his chest, where a jagged piece of metal protruded from it. The green light ceased from his fingers as he reached down to touch the object of his undoing.

"It matters naught if you render this flesh useless." The words came out as a ragged rasp. "The End is eternal, as is the darkness. As long as the line of Freius lives, the seed of chaos will thrive."

He then slid down, and his body hit the floor. Behind him stood Annetta, holding the hilt of Severbane. She then took a few steps and looked down at Korangar. "My father always said there could be no good without evil to stabilize it, nor any evil without good to defy it."

Korangar laughed at hearing this, and coughed. "Nothing is ever black and white. Every story has a shade of grey."

A final great breath filled his lungs. A small puff of greenish smoke wafted from his open mouth as he exhaled, and with it, Korangar was no more.

Chapter 50

Annetta's knees buckled seconds later as a wave of dizziness passed through her. She braced herself using the shield trying to find a centre of balance.

Jason rushed to her side, seeing her stagger. "You okay, Anne?"

"I've been better," she groaned, sheathing the broken sword.

Their conversation came to an abrupt end when Titus howled once more, clutching his head. "No! Stay away! I won't let you!"

"Titus?" Venetor reached a hand towards his son. "What's wrong?"

"I'm sorry, father." Titus shook his head and withdrew further from him. "It's too late."

"Too late for what?" The Gaian king's eyes narrowed.

Titus then stopped his throes of pain. His head snapped forward, his eyes glowing green as a vicious grin crossed his face.

"Did you honestly think I would be bested so easily?" The unmistakable voice of Korangar came from Titus. "You mortals are all so tied to your perceptions of one life and body, yet you forget the most fundamental of notions. The soul is eternal, and as long as the Freiuson line endures, I shall be reborn."

Those gathered gripped their weapons tightly as Korangar exploded once more into laughter and then stopped, clutching his head in agony as the body of Titus dropped to the floor. Twisting and moaning, he looked up with a tear streaked face. "Please, if any of you know mercy, then kill me."

"No, absolutely not." Venetor barked the command both to everyone around him and to Titus. He then moved with demonic speed and gripped his son by the shoulders. "You are stronger than this thing. You are the Crown Prince of Gaia."

It was then Titus's turn to grip his father's shoulder back. "Please, you don't understand the extent of this evil inside of me. Snuff it out while you have a chance. You have to. It's the only way."

Venetor's eyes stared widely at Titus. "No. I can't. You're my son. It's... It's against our laws."

"Father, please, I don't know how much longer I can hold him at bay." Titus pleaded with a strained face. "I was your son, but now... I..."

Titus's eyes flickered green. His grip on Venetor's shoulder intensified until his nails dug into the scale mail shirt. Titus's face twisted in malicious intent. "What's it gonna be, old man?"

Puc moved towards them. "Venetor, let me help. I may be able to place a seal-"

"Seal all you like. His son is dead," Korangar spat.

Puc halted, unsure of what to do next. At the same time, all traces of mercy vanished from Venetor's face as he removed one hand from Titus's shoulders. "May the Unknown have mercy on me."

Annetta watched in horror as a familiar purple and blue light flared in Venetor's closed fist. He pulled it back, and after a moment of hesitation, he rammed it into Titus's chest. Titus's eyes widened with shock and stared blankly into space before him for a split second. He then exhaled and went limp in his father's arms.

Tears welled in the corners of Venetor's eyes, but the rest of his face remained calm. From the short time Annetta had known her uncle, she knew that mourning was not something he would do in public. He'd lost his wife mere months ago, and now, his son too. It was enough to break any man, but Venetor wouldn't show weakness. The King of Gaia had to remain untouched emotionally from the loss in battle for the sake of his people. He carefully laid Titus's body on the asphalt and closed his eyes.

Venetor then stood up and was about to say something to those around him when the ground began to shake. The sky darkened once more as harsh winds picked up, blowing loose debris in all directions.

Annetta and Jason shielded their faces, and looking up, they both saw a streak of lightning flash across the sky, blotting out everything to white. When the light subsided, two figures stood in their midst. One was a slight woman with short red hair, while the other was a man with a hooked nose that had short spiked blond hair. They both wore black suits, and identical grim expressions.

"When did we end up in an episode of the X-Files?" Jason's nose wrinkled.

"Does it really surprise you with everything that's happened?" Annetta glanced sideways at him.

The blond one then turned in their direction, a sly smile adorning his slim-featured face. "Silence, mortal."

Sparks encircled his body once he said this. Realization then crossed both Annetta and Jason's faces.

"Bwiskai?" Annetta asked and then glanced at the woman. "Fulgura?"

The woman nodded. "It is who we are, young Annetta Severio."

"We came as soon as we heard the news that the White Knights had been dispatched to Earth, though it seems our timing has been rather late given the state of events," Bwiskai said as he observed the crumbling buildings.

"Yeah, we could have used you like… five hours earlier, but no big deal. Our home city just got destroyed." Jason quipped.

It was Fulgura's turn to look around. Her eyes found where Titus lay, beyond Venetor who was kneeling with his hands on his head. She then moved towards them, her heels clicking lightly as she went.

"Forgive me, Angel, for I have sinned," Venetor spoke as she walked past him, keeping his eyes downcast.

Fulgura paused beside him. "What is it that burdens your soul?"

"I have killed one of my kin." He looked up with a tear-streaked face. "I killed my son to prevent Korangar from claiming his body. By doing so, I have violated the ancient laws of my people."

Venetor lowered his head after he finished speaking and remained kneeling. Fulgura laid a hand on his shoulder gently, which prompted him to look up again.

Her eyes, though crimson, were lined with compassion. "You have broken no laws, Lord of Gaia. None in the eyes of the Unknown, that is. You acted to preserve life. Your son's life was forfeit the moment Korangar took hold of his body."

"Enough dallying, Fulgura. We have a job to do." Bwiskai crossed his arms.

Feeling less faint, Annetta rose to her feet. "And what job is that?"

Bwiskai turned and glared at her, causing more sparks to encircle his body. "Earth was not prepared for the awakening. They are not yet mature enough to come into the knowledge of the Unknown and to walk among the other worlds. They must first make their own way, and blunder through their own mistakes. Only then will they be able to come into the light. Our job now is to restore the Earth to as it was before the attack."

"You mean everyone is going to come back? That's awesome!" Jason could hardly contain a grin.

Fulgura, who had knelt over Titus's body and was performing some prayer, rose from her trance to face him. "Not quite, young

Kinsman. While many will return to the world as they were, a price must be extracted, and some will have to remain on the other side. It will be up to the souls of those departed as to whether they will come back or not."

Jason's smile faded. "Nothing ever comes free in this world."

"I am afraid that equivalent exchange is necessary on this plane of existence, as well as most others," Puc interjected, and then looked over at Fulgura. "What is it that you will require us to do?"

"Your task in this venture is done, First Mage," she replied. "You but need to remember and record so that future generations, should they need, know of the events that transpired here today."

"I will see it done." He nodded.

"Good, then our task must begin. We will transport you and the armies to where the Eye to All Worlds lies to remove you from the city once it reawakens." Fulgura got up and walked over to where Bwiskai stood. "We will also restore the city to what it was before the attack. We will also bring back as many people as we can although some we may not be able to bring back. A portion will need to remain in the afterlife but souls will have a chance to volunteer and stay behind. Their deaths will be explained naturally to those they hold dear."

"Only the memories of those of the Four Forces and the Gaians shall remain intact, as well as those of you gathered here. The rest of humanity will carry on as they were before." Bwiskai stated.

The two Angels then raised their hands skyward and began humming in a low and indistinguishable melody. Annetta tried to listen to it, but could not pick out anything resembling a rhythm of any kind, yet it all seemed to flow. Before she could say anything to Jason, light emanated from both Fulgura and Bwiskai, their bodies radiating. When Annetta did manage to look at them, she saw a faint glimpse of the original forms she'd met them in. The spectral forms of the birds flashed before her eyes, further intensifying the light until everything around her faded to white.

ဆာ

Jason blinked back sunspots as his eyes fluttered open. Blades of tall green grass obscured the sky above and he swatted them away with his hand, rising with a grunt. He oriented himself and saw that he'd been transported to the field around Severio castle just as Fulgura had said. Others around him also popped up from the grass groggily.

"I guess I now know what respawning feels like." He grimaced, flexing his hand which had fallen asleep.

A startled Sarina poked out of the grass beside him, shaking unkempt hair from her face. "Where are... oh."

"It looks like the Angels kept their promise." He motioned to the castle in the distance.

The sound of feet shuffling through the grass startled Jason, and he felt someone jump on him from behind. He grabbed the wrist that encircled his neck and noticed how small it was. He then caught sight of a very familiar green sweatshirt.

"Liam?" His eyes widened.

His brother's familiar laugh filled his ears as Liam removed his hands and faced him.

Jason's mouth hung open for a good minute as he took in his brother's overly large green hooded sweatshirt and jeans, the last things he'd been wearing when he'd seen him in Q-16.

"How are you... how are you here?" He managed to ask.

"I was told to go back." Liam shoved his hands into his jeans matter-of-factly.

"Told? What do you mean told? By whom?" Jason regarded him skeptically.

Liam's beaming smile faded as he looked down at his sneakers. "Uhm... by dad."

"Dad?" The word felt strange on Jason's tongue.

Liam nodded. "Yeah, he said he wanted me to go back, and that he had to stay. When I asked him why, he said so that he could always be with us where he was now. I didn't really understand what he meant by it. He's not actually here."

"No, he's not," Jason confirmed. "But wherever he is, maybe he can see us."

More feet came pounding towards him. Jason got up from where he was sitting and helped Sarina up as well. When he turned, he saw that it was Darius and Jansen. On the opposite end, Jason saw Atala and Venetor as well as Puc and Skyris. Others around them were also beginning to stir, creating the illusion that the seas of grass were giving birth to a multitude of creatures.

"Hey, little man." Darius greeted Liam. "You look a little worse for wear."

"You don't know the half of it," Liam replied.

"Liam!" Xander's voice boomed from across the field.

Turning in its direction, Jason saw Xander racing towards them, followed by Matthias, who also looked to have acquired his own set of injuries while in the Lab. The right side of his face was wrapped in bandages, with some gauze sticking out. Jason worried briefly about what it could mean, but was distracted by the reunion of Liam and Xander, who'd thrown their arms around each other in a hug.

"I thought you were dead." Xander pulled away, examining his friend from head to toe.

"I was... it's kind of a long story."

Xander then seemed to remember something and looked around. "Has anyone seen my sister or my parents?"

Before Jason could even begin to think how to explain, the form of Venetor towered over Xander from behind. The boy veered around to see what was creating the shadow that had just overtaken him.

"I think its best you come with me so I can explain," he said in a gruff voice, and then turned as if to walk away. "Alone."

It was clear from the smile fading on his face that Xander understood something was amiss, and the boy nodded before going off with Venetor. They walked past Matthias, who then came within hearing distance of the group that was slowly converging around Jason, Sarina and Darius.

"Matt, what happened to your face?" Sarina pointed at the wrappings.

He moved his head sideways so that he could see her with his good eye. "Amarok."

"Amarok? You mean in the city?" Jason's eyes widened.

"No, in the Lab." Matthias shook his head.

"How? I thought teleportation was locked so that only authorized psychics could get in." Jason turned to Skyris.

"He didn't teleport in." Matthias crossed his arms. "Amarok came down with some of the humans. He was dressed as a civilian when I ran into him."

"Did he escape? Any idea what he was doing down there?" Jason fired off questions.

Matthias raised a gauntlet-clad hand to slow him down. "He did get away, and I don't know. I did catch sight of a vial he was holding when we fought, but I was a little preoccupied with his vambraces to ask questions."

"It seems we are yet again one step behind," Puc concluded, and then looked at Matthias's face. "I should have a look at that. Somehow I doubt your skill with a first aid kit is sufficient for what I may find."

"Assassin, not a cleric." He rolled his good eye and sat down, allowing Puc to examine him.

Jason took another look around at the bands of Gaians, Minotaur, Soarin, Ogaien and Water Elves that were beginning to fill the plains around the castle as they awoke. It reminded him of the aftermath of the battle against Mislantus. The more he thought about it, though, the more he realized how different this fight had been.

"Things are going to change now, aren't they?" he asked no one in particular, simply needing to say the words to make them real in his mind.

"That's how life goes." Skyris's voice cut through his thoughts, and he looked over at her. "It's always changing, moving forward and never taking a second glance back."

"M'Lady!" A thick voice then boomed from behind them all, and pivoting around, they saw Gladius bounding towards them, his plate mail clinking. "M'Lady, is the king anywhere near? I have just received news through my C.T.S. from tha Intergalactic Federation of tha election results."

"I'm not sure if my brother will want to know of another loss right now, Gladius." Skyris crossed her arms. "Titus is… well."

Despite the joy of having been reunited with her own son, tears welled up in Skyris's, and Gladius immediately came to embrace her. "I'm sorry, M'Lady. He was a good lad and would have been a wise king."

He withdrew from the embrace and continued. "I have not, however, come with such news. Gaia has won."

Skyris blinked, as if not hearing him correctly. "Won? But he walked out on the final speeches."

Gladius raised a meaty finger. "Aye he did, to help his sister planet. Tha other planets were outraged when the Greys wanted to continue without him. Tha entire assembly banded together against them, including the candidates. There hasn't been an uprising like that against any faction in a long time."

The colour drained from Skyris's face at hearing this. "Well, I'll be damned."

460

Jansen, who had been standing beside Darius then interrupted. "Hey guys, has anyone seen Annetta anywhere?"

"Not since we came here." Jason focused his telepathy on her. *'Hey, Anne, can you hear me?'*

Something was wrong with the connection Jason realized, and it wasn't just the fact that he got no answer from Annetta. It was like she wasn't even there to begin with. He furrowed his brows. "I can't seem to reach her."

"Maybe she blocked you off." Matthias offered as an explanation.

Jason stroked his chin, feeling a few longer thin hairs. "I guess, but it's never happened before. Not like this."

Puc got up, having concluded his examination of Matthias's face. "She is in mourning, and all grieve differently. The loss of a parent is catastrophic, and can leave a person feeling less than whole. To lose both at once is double the blow."

Jason nodded. Though it appeared that his own father had not come back, he was never as close with him as Annetta had been with her own parents. "What should we do?"

Puc reached into his robes then and produced shattered pieces of metal. Only when Jason looked closer, did he see the bits of writing on what had once been Severbane.

"We give her time, and allow for that which was broken to mend."

৪৩৫৪

Elsewhere on a plateau of limestone obscured by pine trees, away from the crowds that were awakening, Annetta looked down with a glazed stare. Her eyes were rimmed red from tears that still stained her face, creating alternating bands of dark and light. Their focus alternated between the landscape before her and the shield which lay beside her, along with the broken hilt of Severbane in its scabbard. She felt numb, as though something had taken out her insides and replaced them with nothing.

Annetta knew eventually that she would need to go down to her friends, and that her brother, too, waited for her. She was faced also with the fact that in the place she had once called home, there would now be two empty seats, and this pained her more than anything else she'd endured. Now more than ever, she craved an escape if only for a while.

Taking a deep breath, she closed her eyes and allowed her mind to wander, to run to where it most desired. The pain would ease in time, and she knew she would see them all again.

Epilogue

Excerpt from the chronicles of the Eye to All Worlds:

Dark have been these days of late, and yet as within all darkness, there have been sparks of light, little holes in the perpetual black that strive to defy it. Nothing in this world is ever a downward spiral, but a series of ups and downs, as Orbeyus once put it.

Earth has returned the state it had been before the attack, and though many could not be returned, the Angels found ways to explain their deaths in ways that the humans would understand.

Gaia has won a great victory, and has taken over as the leading planet for the Intergalactic Federation. I pray the Unknown grants wisdom onto Venetor Severio, so that he may lead the Federation into a new era of peace and prosperity.

Jason and Sarina have resumed their studies at the university. Jason has severed his ties with his mother Talia for the most part, who has denounced Q-16, and wants nothing more to do with it. I was also tasked with binding Liam's abilities until his eighteenth birthday, at which time he may choose to return to the Lab, and not before.

Matthias didn't lose an eye as he thought he might, though his sight was weakened on the right. Skyris is currently working to find a way to repair the damaged tissue, but it may take time, as all things do.

Darius, or I suppose now I should say my son, has decided to accompany the young woman Jansen back to the Sisters of Wyrd to help solve the mystery of her abilities. The riddle has left us all puzzled and strained for answers, but I have faith in Lysania's talents to find the truth.

Venetor has taken young Xander to Gaia. Greif has a strange way of bringing people together, and I daresay this has been one of those instances. I have never had any inclination to like the man, but seeing his compassion towards the boy in his hour of greatest need has softened my resolve and opinion of him. I suppose there is also the issue of him finally allowing Skyris to make her own choices about her romantic life instead of being a pawn in a potential political marriage.

Annetta has declined Venetor's invitation to also join her brother on Gaia. Her conviction that she must remain on Earth as its guardian, it seems, is stronger than the grief she now carries in her heart. A warrior if ever I met one, and a reflection of the ideals my dear friend once carried as his torch. Be proud, Orbeyus, and know your legacy is protected.

I suppose this is where I write of my own aftermath of Korangar's fury, and that is that after much thought, Skyris and I have decided at long last to wed. I hope wherever you are, Orbeyus, my dear friend, you will be with me in spirit on that day.

Should you, dear reader, happen upon this chapter in the lives I have recorded, understand that this is but a fragment of a much larger story, one which stretches over the years. It is inaccurate to judge any life based on a single experience, for bias is the bane of all rational beings. Look deep, and remember that there are many pages to every tale.

-Puc Thanestorm
First Mage of Aldamoor
Chronicler of Severio Castle through the lives of Orbeyus, Arieus and Annetta Severio, Defenders of the Eye to All Worlds

Acknowledgements

As I wrote in both previous acknowledgements for Q-16 and the Eye to All Worlds and Q-16 and the Lord of the Unfinished Tower, a writer is never alone. First and foremost, a huge thank you to my parents for always being patient with me. Whether I was writing or engrossed in late night edits, they always understood of the time it takes to write a novel. To my brother for his continued encouragement. I promise one day the audiobooks will be available for you or perhaps by then, you'll get to read these. I also cannot forget my four-legged companion Meesha, who made it a point to come and guard me when I was writing. Involved in this process, as always, and I thank him much for his time, was my editor Anthony Geremia, who was quick to point out when Annetta and her friends were doing something out of character. Even us authors need to be reined in some of the time. To Sylvia Powers who once again came to the rescue with beta reading and edits, thank you for your help. To Anthony "Letch" Letchford for his fantastic cover art. Thank you for helping bring my vision to life. It's here I should also mention my champion and M.V.P. at pretty much every convention since the start, Chris Barfitt, who has made sure this author has not collapsed on more than one occasion from dehydration or lack of eating. Thank you for always taking into consideration also that an author is two parts crazy and one part sane. Finally, to all those I have met at conventions, authors and readers alike, I thank you for your support and encouragement. As many of you know, the Q-16 series for me is a labour of love and is done on my off time when I'm not at my day job. It takes a lot of discipline on my part as well as personal sacrifices, usually in the form of spare time that would otherwise be used gaming, watching movies or consuming some other type of media. Seeing others share my enthusiasm for the Lab and its inhabitants make this well worth it. If there are any I have missed in here, I apologize and know that whatever support, wisdom or smile that you gave was not a gesture I have forgotten. Until the next adventure, keep it awesome!

About the Author

A.A. Jankiewicz (known to most as Agnes) hails from the city of Pickering, Ontario. Her debut novel 'Q-16 and the Eye to All Worlds' was published as part of her thesis project at Durham College as part of the Contemporary Media Design Program. Prior to that, she graduated from York University with a BFA in Film Theory, Historiography and Criticism. When she's not busy plotting the next great adventure, writing, doodling, tinkering in the Adobe suite programs or mellowing out with her friends, she enjoys walks with her four-legged companion Meesha. When not at work she is working on the next instalment in the Q-16 series.